When the trials begin,
in soul-torn solitude despairing,
the hunter waits alone.
The companions emerge
from fast-bound ties of fate
uniting against a common foe.

When the shadows descend,
in Hell-sworn covenant unswerving
the blighted brothers hunt,
and the godborn appears,
in rose-blessed abbey reared,
arising to loose the godly spark.

When the harvest time comes,
in hate-fueled mission grim unbending,
the shadowed reapers search.
The adversary vies
with fiend-wrought enemies,
opposing the twisting schemes of Hell.

When the tempest is born,
as storm-tossed waters rise uncaring,
the promised hope still shines.
And the reaver beholds
the dawn-born chosen's gaze,
transforming the darkness into light.

When the battle is lost,
through quake-tossed battlefields unwitting
the seasoned legions march,
but the sentinel flees
with once-proud royalty,
protecting devotion's fragile heart.

When the ending draws near,
with ice-locked stars unmoving,
the threefold threats await,
and the herald proclaims,
in war-wrecked misery,
announcing the dying of an age.

—As written by Elliandreth of Orishaar, c. −17,600 DR

FORGOTTEN REALMS®

THE SUNDERING

THE COMPANIONS
R.A. Salvatore

THE GODBORN
Paul S. Kemp

THE ADVERSARY
Erin M. Evans

THE REAVER
Richard Lee Byers

THE SENTINEL
Troy Denning

THE HERALD
Ed Greenwood

TROY DENNING
THE SENTINEL

FORGOTTEN REALMS®

THE SUNDERING

Book
V

THE SENTINEL
©2014 Wizards of the Coast LLC.

Published by Wizards of the Coast LLC. Manufactured by: Hasbro SA, Rue Emile-Boéchat 31, 2800 Delémont, CH. Represented by Hasbro Europe, 2 Roundwood Ave, Stockley Park, Uxbridge, Middlesex, UB11 1AZ, UK.

Prophecy by: James Wyatt
Cartography by: Mike Schley
Cover art by: Tyler Jacobson
First Printing: October 2014

9 8 7 6 5 4 3 2 1

ISBN: 978-0-7869-6543-4
ISBN: 978-0-7869-6548-9 (ebook)
620A6854000001 EN

The Hardcover edition Cataloging-in-Publication data is on file with the Library of Congress

Contact Us at Wizards.com/CustomerService
Wizards of the Coast LLC, PO Box 707, Renton, WA 98057-0707, USA
USA & Canada: (800) 324-6496 or (425) 204-8069
Europe: +32(0) 70 233 277

Visit our web site at **www.dungeonsanddragons.com**

For Karina Hayday

CHAPTER ONE

2 Uktar, the Year of the Nether Mountain Scrolls (1486 DR)
Marsember, Cormyr

THE EYES WERE THE FIRST SIGN OF TROUBLE, A PAIR OF steel-blue ovals staring out from beneath a storefront awning across the street. Focused and intense, they were watching something on the wagon-choked boulevard, fixing on it the way a predator fixes on prey.

"Those priests have to go," said a hoarse voice down in front of Kleef. "You can see that, can't you?"

The voice belonged to a ruddy-cheeked cloth merchant. A moment before, Kleef had climbed onto the side of the man's wagon, trying to see what was clogging Starmouth Way. The merchant had immediately begun to harangue him about removing a group of street-corner priests who were attracting a crowd and blocking the square ahead.

Kleef continued to ignore the fellow and continued to studied the steel-blue eyes across the way. So bright they almost seemed to glow, the eyes were set beneath a heavy brow, in a gaunt, gray face that appeared to shift hues with the shadows. The shoulders beneath were broad and sturdy and covered by a dusky cloak that seemed to blur at the edges. Through the press of the crowd, it was difficult to tell much more about the figure—except that he had a commanding

1

presence that seemed to insulate him from the jostling mob.

As a topsword in the Marsember Watch, Kleef Kenric had more experience fighting back-alley cutthroats than Shadovar spies—but he was fairly certain he was looking at one now. He had been warned to expect them before the actual assault began, and scouts from the Purple Dragons had been arriving since yesterday with reports of the enemy's approach.

Hoping to spot the Shadovar's quarry, Kleef shifted his attention to the middle of the boulevard. It took only a moment to find the likely target: a beautiful woman whose long, flame-red hair cascaded down the shoulders of her fine green cloak. She was moving against the traffic, glancing back as though aware she was being stalked. Even from a distance, Kleef could see that her eyes matched the emerald-green hue of her cloak. Following close on her heels was a slovenly little man with a round head and a thin frame, dressed in a drab gray robe that hung on him as though it had been draped over a skeleton. Despite the press of the crowd, people were moving aside to let them pass, smiling and nodding at the woman but scowling and wrinkling their noses at her companion.

Kleef had only been watching the pair for a moment when a mule cart piled high with furniture and children pulled alongside him, blocking his view. Almost instantly, the cart's progress was blocked by the wall of wagons that had already attempted the same maneuver, and Kleef found himself staring into the wide-eyed faces of three young boys, all sitting upon an overturned table. The youngest was clutching a small white dog that flattened its ears and began to bark at him.

The cloth merchant grew more impatient. "Well, Watchman? Are you going to do your job or not?" He waved the handle of his ox whip in front of Kleef's eyes, then pointed it up the clogged boulevard. "Those charlatan priests are the problem. You have to get rid of them."

Kleef dropped his gaze to the merchant, a ruddy-cheeked man with a slim crescent of chain mail peeking out from the neck of his silken robes. Seated on the bench beside him were a haggard-looking woman and two young, weary-looking girls.

"I see a lot of things," Kleef said. As he spoke, he tried to peer past the mule cart and catch another glimpse of the Shadovar. "I can't fix them all."

"But you *can* remove the priests, can you not?" The merchant slipped a hand beneath his robes and withdrew five gold lions. "Surely you see how they're bringing the entire evacuation to a halt?"

Kleef felt his lip curl at the offer of a bribe. But with an enemy spy already inside the city, now was hardly the time to slap an ordinary merchant in the stocks. Kleef started to step off the wagon.

"Perhaps you didn't understand me, Watchman." The merchant's voice grew more urgent, and a metallic jingle sounded from his palm. "With the crowds they're drawing, those priests are endangering everyone. You *need* to clear the streets."

Kleef glanced over to find that the palm now held ten gold coins. He stopped mid-descent, one boot still on the wagon's footboard and the other on the boarding step. Despite the insult of the gold, the merchant was right about one thing: Starmouth Way was so choked by top-heavy carts and wagons that it was impossible to see even fifty paces ahead—and it was as much Kleef's duty to keep the evacuation moving as it was to watch the Shadovar spy.

And the merchant was right about the priests, too. Kleef could not actually see them, but they were clearly audible, using the magic of their gods to make their booming voices heard above the din of the evacuation, above the creaking axles and lowing oxen, the shouts of impatient evacuees and the wails of frightened children. From the sound of it, at least one priest stood preaching on each of the four corners of the square ahead, and each priest was heralding the end of the world, swearing that his god alone could offer salvation.

It was no wonder crowds were stopping to listen. There

were streaks of greenish-blue flame in the sky, and just that morning, the streets had shaken so hard that an entire neighborhood in the Canal District had slid into the water. People wanted to believe that the right prayer would return their lives to normal—that if they offered a large enough donation to the priests, or made a large enough sacrifice, it would save them from the coming cataclysm.

Fools.

The gods might spare them, but the Shadovar would not. From what Kleef had heard, the entire kingdom of Cormyr was falling. Riders from the Purple Dragons arrived at the King's Tower every day to bring news of a fresh disaster— Myth Drannor was besieged, the Netherese were storming Arabel and marching south toward Suzail, the shadow fiends had escaped their prison in Wheloon and would soon be descending upon Marsember. By some accounts, the fiends might even arrive before the next dawn—news that had not been shared widely, lest the evacuation turn into a riot.

The merchant continued to offer the coins expectantly. Kleef pulled himself higher and craned his neck, trying to catch sight of the Shadovar as he weighed his responsibilities. On the one hand, it was important to stop the spy. On the other, it was his duty to keep the evacuation moving. Without a doubt, the Law of Service—the law of his god, Helm—prohibited the taking of bribes. But Helm had been silent for a hundred years, and these were unusual times. Kleef was beginning to see how the merchant's gold might allow him to go after the spy *and* clear the priests from the square.

A curtain of sapphire light flashed across the western sky, and Starmouth Way surged a few inches upward, cracking and crunching as cobblestones popped free of the street. In the next instant, the lowing and braying of terrified draft animals was echoing off the swaying storefronts, and the merchant's moon-faced wife began to grow impatient.

"Hantur, this is no time to be cheap!" she said. "With this

4

mob, you're asking the good watchman to take his life into his hands. Give him twenty."

"*Twenty* gold lions?" Hantur gasped. "That's as much as he earns in a month!"

"And you had me up all night rolling cloth worth a thousand times that," she countered. "With the portals corrupted and the travel-wizards dead or gone, you'll pay him twenty platinum *tricrowns,* if that's what it takes to get us out of this city."

Hantur scowled, but he reached under his robe for more coins. It made Kleef's stomach turn to even consider taking the bribe, but he knew that most of his fellow watchmen would have laughed at his aversion. The Marsember Watch had been founded in a cesspool of corruption nearly a century ago, when the merchant's guild had decided the city needed its own militia to protect its members' interests—and to prevent the local garrison of Purple Dragons from interfering with the way they conducted business. And not much had changed in the last hundred years.

Hantur's hand came out again, filled with more gold. "Twenty lions," he said to Kleef. "If you want more, go rob someone else."

Kleef sighed. "*Ten* gold lions is enough," he said, putting his hand out. "And offer no more bribes. In this madness, there are too many who will see it as a chance to take your entire purse."

Hantur frowned, clearly insulted. "I know how to conduct my own business, Watchman." The merchant dropped ten gold into Kleef's palm, then tucked the rest back inside his robes. "Just get on with your job—and be quick about it. This wagon should be halfway to Suzail by now."

Kleef felt his jaw clench at the merchant's tone, but he supposed such treatment was to be expected when a watchman opened his hand for gold. He cast one last glance across the boulevard and, finding the mule cart still blocking his view, dropped off the wagon. He moved to the near side of the street, where his small troop of uniformed drunkards and wastrels stood waiting in an alcove, their short swords still sheathed and their halberds resting against their shoulders.

Kleef motioned for his troop to gather around, then said, "We can't have the evacuation choked off like this." He turned to the largest man, a heavy-jawed brute with legs like tree trunks. "Tanner, take the troop and remove those priests from the square."

"And do *what* with them, Topsword?" Tanner gave him a sly grin. "Dump their bodies in the lagoon?"

"If it comes to that, yes." Kleef could see the surprise in the faces of his men, for he had never been one to tolerate the mistreatment of prisoners. "It might be less work to just escort the priests outside the city walls and order them to stay there, but do what you need to do. If we don't get those wagons rolling through Wilhastle Square before the assault begins, we'll have a riot on our hands."

Kleef held out his hand, displaying the coins the merchant had given him, then added, "Clear the square within a quarter hour, and there's a gold lion for each of you."

His first blade, a young Shou from the now-flooded quarter of Xiousing, scowled in open disapproval. The rest of the troop looked confused and suspicious.

"That's a mean joke," said the oldest man, a gray-stubbled fellow named Rathul. "We're selling our lives cheap as it is. There's no need to rub our noses in—"

"Does it look like I'm joking?" Kleef interrupted. "Clear the square, and the gold is yours."

The men continued to look wary.

"Right," scoffed Ardul, a fuzzy-cheeked youth. "So you can flog us for taking a bribe? This must be another one of your tests."

"No test," Kleef said, allowing his frustration to color his voice. "Times are desperate, and I need you to clear that square without Jang and me. *Now.*"

Tanner frowned. "So, we'll all be in the square, while you and Jang are . . . doing *what*, exactly?"

Normally, Kleef would have rebuffed the question with a curt reminder of who gave the orders. But not much was normal right then. Dozens of senior watchmen had already deserted their posts, and that morning, even the day-watch oversword had failed to report for duty.

Kleef sighed and pointed across the street. "Jang and I will be back there somewhere, watching a Shadovar spy."

"The Shadovar are inside the city?" Jang gasped. "Already?"

"I believe I've spotted *one*," Kleef said, hedging a little, since he had not yet confirmed his suspicions, and he did not want his men to panic or rethink their priorities. "Maybe I'm wrong, but Jang and I need to check it out."

Tanner raised his brow, studying Kleef with grudging respect. "Just the two of you? Alone?"

"No choice," Kleef said, knowing that Tanner and the rest of his troop's ready blades would be more hindrance than help against a Netherese shadow warrior. "Someone has to clear the square. Besides, if I bring more men, he'll see us coming."

Tanner's gaze drifted back to the coins in Kleef's palm. "Makes sense," he said. "But maybe you should leave the coins with me, just in case you don't—"

"Sorry," Kleef said, closing his hand. "Clear the square *first*. If I don't return—"

"Don't worry, we'll come and find you." Tanner grinned, displaying a set of broken brown teeth, then added, "Or whatever is left of you. You'll be carrying our gold, remember?"

With that, the big man turned and, using his halberd to shove and poke his way through the crowd, led his companions toward Wilhastle Square. Kleef motioned for Jang, then started down the street in the opposite direction, bulling his way through the pedestrians. It was difficult to see anything on the far side of the wide street, but Kleef knew his best chance of locating the Shadovar again lay in finding the red-haired woman.

Jang seemed to slip through the crowd like an eel, and he easily kept pace with Kleef. "Now *you* are giving bribes?"

"Not really," Kleef said.

Jang was the only man under his command whose respect truly mattered to him. The Shou wielded a blade almost as well as Kleef did, and he followed a code of honor as strict as Helm's Law. Unlike Kleef, however, Jang hadn't devoted his life to faithful service; he was simply an honorable man, and Kleef both admired and envied him for that.

"I just needed a way to keep the troop from deserting the instant we're out of sight."

"By offering *them* a bribe," Jang insisted. "It is good that you follow Helm. A dead god will not punish you for ignoring his laws."

Kleef winced. He *was* stretching Helm's Law of Service, but he saw no alternative. He knew his troop too well to think they would clear the square without the promise of gold. Moreover, Helm had been gone so long that even his most devoted worshipers considered his Law more of a guideline than an inviolable code. Under the circumstances, was it wrong of Kleef to think the same way?

After twenty paces, Kleef glanced over the backs of two stamping mules and caught a glimpse of green wool slicing through the crowd near the middle of the street. He tugged Jang's sleeve and stepped into the slender gap in front of the mules' noses. The beasts brayed and balked, but Jang quickly grabbed their halters and calmed them with a few words of whispered Shou.

Kleef located the flash of green again, about ten paces away and still pushing against the traffic. The woman had wisely concealed her hair by raising the hood of her cloak, but the green was so bright and distinctive that it drew almost as much attention.

Still, something seemed wrong to Kleef, and after a moment, he realized the woman was not moving through the press of bodies as easily as she had before. Now she was shouldering her way ahead, not looking back at all, and there was no sign of her short companion.

"Stinking Hells!" Kleef pointed at the green hood. "Fetch the one in the green cloak. I have questions."

Jang acknowledged the order with a curt nod and slipped into the crowd. Shaking his head at his own folly, Kleef shoved through the mob in the opposite direction, until he found a spot where he could view the far side of the street. Here, the river of pedestrians was roughly ten people wide. In the absence of wagons, they were pulling handcarts and carrying heavy rucksacks, creeping toward Wilhastle Square at a tortoise's pace.

Kleef stepped onto another wagon to get a better look. Neither the red-haired woman nor her short companion were anywhere in sight, but a dusky-robed figure was skulking along the walkway, moving against traffic and still keeping a watchful eye on the middle of the street. The man's eyes were not visible, but there was a vague haziness around the edges of his silhouette, a kind of murkiness that suggested shadow magic, and Kleef began to hope that he had found the spy again.

Then the figure looked directly at him, revealing an ashen face with a long chin and brown, faintly glowing eyes. His gaze slid past Kleef without pause, then he turned around and began to move through the crowd again. As the man drifted away from the buildings, his drab robe faded to gray, and he grew indistinguishable from the rest of the mob.

Kleef resisted the impulse to go after him. He had never seen a Shadovar before today, much less hunted one. But he had been told by a member of the Purple Dragons that there were several kinds of Shadovar, and that the ones with the lambent eyes—the *shades*—were the most cunning and dangerous. So, trailing the spy now seemed unlikely to accomplish anything more than leading Kleef into an ambush. It would be much smarter to find the red-haired woman, then ambush the shade when he attempted to take his quarry.

Jang returned to Kleef's side, engulfed by a cloud of fragrance so sweet and fresh that it masked the stench of manure and urine that pervaded the street. The Shou's hand was locked on the elbow of the slender figure wearing the green cloak. Kleef reached out and snatched back the hood, exposing the dirty blond hair and sunken-cheeked face of a teenage street urchin. A *boy,* no less. No doubt the cloak was the source of the perfume.

Kleef ordered Jang to keep watch for Shadovar, then grabbed the urchin by the back of his neck and pushed him off the street, seeking the privacy of a doorway. Once he felt certain he could question the boy without being observed by the spy, Kleef took the front of the cloak and rubbed the soft green cashmere between his fingers.

"Nice cloak," he said. "How did you come by it?"

The urchin raised his chin. "I didn't steal it, if that's what you mean. It's mine."

"That so?" Kleef knotted his fist into the cloth, then lifted the urchin off the ground and made a show of sniffing around his collar. "Pretty nice perfume for a guttersnipe like you—especially a *boy* guttersnipe."

"I'm no boy," the urchin said. "I'm a man."

"A *boy* . . . who smells as sweet as a noblewoman." Kleef lowered the urchin back to the street, but continued to hold the cloth. "You can keep the cloak, but I need to find the lady who gave it to you."

"I have no idea what you're talking about," the urchin said. "I took this cloak off a cart."

Kleef raised a brow. "You're admitting you stole it?" he asked. "*Confessing* to thievery, just like that?"

The urchin paled. "I mean, it fell off a cart, and I picked it up." He looked away. "If you want my thumb for that, I guess I can't stop you."

"You'd give up a thumb for the red-haired woman?" Kleef was truly surprised. Marsember's street urchins were not the kind to make noble sacrifices. "Who is she to you?"

The bewilderment that washed over the urchin's face told Kleef all he needed to know. The boy had no idea who the woman was—or even why he was trying to protect her. She had probably charmed him with magic.

"Look," Kleef continued, "if you truly want to help the lady, you *will* tell me where she went. She's being hunted by a dangerous sort. She'll be much better off if I find her first."

"You expect me to believe that?"

"I *expect* you to answer me." Kleef took a deep breath, then switched to a more kindly, fatherly voice. "Since you're a man, I'll tell it to you straight. It's not *me* this woman is running from. It's the Shadovar."

"There are *Shadovar* in the city?"

"At least one—a shade no less—and he's hunting your red-haired lady." Kleef released the urchin. "Now, will you help her or not?"

The urchin looked uncertain for a moment, then finally nodded. "She's so beautiful," he said. "I can't believe she asked *me* for help."

"Go on," Kleef urged. "Everything you remember."

"There isn't much," the urchin said. "She just smiled at me and said she would consider it a kindness if I took her cloak and wore it."

"That's all?" Kleef asked.

"That's all she *said*," the urchin replied. "But there was a look in her eyes. It felt like we had known each other forever. I could tell she liked me . . . she liked me a *lot*."

Kleef nodded to himself. Charm magic, for certain. "And I suppose she told you to pull up the hood?"

The urchin shook his head. "That was my idea," he said. "I knew she was being chased, and I wanted to draw them off."

"*How* did you know she was being chased?"

The urchin frowned, clearly confused. "I don't know. I guess it was the way her manservant kept watch," he said. His face brightened, remembering. "And the servant said something like, 'There is one of the devils now,' and then he led her away."

Kleef felt his belly sinking. " '*One* of the devils?' " he asked. "You're sure he said that exactly?"

The urchin nodded. "That's what I heard. And then he grabbed her arm and pulled her into Backstabber Alley, just like I said."

Actually, the urchin hadn't said anything about Backstabber Alley, but it seemed an honest mistake. Kleef reached into his belt pouch and removed a Watch flan—a steel meal token the Watch used to buy the cooperation of the hungry—and passed it to the boy.

"Take that to King's Tower and tell the gatekeeper you've been of service to Kleef Kenric," he said. "Got that? He'll see that your belly is filled before you leave Marsember."

The urchin took the flan. "Kleef Kenric. Got it." He paused, then frowned. "Wait—are you throwing me out of Marsember?"

Kleef frowned. "I'm trying to look out for you, boy. The shadow fiends of Wheloon have escaped their prison, and they're marching against us. Even the lord marshall doubts we can hold the city, and with the war against Netheril going the way it is, there won't be any help from the Purple Dragons."

The urchin shrugged. "What do I care who rules this city—or the Realm?" he asked. "Either way, I sleep in a doorway. But I hope you help the lady. I liked her."

"I'll do what I can," Kleef promised. He thought about trying to persuade the urchin to leave, but then realized a boy alone wouldn't be much safer on the open road than he was on the familiar ground of the city. He took a few more Watch flans from his belt pouch and gave them to the waif. "I suppose every man has the right to face his doom how he will. The Watch will be looking for bolt-loaders to help man the walls. You could join them, if you decide you want to make your death count for something."

The urchin looked at Kleef as though he were daft. "Thanks, but I won't." He closed his hand around the meal tokens. "Can I go?"

Kleef nodded. Fighting to overcome a rising tide of bitterness and despair, he started back toward Jang. Raised in a household devoted to Helm, Kleef had joined the city Watch as soon as he was of age. Like his father and grandfather before him, he had dedicated his entire life to bringing Helm's Law of Service to his fellow watchmen. But the corruption of the order's founders simply ran too deep. After three generations of effort, the Kenric line had nothing to show for its faith but the knowledge that they had stayed true to the teachings of a dead god. If the inhabitants of Marsember had no interest in helping to save their city, the Watch had only itself to blame.

Kleef returned to Jang's side.

"I have seen no sign of any Shadovar," the Shou said. "I hope you learned something."

"I did." Kleef motioned for Jang to follow him, then started plowing through the crowd, angling up Starmouth Way. "It seems the woman and her manservant are headed down Backstabber Alley."

"A bad choice for someone who is fleeing a Shadovar," Jang said. Backstabber Alley was aptly named, for it was a crooked and narrow gauntlet, lined with dark doorways and crannies where trouble invariably lay waiting. "They must not be familiar with the city."

"Probably not," Kleef agreed. "We'll circle around fast and take Rover's Way, then catch them at the other end of the alley. That way, we can take them by surprise—and the Shadovar spies, too, if they've caught up."

"*Spies?*" Jang asked, slipping to his side. "There is more than one?"

"That's the way it sounds."

They reached High Bridge Road. It was filled with foot

traffic, all flowing away from Starmouth. No doubt most of the pedestrians hoped to detour around the jam in Wilhastle Square. To make up for lost time, Kleef did his best to run along the edge of the street, shouting, "Make way for the Watch!" while shoving dawdlers aside with well-placed forearms. He and Jang often had to bound over handcarts, and twice, Kleef found it necessary to throw a slow-moving crone over his shoulder and carry her a few paces until he found a safe place to deposit her. By the time they reached Rover's Way, a narrow cross-lane that led to Backstabber Alley, both men were sweating and breathing hard.

Kleef slowed to a walk and slipped his greatsword, Watcher, off his back, then unsheathed it and returned the empty scabbard to its place. Jang drew his own blade—a slender Shou katana—off his hip, and together they turned the corner into Rover's Way. Though the lane was nearly ten feet wide, it was so littered with discarded belongings that a donkey cart could not have passed through. Pushing their way past all the paupers picking through the refuse, Kleef and Jang advanced nearly a hundred paces before they finally saw Backstabber Alley opening onto Rover's Way on the right.

As they approached the mouth of the alley, Kleef listened for screams or the sound of running boots, anything to suggest the Shadovar had caught their quarry. He heard only the nervous murmurs of the paupers on Rover's Way, who were quick to shy away from two watchmen with drawn blades. In normal times, Kleef would have also heard the *bang* of slamming shutters overhead and the thud of crossbars falling across doors, but times were not normal. The residents of Rover's Way had already fled, leaving their homes open to the urchins and thieves in hopes of one day returning to find the doors still hanging on the hinges.

The two watchmen were a dozen steps from Backstabber Alley when a small cone of blue radiance flared in front of

Kleef. Stunned, he dropped into a fighting crouch, his eyes scanning left and right for the source of the spell.

When he found none, Kleef's blood ran cold.

He removed a hand from Watcher's hilt to wave Jang back. As his other hand rebalanced the sword, rolling it slightly downward, the blue cone faded to a glow. It was only then that Kleef realized the blue light was emanating from a decoration on the crossguard of the sword itself: a blue agate surrounded by the etching of a large eye—*Helm's Eye.*

Kleef's jaw dropped. Watcher had been in his family since the time of Ildool, and there was no doubting its magic. In the hands of a true Kenric, it was as light as a dagger, yet no one outside the family had the strength to wield it. A set of runes etched into the blade read STAY TRUE AND SO WILL YOUR STEEL, a motto that had proven itself accurate time and again as the greatsword cleaved oak shields and steel armor. But as far as Kleef knew, that was the extent of the sword's power. Never had anyone mentioned a blue light, and Kleef had never seen the agate glow as it did now.

Jang touched his shoulder and whispered. "What does that mean?"

Before Kleef could reply, a trio of dusky figures stepped out of a doorway opposite Backstabber Alley, all three with the lambent eyes of shades gleaming beneath their cowls. The figure in the lead swung a hand, and a scythe of darkness swept across Rover's Way, slicing through a half-dozen paupers who had been scurrying up the lane ahead of Kleef and Jang.

A panicked voice, nasal and male, rang out of Backstabber Alley. "Go back! We're trapped!"

By then, the three shades were springing toward the mouth of the alley, and Kleef and Jang were charging up Rover's Way to attack the trio's flank.

Kleef arrived first, bringing Watcher around in a chest-high strike that took the nearest shade from behind. The blade dragged a bit as it sliced up through the warrior's shoulder.

Kleef pivoted, putting all his strength into the attack, and felt the sword drive the rest of the way through. The shade's torso came apart in a spray of blood and darkness.

Jang was already on the second shade, his slender katana hissing and whistling as he attacked high and low, severing first tendons, then limbs, and finally rising toward the neck.

Kleef glimpsed the third warrior spinning to attack Jang from behind. Kleef stepped forward, using a shoulder to bull the shade off balance, then leaned away and brought Watcher up in a one-handed slash. The blade entered beneath the warrior's armpit and did not stop until it was halfway through his chest. Kleef used his free arm to knock the dying shade off his sword, then brought his weapon back around to send the fellow's head tumbling.

Like the rest of the Watch, he had been told to behead a shade every time, that it was the only way to be sure that the shadowstuff would not heal him. He glanced over and found Jang already spinning away from his headless foe, putting his back to the wall on the far side of the alley mouth. Kleef did the same on his side, and by the time the third body had hit the cobblestones, he and Jang were flanking the mouth of Backstabber Alley.

From inside the alley came the sound of running. Two sets of feet—one clumsy and loud, the other light and graceful. Kleef caught Jang's eye and waggled two fingers, then held his palm open and level, indicating they should let both runners pass.

Jang nodded, and the odd little man Kleef had glimpsed earlier burst from the alley. Gaunt and round-headed, with bulging eyes and thick lips, he was clutching a gray satchel to his bony chest. He hopped over the carnage in the street with no hint of revulsion or surprise, then turned right and raced up the lane without a backward glance.

The red-haired woman appeared an instant later, her green eyes going wide at the sight of so many bodies cut into so many pieces. Absent her cloak, she was wearing a silk tunic belted over leather trousers. Her right hand carried a slender short sword. Despite her practical attire, she was lovelier than any woman Kleef had ever seen, and when she glanced over at him, he felt the same sense of warmth and familiarity that the urchin had described.

Kleef pointed up the lane in the direction her manservant had fled, then silently mouthed the word, "Go."

She responded with a smile that made Kleef go even warmer inside, and he began to wonder just what he had gotten himself into.

Then the agate on Watcher's crossguard began to glow more intensely, and Kleef glimpsed a blur of motion across Rover's Way. He turned to find another shade emerging from the same dark doorway as the first three warriors. To Kleef, it seemed the dark figure was not just stepping out of the shadows—he was dividing from them.

The woman's face grew pale, but she flicked a hand in the enemy's direction. A trio of white darts appeared at her fingertips and streaked across the lane. Her target dropped to one knee, crouching behind his arm and raising a shield of swirling shadow.

The first dart hit the shield and sizzled out of existence. The second vanished in a crackling flash that also took down the shield. The third sank into the warrior's ribs, buckling him forward. He sprawled in the lane, writhing in pain and bleeding shadowstuff onto the cobblestones.

By then, the woman was five paces up Rover's Way, and Kleef was leaping across the lane. He beheaded the fallen shade with a single swipe, then stepped into the doorway from which the warrior had emerged. A blazing blue radiance shone from Helm's Eye, dispelling the darkness within. He found himself looking at a small foyer, in which a ropy, half-formed silhouette was being pushed into the far corner by the light of his sword. Kleef glimpsed a gray, grimacing face, then the dark figure melted into the last remnants of shadow and vanished.

Kleef had been warned that Shadovar warriors could sometimes move through shadows, but with Jang's slender sword singing in the lane behind him, he had no time to consider what he had just seen. He whirled out of the doorway with Watcher still aglow and found Jang dancing around in front of him, his slender sword chopping and slashing in a shadow-cleaving blur. Already, a pair of gray limbs lay oozing darkness onto the street, and the warrior who had lost them had dropped to his knees. Jang's blade whistled back around and sent the shade's head flying.

A piercing hiss sounded from the black mouth of the alley. Jang stumbled backward, his sword arm falling limp and his katana flying free.

Kleef leaped forward, snatching the katana on the fly. "Jang, with me!"

He retreated a few paces down Rover's Way, away from the woman, then turned to Jang. Part of the Shou's breastplate had shattered, and his right shoulder and breast were exposed, revealing a patch of flesh that look bruised, black, and icy. His right arm hung useless, but at least he was keeping up. Kleef held the katana out and was relieved to see Jang take the weapon with his left hand.

"Time for you to withdraw," Kleef said, nodding his friend down the lane. "Report to the King's Tower."

Three more shades spilled from the alley's mouth. The first two turned away, continuing after the woman and her manservant. The last one stepped into the middle of the street and turned to face the two watchmen, studying them with the bright, steel-blue eyes that had first caught Kleef's attention.

"Go." Kleef pushed Jang behind him, back toward the entrance to Rover's Way. "Tell the lord marshall we have Shadovar assassins in the city."

"And leave you behind?" Jang gasped. "Never."

"It's not a suggestion, Jang. Someone needs to report." As

Kleef spoke, he continued to watch the last shade—who was merely watching *him*, not yet advancing. "Tell the lord marshall it looks like they'll end up in the Canal District. Have him send reinforcements down High Bridge Road."

"And that is where we'll meet?" Jang asked, his voice still reluctant. "High Bridge Road?"

Kleef nodded. "I'm going to keep an eye on the chase," he said. "But I'll look for you there."

As Kleef spoke the words, the agate on Watcher's crossguard glowed brighter—this time, casting its blue beam a dozen paces down the lane. Kleef adjusted his stance so the light fell directly on the steel-eyed warrior.

The Shadovar merely grinned, showing a pair of white fangs as long as fingers. Then he raised his arm and vanished behind a shield of darkness.

CHAPTER TWO

WITH THE RESIDENTS OF MARSEMBER FLEEING THE CITY BY any means possible, every noble in town should have been out in the streets, bolstering the courage of the people and inspiring them to take arms against the coming invasion. Instead, Lady Arietta Seasilver—a Chosen of Siamorphe, the patron goddess of nobility —was trapped on her own balcony, a virtual prisoner in her own rooms. Forty feet below, the family servants were scurrying back and forth to House Seasilver's private quay, loading her father's galleass with coin chests and serving silver, ceremonial armor, bejeweled weapons . . . even crate after crate of fine wine.

The sight set Arietta's teeth to grinding. When she looked north across Deepwater Canal, she could see over the city rooftops far into the northern plain, where churning clouds of dust marked Netheril's push into Cormyr. When she leaned over her balustrade and looked to the northeast, she could see a curtain of gray smoke on the horizon—the shadow fiends of Wheloon, burning all they passed on their march to Marsember. If ever the realm had needed every sword it could raise, that time was now.

But instead of rallying the people to the city's defense, her father was fleeing to Elversult with all his prized possessions. Clearly, it was not for nothing that Grand Duke Farnig Seasilver was known in local taverns as "Farnig the Feckless." With Myth Drannor under siege and the eladrin doomed, could he truly be fool enough to think he would escape the Shadovar by simply sailing across the Dragonmere? Cormyr was all that remained to stop the Army of Night, and if the kingdom fell, the Netherese would claim all of Faerûn—perhaps all of Toril.

The clack of a turning lock echoed from the interior of Arietta's chambers. She asked Siamorphe for the strength to be patient and the courage to be direct, then returned to her sitting room. As she had anticipated, a statuesque noble-woman with high cheekbones and a blade-straight nose was arriving from the anteroom. Beyond her, still closing the heavy oak door to the suite, were two burly soldiers in white tabards with wyvern sigils—the same two men who had been standing outside Arietta's door every day for nearly a month.

Arietta flashed the woman a practiced but joyless smile, then went to greet her.

"Mother, what a pleasant surprise." She intercepted the Grand Duchess Elira in the center of room and kissed both cheeks, then motioned to one of the ornate armchairs flanking the fireplace. "Please, sit."

As they settled opposite each other, Arietta's lady-in-waiting, Odelia, hurried in from the dressing room.

"Your Grace," said the girl, curtsying to Arietta's mother. "Please forgive me for not being at the door to welcome you." Rosy-cheeked and doe-eyed, she had a joyful beauty, and Elira often complained that the servant drew too many eyes away from Arietta. "I was packing gowns and did not hear you arrive."

Considering the arrival had not been announced by the guards or preceded by a knock, it was little wonder.

Elira smiled with practiced warmth. "Think nothing of

it," she said. "With those dreadful shadow fiends on the way, we must all be a little forgiving of ourselves. I'm sure you'll return to your usual behavior soon—once we've set up the new household in Elversult."

Tears welled in Odelia's eyes, for she would not be going to Elversult. Concerned that he might be overloading his ship, Duke Farnig had decreed just that morning that only servants who could handle an oar or a weapon would be accompanying the family. All others would be left in Marsember to defend the townhouse.

Doing her best to hold her emotions in check, Odelia inclined her head. "Your patience is most kind, Your Grace." She looked to Arietta, always careful not to usurp her mistress's role as hostess. "Will you be needing anything, my lady?"

Arietta looked at her mother. "May I offer you something?" she asked. Her tone was sweet, but she was seething inside— her mother's remark to Odelia had not been innocent. "Some pear cider, perhaps, or apple wine?"

The cider had gone bad, and Elira hated apple *anything*.

Elira replied with a shrewd smile. "I am afraid we haven't the time." She waited until Odelia had withdrawn, then finally deigned to comment on her daughter's attire. "Arietta, really. It's not as though your father is lacking for guards. Won't you find that armor rather hot aboard the *Wave Wyvern*?"

"How nice of you to be concerned," Arietta replied. "But it won't be a problem, since I won't be aboard."

Elira rolled her eyes. "I thought we had finished that conversation."

"We did," Arietta replied. "You made it clear that you and Father intend to flee the realm in its time of need. *I* intend to defend it. There is nothing more to discuss."

Elira sighed and looked to the ceiling. "I could have sworn that Chauntea sent me a daughter."

"She sent you a Seasilver," Arietta retorted. "And with that name comes a duty to the realm."

"A duty that is your *father's* to observe," Elira said, narrowing her gaze. "And he is doing precisely that."

"By fleeing the war?" Arietta scoffed. "I think not."

"Then we agree—you *don't* think," Elira said. "Because if you did, you would remember that your father is in line to the throne."

"*Twelfth* in line!" Arietta pointed out. "He won't be ascending anytime soon."

"Be that as it may," Elira said, "he must survive. He owes it to the king."

"He *owes* it to the king to flee the war?"

"Just so," Elira said. "Arietta, you must consider the larger picture. Your half-uncle Erzoured is undoubtedly scheming with the Shadovar, while anyone with the Obarskyr name is obliged to stay in Cormyr to fight. We must make certain that a legitimate heir remains to claim the throne. And that duty falls to your father."

Arietta was surprised to see the wisdom of her mother's argument. She began to wonder if she had judged her father unfairly. "And the king has asked this of him?"

Elira flashed a condescending smile. "The king didn't *need* to ask, my dear. Your father understands what is required."

"He *understands* . . ." Arietta could only shake her head, too accustomed to her father's self-serving rationalizations to be shocked. "Has Father at least thought to send word, informing the king of his plans?"

Elira waved a hand dismissively. "The king has other things to worry about. He does not need to concern himself with the safety of your father's sea-crossing."

"Of course not," Arietta said. "And I doubt that he *would*. In fact, if the *Wyvern* were to go down at sea, it would probably be a great relief to His Majesty. There would be one less craven grand-nephew in his line of succession."

"*That* is most uncalled for," Elira snapped. She glanced toward both doors to make certain no servants were eavesdropping, then leaned closer and spoke quietly. "Your father is merely looking toward the future. After Cormyr falls—and it will—the people will *need* a king in exile to keep their hopes alive."

"And do you actually expect the people to find hope in a coward?"

Elira glared. "If I were you," she warned, "I'd be mindful of that tongue of yours. It's the reason you are still unmarried at four-and-twenty—and it's why Aubrin has refused to honor your secret understanding."

"Mother, there *is* no understanding—secret or otherwise," Arietta said. "I wish you would stop telling people that. He said four words to me, and not one of them implied love."

"Love? *Pshaw.*" If Elira had noticed the catch in her daughter's voice, she betrayed no sign of it. "Love is for people who don't matter. *You*, my daughter, are a Seasilver."

"Which is why I would never swear a false vow," Arietta said, "or accept one from anyone else."

"Vows? *Pshaw!*" Elira threw up her hands in exasperation. "This foolishness has gone on long enough. I'll see you aboard the *Wyvern,* Arietta." She rose and started for the door. "We set sail within the half hour."

"Thank you for the update," Arietta said, also rising. "But I have decided to stay."

Elira waved a hand over her shoulder dismissively. "Your father is not giving you that choice." Upon reaching the anteroom, Elira stopped and turned, cocking her head as if a thought had just occurred to her. Her voice softened. "He says you have enough space in your cabin for ten trunks." She gave a little smile. "How would he know if one of those trunks held Odelia?"

Arietta's stomach grew cold. "I know what you're doing, Mother." Elira's suggestion was, of course, a manipulative ploy. If Arietta agreed to come along nicely, her mother would look the other way and allow her to smuggle Odelia aboard. If not . . . well, then Odelia's abandonment would be on Arietta's shoulders. "It won't work."

Elira shrugged. "The girl's future is yours to decide," she said. "But tell me, Daughter, have you forgotten the teachings of Siamorphe?"

"You know that I have not."

"And doesn't she teach us that it is the duty of all vassals to obey the commands of their liege?"

Arietta began to feel ill. "Of course."

"Well, there you have it. Farnig is your liege as well as your father. To disobey him is to disobey your goddess."

"But my *liege* has duties, too," Arietta objected. "Father should be leading the fight, not running from it with every bauble he owns."

"What good would it do for him to throw away his life *and* his treasure? That would only bolster the enemy further. You mustn't defy your father, Arietta, not in this. He always says that *you* are his greatest treasure—and he won't lose you to the Shadovar, either."

Arietta met her mother's gaze. "It would be better if he treasured the people of Marsember."

"Better for the Shadovar, I think," Elira countered. "Thirty minutes, Arietta. I'll send someone to fetch your trunks."

Elira strode across the anteroom and struck the door with the heel of her hand, causing a surprisingly loud *boom* for such a thin woman. Again, the lock clacked open. The two guards slowly opened the door and peered inside, as though they feared Arietta might be waiting to attack or bolt past her mother.

Arietta shook her head in exasperation. Her father had been keeping her a near prisoner for almost a month now, ever since the sergeant of his guards had discovered her in a tavern one night, disguised as a common minstrel and singing onstage. Arietta had tried to bribe the man to keep her secret, but he had pocketed her coin and used it to prove the truth of his story when he told her father. As a reward, her father had tripled the payment.

With the door locked again behind her, Arietta turned and found Odelia holding a seldom-worn gown in her arms. From her hopeful expression, it was obvious she had been eavesdropping. Elira's plan to make her a stowaway was the girl's best hope of survival.

"So, you've heard?" Arietta asked, knowing that Odelia would never be so bold as to bring up the subject herself. "My father says we have room for ten trunks."

"Then . . . you may have some difficult choices to make," Odelia said carefully. "I have already packed fifteen."

"You may choose which trunks will stay and which will go," Arietta said. "Just make certain you can hide inside one of them."

"Are you sure?" Odelia asked, her face brightening. "I know it's your mother's idea, but if your father learns that you have defied him yet again—"

"We don't have much time," Arietta interrupted. The last thing she wanted to discuss was obedience to her father. "You *do* want to go to Elversult, do you not?"

Odelia was quick to nod. "Of course, my lady," she said. "My place is at your side."

"Then you worry about the trunks, and let me worry about the grand duke," Arietta said, ignoring the question of whether *she* would be going to Elversult. She was a Chosen of Siamorphe, which made it her duty to inspire her people *and* obey her liege. It was not clear to her yet how she could do both, but she was determined to find a way. "Just be sure you can open your trunk from the inside."

Odelia looked surprised. "Won't you be able to let me out?"

"Best to play it safe, I think," Arietta said with a shrug.

A muffled clamor sounded from somewhere down in the streets, and a man's voice called for the crowd to make way.

"Finish the packing," Arietta said, heading to the balcony

to investigate. A man was charging along the opposite side of Deepwater Canal, heading east toward the bridge. He looked like a typical thug of the Marsember Watch, carrying a greatsword in a single hand and bellowing for people to clear his path. Arietta saw no one fleeing directly ahead of him. But on High Bridge Road, a red-haired woman and a short disheveled man had just emerged from a narrow footlane to the north, and they were headed south toward the canal. It appeared the big watchman was rushing to intercept the pair before they reached the bridge.

The two citizens were clearly in a hurry; in fact, the man looked utterly panicked. But the red-haired woman had an air of refinement, and she was dressed in a silk tunic that appeared to be both finely tailored and cinched by a silver belt. The watchman, on the other hand, belonged to an organization filled with notorious brutes who often abused their power. If there was a criminal below, Arietta suspected it was the man wearing the armor and cape.

Remaining at the balustrade, she called over her shoulder. "Odelia! Bring my bow and quiver!"

Odelia stepped out of the dressing room, looking confused and harried. "My apologies, but did you ask for—"

"Bow and quiver!" Arietta pointed toward the bedchamber, where she kept her most precious possessions—her weapons and her lyre. "Quickly!" she commanded. "A gentlewoman's life may depend on it."

When Arietta looked back to the streets, the woman and her slovenly companion were already racing onto Deepwater Bridge. The watchman was quickly closing in from the side, still bellowing and knocking people out of his way. He vaulted over a mule cart and landed near the foot of the bridge. But instead of turning to cross the canal, he stopped and looked up the footlane from which the woman and strange little man had come.

For an instant, Arietta thought the watchman might be

waiting for the rest of his troop. But then he brought the giant sword around in a middle guard and stood at the foot of the bridge, turning his back on the fleeing pair. Arietta began to wonder if she had misjudged the situation. Could he possibly be *protecting* the woman?

A blue aura shone around the hilt of the watchman's sword, and he sank into a defensive stance, as if bracing to meet a charge. For a moment, none came, then two dark silhouettes emerged from the footlane, their forms swaddled in shadow. When they saw the watchman, they paused, and a third figure emerged from the footlane to join them. This one had two dots of steel-blue light shining out from beneath his hood.

A shade of Netheril, if one of Arietta's former suitors was to be believed. A Purple Dragon, the fellow had been fond of trying to impress her with his experiences fighting off Netherese border raids, and he had told her that shades could always be identified by their lambent eyes. He had even named the eye color of several of the princes, but Arietta had already grown weary of his bragging and stopped paying attention.

"Odelia!" Arietta called, swinging her hand behind her. "My—"

Arietta felt a shaft of polished yew slapping into her palm, and she brought the bow in front of her to string it. The trio of shades had started to advance again, moving cautiously. By the time she had flipped the bow and slipped the string over the opposite tip, the leader was whipping one hand forward in the air, his blue-gray eyes fixed on the watchman.

A crescent-shaped blade of shadow materialized in front of the shadow warriors and came spinning, past half a dozen people on High Bridge Road. One unfortunate man dropped to his knees, clutching his side. Unimpeded, the dark disc continued toward the watchman, who whipped his heavy sword downward to block. When the disc hit his blade, the shadow divided into two pieces that wobbled past on either side, then dissipated against the stone railing of the bridge. The few people remaining on the street screamed and scattered.

Arietta reached back again with her hand. Before she could even say "arrow," she felt a thick shaft slap into her palm. She quickly nocked the heavy boar-arrow Odelia had given her, but instead of taking aim, Arietta held her bow low, so it would be hidden by the balustrade. Firing too soon would be a mistake. Her weapon was a hunting bow, not a longbow, and despite the flattery of her retainers, she understood that she was not truly a master archer—not yet. The shades were still too far away, and even the watchman was near the limits of her accuracy.

The shades advanced slowly, the leader's blue-gray eyes enlarging from dots of light to larger disks. His companions remained two paces behind him.

Odelia crouched behind her and whispered. "Are those . . . are those the shadow fiends of Wheloon?"

Arietta shook her head. "They don't look monstrous enough. I think those are just normal shades."

"*That* is normal?" Odelia gasped. "We are doomed!"

"Not if we keep our heads," Arietta said. "The Shadovar are not the only ones with magic at their fingertips."

Two more shades emerged from the footlane and started toward the bridge. The watchman held his ground, as if determined to deny passage to all five of his foes. The red-haired woman had stopped halfway across the bridge and was looking back toward her protector—until her slovenly companion rushed back to tug at her sleeve.

"There's going to be a battle," Arietta said. "Odelia, leave my quiver and sound the alarm. Tell the guards at my door that there are Shadovar on the bridge. Then go to the Bridge Gate and tell the guards they must open our house to the woman and her companion—and to the watchman, too, if he reaches us."

Odelia hung the heavy quiver from its hook on Arietta's belt, then hesitated. "Shouldn't the orders come from your father?"

As Odelia spoke, the Shadovar leader drew a scimitar with a blade that looked like black glass and charged toward the bridge.

"No time!" Arietta fixed her gaze on the pair of gleaming eyes, trying to gauge her target's speed by counting her own breaths. "Tell them the gentlewoman is a friend of my mother's."

"You wish me to *lie*, my lady?"

Arietta exhaled in exasperation. "Yes, Odelia. I insist!"

The Netherese warriors moved at a speed Arietta could scarcely believe. She raised her bow and drew the string back to her cheek.

By then, the shade's leader was only two strides from the watchman.

Arietta set her aim on the empty space just above the watchman's shoulder and, exhaling, let the bowstring sing. The arrow streaked away in a yellow blur, flashing across the canal in less time than it took her to finish emptying her lungs.

The shaft caught the leader high in the torso, piercing his black armor and sinking a hand's length into his chest. The impact was enough to stop his charge and send him sprawling back into the street.

If the watchman was surprised, he showed no sign of it, instantly stepping forward to finish his foe. His attack was intercepted on the way down by a pair of dark blades, both of which shattered beneath his huge sword.

Arietta struggled to find another target, but with the melee now acting as a shield, she risked hitting the watchman if she loosed another arrow. Then a shade broke to the left, and Arietta let fly, hoping to drive him back before he could slip past the watchman onto the bridge. The warrior saw it coming and swirled a hand through the air, raising a shield of murk between himself and the approaching arrow.

The arrow sank into the darkness and briefly vanished. An instant later, the shade stumbled out from behind his shield, both hands falling away from the arrow now buried in his heart.

Arietta drew back her bowstring, looking for her next target. But the watchman had begun a strategic retreat, pivoting back and forth across the bridge, using his huge sword to hold two shades at bay while the red-haired woman and her companion fled. Arietta could not find the fifth shade, and she could not find a clear shot at the two on the bridge.

Then she saw the leader, still lying on High Bridge Road, struggling to pull her first arrow from his chest.

Impossible.

Arietta's arrows were a gift from King Foril, created by one of Cormyr's most powerful War Wizards, Glathra Barcantle herself. They were, in effect, a royal apology. Arietta and her father had been riding with the king's hunting party when a wounded boar had charged her. Arietta had planted half a dozen shafts in the poor creature before it finally unhorsed her. Afterward, it had emerged that King Foril himself had fired the arrow that enraged the beast. To make amends, the king had asked Glathra to create an entire quiver of arrows that would stop anything Arietta struck.

Anything except Shadovar warriors, it seemed.

She loosed again.

The shade looked in her direction and raised a hand. In the next instant, she watched her arrow sinking into a small shadowy shield, but instead of passing through, the arrow simply vanished.

Hoping that three arrows might succeed where two had failed, Arietta nocked again and set her aim on the shade's chest—then felt her blood go cold as Odelia's scream erupted in the sitting room behind her.

Arietta dropped low and spun around. Her lady-in-waiting was swaying on her feet, her face frozen in a shocked expression, her body cleaved from collar to breastbone by the gore-dripping blade of a thick black sword. The Shadovar who held the blade was still hanging from a shadowy corner of the ceiling, like a descending spider.

Arietta started to aim, but the warrior was already pointing four fingers on his free hand in her direction. She loosed anyway, then flung her bow at him and dived for the floor, rolling forward and snatching an arrow from her quiver. She saw her chairs and fireplace flash past to her right, then cold bands of shadow angling toward the patch of floor she'd just left, slicing through everything they touched. She came up on her knees just as the shade dropped to the ground in front of her, his dark sword rising to strike. She plunged the arrow up into his abdomen.

The shaft went vertical as the arrowhead drove up toward his heart. The warrior screamed in anguish and dropped his sword, reaching down to clutch at the arrow with both hands, struggling to pull it free. Arietta kept pushing, hard, and sent him stumbling backward—straight into the swinging sword of a charging guard in a white tabard. The shade's head bounced off the wall, and Arietta barely had time to spin out of the way before it landed on the floor beside her.

"My lady!" A big hand reached down and pulled her to her feet. "Are you—"

"I'm fine."

She jerked her arm free, then turned to find the shade's decapitated corpse sprawled over Odelia's motionless form.

"Sorry, my lady," the guard said, no doubt noting the horror in her eyes. "They say you have to remove their heads."

Arietta nodded, then pointed at the shade. "Could you remove that, please?"

The guard bent down and quickly pulled the shade aside, revealing a gore-filled cleft in Odelia's chest that left no doubt about her fate. Heart breaking, Arietta uttered a quick prayer and knelt down to close the girl's eyes.

The second guard—a lanky fellow named Mannus—stepped through door and began to scan the room.

"Was that the only one?" he asked, gesturing at the dead shade. "How did he get in?"

Arietta pointed toward her still-open balcony. "I'm not sure, but they're out on High Bridge Road." She paused, suddenly angry at Mannus, then rose. "Where *were* you?"

Mannus's face colored with guilt, but instead of apologizing or explaining, he motioned the second guard to the balcony.

"Secure those doors, Suther." He turned back to Arietta. "Did he come across the balcony?"

"No," Arietta replied, "and I was standing right there."

"Maybe you couldn't see him," Mannus said. "I've heard some of them can walk between shadows."

"Apparently, you heard correctly," Arietta said bitterly. She retrieved her bow from the floor, then turned to confront the guard. "This should not have happened, Mannus. I sent Odelia to alert the house and go to the Bridge Gate. Why was she still here?"

Without waiting for his reply, she turned on her heel and headed to her bedchamber.

Mannus trailed after her, but stopped at the door. "My apologies, Highness," he said. "We thought Odelia's warning was a trick. Your father—"

"A *trick*?"

"Your father warned us to be wary," Mannus continued. "He would have our heads if you fooled us and slipped away."

Struggling to bring her temper under control, Arietta stepped toward her bed. There was no time to sit and calm herself, but she was still careful to inhale deeply and exhale completely, telling herself that nothing could be accomplished by rage, that nothing would bring Odelia back.

The tactic failed miserably. By the time she had retrieved her sword scabbard from its hook beside her pillows, she was more furious than ever—at the Shadovar, at Mannus and Suther, and most of all, at her father. It was *his* order the two guards had been following, and now Odelia was gone. Her father would answer for that—even more surely than his guards.

Arietta turned to find Mannus blocking her path, eyeing the jewel-encrusted scabbard in her hand. His expression suggested he thought it ridiculous for her to even own such a weapon, much less wield it. She used the tip of her bow to push the guard backward, then proceeded to herd him across the sitting room.

"Do you really find me that ridiculous, Mannus?" she demanded. "Do you really think me so foolish as to sound a false alarm at a time like this?"

"It wasn't our fault," Suther protested. "My pardon for saying so, but you're a very headstrong wo—"

"*Headstrong*?" Arietta whirled on the man, bringing the flat of her scabbard up under his chin. "Is it 'headstrong' to think that my father's place—that *our* place—is with the people? War is upon us, you idiot!"

Suther appeared too confused and flustered to answer.

Mannus came to Suther's rescue, gently pulling him out of the way. "It's not our place to decide such things," he said. "But the grand duke—"

"You're right, Mannus." Arietta secured her scabbard on her hip, opposite her quiver, then added, "It is not your place to decide *anything*. And I order you to come with me."

Still holding her bow, Arietta hurried from her chambers into the central tower, the Turret of Heavens, and began to descend the long flight of stairs that spiraled down the outer wall. The turret was open all the way to the Golden Hall on the ground floor, and looking over the balustrade, Arietta could see a steady stream of servants carrying armfuls of linens.

She began to call down, "Shadovar on the bridge! Sound the alarm!"

Mannus and Suther added their voices, shouting commands to prepare the house. By the time Arietta had reached the second level, heaps of abandoned linens lay strewn across the marble floor, and the bang of slamming shutters echoed from every corner of the house.

Arietta reached the bottom of the stairs to find a grizzled

sergeant—the very sergeant who had told her father about her adventures as a tavern minstrel—waiting with half a dozen armored men.

"Lady Arietta, the *Wave Wyvern* will depart as soon as we're aboard." The sergeant extended an arm to his left, in the direction of the walled yard that protected the ship's mooring. "Your father has sent me to escort you."

"Thank you, Carlton," Arietta stepped directly toward him—then bent backward at the last possible moment and ducked under his arm. "But we both have more important things to do."

"My lady!"

Carlton spun and grabbed for her, but she was already slapping her bow tip into the helmets of two men, using it to startle them apart before she pushed between them.

"Lady Arietta!" Carlton roared. "Your father has ordered me to bring you to the ship!"

"Then you'll have to catch me." Arietta broke into a sprint, racing out of the Golden Hall and into the swirling gray seascapes of the Corridor of the Kraken. She called over her shoulder, "And be quick about it!"

"Be . . . *quick*?"

A cacophony of clanking and yelling broke out as the twelve guards took up the chase, with Carlton threatening all manner of dire consequences if Arietta did not stop immediately. The more he threatened, the more determined she became. If the choice lay between obeying her feckless liege and serving the people, then Siamorphe's will seemed clear. Arietta would not offend her goddess—not when a brave man was out there on the bridge alone, doing what her *father* should have been doing—leading the fight against the Shadovar.

Carlton's threats faded into the general din of the house as Arietta rounded a corner and entered the Hall of the Sirens. Halfway down its length, she turned abruptly and ducked down an intersecting corridor, crossed a small foyer, then raced out into the carriage court used for domestic deliveries and casual access.

Thirty paces away, the gate that opened toward High Bridge Road hung closed and barred. A pair of square watchtowers rose to either side of it, and Arietta counted two guards on each one, looking away and peering toward the action on the bridge. Knowing Carlton would soon reappear, Arietta yelled up at one of the towers.

"You there!" she cried, still running. One the guards glanced back into the yard. "Open the gate!"

The double-chinned guard gaped at her in surprise. "Lady Arietta? Is that—"

"*Now!*" Arietta commanded, halfway to the gate. She slowed just long enough to make her point clear. "My mother will have your heads if something happens to that woman. She's a dear friend of the family!"

The guard's expression grew alarmed. He relayed her command to the others, then stooped and disappeared. An instant later, the remaining three guards were shouting warnings down into the street, and the double-chinned guard had entered the yard from the tower. To Arietta's relief, he rushed straight toward the heavy wooden gate, putting his hand on the crossbar to lift it.

And that was when Carlton emerged from the house behind her, still shouting her name and demanding that she stop. The double-chinned guard—Fiske, she remembered he was called—looked up and scowled, one hand still resting on the bar.

"Carlton, come quickly!" Arietta yelled. Praying to the goddess to make her voice loud enough to drown out her pursuer's, she swung her bow toward the gate, as if urging Carlton and his men to follow her. "They're bound to be on her by now!"

Outside the gate, Arietta heard the clang of iron bolts ricocheting off cobblestones, followed by muffled cries of surprise. She looked up and saw that her father's guards were not aiming their crossbows at the Shadovar on the bridge. Instead, they were shooting straight down, in front of the gate. It seemed they were attempting to clear the area so no commoners would be tempted to seek shelter inside the house.

Another of her father's orders, no doubt.

Still ten steps from Fiske, Arietta nocked an arrow and raised her bow, ready to pin the man's hand to the wood if need be. But the guard was merely being cautious, peering out a spyhole before he drew the bar back.

"*Now*, Fiske!"

Arietta let fly. Her arrow thunked into the wood at the base of the gate, and Fiske looked up, his thick-lipped mouth hanging agape. Arietta nocked another arrow.

"Open it now!"

Fiske lifted the crossbar and pulled his side of the gate open, just far enough for Arietta to slip out. She had to pause in the alcove between the towers, for the scene in the street was madness. A panicked mob was fleeing the fight on the bridge, trying to squeeze through a maze of toppled handcarts and spilled possessions. Her father's guards were shouting down from their towers, warning people to stay clear of the gate—and reinforcing their orders by pinging iron crossbow quarrels off the cobblestones below.

Arietta looked up the street toward the canal, where the watchman was at the center of the bridge—bloodied, but his greatsword slashing back and forth as he executed a *very* slow retreat. She counted three Shadovar against him, the nearest pair harrying him with wedges of flying shadow while the third tried to dart past along the bridge railing.

As she watched, the watchman's sword lashed out, and the third Shadovar's dark head went tumbling into the canal. The other two countered with an onslaught of sword-work, their blades whirling and slashing as they pressed the attack.

The watchman blocked and parried, then retreated a step.

One single step.

If the man wasn't a knight, he soon would be. Arietta would see to that herself—assuming he survived, of course.

Knowing that Carlton and his men would soon come

through the gate behind her, Arietta took a deep breath, then stepped out into the street and looked up at the tower guards.

"You up there! Stop that!" She used her bow to point toward the battle. "Come with me to the bridge!"

The rain of quarrels diminished, and the eldest guard, a long-faced brute with a drooping mustache, leaned over and frowned back at her.

"What, are you mad?" he called down. "Your father would have our ears!"

"Yes, but he'll have your *heads* if you let me go out there alone." She smiled sweetly, then shrugged. "The choice is yours, of course."

Arietta heard the gate creaking open behind her, but she did not look back. She was already charging up the street.

CHAPTER THREE

IT WAS ALMOST TOO EASY. BY ALL RIGHTS, KLEEF SHOULD have been dead by now. His boots were slipping in his own blood, his arms and legs ached with the ice-cold burn of shadow-inflicted slashes, and his shoulders had grown so weary he could barely swing his sword. Yet somehow, he was still holding the bridge, *alone,* against an endless stream of shades.

It made no sense.

The enemy arrived in twos and threes, rushing in behind flurries of umbral magic and slashing blades, attacking so fiercely Kleef dared not look away. He had no idea what had become of the red-haired woman or the mysterious archer who had come to his aid, and he had long ago lost track of the Shadovar leader—the one with the steel-blue eyes. And yet, his foes never seemed to press so hard that he would be forced to flee, as though they wanted to kill him on Deepwater Bridge or not at all.

At first, Kleef had attributed their caution to Watcher. The agate on the sword's crossguard continued to glow whenever Shadovar drew near, and they tended to cringe and dodge when it shined in their direction. But the blue light never seemed to cause any injury that would explain their reluctance to mount a full charge, and, he had eventually decided that his opponents were simply trying to keep him from seeing what was happening behind him.

Kleef retreated three quick steps, hoping to buy a moment to look behind him and see what had become of the red-haired woman. Another hissing disk came flying from the right and a cloud of black darts from the left. He ducked the darts and used Watcher to deflect the disk, and his latest trio of foes came rushing in behind a flurry of kicks and slashes.

Kleef stood his ground for two heartbeats, then blocked and pivoted, sending the middle shade flying with a knifehand to the throat. He brought Watcher around in a single-handed chop that buried the sword deep in the collar of the one on the left. He spun away, ripping the blade free and leading with a heel sweep that would prevent his last attacker from slipping in behind him.

Then Kleef glimpsed a yellow streak flying in from the south end of the bridge. He drew up short, just in time to see an arrow take the last shade in the side of the head. The impact lifted him off his feet and sent him flying.

Kleef quickly beheaded all three of his downed foes, then was astonished to look up and find no more Shadovar charging in to attack. For the moment, at least, they had run out of warriors.

Kleef glanced behind him, toward the south end of the bridge.

Twenty paces away, a tall, fair-skinned woman was racing toward him, her blonde hair flying over the shoulders of her ornate hunting armor. She came to a stop ten paces away, nocking a fresh arrow and looking for another target. With pale blue eyes and a wide, full-lipped mouth, she looked vaguely familiar—and entirely out of place charging into battle against the Shadovar.

When she saw Kleef staring at her, the woman cocked an eyebrow. "Oh, I'm sorry," she called. "Did you want to kill *all* of them yourself?"

Kleef frowned. "What?" Then, recognizing her sarcasm, he quickly added, "No."

Leaving it at that, he shifted his attention to the street behind her. The crowd was too dense and churning for him to spot the red-haired woman, or much of anything else. But at least he saw no obvious battle snarls to suggest the Shadovar had found her.

The blonde archer cried out, "*Drop!*"

Kleef obeyed instantly. He still hadn't hit the ground when her arrow sizzled past, barely a hand's width from his ear, and thudded into its target. He looked up to find another trio of shades almost upon him. A fourth lay behind them, clutching at the arrow in his chest and writhing in pain.

Kleef rose to one knee and swung his sword into the dark tangle of legs coming toward him, and the air erupted into screams. He switched to a one-handed grip and sprang back to his feet, then blocked, ducked, and shouldered forward between two of his attackers. He spun around behind the one on the left end and sent the shade's head flying, then saw a geyser of dark blood erupt from the middle one as an arrow tore through his throat.

The one on the right end was already five paces past Kleef, halfway to the archer. Holding her bow in one hand, she drew a slender sword and blocked his initial attack, then brought the bow tip around to harry her attacker's feet. The shade leaped back, then forward again, and only a timely pivot saved the archer from having her armor sorely tested.

By then, Kleef was within striking range. He brought Watcher around high and sent the shade's head flying.

A gout of dark blood arced from the neck stump, spraying the woman's golden hair and the left side of her face. Her blue eyes went wide.

"Uh, sorry," Kleef said, kicking the body away before it could fall on her. "I didn't mean to—"

"It's quite all right," she said, forcing a smile between lips

41

curled in revulsion. "You were only trying to help."

Seeing her up close, Kleef felt even more certain he recognized the woman from somewhere—but now was hardly the time to figure it out. He merely nodded, then turned to see whether a fresh wave of attackers had arrived.

And they had. This time, there were more than a dozen, standing in two murky ranks about two-thirds of the way across the bridge. When they did not advance, Kleef began to fear they were simply giving themselves enough room to unleash an onslaught of shadow magic.

Then he began to hear boots pounding up the bridge behind him, and he glanced back to find at least ten men-at-arms charging from the direction of House Seasilver. Their white tabards bore a pale purple wyvern—the sigil of Duke Farnig's household guard—and they quickly began to gather around the blonde archer.

Kleef stepped over to a gray-bearded man wearing the crimson shoulder-braid of sergeant of the guard, then warned, "Don't cluster—not against shadow magic." He waved a hand across the width of the bridge. "Form a battle line here."

The sergeant's expression turned resentful, and his men-at-arms frowned.

Then the agate on Watcher's crossguard flared to life again, and the gazes of all ten men-at-arms dropped to the blue stone. They began to stand a little straighter, their faces started to harden with determination, and Kleef found himself trying to hide his confusion. Clearly, there were a few things about Watcher his father had neglected to tell him.

Finally, the sergeant barked, "You heard the man. Single rank!" He glanced at Kleef, then added, "No one passes!"

The guards responded with a spirited cry and assumed their positions in front of Kleef, their hands filled with daggers and swords. The woman stepped to Kleef's side, her sword back in its scabbard and a fresh arrow nocked on her bowstring.

Kleef stole one last glance over his shoulder, searching for any sign that more Shadovar might be emerging from the shadows to attack from behind them. At first, he didn't see anything except the continued mayhem of too many people fleeing up High Bridge Road. But his eye was soon drawn to movement near the Bridge Gate of House Seasilver, and he glimpsed a flash of red hair as it disappeared through the narrow gap of the closing gate.

"The enemy is in *front* of us," the archer said. "And you're welcome, by the way."

It took Kleef a moment to catch her meaning. "Uh . . . right." He looked back to the Shadovar and was alarmed to find them swirling their hands, creating shields of raw shadowstuff. "Thanks for your help."

"Think nothing of it." Given the sarcasm of a moment before, the woman sounded surprisingly sincere. "Your stand has been an inspiration to us all."

As she spoke, the second rank of Shadovar began to rub their hands together, drawing wisps of darkness from their murky auras and packing them into pulsing balls of shadow. Unable to locate the steel-eyed leader, Kleef simply pointed at the middle of the second rank.

"That one. Second rank, center."

"That one *what*?" asked the archer.

"Kill him," Kleef said. "*Now*."

The woman brought her bow up and loosed the arrow in the same smooth motion, and an eye blink later, her target went stumbling backward with an arrow sprouting from his chest. The ball of shadow seemed to melt in his grasp and began seeping through his fingers, dissolving everything it touched. By the time his body hit the bridge, his elbow was gone, and the rest of his arm was draining into the dark cracks between the cobblestones.

The warriors to either side of him raised their arms, preparing to hurl their balls of shadow. Kleef called for a charge and started forward, the archer and Duke Farnig's men-at-arms running at his side.

The shadow orbs came flying.

The torsos of two guards melted into darkness as they took the hits full in the chest. Kleef brought Watcher around, Helm's Eye flashing as he deflected two of the dark balls, sending them arcing over the canal. A third orb managed to slip past him, and he turned to see the archer trying to pivot away from it.

No time. Kleef kicked the back of her heels. Her feet flew out from beneath her—and her head dropped out of the shadow ball's path half a heartbeat before it streaked past.

The woman landed on her backplate, and Kleef was glad to see she had the good training to tuck her chin to prevent her head from hitting. They had already fallen five paces behind the charge, so he grabbed her by her bow arm—and finally recalled where he had seen her face.

"I know you."

"I shouldn't be surprised," she said. "Though I hardly—"

"You're that minstrel who used to sing at The Old Oak," Kleef interrupted, yanking her to her feet. "Elver . . . Elberta . . ."

"*Elbertina*." The woman's tone was irritated. "But that was my stage—"

A tremendous battle cheer sounded behind the Shadovar, and it was quickly answered by Duke Farnig's men-at-arms. Kleef looked up to see nearly a dozen halberds swaying in the air behind the Shadovar lines. The Marsember Watch had arrived.

"Reinforcements!" Elbertina raced after Farnig's guards. "*Now* we have them!"

But the shades were in no mood to continue the fight. They broke toward both sides of the bridge, flinging lines of shadow around the balustrades. As their ranks parted, Kleef was surprised to see that the "reinforcements" were his own men, with Jang leading the troop.

The shades began to leap off the bridge, trailing their shadow lines behind them like ropes. As they hit the ends, they swung back and disappeared under the belly of the bridge. Kleef reached the balustrade half a step behind the last warrior, but by the time he leaned out to slash the dark line, the fellow was already dropping into the murk beneath the span. Kleef did not hear a splash.

Elbertina reached his side, leaning over the balustrade to peer into the empty waters. "Where did they go?"

"Good question," Kleef said. He turned and looked back toward House Seasilver. "I have a feeling we won't like the answer."

Joelle Emmeline stood just inside a small carriage court, peering through a narrow gap between two barely open gates. She was looking back toward the bridge where the battle had been, studying the big watchman who had just saved her for the second time that day. With rugged features and dark hair curling out beneath his helm, he was as handsome as he was deadly, and she could not help thinking that the Lady had sent him to her. He certainly appeared capable of protecting her. And if he proved to be as talented in the gentler arts as he was in combat? Well, then—the long journey ahead might even become a pleasure.

"Have you gone *mad*?" demanded a nasal voice beside her. "You will let in the . . . shadows!"

The gates banged shut, and Joelle looked over to find her companion with his hands pressed to the oaken planks. Dressed in a drab gray robe and exuding a foul odor that seemed impossible to scrub off, the little round-headed man looked more like a beggar than one of her fellow Chosen. For the hundredth time, she found herself questioning whether he had truly been sent by the gods to help her save Toril.

"Aren't you curious about him, Malik?" Joelle asked. She helped him slide the heavy crossbar back into place. "Not the least little bit?"

Malik's face grayed with irritation. "About a big oaf with a big sword and a big thirst for using it?" he asked. "His type is as common as vermin in this vile place. I could stand on any corner of the city and hire a hundred just like him."

Joelle flashed her radiant smile. She smiled often—and when she did, it was always radiant.

"How sweet," she said. "You're jealous."

A pained look came to the little man's face. "Why should I be jealous? You will never belong to someone like me—and I am wise enough to know it."

"*Belong*?" Joelle chuckled, her voice gentle but chastising. "Love isn't a yoke, Malik. It's a gift to be shared freely—or not at all."

"And it is one you will never share with me."

"You're wrong about that, Malik." She laid a hand on his shoulder. "I have *already* given you my love. And you would see that, if only you would give yours to me."

"I'm here, am I not?" Malik's tone was resentful. "If joining you in this madness isn't love, I don't know what is."

"You're here because your god commands it," Joelle reminded him. "That's obedience, not love."

Malik looked away, as he always did when he did not wish her to see into his heart, then picked up the small woolen satchel he had stolen off a cart soon after the Shadovar began chasing them.

"Enough blather," he said. "We have to move on. It's not safe here."

Joelle turned toward the interior of the cobblestone court-yard, where dozens of other refugees who had pushed through the gate milled about. Many had begun peering into the windows of the carriage house and into the arched doorways of the great house itself, nervously murmuring to one another. If any guards had remained behind when the archer led her company out to join the fight on the bridge, they were nowhere to be seen.

Joelle allowed Malik to take her arm and lead the way around the courtyard's center monument—a grotesque statue of a diving wyvern. On the far side, he stopped suddenly and clutched the small satchel to his chest.

Joelle followed his gaze and immediately spotted the source of his alarm: a pair of steel-blue eyes shining out of the murk beneath one of the arched doorways. In a single fluid motion, she snatched a trio of throwing darts off her belt and whipped them toward the eyes.

The enchanted darts blazed with the all-consuming heat of Sune's passion, and a chorus of alarmed cries filled the courtyard as panicked refugees raced for cover. Joelle kept her gaze fixed on the doorway, where the dusky silhouette of her target became visible. Swaddled in a dark cloak that blurred into murkiness at the edges, he was tall and lanky, with a long chin, gaunt cheeks, and the glowing, metal-colored eyes of a Prince of Shade.

Yder Tanthul, of course. He was one of the Shadovar's greatest living warriors—and the bane of Joelle's existence.

He caught her first dart on a shield of shadow, which dissolved instantly into magical flame. Unfazed, Yder pivoted aside, allowing the next pair to thunk into the door behind him. He smiled and extended a hand.

Joelle tensed her legs, gathering herself to spring away, but it was Malik who cried out in alarm.

"Help me!" He began to lurch forward, fighting to keep the satchel clutched to his chest. "The Eye! He has the Eye!"

Joelle drew her slender sword and, praying for Sune's help, stepped between Malik and Yder. Instantly, her long red hair began to emit a faint aura of fiery light. All eyes swung in her direction, and the panic in the courtyard waned as refugees stopped to gape at her divinely enhanced beauty. When she smiled, gasps of awe rippled through the crowd.

Only Yder seemed immune. He emerged from the doorway, hissing and cursing, his hand spraying a beam of shadow in her direction. Joelle spun away and dived into a forward roll, then heard a cold sizzle as the shadow beam grazed the statue behind her. An instant later, the entire courtyard shook as the stone wyvern crashed down and shattered against the cobblestones.

The shadow beam reached the gate and crackled through the heavy oak planks. Cries of alarm and anger echoed across the courtyard. The refugees whirled on Yder in a rage, their hands filled with daggers or clubs or anything else they could use as a weapon. By the time Joelle had returned to her feet, the shadow prince had been swallowed by a screaming mob.

Malik was gone, too, of course. His god, Myrkul, had bestowed on him the ability to vanish like a ghost, and he practiced it often—especially when danger threatened. That left Joelle to handle Yder alone, and when she looked toward the courtyard entrance, she found several of his shadow warriors already climbing through the shattered remains of the gate.

Knowing that Malik would try to conceal his odor by hiding in the worst-smelling place possible, she turned toward the carriage house annex and raced inside. At the near end, a trio of expensive coaches sat side by side. A line of open stalls stood along the back wall, still lined with hay and manure, but otherwise empty. A ladder between two stalls led up into the hayloft. At the end closest to the main house were two large doors, one marked "Tack Room" and the other "Clean Shoes Only."

Joelle glanced back into the courtyard and found the Shadovar still busy trying to fight off the enraged mob. She felt genuine remorse to see so many felled by the glassy black blades, but their sacrifice was necessary. If she and Malik did not survive to complete their mission, those same people would suffer a fate much worse than death—as would all of Toril.

She barred the carriage house doors, then turned to look for her companion.

"Malik?" She grabbed a pitchfork and began to stir the piles of hay and manure in the stalls. "Malik, we have to hurry!"

Joelle was on her third stall when she heard a soft clunking from the far end of the annex. Her companion emerged from the tack room, one hand holding his curved short sword, the other clutching the gray satchel hung over his shoulder.

"Is it safe?"

"For the moment," Joelle said. "But we need to move, and quickly."

Malik frowned. "I have only been waiting on *you*," he said. "Next time, I will not be so gallant."

Malik left the tack room, then led the way through the adjacent door into a long service corridor that ran along the back side of the mansion. The passage had limestone floors and iron candle sconces on the walls, and it was littered down its entire length with abandoned furniture and trunks of discarded clothing. Ahead, several exhausted servants stood in the mouths of intersecting hallways, leaning against doorframes and eyeing the cast-off goods with expressions of shock and resentment.

Malik closed the door to the stable and pressed his palm to it, calling upon the god of the dead to hold it fast. Then he turned and led the way into the house. If any of the servants raised a brow, Malik returned their gaze with a bulging-eyed glare that made most recipients blanch and turn away.

The strategy worked until they had advanced roughly halfway through the house. There, an imperious looking man in velvet robes stepped out to block their path. He had an arched nose and close-set eyes, and his velvet robes bore the same wyvern sigil as the guards' tabards. He was obviously a high-ranking member of the household staff—probably the majordomo himself. The man eyed them up and down, then spoke in a plummy voice.

"Do I know you?"

"No, and you are safer for it," Malik answered. He brandished the gray satchel slung over his shoulder. "But have no worries. We are not here to take your master's cast-off belongings, only to deliver to him a most marvelous gift that has been sent by the gods themselves."

The man stared down at Malik's soiled clothes and the grimy satchel, then wrinkled his nose and turned to call over his shoulder.

"Kegwell, come here," he said. "And bring your men. I have a job for you."

The clamor of steel and boots echoed down the hallway. Joelle silently cursed Malik's love of the lie. Sometimes, it seemed that he would rather invent an implausible story than tell a convincing truth. She grabbed his shoulder and pulled him back, then stepped into his place.

"Please accept my apologies, my good man." Joelle smiled, and the majordomo's expression quickly softened. "My traveling companion can be quite inventive when he's frightened."

Malik huffed in indignation, but the man ignored him and turned to Joelle. "I don't believe I know you, either, my lady."

"Lady Emmeline, of Berdusk." Joelle did not present her hand, aware that no noblewoman of Cormyr would grant such liberties to a mere servant. "I do hope you'll be good enough to let us pass. The fighting in the streets is quite ferocious."

As Joelle spoke, five men in white tabards over chain mail emerged from the hallway behind the proud-looking man. She smiled at them, and their countenances immediately changed from bellicose to friendly. Her smile almost always had that effect on people. The lead guard, a grim-faced man with a drooping mustache, allowed his gaze to linger on Joelle as he spoke to the man who had summoned his team.

"You called for us, Master Greymace?"

"Yes, Kegwell, I did."

Greymace frowned at Joelle and Malik, his gaze sliding back and forth between the two as he tried to make sense of the apparent differences in their social rank. Finally, his gaze settled on Malik.

"The rabble is beginning to make its way into the house," he said. "Escort these two from—"

Greymace was interrupted when a muffled *boom* reverberated from the carriage house annex. Malik glanced back, then removed the satchel from his shoulder and astonished Joelle by shoving it into Kegwell's arms.

"You must take that to your master's ship!" His voice had assumed a commanding urgency. "It will protect him from the shadow fiends!"

"Shadow fiends?" Kegwell looked up the corridor toward the boom. "Here?"

"Who do you think that *was*?" Joelle asked, starting to see where Malik was going with this particular lie. She turned to Greymace and shooed him down the corridor. "We must hurry. I think your master has been their target all along!"

Greymace studied the satchel and frowned doubtfully—until another *boom* rumbled from inside the carriage house. Eyes lighting in alarm, he motioned for Kegwell and the guards to follow, then started down the corridor at a brisk pace.

"The duke cannot wait for his daughter any longer," he said. "The *Wyvern* must depart at *once*."

They had barely taken five steps before a tremendous crackle-and-clatter sounded behind them. Joelle glanced back to see a long blade of shadow cleaving the stone wall that separated the stables from the main house.

"Run!" she yelled. "They're coming!"

The guards did not need to be told twice. Two of them grabbed Greymace by the arms and broke into a full sprint, pulling the majordomo down the corridor with them. Kegwell followed close on his heels, clutching the heavy satchel under his arm and commanding his men to run faster, and soon they were all racing out of the passage into a large courtyard strewn with crates of unwanted books, draperies, and porcelain.

On the far side of the yard, a hundred-and-fifty foot galleass was docked at a private quay, its deck rails lined by men-at-arms wearing the white tabards of the house guard. On the raised quarterdeck stood a tall, handsome figure in golden scale mail—undoubtedly the master of the house. He had long coppery hair and a pointed beard, and he was using a magnificent sword in a bejeweled scabbard to point and gesture as he bellowed orders to the crew on the main deck.

A thunderous *crack* echoed out of the service corridor. Joelle returned to the door and looked up the length of the passage to where the dark form of Prince Yder Tanthul was just stepping through the remnants of the carriage house wall. She pulled a trio of darts from her belt and sent them sailing down the hall, then spun back toward the galleass . . . and felt Malik's hand close around her elbow.

"Let the fools go," he said, pulling her aside. "They're doomed anyway."

Joelle frowned and—watching Kegwell race up the gangplank with Malik's satchel—tried to pull free. "But the Eye—"

"Will never be aboard that ship." Malik pulled her toward the front of the mansion. "And neither will we."

Arietta stepped onto her father's private quay and could scarcely believe what she saw. The *Wave Wyvern* was already two hundred yards up the canal, with all oars pulling and dozens of archers at the rails. She could barely make out her father—a copper-haired figure in gold armor—standing on the quarterdeck, peering at something being held by another figure in robes—probably his majordomo, Greymace. After a moment, he reached toward Greymace, then raised what appeared to be a large hammer. He studied the hammer for a moment, then cocked his head in confusion and looked back at the majordomo.

The quay drummed with the sound of running boots as her companions caught up to her. The big watchman—he had introduced himself as Kleef Kenric—took a position at her side and began to issue orders, dispatching men to murky corners and dim alcoves to watch for any sign of Shadovar. The sergeant of her father's guard joined them on her other side, then gaped at the departing galleass in disbelief.

"The *Wyvern* left without you," Carlton said, shaking his head. "I can't believe the duke would do that!"

"Why not?" asked one of Kleef's subordinates—a heavy-jawed brute who was half a head taller than most of his fellows, but still half a head shorter than his superior. "He's a noble, ain't he? There's not a one of 'em that ain't a coward—"

"That's enough, Tanner," interrupted Kleef. "Why aren't you looking for Shadovar, like I ordered?"

Tanner eyed his superior with open resentment for a moment, and Arietta saw in his face a bitter hopelessness that was all too frequent in Marsember. It was the sour recognition that the local nobility would do nothing to protect the common people or see to their welfare, that the city's rulers were little better than tyrants who used their power and wealth only for their own benefit.

After a moment, Tanner finally seemed to find the courage to speak what was on his mind: "You haven't given us what you promised for clearing the square, Topsword. I hope you're not thinking of holding out—"

"Your gold is right here." Kleef pulled out a purse and jingled it in his palm. "I'll divide it *after* we're finished with the Shadovar."

Tanner looked as though he would object for a moment, then his eye dropped to the agate on the crossguard of Kleef's sword. He seemed transfixed for a moment, then finally nodded.

"Fair enough. You've always been a man of your word." A cynical grin crossed his face, and he added, "Otherwise, you'd be a blademaster by now."

He turned to leave, and Arietta scowled at the purse in Kleef's hand. "You must bribe your men for every task? With *gold*?"

Kleef looked embarrassed. "Never have before," he said, tucking the purse back beneath his breastplate. "But these are strange times."

"Strange indeed," Arietta said. She abhorred the corruption of the Watch—but who was she to judge, when her own father was abandoning Marsember with a quarter of the city's wealth stowed below his decks. "I'm sure they have earned every coin."

As she spoke, a sudden outcry echoed across the water from the direction of the *Wave Wyvern*. Arietta looked up the canal to find the tall, bright-eyed silhouette of the Shadovar leader looming over her father, menacing him with a dark blade. Her heart leaped into her throat, and she saw that the archers had disappeared from the rails.

"There are your Shadovar!" Carlton gasped. "How did they cross—"

"Walked through shadows," Kleef explained. He stepped to the edge of the quay and peered over the edge. "Is there another boat?"

"Not one that can get us there in time," Arietta said.

As she spoke, bodies and parts of bodies were already tumbling over the *Wyvern*'s deck rails. She nocked an arrow and drew the string back—only to have Kleef's big hand grab her arm.

"Hold," he said. "You might hit the grand duke."

Arietta looked to him in surprise. "You would care?"

"About Farnig the Feckless?" Kleef snorted and shook his head. "But I have my duty. I must do what I can to protect him."

Continuing to hold Arietta's arm, he looked back toward the *Wyvern*. When her father finally summoned the courage to attempt drawing his sword, Kleef sighed and released her arm.

"*Now* you can loose your arrow," he said. "The man is as good as dead already."

A cold hollow formed in her stomach, and Arietta raised her bow again and let fly. The shade's blade swung, and her father's body hit the deck while her arrow was still in the air.

"My lady!" Carlton gasped.

Arietta ignored him and watched in disappointment as her arrow barely cleared the taffrail and dropped out of sight. If the shade noticed the attack at all, he gave no sign of it.

Carlton reached for her arm. "My lady, are you—"

"I'm fine," Arietta said, cutting him off. The watchmen still seemed to think she was a minstrel, and the last thing she wanted right now was to reveal her true identity to Kleef Kenric or his men. "We'll say nothing more about it."

She pulled free of his grasp and turned away from the canal, only to find Tanner marching the red-haired gentlewoman toward the quay. Next to him, two more watchmen had the red-haired woman's manservant by the arms, dragging him along as he kicked and struggled.

"Are you mad or daft?" the little man exclaimed. "We must be gone before the fiends discover we are not aboard. Your lives will depend on it!"

CHAPTER FOUR

Y DER TANTHUL STOOD ON THE GALLEASS QUARTERDECK, clutching an empty satchel in one hand and a captive's throat in the other. The captive reeked of sweat and fresh urine, so Yder knew it would not be long before his velvet-robed prisoner told him what he needed to know. He lifted the man until his heels left the deck, then held out the bag.

"I want the thieves who gave this to you." Yder spoke in a low, wispy voice that the prisoner would hear as much inside his head as in his ears. "And I want the Eye."

"The . . . eye?" the prisoner croaked. He had an arched nose and close-set eyes, and when he spoke, it was in a strained voice. "*Whose* eye?"

Yder shook the satchel in the man's face. "The stone they were carrying in this bag," he said. "The Eye of Gruumsh."

At the mention of Gruumsh, a flash of terror shot through the prisoner's eyes, and Yder knew he recognized *Gruumsh* as the name of the orcs' one-eyed god of savagery. But if the man understood the significance of the Eye itself, he didn't let it show. He merely studied Yder in confusion, then finally raised his brow in a practiced expression of deferential helpfulness.

"A stone?" he asked. "And just how large . . . might the Eye of Gruumsh be?"

The prisoner let his gaze slide back to the satchel, silently suggesting that perhaps the stone might still be inside, and Yder realized that the fool took the *Eye of Gruumsh* to be the name of a mere gem—something akin to the *Titan's Tear* or the *Star of Halruaa*.

Yder tightened his grasp on the man's throat. "I am weary of hearing questions in the place of answers," he said. "Where are the contents of the satchel?"

The prisoner's eyes bulged. "There." He pointed to a forge hammer lying on the deck next to the gold-armored buffoon Yder had killed just a few minutes earlier. "They . . . your thieves . . . they said it would protect Farnig from . . . your kind."

Yder recognized the grand duke's name and knew that his father—Netheril's ruler, the Most High Telamont Tanthul—would be pleased that Yder had killed a Cormyrean royal. But Yder hadn't come to Marsember to please his father *or* kill Farnig—and so far, he wasn't having much success doing what the Mistress of the Night *had* sent him to do.

He tossed the empty satchel aside, then lowered his free hand toward the forge hammer and extended a shadow finger to retrieve it. He studied the tool for a moment and, feeling no magic in it, held it before the prisoner's eyes.

"Who said this trifle would protect the grand duke?" Seeing that his captive was about to pass out, Yder loosened his grasp. "Describe them."

The prisoner took a ragged breath, then said, "It was a red-haired beauty and her manservant." His voice was hard, as though he was angrier at the ones who had deceived him than at his tormentor. "She introduced herself as Lady Emmeline of Berdusk, but I knew the moment her servant arrived that she was no lady. A true gentlewoman would never tolerate such an odor."

Yder nodded and returned the prisoner's feet to the deck. His spies had already identified Joelle Emmeline as an accomplished Berduskan jewel thief with unusual powers of beguilement. Her foul-smelling "servant" was actually an accomplice, a barely competent spy and murderer who went by the name Malik el Sami yn Nasser.

There were reports of Malik claiming to be a Chosen of the dead god Myrkul, but Yder had his doubts. The spy's name was the same as that of the Seraph of Lies who had served Cyric the Mad a hundred years earlier. Besides, with the entire world on the verge of a new age, the gods were vying for worshipers like rival crime guilds fighting for turf, dispatching their Chosen to advance their interests and sabotage the plans of their rivals. And sending an impostor to steal another god's domain seemed like exactly the kind of scheme that Cyric—the god of strife—would relish.

Still holding the prisoner by his neck, Yder turned to study the main deck. Soaked in blood and strewn with corpses and moaning wounded, the *Wave Wyvern* looked more like a charnel house than a ship. Most of the casualties wore tabards over chain mail, but Yder had suffered losses, too. A long row of dusky bodies lay atop the center cargo hatch, their severed heads tucked under their arms and wisps of shadow still seeping from their neck stumps.

He saw no sign of Malik or Joelle—or the Eye.

He began to seep black wisps of shadow, a sign of his growing frustration. He had brought along only fifty of his Night Guards, believing that number more than adequate to hunt down a single pair of thieves. But the big watchman had proven a nasty surprise—first by stepping forward to protect the thieves at all, then by killing a quarter of Yder's company almost by himself. It was not the kind of resistance his spies had led him to expect from the Marsember Watch, and he could not help seeing the hand of his goddess's enemies in the unanticipated interference—and especially in that blue agate on the watchman's sword. The way it glowed when he and his warriors came near, the way it weakened and blinded them, pointed to divine favor.

And now the hulk had sounded the alarm and was actually leading a hunt for him and his warriors. It would be a simple matter to summon reinforcements from Shar's Hall of Shadows in Thultanthar, but that carried even greater peril. Less than two years earlier, Yder's brother Rivalen had attempted to initiate Shar's world-destroying Cycle of Night, and now many of Netheril's most important figures—including the Most High himself—feared her power over the empire. If Yder removed too many warriors, someone was certain to raid her temple and undermine her power in Netheril.

And that was a risk Yder dared not take. Rivalen had failed to bring the Cycle to a successful close, but Shar remained one of the most powerful deities on Toril—and one who intended to grow even more powerful by eliminating the boundary that separated her Shadowfell from the world of stone and soil.

After a few moments, Yder grew certain that the thieves could not be among the dead. Had they been, one of his warriors would have informed him by that point. He turned back to the prisoner.

"Where are these liars now?" he asked. "Why can't we find them?"

A look of confusion came to the majordomo's face, and he glanced forward. "They should be here," he said. "They were right behind us when we boarded."

Whispering through the shadows, Yder ordered the survivors of the battle to continue the search for the thieves and their prize below decks, then turned back to the majordomo.

"Did you actually *see* them board?" he asked. "Or do you assume?"

The majordomo's eyes widened. "I didn't see them, no," he admitted. "The situation was chaotic, and they were behind me."

Yder resisted the temptation to crush the man's throat. "Then why do you believe they followed you aboard?"

"Where else could they have gone?" he asked. "You were coming right behind us."

"And they knew it," Yder said, more to himself than the prisoner. "That was my mistake."

Yder looked aft, debating the wisdom of returning to shore. Cyric's blessing—at least he *assumed* it was Cyric's blessing—kept the Eye and its bearers hidden from the divination magic of even the Mistress herself. So if he lost track of his quarry now, there was a chance he would never be able to find them again.

But the big watchman had no doubt sounded the alarm, and that meant the entire Marsember Watch would soon be mustering to hunt down his company. If he returned to the city to search for the thieves, his Night Guards would be outnumbered ten-to-one. And *that* meant he would lose a lot more of his force—probably *most* of it.

Fortunately, Yder saw no reason to believe that he *needed* to find his quarry in Marsember. Contrary to what the prisoner had seemed to think, the *Eye of Gruumsh* was not a giant gem, and the thieves had not come to the city to sell it. They had probably come to Marsember because it was a port—and that meant they intended to board a ship.

And now Yder had a ship of his own.

In their haste to escape Marsember with their lives, the Shadovar were fleeing in their stolen vessel with all oars pulling. Malik could hear the cries of their wounded captives echoing off the buildings that lined the canal banks, and he could see their craven leader standing on the quarterdeck, looking back toward the great arcing bridge where Kleef Kenric and his brave fools stood watching in anger and despair.

The crazed watchman had hoped to reach the High Bridge in time to drop onto the *Wave Wyvern*'s decks and avenge the death of his murdered duke, and so the entire group had spent the last ten minutes racing through the streets like madmen. But Malik had wanted to avoid being seen by the Shadovar, and it was on that account that he had contrived to stumble and fall so frequently that his companions had finally begun to drag him along by his elbows. Even so, he had managed to slow the company enough to save it from the slaughter that would surely have followed had it arrived in time to execute Kleef's foolish plan, and the group had raced onto the bridge to find the *Wave Wyvern*'s stern just beyond leaping distance.

Taking care to keep one of Kleef's courageous buffoons between him and the Shadovar at all times, Malik reached out to tug on the topsword's tattered cape.

"It is a sad thing that we have missed our chance to deal those Shadovar devils the death they deserve," he said. "But Lady Emmeline and I have urgent matters beyond the Lake of Dragons. If you and your men will kindly escort us to Starmouth Harbor and help us find the ship we have hired, I'm certain you will find Lady Emmeline most grateful."

"Indeed," Joelle said. Like Malik, she was taking care to remain hidden from the Shadovar—in her case, by standing directly behind the big watchman. "Most grateful."

She took Kleef's arm and graced him with a beaming smile, and Malik knew they would soon be on their way to the harbor. As a Chosen of Sune, Joelle had but to smile at a man to bend him to her will—and when she deigned to touch him, he became her happy slave. Malik knew this from his own experience. It was the only reason he been foolish enough to accompany her into the orc stronghold at Big Bone Deep and remove the Eye of Gruumsh from the great statue in the Hidden Temple of Nishrek.

As Malik had foreseen, Kleef nodded at Joelle, then turned to his followers. "This is a matter for the Royal Navy now," he said. "We'll escort the lady and her manservant to Starmouth Harbor and report to the lord admiral. He'll alert the fleet to watch for the grand duke's ship, and perhaps one of his captains will be able to take vengeance."

"What about Her Grace?" demanded the archer, Elbertina. Though she had spoken very little until now, she had been one of the most determined runners, leading the company the entire way. "And the rest of the household?"

"The Seasilver family is aboard?" Kleef asked this not of Elbertina but of the grizzled sergeant of the household guards, Carlton. "Duke Farnig hadn't sent them ahead?"

For some reason Malik did not understand, Carlton glanced at Elbertina before he spoke. Perhaps she had been the grand duke's private bodyguard or his personal bard—or some other assistant of an even more confidential nature.

After a moment, Elbertina nodded, and Carlton said, "The grand duke felt his family would be safer crossing on the *Wyvern* with him. Her Grace is aboard."

Kleef cursed, then said, "You didn't mention Lady Arietta. Is she aboard, too?"

Again, the sergeant's gaze slid to Elbertina.

"Arietta wasn't aboard," she said. "She was . . . away from the residence."

The words scratched at Malik's ear, for it was a gift of Cyric the One and All that he could always tell when someone spoke a lie, and he knew her hesitation had not been innocent. The minstrel was keeping something from them—something she and the sergeant both knew about Lady Arietta.

If Kleef noticed her falseness, he did not show it. The big oaf merely turned to watch the *Wave Wyvern* as it departed the canal, his brow furrowed with the effort it took him to see what was obvious. The ship was already entering the open sea, and even now the shades were stepping her masts. There was no way to catch the vessel.

Still, Kleef pointed to a pair of canal boats moored at a quay at the far end of the bridge.

"There," he said, starting across the bridge. "We can still catch them."

"And then what?" asked Joelle, taking his arm. "Even *you* can't board a fighting ship from a pair of oversized canoes—not against shades."

"We need to try," Elbertina insisted. Her loyalty to Duke Farnig and his family must have been great, for her voice was cracking and her eyes were swollen and wet. "If they don't murder Her Grace outright, they'll hold her hostage the rest of her life."

"And how will getting yourselves killed change that?" Joelle asked, her voice filled with comfort and reassurance. "It's better to be patient and look for a real opportunity to save her."

"What opportunity?" Kleef asked. "The Lake of Dragons is a big place. By the time we reach Starmouth Harbor and report, the *Wyvern* will be far from shore. And by the time the lord admiral sends a flotilla after it—*if* he sends a flotilla—it will be lost in the Sea of Swords."

Joelle shook her head. "No, it won't," she said gently. "It will be waiting for us somewhere at sea. And if you do as I suggest, the Shadovar will come to *you.*"

"How can you know what the Shadovar will do?" Malik asked. He was starting to grow worried, for it was plain to see that Joelle had set her fickle heart on Kleef and would say anything to have him—even the truth. "They have what they came for. The duke is dead and they have his wife. We should say our farewells to our brave friends and let them go after her before it's too late."

Malik took Joelle's arm and started to pull her away—only to have his path blocked by Jang, the narrow-eyed Shou who served as Kleef's second-in-command.

"But you are wrong," Jang said. "The Shadovar *do not* have what they came for. It is you and Lady Emmeline they have been chasing."

Kleef nodded. "It's true," he said, turning to Elbertina. "I only noticed the Shadovar in the first place because they were stalking these two."

Elbertina lowered her brow and studied Malik for a moment, obviously weighing Kleef's words—and perhaps what she had observed for herself—against the brilliance of Malik's suggestion. Finally, she nodded to herself and turned back to Joelle.

"Very well. I'm listening."

Joelle smiled, and Malik knew that the oaf and his followers would soon be traveling with them—a tragedy that would certainly make it more difficult for him to claim Joelle for himself and to perform the task his true god had set before him. Still, Malik would never have been pulled from the Plane of Nothingness, where Cyric had left him to roam lost and dead for a hundred years, were he not the most resourceful of all the Chosen now wandering Toril. By the time the fateful moment arrived, he would be long rid of Kleef and his troop of fools—and free to make Joelle his forever.

"The good watchman is correct," Joelle said, nodding at Jang. "The Shadovar *are* chasing Malik and me. If you want to find them, come with us."

"And what good will that do?" Malik asked, making one last attempt to divert his competition. "If the Shadovar see watchmen aboard our ship, the duke's wife is as good as dead."

Joelle shot him an angry look—a devastating frown that almost crushed his putrid heart—and then she said, "Then we mustn't let them see any watchmen." She turned to Kleef and spoke in a warm voice. "I don't believe she's dead. The Shadovar are too cunning to kill a valuable hostage without good reason. As long as the grand duchess makes no trouble, she'll be held as a bargaining chip—or perhaps to install as a straw queen after they've conquered the realm."

"Duchess Elira has no value on that account," Elbertina clarified. "She has no direct claim to the throne. If the Shadovar are here to capture a royal heir—"

"But they're *not*," Kleef reminded her. "They were chasing Lady Emmeline—"

"*Joelle*," Joelle corrected. Her voice grew sultry, and she touched his arm. "*Please*."

Kleef nodded and continued, "They were chasing Joelle and her manservant."

Malik objected that he was no manservant, but the big oaf

continued to talk over him, and no one paid him any attention.

"Capturing Her Grace was a happy accident," Kleef continued. "My guess is the Shadovar won't be in a hurry to kill anyone. They'll want to take stock and consider their options."

"Then it seems we're decided." Joelle took Kleef's arm again and turned away from the canal boats. "Which way to the harbor? Our captain—"

"Not yet," Elbertina said, signaling for Kleef and the others to remain on the bridge. "First, I want to know why."

"Why the Shadovar are chasing us?" Joelle asked. "Or why I want you to come with us?"

Elbertina shook her head. "Neither. You're the one who brought this trouble to my . . . to the grand duke's door." She glanced in Kleef's direction, then continued, "I want to know why I shouldn't have the good sergeant and the topsword seize you, then offer to trade you for the grand duchess and her sons."

Kleef's brow shot up at the suggestion that he would do any such thing at the request of a mere minstrel, but the grand duke's sergeant nodded as though he thought it an excellent idea. Malik scowled and quickly reached out to tug Joelle's hand away from the huge arm it was holding.

"You see?" Malik demanded. "This is the tragedy that comes of helping strangers."

He tried to pull Joelle away, but she only glanced toward the departing *Wave Wyvern* and frowned at the murky fog that was rising up to engulf it. She studied the scene in silence for a moment, then finally shook her head.

"No, Malik," she said. "They deserve to know the truth."

"They deserve to know nothing," Malik said, starting to panic. "Least of all the truth! Are you so eager to damn us both to the Great Pit of Hells?"

Joelle gave him a patient smile. "Malik, we're Chosen," she said. "That's not going to happen."

"Not to a Chosen of Sune, perhaps," Malik retorted quickly. "But I am a Chosen of Myrkul. How is a dead god going to protect me from the Mistress of the Night?"

Joelle's smile grew condescending. "As long as Myrkul lives in your heart, he's not truly dead, now is he?" She pointed at the magic pocket hidden inside Malik's drab robe. "Show them the Eye."

Malik recoiled as though she had struck him. "Are you mad?" he demanded. "*He* will see us."

"*He* already knows who we are," Joelle said. "And Kleef needs to understand that there's a reason our paths have crossed."

She glanced at Kleef, who was scowling at her and Malik as though he thought them both mad. Elbertina, on the other hand, was watching them with a wide-eyed expression of relief and . . . could it be recognition?

"Who is this *he*?" Kleef demanded. "And stop stalling, or I swear I'll do as Elbertina suggests."

His hand dropped to the hilt of his sword, and blue light flared from the agate in the crossguard.

The glow prompted Joelle to grab Malik by the elbow and squeeze. "Show him," she hissed. "*Now.*"

Malik sighed. "As you command," he said. "But must we show everyone? And do it in plain sight of the Shadovar?"

Without waiting for a reply, he started to shuffle down the bridge toward the shelter afforded by the tall buildings that lined the street. The others followed, and soon he was standing in the doorway of a shuttered spice shop with Joelle, Kleef, and Elbertina.

Malik reluctantly slipped a hand inside his robe. It took a moment to find the line of rough thread that marked the mouth of the pocket—and once he had, he was so nervous he had to thrust his arm inside up to the elbow before Cyric's magic responded to his thoughts and he felt the Eye resting in his hand. He was seized at once by a terror so cold he began to shiver, and he could not help looking back to Joelle.

"Are you certain you wish to do this?" he asked. "Once

they have seen the Eye, we can never undo it."

"You have no choice," Kleef warned. "Show us the reason the Shadovar are chasing you, or I'll deliver you to them myself."

Malik had to bite his tongue to keep from answering with a threat of his own. He lifted the Eye from its hiding place, the mouth of the pocket stretching around the huge orb, until he finally had to slip his second hand beneath it and support the thing in front of his belly.

Made of milky quartz, the orb was far from perfect. It had lumps and flat spots, and crooked veins of red iron that came together in front to join a scraggy disk of false gold. In the center of the sparkling disk was a small circle of obsidian—which was rapidly expanding, as Malik could see by the raised brows and dropped jaws of the others.

The red veins began to pulse and writhe, and the stony eye spun in Malik's hands, turning its dark gaze on Kleef and Elbertina.

The minstrel gasped and raised a hand to shield her face, but Malik could tell by the way she trembled and stumbled that she had been touched by its savage lust and dark appetites. The big topsword merely paled and clenched his fist around the hilt of his sword, but even he looked as though he were about to leave his morningfeast on the steps of the spice shop.

Malik shot a questioning look in Joelle's direction, and she was quick to nod.

"That's enough," she said. "You can put it away."

Malik slipped the Eye back into its magic pocket and began to feel a bit more steady and confident. Kleef glared at the robe into which it had disappeared for a moment, then turned to Joelle.

"What *was* that thing?" he demanded.

"The Eye of Gruumsh," Joelle said. "Malik and I took it so we can save the world." She stepped closer to Kleef, so close it was easier to describe what was *not* touching him than what did. "And you, my friend, are going to help us."

CHAPTER FIVE

Ringfinger Wharf was creaking and swaying beneath the weight of the refugees packed onto its spongy decking. Despite his height, even Kleef found it difficult to see anything beyond their heads except the masts and bulwarks of ships at berth. There were at least five large vessels moored along the pier, all three-masted caravels or barkentines with lines of passengers still ascending their gangplanks. But at the seaward end was a small gap with a pair of slender masts barely rising above the crowd, and if there was anyone boarding the unseen vessel, the mob in front of it did not appear to be growing any thinner.

Guessing that his charges had hired the small vessel that wasn't currently taking on passengers, Kleef started toward the seaward end of the wharf. With his own watchmen on his left, and Carlton's men-at-arms on his right, the crowd parted before him like water before a prow. It soon grew apparent that the throngs were clustered most densely around the gangplanks of the five large ships, where armed members of the ship's crew stood guard as their officers sold berths.

As Kleef and his companions continued to push forward, an angry din began to build ahead. Soon, they reached the end of the wharf and found a mob of people standing along the edge, yelling down at an unseen vessel, simultaneously offering unthinkable bribes and threatening dire acts of piracy.

Before pushing through the crowd, Kleef paused and turned to Joelle. "Will the captain know you?"

Joelle nodded. "By sight," she said, "as I will him. But how can you be sure this is the right ship? I haven't even told you what it's called."

Kleef looked around the wharf, confirming that this was the only vessel not yet taking on passengers. "It's the one." He motioned Jang and Carlton forward, gesturing for them to clear the way. "We'll need to board quickly, if we don't want half the city coming with us."

Jang led the way into the crowd, bellowing orders to make way for the Watch and shoving aside those who were too slow to obey. But even with more than a dozen armed men helping him, the mob seemed to sense that someone was about to board the vessel and quickly began to push back. Finally, Kleef unsheathed Watcher and brandished the blade above their heads.

"Stand aside *now*!"

All eyes turned toward Kleef. A hush fell over the area, but the crowd seemed more transfixed than intimidated by the sight of his drawn sword, and no one moved.

Then Elbertina stepped to his side. "I suggest you do as he commands," she said, speaking in a soft voice. She still carried her weapons, and had slung a leather rucksack she had fetched from the grand duke's mansion over one shoulder. "This company is on a mission for the Crown, and anyone standing in its way *will* pay a heavy price."

A murmur of discontent rolled through the crowd, but it reluctantly opened a path. Kleef led the way forward and soon found himself staring down at the deck of a small ketch. The vessel was manned by only a short, dark-skinned captain with a close-cropped beard and a sharp nose.

Kleef stepped to the edge of the deck and looked down at the gnome, who was standing amidships behind a chest-height deckhouse, resting a peculiar six-armed crossbow on its roof. With six quarrels arranged in vertical firing slots, and six strings tensioned behind them, it was an odd contraption—but one that looked dangerous enough to hold an angry crowd at bay.

When the gnome saw who had stepped to the edge of the wharf, he pivoted the weapon, aiming at Kleef's chest.

"I've done nothing that's any concern of yours, Kenric," he said. "Go and bother someone who deserves the trouble."

Kleef rested Watcher's tip on the edge of the wharf. "Falrinn, didn't I tell you what would happen if you ever showed your face in Marsember again?"

"Try that, and I'll ventilate your chest armor," Falrinn Greatorm warned. "Besides, I'm not *in* Marsember. I haven't set foot off the *Lonely Roamer.*"

Joelle stepped to Kleef's side and looked down at the gnome. "Captain Greatorm, I presume?"

Greatorm's face lit briefly in surprise, then he scowled in Kleef's direction. "Has this windbag been bothering you, Heartwarder?" he asked. "Say the word, and it never happens again."

"That's a very sweet offer," Joelle said, smiling. "But no. We're going to need him."

The gnome glared at her out of one eye. "Why would we need the likes of *him*?" he demanded. "I have plenty of ballast."

Joelle chuckled. "They *told* me you were quite the wit."

She sprang across ten feet of open water and landed atop the *Roamer*'s deck as light as a bird. The gnome scowled at her audacity in boarding his ship without permission, but before he could object, she stepped to his side and placed a hand on the crossbow.

"Kleef is very good with a sword," Joelle continued. "You'll be glad to have him along when the Shadovar find us."

As soon as Joelle mentioned the Shadovar, the crowd began to murmur and back away from the *Roamer*—and the aggravation in Greatorm's face changed to reluctance.

"*Shadovar?*" The gnome shook his head. "No one said anything about shadowalkers when I took this job."

"Then we'll renegotiate," said Elbertina. She pulled a small purse from her rucksack and tossed it onto the *Roamer*'s deck. "That will be enough."

"And remember that this is Starmouth Harbor." Kleef brandished his sword. "And that I have good enough reason to seize your boat."

Greatorm's expression grew hard. He glowered over at Joelle for a moment, then finally turned to the purse on the deck.

"That silver in there?" he asked. "Or gold?"

Elbertina closed her rucksack, then flashed him a condescending smile. "It's platinum."

Greatorm's face lit with delight. "In that case, welcome aboard," he said. "But I can only take eight of you. This isn't the *Queen Filfaeril*, you know."

"Eight is madness!" Malik objected. "The Shadovar have many times that number!"

"Aye, and I was hired to *dodge* trouble, not look for it," Greatorm said. "Eight is all I can carry. We take any more, and those Shadovar you're worried about will run us down before we leave the harbor."

"Then eight will have to be enough," Elbertina said.

She gathered herself up and leaped down onto the deck. Though her landing was a bit heavier and less graceful than Joelle's, she managed to keep her feet and avoid smashing the lyre tucked beneath the flap of her rucksack. Still, Kleef did not jump down behind her. Greatorm was the kind of stubborn smuggler who always thought ahead and never gave up. Kleef actually liked that about him, but he suspected the gnome was just trying to limit the odds he would face when the time came to double-cross them.

71

Kleef turned to his troop and summoned Rathul, who had spent three decades in the Cormyrean navy before a third ship-sinking finally convinced him to seek a livelihood ashore.

"What do you think?" he asked. "How many can Falrinn take in this boat?"

Rathul studied the ketch for a moment, his rheumy eyes taking it in from bow to stern, then finally shrugged. "I'd say twenty or twenty-five, as long as the day is clear and you don't leave harbor." As he spoke, his gaze grew unsteady and his hands began to tremble. "But to go to sea, you need provisions and you need to be ready for heavy weather. I would have said fifteen or so, but you'd better take the captain at his word. He knows his own vessel."

Kleef glanced at Rathul's trembling hands. "Don't worry, Rathul," he said. "You won't be coming with us."

Rathul scowled. "Why not?" he asked. "I have more experience at sea than any man here."

"You're *volunteering*?" Kleef asked, surprised.

Rathul looked confused for a moment, then finally nodded. "I guess so," he said. "The Shadovar catch you out there, you're going to need someone who knows how to sink a ship."

"True enough, but . . ." Kleef made a point of looking at Rathul's hands. "Are you sure about this?"

Rathul glanced down, then smiled. "This?" he asked, raising his hands. "Don't you worry. They'll be steady enough, once they're holding a boarding axe."

"Then, good," Kleef said. "Thank you."

He turned to select the rest of the crew and was surprised to find not only Jang but his entire troop stepping forward. And standing next to them were Carlton and his men-at-arms.

Kleef didn't know what to make of so much unexpected bravery. "Look, coming along won't be any better than staying here to defend Marsember. In fact, it'll probably get you killed. The Shadovar are still looking for our friends."

"Which means you'll need help protecting them,"

Tanner said. He hesitated, clearly as surprised as Kleef by his words, then shrugged. "You deserve better than we've given you, Topsword. You've been fair, even when we didn't respect you the way you'd earned. Maybe we just figure we owe it to you to do our duty for once."

"That's right," said Ardul. "I'll go, too."

"Well, the boat won't hold all of us," Carlton said, stepping to Kleef's side. "Even I can see that."

Kleef nodded and turned back to the *Roamer*, which Greatorm was slowly drawing toward the wharf by means of a windlass connected to both of the ship's mooring lines. Joelle was standing well forward, ready to grab a boarding ladder fixed to the wharf, while Elbertina was standing behind the gnome, ready to draw her sword if he tried anything shifty. Kleef liked her instincts.

He shifted his attention to the gnome. "How many of us can you take?" he asked. "Truly?"

Greatorm barely looked up. "*Eight.*"

"Twenty," Kleef countered.

Greatorm's head rose, an expression of true fear on his face. "No more than twelve," he said. "And if the seas turn heavy, you'll be dumping your armor."

Kleef looked to Rathul, who gave a curt nod. "At sea, armor is a mixed blessing anyway."

Kleef turned back to Greatorm. "Done."

Greatorm let out his breath. Then Carlton picked three of his own men-at-arms to accompany them, and Kleef distributed the merchant's bribe among the surviving members of his troop. Ten minutes later the *Roamer* was pushing away from the wharf.

The gnome ducked into a compartment beneath the windlass, then a muffled clunk sounded below decks. The windlass began to rise, drawing beneath it a trio of tall, slender sails mounted around a vertical axis. When the sails reached a height of six feet, another thump sounded, and Greatorm reappeared. He removed a locking pin from the base of the structure, and two of the small sails immediately caught the wind and began to spin. The *Roamer* began to move forward as though propelled by invisible oars and soon fell into the long line of ships departing Starmouth Harbor.

Kleef took a moment to assign watch zones and order his men and Carlton's to remain hidden behind the ketch's bulwarks. Then he stepped to Jang's side and spoke in a quiet voice.

"All this volunteering doesn't feel right," he said, nodding to Tanner and the others. "What are they up to?"

Jang shrugged, then answered just as quietly. "It must be the platinum." He glanced aft, to where Elbertina and Malik stood near the strange windmill. "I think they smell treasure on the minstrel."

"Could be," Kleef agreed. "If anyone gets too interested in that rucksack of hers, discourage him."

"I will," Jang said. He glanced down at Kleef's bloodied limbs. "How are your wounds?"

"Sore," he admitted. "But I'll last until we find the duchess. You?"

"Well enough," he said. "One of the battle-priests saw to me when I reported to the King's Tower."

Kleef had thought as much. "Good. And speaking of the Tower, what was the lord marshall's reaction when you told him there were Shadovar in the city?"

Jang shook his head in disgust. "It wasn't to send reinforcements," he said. "He ordered the Tower doors barred and the portcullises dropped. I barely made it out in time to collect the troop and come after you."

Kleef gave him a bitter smile. "I guess the old marsh buzzard thought he was finally going to be rid of me."

"Perhaps so," Jang said. "His eyes *did* brighten when I told him you had gone after the enemy alone."

"Well, I guess that's fair," Kleef said. "I truly hope *he's* alone when he meets the Shadovar."

Jang chuckled darkly, but stopped when Joelle emerged from below decks carrying a wooden toolbox and a bucket of water. When she caught Kleef's eye and smiled, the Shou took his leave and went to keep watch over Elbertina.

As Joelle approached, Kleef glanced into the toolbox she was carrying. Inside were dozens of different needles, threads of all thicknesses and materials, and small rolls of canvas that could only be sail patches.

"Expecting a storm?" he asked.

"Soon enough." Joelle took his arm, then drew him toward the center deck and sat him atop the hold cover. "And I want to be sure you're patched up before it hits. Let me see how bad your wounds are."

Kleef eyed the bent, rusty needles in the mending kit. "Not bad," he said. "I'll last until we've recovered the duchess."

"I have no doubt." Joelle dipped a hand in the bucket, and the water inside began to glimmer with a faint silver light. "It's what comes after that I'm worried about."

Kleef frowned. "Protecting the Eye of Gruumsh?"

"Exactly."

"I haven't said I'd help with that," Kleef said.

"But you will." Joelle soaked a piece of cloth in the water bucket. "You're a good man."

"That doesn't mean I can ignore my duty," Kleef replied. "I'll do what I can for you, but I'm here to rescue the grand duchess."

"And *we* are serving as bait to improve your chance of succeeding." Joelle looked up and locked gazes with him. "Doesn't one good deed deserve another?"

She smiled, and Kleef began to feel guilty for being so reluctant. Clearly, she and Malik would be taking extra risks by deliberately *allowing* the Shadovar to find them, and she was right—that deserved some consideration.

Finally, Kleef nodded. "Within reason," he said. "Now, tell me why you and Malik stole the Eye of Gruumsh in the first place—and why the Shadovar are so desperate to get it back."

Joelle thought for a moment, then motioned to the bloody armor covering the main parts of his limbs. "Will you take off those vambraces and cuisses so I can see to your wounds?"

Kleef glanced into the bucket of still-glimmering water. In the absence of a good battle-priest, it was probably better to trust to Joelle's healing abilities than to do without. He began to undo the buckles on his armor.

"You understand, I promise nothing in return," he said. "My duty is to Marsember first."

"How could I forget?" Joelle asked. "But you will not save Marsember by letting Shar give the rest of the world to the Shadovar."

Joelle smiled again, this time with an expression of forbearance, and Kleef began to feel just a bit foolish. Clearly, he was defining duty a bit too narrowly, guarding only the hand when the foe was striking at the head.

"You have a point," he admitted, "as long as you're not exaggerating."

"I'm not," Joelle said. "You'll see that soon enough."

She had Kleef remove the doublet and hose he wore under his armor and began to clean his cuts with water from the bucket. There were more than a dozen, mostly around his knees and just above his wrists, but none were deep enough to have slashed any tendons or major blood vessels. Still, Kleef was relieved to discover that as Joelle worked, a pleasant numbness overcame the stinging ache of his wounds.

"So," Kleef said. "The Eye of Gruumsh. Where did it come from?"

"The one you saw came from an orc stronghold in the Stonelands," she said, not looking up. "Malik and I recovered it from the Hidden Temple of Nishrek in Big Bone Deep."

Kleef didn't know whether to be impressed or skeptical. Big Bone Deep was the stuff of legend, home to an infamous tribe of orcs known as the Spleen Eaters. According to folklore, they had lived in the Stonelands since before the Storm

Horns were mountains, and they were credited with a hunger for human flesh so ferocious that no human had ever seen their lair and survived to tell about it.

But, incredible as the claim was, that was not what gave Kleef pause. "The one I *saw*?" he asked. "You mean there's more than one Eye of Gruumsh?"

"In a manner of speaking, yes." Joelle dipped her cloth in the bucket and squeezed. Dirt and blood jetted into the water, then vanished without fouling it. "It's the same Eye, but it can be perceived in different ways."

"What's that mean?" he asked.

"You've already experienced it," Joelle said. "When Malik showed you the Eye, first you saw a rock. Then, after a moment, you glimpsed its true nature—I saw the horror in your face."

"That felt like magic to me," Kleef said. "*Dark* magic."

"What did you expect?" Joelle countered. "That's how it feels to have a god look at you. Terrifying and magical and mysterious."

"Maybe," Kleef said. If there was one thing twenty years of night duty on the Watch had taught him, it was to be suspicious of ready explanations. And Joelle *was* trying to recruit him—he couldn't forget that. "Let's say Big Bone Deep really exists, and that you and Malik actually raided this hidden temple and lived to tell about it."

Joelle looked hurt. "You don't believe me?"

"I have a suspicious mind," Kleef said. "I still don't see what's so important about a big ball of quartz."

Joelle's smile grew frosty—and Kleef felt crushed.

"I thought I explained that." Joelle paused, then continued in a tone that suggested she found Kleef a little slow. "The Eye of Gruumsh is a 'quartz ball' only in its physical aspect. In its divine aspect, it's a center of power—the medium through which Gruumsh perceives all of Abeir-Toril."

"And that's why you and Malik had to steal it?" Kleef asked, not quite sure why he suddenly felt the need to prove he was smarter than Joelle seemed to think. "To protect the world from orcs?"

Joelle looked confused for a moment. "I suppose 'protecting' *is* how you would perceive our task," she said. "But it's more complicated than that. It's not the orcs we're trying to stop, and we didn't actually steal the Eye—at least not the divine one. Luthic gave it to us."

"*Luthic*?" Kleef asked. "Gruumsh's mate?"

"The goddess of caves," Joelle corrected. "Why do men always assume that when a female beds a male, she becomes *his* property and loses *her* identity?"

"I wouldn't know." Kleef's reply came without hesitation, for he had questioned enough scofflaws to know when someone was trying to rattle him. "Why would Luthic give you her mate's only eye?"

Joelle studied him for a time, then spoke in a soft voice. "There's no need to make this into an interrogation, Kleef. I'm happy to tell you everything."

"Thanks," Kleef said, not changing his tone at all. "Why would Luthic give you her mate's only eye?"

Joelle sighed. "It's a gift."

"For you?" Kleef glanced aft toward Malik. The little bug-eyed man had Elbertina trapped against the port bulwark, engaging her in a conversation she was obviously too polite to end. "Or for Malik?"

"Malik is just the bearer," Joelle clarified. She set the cloth aside, then began to fish through the sail-mending kit. "The Eye is for Luthic's lover, Grumbar."

"Luthic is mating with an earth primordial?" As much as Kleef found himself *wanting* to believe her, he was growing more skeptical by the moment. Affairs between gods, he could imagine. An affair between a goddess and an earth primordial . . . well, he didn't *want* to imagine that. "Are you sure?"

Joelle looked up long enough to waggle her hand back and forth. "That's how we heartwarders perceive it." She withdrew a hooked needle and a length of sail thread from the kit, then slipped them both in the bucket. "I suspect you Watchers might see the Eye differently—perhaps as a reward for her faithful protector."

Kleef began to find the explanation a bit more reasonable. "What would Grumbar be protecting her from?"

Joelle shrugged. "From her mate, perhaps. Gruumsh *is* the god of savagery, after all." She removed the needle and thread from the still-glimmering water, then added, "But I really wouldn't know. As I said, that's how *you* might see things."

Kleef frowned. As a follower of Helm's Law, he had a duty to protect the weak, and the vow was so deeply ingrained that he found himself clenching his teeth in outrage.

"How many ways are there to see this gift?" he asked.

"As many ways as there are faiths," Joelle replied. "The important thing is that Malik and I are trying to stop the Mistress of the Night."

"*Shar*?" Kleef asked. The longer Joelle talked, the stranger this supposed love triangle began to seem. "What does she have to do with Luthic and Gruumsh?"

"You're forgetting Grumbar." Joelle began to thread the needle, which had emerged from the water bucket as clean and shiny as a brand new one. "And Grumbar is the key to Shar's plan."

She began to close Kleef's wounds. He watched her sew a cut above his knee for a moment, crisscrossing her stitches in a tight, uniform pattern. To his surprise, her work did not cause him much pain—only a little pressure as the needle pushed through the skin, then a little tugging as the thread was drawn through behind it.

After a moment, he said, "All right. Tell me about Shar's plan. And maybe you'd better start at the beginning."

"If you like." Joelle finished stitching the first cut and moved to one on his thigh. "What do you know of the Cycle of Night?"

"Other than the name you just mentioned, nothing."

"Then perhaps I won't start at the *very* beginning." Joelle spoke without looking up. "But, surely, you've noticed that Faerûn is in a time of great change."

"Hard to miss," Kleef said. He glanced back toward the now-distant harbor, where waves were breaking over a shoal of warehouses that had been submerged during the Great Rain. "It feels like the whole world is having a nightmare."

"In a sense, it is," Joelle said. "Abeir and Toril are separating."

"So the doomsayers say." Kleef had stood watch over enough street-corner sermons to know that most sages believed the world was really *two* worlds that had been separated at the dawn of time, and then forced back together in a great cataclysm of destructive magic a hundred years ago. "I won't claim to know if they're right."

"Then you need to open your eyes and look at the world around you," Joelle replied. "The earthmotes are falling, the plaguelands are vanishing, and even magic has returned to the old ways. The ground heaves and rolls like a restless sea, lakes freeze one day and boil the next, and Faerûn is at war from Mirabar to Al Qahara. How can you know all that and doubt the truth of what I'm telling you?"

"Because I don't *know* all that," Kleef said. "I *know* only what I've seen with my own eyes, inside the walls of Marsember."

"But even that must be enough," Joelle insisted. "I was in the city for less than a day, and I saw buildings shake like drunkards."

"True enough," Kleef said. With his own eyes, he had seen three different earthmotes plunge into the Dragonmere, and twice he had been nearly been knocked off his feet when the street suddenly writhed beneath his boots. "But even if the doomsayers are right, that doesn't explain the wars. If the world is coming apart, why should so many people waste their last days fighting over it?"

Joelle shrugged. "Because mortals are the weapons of gods,"

she said. "And the gods are fighting to control the world that comes after. That is certainly true of Malik and me—and if we fail, Faerûn will suffer for it. All Toril will suffer."

"Because of Shar's plan?" Kleef asked. "*She*'s causing the worlds to separate?"

Joelle shook her head. "Taking advantage of it, certainly. But what single god could sunder the worlds?" She waved her hand vaguely skyward, as if the shimmering heavens above could encompass all the upheaval that had seized Faerûn in the last two years. "Were Shar *that* powerful, the Cycle of Night would never have been stopped."

"What *is* this Cycle of Night?" Kleef asked. He was starting to wonder how Joelle—or any mortal—could know all she claimed about the affairs of gods. "That's the second time you've mentioned it."

Joelle stopped sewing and looked up. "Oblivion," she said. "Shar is the Lady of Loss, and her appetite is insatiable. She feeds on her own divine children, and through them gains the strength to devour an entire world. Had her son Mask not tricked her, she would have swallowed all of Abeir-Toril."

Kleef scowled. "As in, *eaten*?" he asked. "I'm not sure I believe—"

"You should," Joelle interrupted. She went back to work, this time closing a cut on his wrist. "You have heard of the Ordulin Maelstrom, I am certain."

"Who hasn't?" Kleef said. Once the capital of Sembia, Ordulin had been destroyed a hundred years earlier by a follower of Shar. Since that time, a growing storm of rain and shadow had swirled around an ever-growing void at the heart of the ruins. "What are you saying, that the maelstrom is Shar's *mouth*?"

"In a sense, yes," Joelle said. "Had Mask not stopped her, the maelstrom would have continued to expand until Shar had devoured everything."

A cold knot formed in the pit of Kleef's stomach. It was a

familiar sensation, the same one he always felt when he caught Tanner or Rathul or another of his men in a lie.

Taking care to keep an even voice, Kleef said, "I don't see how that can be. Mask is dead."

"No god is ever truly dead, so long as he lives in the heart of a single worshiper," Joelle said. She looked up from the wound she was closing on Kleef's forearm. "You should know that better than anyone else, Watcher."

Kleef scowled, annoyed by her use of the name once given to Helm's faithful. "Those are pretty words, but you won't win my help through lies," he said. "The Lurking Lord has been dead for a century."

"And now he is back." Joelle returned to her work. "As is Lathander, and no small number of other gods—perhaps even Helm."

"If the Vigilant One has returned, he has not bothered to tell me about it."

"Hasn't he?" Joelle asked. She tied off a stitch, then looked up. "You are a fine swordsman. But had you truly been alone today, you could never have held that bridge—not for so long, against so many."

"I had help," Kleef replied. "The *human* kind."

"Eventually," Joelle said. "But we both know you should have been killed half a dozen times over before they arrived."

Kleef thought back to the blue glow that had been shining from the agate in Watcher's crossguard, then reluctantly nodded. "There may have been some magic," he allowed. "But that doesn't mean dead gods are rising."

Joelle sighed in exasperation. "Then perhaps we should talk about what you *will* believe," she said. "Now that Shar has been stopped from devouring the world—*however* that happened—she has a new plan."

Kleef glanced aft toward Malik. "One that involves the Eye of Gruumsh?"

"No, that is *our* plan," Joelle said. "Shar's plan is to drive

Grumbar away, since his earthly essence is what keeps her Shadowfell separate from the physical world. If she can make him leave with Abeir when the worlds divide, her essence will be free to spill across all of Toril. Shar will become even more powerful than she is now—and master of her fellow gods."

"And what's that have to do with Luthic?" Kleef asked. Joelle gave him a look of strained patience, and once again, Kleef suddenly felt the need to prove that he wasn't the idiot she seemed to believe he was. He took a chance and asked, "Is Luthic what keeps Grumbar on Toril?"

Joelle smiled—and sent a flood of warmth pouring through Kleef. "Indeed," she said. "Grumbar's passion for Luthic has no limits. If Shar can overcome that, Toril is hers."

"Sounds like that might be hard to do."

"Not as hard as you might think," Joelle said. "Shar has threatened to reveal their dalliance to Gruumsh One-Eye—and if that happens, the Savage One's anger will know no bounds."

Kleef nodded. "That would be bad," he said. "Kings have been known to go to war over such things."

"So have gods," Joelle said. "So Shar has convinced Grumbar that the only way to protect Luthic is to leave her— to depart with Abeir when it separates from Toril. And if he doesn't, Shar will make certain that Gruumsh discovers their dalliance."

"And Grumbar buys that?" Kleef asked. "He's not willing to fight for her?"

"He might be—if Shar hadn't also planted the idea that Luthic never loved *him* at all," Joelle said. "Shar has Grumbar thinking that Luthic was only trysting with him because he was the earth primordial—because his favor allowed her to extend her grottos into every last corner of Toril."

"Any truth to that?" Kleef asked.

Joelle shrugged. "Enough for it to work," she said. "Grumbar has just about given up any thought of remaining on Toril. He isn't even *trying* to secure the dominion of stone and earth in this plane."

Kleef fell silent, trying to come to grips with the idea of thinking about gods and primordials on the level of common city folk. Joelle's description of the love triangle sounded like the trouble behind a hundred house brawls he had been called to break up, and he could not help feeling it all made just a little too much sense.

"How sure are you about all this?" he asked. "It's hard to believe the gods conduct their lives no better than we do."

"Because we are seeing them through *our* eyes," Joelle said. "We can only understand them in terms of ourselves. To Malik, it probably looks like Grumbar is dying of a broken heart. To you, it might seem that Grumbar is leaving out of honor, because he endangered Luthic by encouraging her to break a vow of fidelity."

"Vows?" Kleef asked. It hadn't escaped his notice that Joelle's explanations all revolved around love. "I thought you said Gruumsh and Luthic weren't married."

"I *said* that Luthic wasn't property, but they aren't married either —at least not to my way of thinking," Joelle replied. "To one of Helm's Watchers . . . well, it's impossible for me to know how you would see their arrangement. But the heart of the matter remains the same—Shar is tricking Grumbar into leaving Toril, and it has fallen to us to change his mind . . . and *that* is what the Eye is for."

Kleef recalled what Joelle had said about the Eye being a gift. "You're going to give it to Grumbar?"

"That's the plan: take it to his temple in the Underchasm," Joelle confirmed. "Luthic stole it from Gruumsh as a symbol of her devotion—to prove she would rather face the Savage One's wrath than lose Grumbar."

"And to tie him to Toril," Kleef said. "Because now that Luthic has made an enemy of Gruumsh, she'll need help to hold him off. Grumbar would be duty-bound to stay and support her."

"I hadn't thought of that." Joelle's tone was approving. "It will be good to have a Helm worshiper helping us."

"I haven't said I'm coming," Kleef reminded her. "I'm not even sure I believe you."

"No?" Joelle kept her eyes on her work. "What part do you doubt?"

"The part where you know so much," Kleef said. "How can you know what the gods are thinking?"

"Is that all that troubles you?" Joelle tied off the last stitch, then finally raised her eyes. "The Lady of Love revealed it to me, of course."

Kleef lowered his brow, his customary suspicion already turning to disappointment. "Revealed it *how*?" he asked. "In a dream?"

Joelle's eyes twinkled. "Something like that," she replied. "It came to me as revelations from the goddess always do—in a moment of passion."

Kleef felt the color rising to his cheeks, but pressed on. "That's not much comfort," he said. "What did you see? What did she say?"

"*See*? *Say*?" Joelle laughed and returned the needle to the mending kit. "Clearly you have never had a divine revelation. I didn't see anything, and Sune didn't *say* anything—at least not that I can remember. She just entered my mind, and I knew."

"You . . . *knew*?" Kleef repeated, scarcely able to believe how close he had come to accepting Joelle's story. "How am I to trust in that?"

"How can you not?" Joelle countered. "You've seen the Eye. You've felt its power. Do you think Malik and I could steal *that* without divine help?"

"Steal it, maybe," Kleef said. He thought back to the moment Malik had revealed the Eye to him—to the cold terror he had experienced as it awakened and looked into him. "But carrying it into the Underchasm? For that, you *will* need the help of the gods."

"Which must be why Helm sent you to us."

Joelle smiled and touched Kleef's hand, and he started to see the sense in her words. The earthmotes had dropped, and the Sea of Fallen Stars had risen to its ancient levels. The entire world was at war, and Cormyr was imperiled as never before. Clearly, change was coming to Toril. Joelle allowed her fingers to linger, and Kleef began to realize just how right she was. With dead gods rising and the heavens themselves engulfed in a power struggle, perhaps Helm *had* returned.

Perhaps he *had* sent Kleef to protect Joelle on her journey. Then Kleef realized what was happening and pulled his hand away. "Don't do that."

Joelle looked mystified. "Do what?"

"Try to charm me," Kleef replied. "It'll never work. I won't turn my back on my duty."

Joelle's voice grew stern. "No one is asking you to ignore your duty, Watchman. Quite the opposite, in fact." She retrieved the cloth she had used to clean Kleef's wounds, then dropped it in the bucket and rose to leave. "We'll remove those stitches in a few hours. Your wounds will be healed by then."

"A few hours?" Kleef's head was already spinning from everything she had told him, and he struggled to figure out why she might make such an outrageous claim. "You didn't cast any healing magic."

Joelle looked back over her shoulder. "Kleef, I'm a Chosen of Sune," she said. "My love *is* healing magic."

CHAPTER SIX

ARIETTA STOOD AT THE *LONELY ROAMER*'S TAFFRAIL, SEARCHING a rolling gray sea for a white triangle of sail or the distant flash of the *Wave Wyvern*'s oars—anything to suggest the Shadovar were pursuing them as Lady Joelle had said they would. She saw only the same forest of square-rigged masts she had been watching for hours now, a fleet of overloaded pinnaces and caravels that had departed Marsember on the same tide as the *Lonely Roamer*.

In Arietta's mind, she kept seeing her father's death, the Shadovar prince looming over him, her father finally finding the courage to reach for his sword. The end had come too quickly to say Duke Farnig had died well, but at least he had not died a complete coward, and she hoped that Lord Kelemvor would judge him less harshly in death than she had in life.

When it came to her mother, Arietta did not know quite what to hope for. Elira Seasilver would be a difficult prisoner at best, and Arietta could not see the Shadovar tolerating such trouble for long. But would they react by throwing a valuable hostage overboard? Or by locking her in the *Wave Wyvern*'s cramped, sweltering brig? The first was a sure death and the second a fate worse than death, and it made Arietta shudder to imagine her mother facing either.

And it made her sick with guilt. It had been Arietta who

had pressured her father to remain in Marsember, Arietta who had delayed the *Wave Wyvern*'s departure by charging out to help Kleef, and Arietta who had given the Shadovar cause to enter House Seasilver at all. Her thoughts had been filled with fanciful notions of duty and glory, and she could see now how silly she had been, how little she had understood the enemy's insidious power. Ultimately, her father's death was on her head—and if the Shadovar killed her mother as well, then *that* would be on her head, too.

Arietta caught a familiar whiff of decay and turned to see Lady Joelle's little manservant approaching. She forced a pleasant smile and turned to greet him.

"Back so soon, Malik?" she asked. "It seems you left my side just minutes ago."

"And so I did," Malik replied. "But I see how you worry for the grand duke's wife, and what friend would allow another to fret when it is in his power to ease her mind?"

Arietta eyed the little man warily. "Are we friends, Malik?" she asked. "That seems rather sudden."

"Perhaps, but I am a shrewd judge of character," Malik explained. "I can see that my kindness will not be wasted on you."

"No kindness is ever wasted," Arietta said carefully. "But you're right, I *do* fear for the grand duchess. I see no reason for the Shadovar to spare her."

"Never make the mistake of believing you know how the Shadovar think," Malik said. He stopped next to her—just downwind, thankfully—and propped his elbows on the bulwark. "There is only one thing we can count on those dusky fiends to do, and that is to find us when we are the most ill-prepared for it."

Arietta raised her brow. "And you think *that* will ease my mind?"

"At least it will help you see there is no use in this endless vigil," Malik said. "The Shadovar will find *us*. They always do."

"That doesn't mean the duchess will still be alive."

"But it does not mean she will be dead," Malik countered. "And you can't change her fate by standing at this rail all day. By now, the Shadovar have either killed the grand duchess or decided to hold her captive, and the only way to learn which is to find them—and the only way to find *them* is to wait until they find *us*."

Arietta contemplated the assertion, trying think of a faster, surer way to locate the *Wave Wyvern*. But even if she *had* known how to track Shadovar across an open sea, an obvious rescue attempt would only place her mother in even greater danger. As much as she hated to admit it, the safest thing was to do as Malik suggested.

Finally Arietta asked, "You're *certain* the Shadovar will find us?"

"In this world and this time, only a fool is certain of anything," Malik said. "But the Shadovar have always found us before, and I see no reason for that to change."

"How long have they been chasing you?" Arietta asked. "Since you stole the Eye?"

"Almost since we pried it from the idol's head," Malik confirmed. "We have been attacked twenty times in forty days. It is a wonder I am still alive."

"And yet you *are* still alive," Arietta observed, "no doubt because you and Lady Joelle are Chosen."

"No doubt." Malik's tone grew resigned and bitter. "It is an undeserved curse that compels us each to do our god's bidding in all things, and to risk our own lives for the benefit of everyone but ourselves."

"And you resent the sacrifice?" Arietta asked, genuinely surprised. As a Chosen of Siamorphe, she had always found her position more of a boon than a burden—until now, at least. "How is that even possible? No god would invest power in someone who lacks devotion."

Malik shrugged. "There are as many manners of devotion as there are gods," he said. "In the end, all that matters is that we obey."

"That's a very bleak view of one's calling."

"I serve a bleak god." Malik turned away, gazing out toward the western horizon. "And if I fail him, I will suffer."

Arietta started to feel sorry for the little man, if only because she was just beginning to understand the true cost of her own faith. Until earlier that day, her devotion to Siamorphe had seemed a purely personal matter, requiring sacrifices from no one but herself. But in expecting her father to honor those same standards, she had gotten him killed and her mother abducted—and that left her feeling confused and regretful, overwhelmed by guilt and questioning whether she had been right to impose her beliefs on her family.

Her faith was being tested as never before, and she could not help wondering what kinds of sacrifices had been required of Malik, how much worse his suffering had been than her own. Arietta laid her hand on top of his and—despite its cold and waxy feel—gave it a reassuring squeeze.

"You won't fail in your mission, Malik," she said. "Once we have seen to the safety of the grand duchess, Carlton and I will be joining you and Lady Joelle—as will Kleef and his watchmen, I'm told."

"*Kleef* will?" Malik's eyes bulged. "Why would he do such a thing? Our journey is a descent into madness!"

Unsettled by the vehement reaction, Arietta removed her hand from Malik's. "From what I have seen, the entire world is descending into madness." She glanced amidships, where Kleef was allowing Lady Joelle to pull the stitches from his freshly healed wounds. "Besides, Kleef is a Helm-worshiper. What kind of Watcher would he be if he turned his back on a mission of such importance?"

"A living one!" Malik fell silent until Arietta looked back to him, then he lowered his voice to a near whisper. "You must convince the oaf to abandon this foolish plan. He will only be in the way."

"In the way of *what*?" Arietta asked. "Lady Joelle seems quite eager to have him along."

"Only until she tires of him," Malik said. "Joelle Emmeline has a heart as fickle as a mountain breeze."

His bitterness took Arietta by surprise. "Malik," she asked, "are you *jealous* of Kleef?"

Malik's face hardened in resentment. "And what if I am?"

Arietta had to bite her lip to keep from laughing. "Malik, it can never happen. Lady Joelle is a gentlewoman, and so stunning she could marry a king." She shook her head in what she hoped would look like sympathy. "And, Chosen or not, you're barely suited to be her manservant. It wouldn't be right."

"*Manservant*?" Malik's eyes bulged. "What do you know? Joelle loves me. She has told me so twice!"

The sharpness in Malik's voice caused Captain Greatorm, standing in his usual place at the helm, to scowl back over his shoulder. Arietta flashed the gnome an apologetic smile, then turned back to Malik.

"And I'm sure she meant it," she said softly. "But not in the way you hope—and Kleef has nothing to do with that."

"Having him gone will certainly make it more likely," Malik countered. A sly grin came to his plump lips. "And it will be better for you, too. As long as Joelle is near, the oaf will have no eyes for you."

The remark stung more than it should have. "You believe I would be attracted to a common watchman?" she asked. "You must be joking."

"Not even a little," Malik said. "I have seen how your eyes sparkle when he looks in your direction."

Arietta felt the heat rise to her cheeks. "You're misinterpreting," she said. "I have the greatest respect for Kleef's courage and swordsmanship. That doesn't mean I'm interested in him romantically."

"There's no use denying it," Malik insisted. "Everyone knows the Chosen can always tell a lie."

Arietta paused, then said, "I don't know that at all, Malik. And I *am* one of the Chosen."

"You?" Malik shook his head. "I have seen nothing to suggest that."

Arietta hid her injured pride with a smirk. "Haven't you?" she asked. "Surely you noticed how bravely the Watch fought today?"

"Who could have missed it?" Malik replied. "Kleef and his men saved my life many times. What does that have to do with you?"

"I'm the one who inspired them," Arietta said. "Leadership is but one aspect of my divine power."

"Truly?" Malik looked doubtful. "And here I thought the *oaf* was their leader. Foolish me."

"I'm sure Kleef does his best," Arietta said. "But the Watch is filled with drunkards and cowards. It's a wonder they arrived to fight at all."

"Then the sooner I am rid of him, the better it will be for everyone," Malik said. "You will be doing us all a great service by ordering Kleef to escort you and your . . . er, Grand Duchess Elira, to a safe place."

The slip of the tongue was not lost on Arietta. "What makes you think I can give orders to a topsword of the Watch?" she asked. "Or that the grand duchess is my *anything*?"

"Did I not just tell you the Chosen can always tell a lie?"

"And didn't I just tell you it's not true?"

"So you did, but that doesn't make you right," Malik said. "How else would I know you aren't the minstrel Elbertina, as you claim, but Lady Arietta Seasilver herself?"

"I see you've noticed how Carlton defers to me." Arietta's reply came instantly, for she was well trained in courtly discourse and knew better than to yield an advantage by hesitating. "But being observant is not a god-granted power."

"Believe what you will," Malik said. "*What* I know is more important than how I know it—and whether I mean to share it."

"And why would I care if you did?"

A sly smile came to Malik's face. "Because *he* would." He glanced forward, to where Kleef and Lady Joelle were still sitting on the hatch cover. "We have both heard what he thinks of the nobility in Marsember."

Arietta rolled her eyes. "*Please*," she said. "I've already told you that I have no interest in him—at least not romantically."

"So you have," Malik said, grinning. "And I have told you *twice* that the Chosen can always tell a lie."

Through his sleep, Kleef heard the familiar thump of a body hitting the floor. It was a common sound in any Watch barracks, where the residents often returned too drunk to find their own beds. But this barracks seemed to be rocking along its length, and Kleef was rolling side to side on hard planks of oiled oak.

A deck, of course.

Next came a long gasping gurgle, and a thick coppery smell that brought Kleef fully awake in an instant. He opened his eyes and saw Rathul lying in front of the *Lonely Roamer*'s helm, one hand clutched to his neck and a dark stain spreading across the planks beneath him. The ship's wheel was spinning free, turning slowly starboard, and Rathul's killer was nowhere to be seen.

Kleef found Watcher's hilt exactly where he had expected, resting in the palm of his left hand. A blue ray shone from the agate on the crossbar, casting a pale radiance over most of the quarterdeck. *Not* helpful.

Being careful to avoid moving his head, Kleef glanced toward the starboard and found a rippling band of shadow pointing across the moonlit sea, to where a brilliant full moon was just sinking below the horizon. Silhouetted in front of the moon was the tiny shape of a vessel with three lateen-rigged masts—many leagues distant but almost certainly the grand-duke's stolen galleass, the *Wave Wyvern*.

Kleef shifted his gaze forward and saw a trio of men lying on the main deck, swaddled beneath their capes—still asleep, by all appearances. His line of sight to the ketch's bow was blocked by the *Roamer*'s helm, so it was impossible to say whether the forward lookout was alive or dead.

When he could not find any sign of Rathul's killer, Kleef rolled once, then whipped his still-sheathed sword around in a circle. He hit nothing and rolled again, this time banging the hilt on the deck to awaken Joelle and Elbertina, who were sleeping in the cabin below. He stripped the scabbard off the blade and came up on a knee facing the *Roamer*'s stern, where a dusky figure with steel-colored eyes stood alone, a pace from the taffrail. In one hand he held a curved dagger, Rathul's blood still dripping from the glassy blade.

"No one else needs to die." The shade's voice was soft and raspy, barely more than a whisper. "Perhaps we can trade: my grand duchess for your thieves?"

Instead of answering, Kleef took a moment to glance around and was surprised to see no other Shadovar trying to sneak up on him. He looked back to the first and stood.

"You can't be serious."

"I came alone, did I not?"

"And killed one of my men."

"Two," the shade corrected. "But only to encourage consideration. Either we trade, or you all die."

Kleef thought for a moment, then spoke in a voice loud enough to be heard below decks. "I have another offer." He glanced behind him again, still fearful of an attack and trying to figure out what the shade was *really* doing there. "Return the duchess and her household unharmed, and I'll let you live."

The shade smiled, showing a pair of white fangs. "Not a tempting offer, I am afraid," he said. "But I think you know that."

Kleef shrugged. "It's the best I can do."

"Not really," the shade replied. "You *could* recover the Eye of Gruumsh for me."

"And let Shar claim all of Toril?" Kleef shook his head. "Not interested."

"You would find the Mistress of the Night grateful for your help," the Shadovar said. "And what would you be sacrificing, really? A man who fights like you deserves more than a bunk in the Watch barracks."

The remark struck more of a nerve with Kleef than he wanted to admit, even to himself. Only officers of the Watch were permitted to take families and live in their own homes, and the lord marshall had made it clear that Kleef would never advance beyond topsword. Had he deserved such a punishment, Kleef might have accepted the sentence without bitterness. But his only crime was being the son of Taggar Kenric, a constal descended from a long line of devoted Helm worshipers who considered it their holy duty to purge the corruption from the Marsember Watch. That Ilgrim Marduth had become the lord marshall of the Watch—just a tenday after Taggar's death—was evidence enough that the Kenric quest was not going well.

When Kleef did not reply, the shade continued to press his case. "Shar cares nothing for ancient names or aristocratic blood. She values ability above all else, and a man like you . . . let us just say that when the Mistress of the Night reigns over Toril, nobles will bow to *you*."

"That's a lot to promise," Kleef said. He didn't believe the offer for a moment, of course . . . but there *was* a part of him that wanted to see Lord Marshall Marduth brought to the justice Kleef's father had not lived to deliver. "And I'm from Marsember, remember? I'm not that gullible."

"Your doubts are wise but unnecessary," the shade replied. "What a Prince of Shade promises, Shar will deliver."

"A Prince of Shade?" Kleef asked. As he spoke, the soft squeak of a step taking weight sounded from the companionway that led down beneath the quarterdeck. It was barely discernible above the gentle sloshing of waves against the *Roamer*'s hull, but audible enough to make Kleef worry about the shade hearing it, too. He brought Watcher around in a diagonal guard, angling the blade so the agate cast its pale beam on the shade's gaunt face. "Is that supposed to impress me?"

Wisps of gray fume rose from the shade's flesh, but he made no effort to escape the light. "You don't strike me as someone who is easily impressed," he said, sheathing his dagger. "That's why I'm giving you this chance to win Shar's favor."

"Thanks, but I'll have to think about it," Kleef said, trying to hold the shade's attention on him rather than the creaking step. "If I decide to accept, which prince do I ask for?"

"There will be no need to ask for me." The shade pulled a small pale cylinder from inside his cloak and flicked it in Kleef's direction. "I shall find *you*."

Kleef brought Watcher up to block and heard something *tink* against the flat of the blade, then *plunk* to the deck. He quickly stepped past the thing, bringing Watcher up in a horizontal attack that found only empty air as the shade retreated—and tumbled backward over the taffrail.

Knowing better than to think the fall had been accidental, Kleef stepped to the far corner of the quarterdeck and cautiously peered over the *Lonely Roamer*'s taffrail. He saw nothing but darkness and water.

Behind him, Joelle called, "*Kleef?*"

"By the Nine Hells!" cried a second female, Elbertina.

A confused murmur began to build amidships as the men sleeping on the main deck were awakened by the alarmed voices. Kleef continued to peer over the taffrail, searching the stern of the little ketch for any shadows that didn't belong.

A gasp sounded somewhere near the helm, then Elbertina asked, "What happened?"

"We had a visitor."

Kleef turned to find Elbertina kneeling in the blood next

to Rathul. Joelle was crossing the quarterdeck toward him. Both women were wrapped in night cloaks, and both held swords in their hands.

"He's gone back to the *Wave Wyvern* now," Kleef continued. "But he claimed to be one of the Twelve Princes."

"*Yder*?" Joelle asked. "He was here?"

"He wouldn't give his name," Kleef said. "But he had glowing blue-gray eyes."

Joelle nodded. "Yder. He's the commander of the guard in the Hall of Shadows in Netheril."

Falrinn Greatorm emerged from below decks cursing and complaining, and a cry of alarm rose from the bow as one of Carlton's men-at-arms discovered the body of the forward lookout. Malik was nowhere to be seen.

Ignoring the outburst, Joelle took Kleef's elbow and asked, "Are you hurt?"

"I'm fine." Kleef pointed to starboard, where the moonlit silhouette of a three-masted galleass sat on the distant horizon. "Yder didn't come to fight, or the *Wave Wyvern* would be turning toward us by now."

"Your man might disagree with that," Elbertina said, removing her free hand from Rathul's slit throat. "Though it's hard to call what happened here a fight."

Kleef had never had much respect for Rathul during their days on the Watch together. But that had begun to change after he volunteered to help rescue the grand duchess, and the sight of the old man lying dead on the *Roamer*'s deck both sickened and angered him.

"That's the point, I think," Kleef said. "Yder was trying to arrange a trade, and he wanted to convince me I had no choice but to accept."

As Kleef spoke, Carlton stepped onto the quarterdeck and joined them. Behind him followed Greatorm, who took one look at Rathul's body and began to mutter about bloodstains. He stepped over the corpse to take the helm, then began to bring them around.

After a moment, Joelle asked, "A trade, Kleef?" Her tone was uneasy. "For what?"

"For you and Malik." Kleef looked around and, still seeing no sign of the little man, asked, "Where *is* Malik? Yder couldn't have—"

"Malik is safe," Joelle said. "When there's an attack, his duty is to hide."

"Very wise," Elbertina said, almost curtly. She looked back to Kleef. "And what was the prince offering in return? The grand duchess?"

Joelle was quick to shake her head. "Yder knows we're too smart for that. We can't even be certain the grand duchess is still alive."

Kleef remembered the pale cylinder Yder had tossed at him, then turned and spotted the thing rolling across the deck. It was a thin, withered finger inside a large yellow ring. "I think maybe we can." He pointed at the finger. "Yder threw that at me before he left."

Elbertina quickly retrieved the finger, and her mouth fell in horror. "It's still warm." She turned the ring up to reveal the incised figure of a diving wyvern. "And that's my . . . That's the grand duchess's signet."

"So, we *do* know Her Grace is still alive," Carlton said. He turned to the helm. "Captain Greatorm, bring us astarboard. We can't let them escape."

The gnome looked at Carlton as though he were mad. "I thought they were the ones chasing *us*?"

"And now that they have found us, we need to move quickly," Carlton said. "The grand duchess has served her purpose. They may not keep her alive much longer."

"And that is a reason to mount an impossible attack?" The question came from down on the main deck, where Malik had just emerged from the companionway and stood looking up at the rest of them. "Perhaps you would care to make it easier for them by attempting to swim to the *Wyvern* in your armor?"

Carlton's eyes blazed with anger. "I don't recall asking your advice."

"But you'd do well to listen to it," Greatorm said. "He's right. They're just trying to goad us into chasing *them*."

Kleef shook his head. "I just don't see that," he said. "Why would they bother?"

"Because sea chases are never quick and never easy," Greatorm said. "And you're sailing with one of the slickest, trickiest captains on the water. All we need to give them the slip is a wisp of fog or a little puff of storm, and they know it."

"They found us this time," Carlton pointed out.

Greatorm's knobby cheeks brightened to crimson. "Because I *let* them. You said you wanted your duchess back, didn't you?"

This seemed to confuse even Joelle. "But now that they have found us, you want to keep running?"

"That's right," Greatorm said. "If we do this right, we won't even *need* to fight those dusky dogs—at least not all of them."

"You see?" Malik said, looking at Elbertina. "That is why you must always trust the captain of your ship."

Carlton continued to look skeptical. "What about Her Grace?" He seemed to be addressing his question not to Malik or Greatorm but to Elbertina alone. "I don't see how running keeps the grand duchess alive."

"Yder will never kill the duchess—not if we can make him believe he can trade her for the Eye." Malik tipped his head toward Kleef. "And even an oaf like Kleef can tell a lie that simple."

Kleef glowered at the insult, but nodded. "I think I can manage that." He turned back to the others. "What bothers me is that Yder came *alone*. Why not bring his whole company and be done with it?"

"I don't know," Joelle said, flashing a confident smile that suggested just the opposite. "Perhaps because he has been trying to kill us since Big Bone Deep and has not succeeded yet?"

Kleef frowned. "That's not much of an answer."

"But one that makes sense," Joelle said. "He has been chasing us since Big Bone Deep, and we have been escaping him since Big Bone Deep. Perhaps he has realized it's time to try another tactic."

"You mean trade," Elbertina said.

Joelle shrugged. "Perhaps," she said. "Or perhaps his true intent was something else entirely. With a Prince of Shade, it's never safe to assume."

"Which is why we can't take a chance on Kleef fooling them," Carlton said. He turned from Joelle to Elbertina. "We need to go after the *Wave Wyvern* now, while we still have her in sight."

Carlton didn't add "my lady" to the end of his sentence, but he might as well have. Clearly, the sergeant was deferring to her judgment—and Kleef could think of only one reason he would do that in a matter concerning the health of Grand Duchess Elira Seasilver.

Kleef turned to the woman he had been addressing as Elbertina. "*Arietta?*" he asked. "I mean, *Lady* Arietta?"

The woman nodded. "As a matter of fact, yes. Arietta *Elbertina* Ifig Seasilver." She did not appear the least bit embarrassed at having been caught in the lie. "Elbertina is my stage name. I tried to explain that on Deepwater Bridge, but there wasn't time."

"So you just kept lying to me?" Kleef was hurt and not quite certain why—and it didn't matter. Now that he knew her true identity, his duty was clear. "But that changes nothing, of course. I am entirely at your command, my lady."

Something soft and regretful appeared in Arietta's eyes, but when she spoke, there was only birthright in her voice. "Thank you, Kleef. I'm certain we'll get along even better than before."

"Until we all drown," Malik replied.

Arietta turned to the little man, her voice harsh. "Truly, Malik? Do you think so little of me?"

Malik looked confused. "Then you are not going to order us to a watery end?"

Arietta glanced back toward the western horizon, where the distant silhouette of the *Wave Wyvern* continued to float in front of the silver moon. She said nothing for a long time, and her expression grew both sad and determined.

Finally, she looked back to Malik. "Of course not," she said. "This is Captain Greatorm's ship, and we should follow his plan."

CHAPTER SEVEN

Sails furled and bow driving, the *Wave Wyvern* was coming hard, a head-sized wedge that just five minutes earlier had been a mere speck on the horizon. Already, Arietta could see the spray of the sea dividing before the prow and the curtains of water dropping from the oars, and it would not be long before she could make out the scaly face of the ship's hissing-wyvern figurehead.

"They're coming too fast." Arietta spoke just loud enough to make herself heard above the waves rippling around the hull of the *Lonely Roamer*'s little skiff. "Falrinn won't have time to reach the reef."

"Captain Greatorm is a better judge of vessel speeds than we are," said Jang. The Shou was seated on the rowing thwart, behind Arietta. "Let us be patient."

"Patience has never been a particular virtue of mine," Arietta admitted. She twisted around to look past Jang toward Kleef, who sat in the stern with his sword resting across his knees. "Kleef?"

"Patience is good," Kleef said. Like Jang and Arietta herself, he had forsaken his helmet and armor for a tunic and trousers. "We can't signal anyone anyway—not unless we want to reveal ourselves."

They were floating behind a rocky little islet no more than fifty paces across, watching their pursuers through the columns of a tilted, half-submerged temple. According to Greatorm, the temple sat atop an earthmote that had plunged into the Sea of Fallen Stars a few months earlier, creating a submerged reef.

The *Lonely Roamer* had spent the last two tendays trying to reach the site at the right time. It had been a tricky operation, since the ketch needed to arrive far enough ahead of her pursuers to circle around the reef and slip through a hidden passage into a pocket of deep water. At the same time, Greatorm had wanted to be sure the *Wave Wyvern* caught up at around mid-tide, when the reef would still be submerged—but not so deeply that the galleass could cross it without running aground.

According to Greatorm's plan, the *Lonely Roamer* would sit in the pocket of deep water and serve as bait, and the *Wyvern* would run aground going after her. Then, when the Shadovar attempted to free the galleass—or left in longboats to continue the chase—Arietta and her two companions would sneak aboard to rescue Duchess Elira and any other captives.

The scheme had as many moving parts as the *Lonely Roamer* herself, and for that reason alone, it made Arietta nervous. From what she had seen so far, the Shadovar were far from predictable, and not even Joelle knew the full capabilities of their shadow magic. But no one had offered any better ideas, and Greatorm had promised that his gnomish fog—whatever that was—would stop the Shadovar from using their shadow-alking abilities. In the end, Arietta had reluctantly agreed that they had no alternative except to try the gnome's plan.

The *Wave Wyvern* was close enough that she could see the figurehead's hammered-silver scales sparkling in the midday sun. But the Shadovar were nowhere to be found. Given their aversion to bright light, Arietta suspected they were hiding below decks, reserving their strength for the battle.

Still, their absence and the calm sea gave the galleass the appearance of a ghost ship, and she could not help fearing that she and her companions were the ones being tricked.

"Something feels wrong." Arietta glanced back again. "Kleef, when was the last time Yder came to you?"

"Last night." Kleef's tone was clipped. "If I had seen him since then, I would have said so."

"Of course," Arietta said, trying not to take offense. "Thank you."

Yder had committed no more murders aboard the *Roamer,* probably because Kleef had tripled the watch and Greatorm was taking pains to keep the Shadovar from locating them after dark. But the prince had been entering Kleef's dreams nightly, pressuring him to betray Malik and Joelle, and the visits were clearly taking a toll. Kleef's eyes were sunken, his cheeks hollow, and he was often sullen and irritable.

Except when he was with Joelle, of course. The good lady was spending most of her time with the topsword, taking meals in his company, standing watch at his side, even sitting next to him as he slept. Arietta should probably have been glad to see her taking such care of him, since Yder never seemed to trouble Kleef's dreams when Joelle was near.

Instead, Arietta found herself a bit jealous. After risking her life to fight at Kleef's side on the Deepwater Bridge, she had felt a certain rapport between them—a warmth and respect that she had expected to grow into an enduring friendship. Sadly, all that had vanished the instant Kleef learned of her noble blood.

At first, Arietta had attributed the change of heart to the typical commoner's spite for the flawed aristocracy of Marsember. But when she attempted to rekindle their friendship, it had grown clear that Kleef's animosity ran deeper. Perhaps he was frustrated that their friendship could never blossom into romance. Arietta had encountered such resentments before, and she knew how quickly a man's affection could turn to hostility when he discovered that his heart's desire was blocked by his station in life.

THE SENTINEL

Arietta turned back toward the Wave Wyvern. The galleass had drawn so near that she filled most of the view between the columns of the half-submerged temple. A dusky shape with tiny bright eyes stood behind the figurehead, his gaze fixed on the pocket of deeper water where the *Lonely Roamer* lay at anchor.

Arietta crouched lower in the skiff. "What's Greatorm waiting for?" she hissed. "Yder *must* sense a trap by now!"

When no answer came, she glanced over her shoulder to find Jang looking back at Kleef, who sat tense and upright, teeth clenched and eyes wide with dread. Fearing that Yder had found a way to visit Kleef during his waking hours, Arietta reached for her bow . . . then felt a dark menace searching for her, something savage and profane, the same unholy hunger that had violated her when Malik revealed the Eye of Gruumsh—and she knew why Greatorm felt so confident in his trap.

He was dangling the ultimate bait.

"What are they doing?" Jang's voice was muffled and hard to hear, no doubt because he was looking in the opposite direction, back toward the *Lonely Roamer*. "Have they gone mad?"

The last thing Arietta wanted to do was reveal herself to the Eye by looking in its direction, but the confusion in Jang's voice was too alarming. If Malik and Joelle were doing something foolish—or even treacherous—she needed to know about it.

Arietta reluctantly twisted around and looked toward the ketch, which was about two hundred paces away, bobbing gently against her anchor chain. The pocket of deep water in which she lay was a little calmer than the shallows covering the nearby reef, a difference that would soon be obvious to any seamen aboard the *Wyvern*. The Eye was nowhere in sight, but several figures could be seen pursuing a larger shape—no doubt Kleef's man, Tanner—toward the bow of the little ship.

"Relax, Jang," Kleef said, finally opening his eyes. "They're

105

just setting the hook."

"You *knew* about this?" Arietta asked.

A tight, half grin came to Kleef's mouth. "My idea," he said. "Yder has been trying to get me to steal the Eye for him. I thought we could use that against him."

"Why didn't you tell us?" Arietta demanded.

Kleef shrugged. "Joelle was nervous about exposing the Eye," he said. "She wanted to keep it a secret until the time came."

Arietta hesitated, feeling a little excluded, then finally nodded. "I see. Well, that makes sense."

Aboard the *Lonely Roamer*, the chase had reached the bow, where Tanner stumbled and fell. His pursuers fell on him immediately, and the profane hunger of the Eye vanished at once. The *Roamer*'s anchor chain began to clatter through the hawsehole, and a dense white fog spilled over her bulwarks and crept across the water toward the reef. In seconds the ketch was no longer visible, and Arietta knew that if all went according to plan, the vessel would soon be escaping through the hidden passage.

"Even better than promised," Jang said. "I had not expected it to be so fast."

"Indeed," Arietta said, still worried. Greatorm had promised that the Shadovar would not be able to dispel the fog, but he had refused to reveal how he created it. "I just wish he had told us how it works. 'Trust me' is not very confidence-inspiring."

"Greatorm is a smuggler," Kleef said. "You can't expect him to give away his tricks."

The fog soon washed over them. It had a salty, acrid taint that burned Arietta's nostrils and made her think of brimstone, and there was a yellow tinge to it that made distant shapes difficult to see.

Shouts of alarm and frustration drifted across the water from the direction of the *Wave Wyvern*, and an urgent creaking grew audible as the oars put on speed.

"Sounds like it's time," Kleef said. "Let's move."

Jang took up their own oars and backed the skiff out of the pool in which they had been hiding, then carefully began to row them around the half-submerged temple. By the time they arrived on the far side of the little islet, Greatorm's gnomish fog had swallowed everything in sight. The only way Arietta could tell that the *Wyvern* was crossing ahead of them was by the *shriek-splash* of her oars.

Then came the deep burbling growl of a keel running aground, followed almost instantly by the crash of tumbling gear and the cries of startled crewmen. The tumult continued for only a moment, then quickly faded as the ship slowed to a dead stop. Jang continued to row, and the *Wyvern* finally grew apparent, a faint darkening in the fog, about twenty paces ahead.

"Hold here," Kleef whispered. "Let's see what they do."

Jang brought the skiff to a stop without so much as the sound of a swirling oar. For the next few minutes, Arietta and her companions sat listening to an angry Yder yell commands and questions in his native tongue. The longer she listened to his raspy voice, the higher the flame of rage and sorrow rose within her. Farnig Seasilver may not have been a paragon of the noble class, but he had still been her father and a grand duke of Cormyr, and he had not deserved the death Yder gave him. That alone would have been reason enough to fight—even had she not understood the importance of helping Joelle and Malik stop Shar from releasing the Shadowfell across all of Toril.

Winches groaned as the Shadovar lowered longboats into the water. Arietta set her quiver at her knee and nocked an arrow, then prayed to Siamorphe to quiet her pounding heart. This would be only the second time she had gone into a life-or-death fight—the first had been when she joined Kleef on Deepwater Bridge—and she found that the waiting frightened her far more than had the actual combat.

At last, a pair of long gray silhouettes glided past the bow of the galleass and faded into the fog. They were trailing no lines and taking care to move as quietly as possible, so it seemed clear that instead of attempting to free his own vessel, Yder had decided to board the *Lonely Roamer* from the *Wyvern*'s longboats—just as Greatorm had predicted.

Jang began to move the skiff forward again, and Arietta scanned the *Wyvern*'s looming silhouette for any sign of a Shadovar lookout. It took only moments to find a dark shape moving aft from the bow. She drew her bowstring taut, but did not loose.

The *Wyvern* had not grounded so solidly that the reef was holding her steady. Instead, she was rolling slightly on her keel, lifting and lowering the target in a steady cycle. Arietta waited until she had the rhythm, then let out her breath and let the arrow fly.

A heartbeat later, it took the dark silhouette in the center of the head and sent him flying back.

Arietta already had her next arrow nocked and, when a second silhouette appeared at the bulwark, she was ready. She loosed instantly this time—and saw the arrow tear through the Shadovar's throat. He stumbled two steps back, then collapsed out of sight.

Not a head shot, but it would have to do. Arietta nocked another arrow and waited, but no more Shadovar appeared as the *Wave Wyvern* changed from gray shape to wooden ship. Once they'd drawn to within a few paces, Jang stopped rowing. Kleef stood and tossed a hook-and-rope onto the bulwark of the *Wave Wyvern*, then held the line steady as Jang ascended hand-over-hand.

The Shou was nearly at the top when a Shadovar peered down at him, his glassy blade already descending to cut the line. Arietta planted an arrow in his dusky face, and Jang was over the bulwark, drawing his slender sword and removing the head before the body had fallen out of sight.

Slinging her bow and quiver over her shoulders, Arietta

took the rope next. While the distance wasn't great, she was not as strong as the Shou, and the rocking of the *Wyvern* made the climb a difficult one. It was nearly a dozen seconds before she neared the top of the rope—and saw Jang reaching down to help her the rest of the way.

"Thank you," she said, clambering onto the deck. "How many remain?"

"I've beheaded the three you hit." Jang pointed to three headless bodies lying on the deck between them and the bow. "I will look for others."

With that, he turned and clambered onto the quarterdeck. Arietta nocked an arrow and kneeled beside the headless body of her last target and tried not to think about the three lives she had just taken. It had been easy to kill the Shadovar when they were the ones attacking, but it felt much different when she was the aggressor. She had to remind herself that her enemies had brought this on themselves, that Yder had killed her father and made a hostage of her mother.

The bulwark crackled beneath Kleef's weight, and a few breaths later he was planting his boots on the deck. He drew his sword and crouched next to her, his eyes scanning the rest of the ship.

"Jang?" he whispered.

Arietta pointed toward the quarterdeck. "He went to check for more guards."

Kleef looked in the direction she had indicated, then nodded in satisfaction when Jang rose from behind the helm and displayed a fist with no upraised fingers.

"Looks like he hasn't found any," Kleef said, turning forward. "Let's finish this."

"You're leaving Jang up here alone?"

"There may be more guards in hiding," Kleef said. "And somebody needs to make sure Yder doesn't come back and surprise us."

Arietta nodded and led him to the forward companionway,

which descended to the rowing deck. As eager as she was to find her mother, their plan called for them to seize control of the *Wyvern* first, and that meant freeing the men the Shadovar had been using as galley slaves.

Kleef paused at the entrance and looked at the agate glowing on the crossguard of his sword, then motioned for Arietta to wait. He kicked the door open and descended the stairs in a single leap.

Arietta peered through the opening and found him six feet below, crouching beneath the low ceiling and spinning, whipping his sword ahead of him in a clearing circle. He caught her eye and dipped his head in a barely perceptible nod, then completed his turn and stepped away from stairs.

Arietta descended the stairs about halfway, then stopped and peered under the railing back toward the rowing benches. Greatorm's fog was not as thick below the *Wyvern*'s decks as it was above, but visibility down there was still even more limited than usual. She had a clear view of only the first three rowing benches, where a dozen haggard men sat with their arms resting on their oars, a few of them too exhausted—or too badly beaten—to even raise their heads.

Kleef pointed his sword at them. "You men," he said. "Are you ready to fight for Cormyr?"

The cheer that came in reply was hardly rousing, but it was sincere, and someone with a gravelly voice said, "Get these shackles off us, and we'll fight."

"Good," Kleef said. "Consider yourselves soldiers again."

He started toward the first bench, and that was when a pair of Shadovar stepped out of the murk behind him. A chorus of half-broken voices croaked warning cries, but Arietta's arrow was already flying toward the shape on the right. It buried itself between the Shadovar's shoulders and sent him sprawling on the deck.

Knowing she had no time to nock a second arrow, Arietta leaped off the stairs, jabbing her bow tip at the figure on the left.

Her blow caught the Shadovar in the back of the head, causing little damage but forcing him to glance back over his shoulder.

That was all the hesitation Kleef needed to whirl around and send the fellow's head tumbling. He continued his spin, deftly lifting the blade over Arietta's head and bringing it down through the neck of the Shadovar her arrow had sent sprawling.

A stunned silence fell over the rowing deck. Kleef worked his sword tip free of the wood in which it had buried itself. He glanced at the agate on the crossguard, which had fallen dark again, then relaxed and turned to Arietta.

"Thanks," he said. "You fight pretty well for an heiress."

"And you're not bad for a clumsy ox," Arietta replied.

The retort drew a chorus of catcalls and cheers from the rowing benches, and she knew that Siamorphe's grace was still working through her. She smiled and turned to address the deck.

"You were my father's best men," she said. "He picked you to escort him on the journey to Elversult because he believed you to be his strongest, most capable men-at-arms. Then the Shadovar came and made galley slaves of you. The next time you meet them, I want you to give them reason to regret that!"

Rather than the enthusiastic cheer she had expected, most of the men merely looked down and tried to avoid her gaze. And those who did speak seemed rather embarrassed and apologetic, promising to do their best and not let the Shadovar take them alive again.

Arietta hid her disappointment with a polite smile. "Well, I'm sure you're all very eager to be free." She turned to Kleef. "Shall we?"

Kleef nodded and started down one side of the aisle, his greatsword rising and falling as he freed the men from their bonds. Arietta went down the opposite side with her own sword, though she was not nearly so fast.

Because her father's ship had not been designed as a slave galley, it lacked the steel eye hooks through which shackle chains commonly ran—and even the shackles and chains themselves. So the Shadovar had improvised with their dark magic, binding the ankles of their captives with thick ropes of pure shadowstuff. And while all of Arietta's weapons were enchanted—she *was* the daughter of a grand duke, after all— she lacked Kleef's strength. Where he simply lopped the lines apart, she found herself sawing and hacking, and she was only halfway down the aisle when she met him coming from the opposite direction.

He glanced over her head toward the men climbing from their benches, then grunted, "Only thirty."

Arietta frowned. "Thirty?"

"Thirty men." Kleef looked back toward her. "And only twenty look strong enough to fight."

Arietta turned to study the men staggering into the aisle behind her. They were filthy and gaunt, with sunken cheeks, lips so cracked they bled, and bare torsos showing through the tattered remnants of their tunics. Their backs were striped by pale welts, and their ribs showed through the gray flesh on their sides. Only their broad shoulders and old scars suggested that they had once been soldiers, and it was obvious that sending them into battle against Yder and his shadow warriors right now would be little short of a death sentence.

"Then it's time to change the plan," Arietta said. "Even Yder can't catch Greatorm in the *Wyvern*'s longboats. All we need to do is deny the Shadovar a ship."

Kleef furrowed his brow. "True enough," he said. "How do we do that without a fight?"

"Like this." Arietta raised her arms, gesturing for the attention of the newly freed captives. "We need to lighten our load. I want you to start dumping cargo—the locked holds first."

An astonished murmur spread across the deck. A red-bearded man whom Arietta recognized as one of her father's personal bodyguards, Balen, stepped forward.

"You're asking us to throw the Seasilver fortune overboard?"

"No, Balen," Arietta said. "I'm *telling* you."

Balen looked confused. "Why?"

Knowing better than to assert an authority her father's men might not respect, Arietta simply turned to another captive—a lanky man with a weathered face and a sun-bleached beard.

"Tell him, Mister Grynwald."

Grynwald, who had served her father as the *Wyvern*'s first mate, smiled and pointed at Balen's feet.

"Feel that?" he asked. "The *Wyvern* is rolling on her keel, and that means she can be freed—if she can shed enough weight."

Balen was quick to shake his head. "Her Grace wouldn't like that."

"She'll like it more than having the Shadovar cut off more fingers," Kleef said. He stepped toward the man, then ran his gaze over the rest of the deck. "Do you really think you're ready to turn the Shadovar away when they return to the ship? Because *I* don't."

When Kleef's comment drew a muttered chorus of agreement, Arietta added, "The Seasilver fortune is lost no matter what." She could scarcely believe her own words, but she had no doubts about their truth. "At least this way, there's a chance we might be able to return and recover some of it."

Balen looked around at his fellows, then reluctantly nodded. "When you put it that way, I guess we have no choice."

"Good." Kleef turned to Grynwald. "You take charge of that."

"As you like," Grynwald said.

Though it did not escape Arietta's notice that all of her father's men were quicker to acknowledge Kleef's authority than her own, now hardly seemed the time to make an issue of it. She merely nodded her approval, then turned aft.

"I don't suppose the shades have been keeping Her Grace in one of the family cabins?"

"No, my lady." Grynwald pointed forward. "They've had her in the Stink."

Arietta's heart fell. "I was afraid of that."

She started forward, barely noticing as Kleef fell in beside her. The Stink was the crew's nickname for the *Wyvern*'s brig, a cramped little cabin tucked into the forepeak of the ship. She could not imagine her mother surviving twenty hours in there, much less twenty days, and she felt her stomach clenching with every step she took.

Kleef insisted on leading the way as they slipped through the bulkhead and into a dim aisle flanked by open bunks. At the far end stood a pair of officers' cabins and the barred door that led into the brig. After pausing a moment to check for lurking Shadovar, Kleef nodded and motioned Arietta forward.

And that was when Jang's voice rang out from the hatchway behind them. "There is yelling. I think it is coming from the *Lonely Roamer*."

Arietta heard Kleef curse under his breath, and they both turned to face the Shou.

"Can you see what's happening?" Kleef asked.

Jang shook his head. "The fog is too thick. But one voice belongs to Carlton, and another to Captain Greatorm."

Arietta did not waste time asking what had gone wrong. Clearly, Greatorm had failed to reach the hidden passage in time, and soon Joelle and Malik and the others would be fighting for their lives.

"We have to go back," Arietta said. "If Yder is catching up to them—"

"Arietta?" The voice was muffled and brittle, and it came from the other side of the brig door. "Is that *you*?"

Arietta closed her eyes—*mostly* relieved to hear that voice—then said, "Yes, Your Grace. We'll have you out in a minute."

"What are you doing *here*?" the grand duchess demanded. "I had hoped you had escaped."

Kleef looked from the door to Arietta, then whispered, "Jang and I will go back to the Roamer." He turned to leave. "You see to Her Grace."

Arietta caught him by the arm. "No, wait."

"Arietta?" Elira called. "Are you still there?"

"Yes, Mother." Arietta squeezed Kleef's arm, hard, and said, "You *wait*."

Kleef sighed, but nodded. "Just make it fast."

Arietta released Kleef and slid the bar aside, then pulled the door open to reveal a dark cramped cabin barely four feet wide and five feet long. Her mother sat on the edge of one of the two bunks, holding a bandaged hand and blinking into the dim light. She looked dirty and frail and starving, and Arietta's heart ached at the sight.

"Hello, Your Grace," Arietta said, stepping through the door. "Come out of there."

The grand duchess studied Arietta for a moment, then looked away. "I'm not sure I can," she said. "Perhaps you should have your man carry me."

Kleef made a disgusted sound. Arietta turned to see him glaring down at her with an expression of impatience.

"I'll meet you at the bow," Arietta said. "Just bring the skiff up."

Kleef turned on his heel and started down the aisle. "That's a small skiff, my lady," he said. "It might be better if you stayed behind, in case we need to pick anyone up."

Arietta put some authority into her voice. "Then leave Jang." When Kleef did not even slow down, she quickly added, "What are you going to do if Yder starts hurling magic at you? Throw your sword at him?"

Kleef stopped at the bulkhead and nodded, then turned to Jang. "You take command here," he said. "*Don't* let the Shadovar retake the ship. Sink it, if need be."

"*Sink* it?" the grand duchess demanded, suddenly finding the strength to rise to her feet. "Do you know to whom this ship belongs?"

Arietta slipped an arm around her mother's shoulders. "He knows, Your Grace," she said, guiding her across the threshold of the brig and out into the aisle. "And he's absolutely right.

We're at war."

Kleef nodded without looking back. "I'll see you in one minute," he said, turning to ascend the companionway. "Don't be late."

The grand duchess tensed. "Arietta, did that man just give you an order?"

"I wouldn't call it an order," Arietta said, guiding her mother down the aisle toward a wary-looking Jang. "It's more of a suggestion."

"I know an order when I hear one," the grand duchess said. "Who is he?"

"He's a topsword in the Watch," Arietta said. "And one of the men who helped take the *Wyvern* back . . . and rescue *you*."

"So he's common."

"He's far from common," Arietta said, thinking of Kleef's skill with a sword. "But he's not noble."

"Then what . . ." The grand duchess stopped to turn and peer up at Arietta. "Don't tell me you've taken a *watchman* as a lover!"

Arietta felt the heat rising to her cheeks. "You must be delirious," she said. "Kleef is a better man than most lords I know, but what you suggest wouldn't be appropriate."

"When has that ever stopped you?" the grand duchess demanded. "Singing in taverns, fighting in the streets like a regular man-at-arms. Why not bed a watchman for good measure?"

"Now you're just being rude," Arietta said. "Kleef risked his life to save you."

"As well he should have," the grand duchess retorted. "If you had just listened to your father, none of this would . . ."

The grand duchess stopped abruptly, but Arietta was already reeling, her heart aching as if from a blow. Her mother had just given voice to her own worst fears, and now she found herself floundering in a sea of doubt again, wondering whether her faith in Siamorphe was just a spoiled noblewoman's silly fantasy after all.

"Arietta, I didn't mean to say that you're responsible," the grand duchess said. "Only the Shadovar are to blame—"

"It's quite all right, Your Grace," Arietta said. "I understand exactly what you meant."

They reached the bulkhead. Arietta removed her arm from around her mother and turned to Jang.

"The grand cabin is in the stern," she said. "Would you see that Her Grace is made comfortable and given food and water?"

Jang cast a wary glance at the grand duchess, then said simply, "Yes."

"Thank you." Arietta started up the companionway, but stopped halfway up and glanced back down at her mother. "And, Jang, *do* remember that you're in charge."

CHAPTER EIGHT

KLEEF WAS ON THE ROWING THWART, FACING AFT AND PROPELLING the little skiff through a miasma of gnomish fog. The sky above was yellow-gray, the surrounding air was yellow-gray, and even the sea upon which they floated was a rippling yellow-gray reflection. The *Wave Wyvern* had dimmed into gray nothingness over a hundred oar strokes ago, and he had no way to tell how far they had come—nor even which direction they were traveling.

But the agate on Watcher's crossguard was growing steadily brighter as he rowed, and occasionally he could hear a voice call out somewhere beyond his shoulder. So far, none of the voices seemed to belong to Joelle, and that gave him hope. Whatever was happening, she and Malik were taking care to stay hidden, and that could only mean that the Eye of Gruumsh remained safe.

Kleef was about to say as much when Arietta's hushed voice sounded from the bow thwart behind him. "*There!*"

He turned to look over his shoulder and found her already nocking an arrow. She pointed the tip ahead and a little to the starboard.

"See them?" she whispered.

Kleef followed the arrow and spotted the dim shapes of

two longboats crammed with shades. The forms were still too distant and indistinct to tell much about the passengers, but the boats seemed to be diverging—either moving toward separate targets or trying to flank a single one.

A male voice—Kleef thought it sounded like Carlton—called out in the fog ahead. It was answered by Tanner's voice, at least a dozen paces away. Both longboats altered course, one angling toward Carlton's voice, the other toward Tanner's.

"Quieter and faster." Arietta's whisper was so soft Kleef could barely make out her words. "Maybe we can take them by surprise."

With two boatloads of shades to face, the advantage of any surprise they achieved would quickly reverse. Still, Kleef had to smile at Arietta's enthusiasm. She had the spirit of a warrior and the pride of a lord, and he didn't quite know what to make of her. Her heart seemed too pure to belong to a noble, yet she had lied about her identity for no reason he could see. It made him wonder if lying was just habit for her, if the practice simply ran in noble blood.

"Kleef, I *said* . . ." Arietta let her complaint trail off, then spoke in a more urgent whisper. "Wait! Hold here."

Kleef let the oars hang in the water, putting just enough pressure on them to slow the skiff without making noise, then glanced over his shoulder again. Arietta was scowling and looking hard to starboard, where the blurry shape of a half-submerged temple could be seen no more than thirty paces distant, sitting on the shore of a rocky islet.

"Something's wrong." Arietta pointed in the direction opposite the islet. "Shouldn't the *Roamer* be somewhere over there?"

"If it's still in the passage," Kleef said. "Maybe Greatorm got lost in his own fog."

"And sailed across half the reef before running aground?" Arietta shook her head. "I don't see that."

Actually, the distance would have been closer to a quarter of the reef, but Kleef saw her point. From what they had seen during the previous day's low tide, it would have been impossible for any vessel with a keel to cross that much of the reef.

"Maybe they're wading," Kleef suggested. "Or swimming."

"It's possible," Arietta said. "But the water would be over their heads in a lot of places, and swimming in this fog would be madness."

Then the voices called out again—this time from a good twenty paces to the left—and Kleef understood.

"They couldn't have moved that far." He spun the skiff around. "It has to be a trick."

Arietta scowled. "That wasn't in the plan." She hesitated, then asked, "*Was* it?"

"Not that anyone told me about." He began to row away from the Shadovar. "I don't even know how they could do it."

Arietta did not even hesitate. "Malik," she whispered. "He's the tricky one."

The longboats had dimmed to gray blurs when Kleef saw a hazy figure rise in the stern of the farthest one. For an instant, he feared they were about to be attacked, but the shade merely extended an arm over the side of his boat. He spoke a few syllables in an ancient, sibilant language that were clearly audible across the water, then cocked his head as though listening for a reply.

A moment later, a deep murmuring groan bubbled across the water, and the shade sat down again.

Behind Kleef, Arietta let out her breath. "What was *that* about?"

"Nothing good," Kleef said. "I don't think we're the only ones who realize the voices are a trick."

He pulled harder on the oars, and both longboats vanished into the fog. An instant later, so did the rocky islet, and Kleef was left with no real sense of where the hidden passage lay.

"Keep a sharp eye up there," he said. "I have no idea where we're heading."

"Just watch our wake," Arietta said. "Keep it straight, and we should be heading more or less in the right direction."

Kleef was impressed. "A minstrel, a lady, *and* a sailor?"

"Not a sailor," Arietta replied. "Just smart."

Kleef was about to ask whether he had just been insulted when a tremendous slurping sound rolled through the fog. It was followed by clacking crossbows and a long chorus of screams. Kleef adjusted their course toward the sounds, then began to row so hard the oars slammed against their locks.

"Faster!" Arietta ordered.

Kleef put his legs into it, pushing against the rear thwart—and snapping it off its mounts.

"Any harder and we'll break up," he said. "What's happening back there?"

"How should *I* know? Just keep . . ." The sentence ended with the twang of a snapping bowstring. "What *is* that thing?"

Kleef glanced back to find a writhing mountain of shadow rising ahead, its blurry darkness so pure that it seemed to shed Greatorm's fog as though it were water. A single enormous eye with a dozen deformed pupils peered out of a pulsing maw, and the maw was surrounded by jointed barbs.

Arietta loosed another arrow, and it was only then that Kleef noticed a flurry of tiny black slivers flying up from below the monster's immense bulk. He followed the line of slivers down to their source, where he found the silhouette of the *Lonely Roamer* sitting in a channel of dark water.

Still rowing, Kleef continued to watch over his shoulder as the shadow creature dipped down and grasped the *Roamer*'s entire bow in its jaws. The screams aboard the ketch grew even more panicked and terrified, and human shapes began to leap overboard. Then the creature lowered the rest of its body to the surface, and the ship began to move backward toward Kleef and Arietta, raising a man-high wave before its stern. A flash of red hair went over the side, and Kleef felt a lump form in his throat.

He doubled his pace, throwing his weight forward and backward so fast the thwart rocked and creaked beneath him, pushing his feet against the hull so hard he feared he would loosen a plank.

The *Roamer* continued to move toward them, coming fast and pushing the wave ahead of its stern. Kleef moved the skiff out of the way just in time to avoid being swamped, but the wake raised the little boat a good four feet above the surrounding sea, and they had a crystal-clear view of the leviathan as it swam past.

Rippling with muscle and sinew, the thing was as big around as a war galley and as long as Ringfinger Wharf. The dorsal fins along its spine were as tall as houses, and the beat of its enormous tail created such a wave that Kleef barely managed to keep the skiff from capsizing.

Once the wave was past, he started to row again. Immediately, he began to hear screaming and splashing, and when he looked over his shoulder, he saw several dim fog-shrouded figures in the water. Some appeared to be swimming better than others, but all were flailing in panic, and a couple seemed to be thrashing their weapons into the sea. Finally, he spotted a fan of red hair about twenty paces away, and a cold hollow formed in the pit of his stomach. Unlike everyone else, this figure was motionless, and it was impossible to tell whether she was alive or dead.

No sooner had Kleef turned the skiff toward her than Arietta pointed in the opposite direction. "Over there, Kleef. It's Malik."

Kleef looked over his other shoulder and saw a small figure, also about twenty paces away. The little man was holding his robe in one hand and his sword in the other, flailing madly as he tried to swim.

Kleef turned away. "Joelle's not moving," he said, continuing to row in the same direction. "We'll save her first."

"Malik has the Eye!" Arietta objected. "We need to get him first."

"He's doing fine," Kleef said. They were only ten paces from Joelle, and now he could see something dark and sinuous circling her in the water. "At least he's still swimming."

"Damn it, Kleef!" Arietta yelled. "If that thing gets Malik, Shar wins."

Before Kleef could look back toward Malik, a splash sounded. He spun around and saw Arietta in the water, head down, legs kicking, and sword in hand as she swam toward the little man. Behind her, a serpentine shadow turned in her pursuit, its body a tiny mimic of the great leviathan that had taken the *Lonely Roamer*.

Cursing the stubbornness of the nobility, Kleef grabbed Watcher and leaned over the side of skiff, slashing it down across the phantom's back. The thing came apart in a cloud of inky darkness that quickly sank out of sight.

"Arietta!" Kleef yelled.

Whether Arietta had heard him or not was impossible to say, but she continued to swim. Kleef glanced back and saw that he had drifted to within five paces of Joelle. He didn't know whether his judgment had been clouded by the heartwarder's charm or his dislike of Malik, but it was clear that Arietta had been right about going after Malik first—and it was just as clear that it was too late to undo his mistake.

Kleef swung the skiff in behind Joelle. Now that he was so close, he could see that she was holding her sword in one hand, her head moving ever so slightly as she watched a sinuous shape circling her. He grabbed his sword again and swung into the water.

The serpent sensed the attack coming and twirled away in a flash—straight onto the tip of Joelle's outstretched sword. It writhed on the blade, whipping its tail around to slash her legs. The water went instantly red and cloudy, and she answered with a quick wrist flick that opened up six inches of flank. The serpent seemed to explode, its insides bursting out through the wound to engulf it in a churning ball of shadow.

Kleef slipped his free hand under Joelle's arm and lifted her into the skiff. Blood oozed from a finger-length gash on her lower thigh, but with Arietta and Malik in the water, there was no time to worry. He lowered her into the stern of the skiff, then set Watcher aside and took the oars again.

Joelle clamped a hand over the wound to stop the bleeding and drew her legs up, then looked around the boat and frowned.

"Where's Malik?"

Kleef nodded toward where Arietta had her sword arm wrapped around Malik, pulling him back to the boat. The little man was thrashing his sword into the water and kicking so hard that Arietta could barely hold onto him.

"And you came after me first?" Joelle asked. "That's sweet, but *Malik* is the Eye-bearer."

"Yeah, that's what Arietta said." Kleef was rowing hard, looking back over his shoulder and trying not to feel guilty. "But I don't see why *Malik* is the bearer. He's a bungler—and not to be trusted, I have a feeling."

Joelle gave him a benevolent smile. "That's the whole point, Kleef," she replied. "Anybody else, the Eye would corrupt. But Malik? He already stands on that side of the temple."

Arietta suddenly let go of Malik and slipped beneath the water. Kleef feared that one of the serpents had dragged her under, but a moment later, she came up with the thing writhing on her sword. Malik screamed and began to slash at it so wildly that Arietta had to hold it at arm's length—and even then, he came closer to hitting her arm than the creature.

Kleef steered the skiff around behind the little man and released the oars, then caught the wrist of Malik's sword hand and squeezed hard.

"Be . . . still."

Once Malik stopped flailing, Kleef hauled him from the water and dropped him into the bow of the skiff, then turned to see Joelle taking Arietta's sword from her. He leaned down to pull her into the boat—only to have her knock his arm away.

"I'll do it myself."

She grabbed the skiff and seemed to rise out of the water like a breaching swordfish, then threw a leg over the side and rolled into the boat. Kleef was relieved to see that she did not leave any blood in the water behind her.

"Get us out of here!" she ordered. "Before Yder realizes they jumped."

Kleef nodded and grabbed the oars—then felt something heavy clinging to the one on the port. He grabbed Watcher in one hand and used the other to push down on the oar handle, levering the blade out of the water.

Clinging to the end was a sodden gnome with an angry gleam in his eyes. "You owe me a ship," he growled. "A good one."

"You can have the *Wave Wyvern*," Arietta said. "All you have to do is find her."

Greatorm's expression brightened. "You're serious?"

Arietta nodded. "I'll give you a letter of transfer," she said. "My mother has family in Westgate, so I imagine the *Wyvern* will head for there—assuming Jang can keep her away from the Shadovar, of course."

"In that case, start rowing." Greatorm crawled up the oar and tumbled into the skiff, then pointed over Kleef's right shoulder. "Shore's that way."

Kleef started to row, but looked to Arietta. "What about survivors?"

"*Survivors*?" Greatorm scoffed. "Do you hear anyone screaming out there? The fry got 'em all."

Joelle nodded. "He's right," she said. "Go on."

Kleef continued to look at Arietta. As a noble of Cormyr, she was the closest thing he had to a commander right now.

She cocked her head, either listening or thinking, then finally nodded. "Keep rowing, Kleef," she said. "Even if there *were* survivors, our first duty is to the mission."

CHAPTER NINE

THE CANEBRAKE LAY STREWN IN A TANGLE OF LEAFY STEMS
and sand-filled root balls that formed a sort of nest around
the abandoned skiff. Yder could see that at one time, the
little boat had been hidden beneath a mound of woven cane.
But someone had come along and torn the camouflage apart
in a rage. The skiff itself had been flipped onto its hull and
bashed into uselessness by what appeared to be clubs and dull
blades. The ground—where it was visible—had been churned
into a lumpy mess by stiff-soled boots, and a broad swath of
trampled cane meandered inland from the moonlit beach.

Yder turned to his most recent second-in-command,
a square-jawed shade who had replaced the three who had
already fallen to Kleef Kenric and his companions. "It seems
we are no longer the only ones chasing the Eye, Ajloon."

"That would be hard to deny, High One." Ajloon pointed a
wispy finger toward the meandering swath of trampled cane.
"But how could a band of orcs know to look for it here, when
we wasted two days searching at sea?"

The scouts had yet to confirm that it had been orcs who
smashed the skiff, but Yder had no doubt that Ajloon's conclusion would prove correct. As the god of savagery, Gruumsh

was the most revered deity of orc tribes everywhere, and word of the theft from Big Bone Deep had no doubt spread quickly. By now, there would be orcish spies posted outside every city, along every road and coast, watching for any hint of the thieves who had taken their god's eye.

And two days ago, they would have felt the same thing Yder had.

"The orcs knew to come here because Gruumsh guided them," Yder said finally. "They felt the Savage One look at them—just as we did."

"Before the *Wave Wyvern* ran aground?"

"Indeed," Yder replied.

His new second-in-command had wisely avoided pointing out that the mistake had been Yder's, but the memory caused angry wisps of shadow to seep from the prince's body. In his eagerness to believe he had won Kleef Kenric for Shar, he had ignored the possibility of a trick—and now a band of orcs was closer to success than he was.

When Yder did not elaborate, Ajloon said, "Truly, High One, your genius has no equal."

"If that were true, we would have the Eye already." Yder's tone was just sharp enough to suggest he was not impressed by such flattery. "I only hope Shar will be patient with me despite my failure."

A sinuous shape rose from the shadows at their feet, coalescing into the dusky figure of a Shadovar scout. Ajloon waited for Yder to nod, then turned to the scout.

"Speak."

"The trail leads to a caravan track ten leagues distant," the scout said. "The ground is too trampled to read clearly, but we found no tracks to suggest that any humans had fled in another direction. I'm confident the orcs are pursuing our thieves."

"And you're certain these are orcs?" Yder asked. "It couldn't be another trick?"

The scout dipped his head in affirmation. "We found

stragglers, High One," he said. "Their tongues had been ripped out, and they had been left to die where they collapsed."

"The orcs are moving fast," Ajloon observed. "And they don't want anyone asking questions."

Yder nodded. "There can be no doubt now. They are after the Eye." He turned to Ajloon. "We depart at once."

"High One, there is more." The scout waited for a nod of permission, then continued, "When we reached the caravan track, we found the footprints of a gnome. He was traveling away from the orcs, toward Alaghôn."

"Alone?" Yder asked.

"So it appeared," the scout reported.

"Interesting," Yder said. Over the last two tendays at sea, they had caught enough glimpses of their quarry to realize the ship was being sailed by a gnome. "So it appears the good ship captain has parted ways with our thieves."

"I'll send a pair of shadow blades to fetch him," Ajloon said.

"Wait," Yder said, raising his hand. "As we rowed to shore, did we not see lights just up the coast?"

"We did," Ajloon confirmed. "A great many."

Yder's frustration began to seep from his body on tendrils of shadow. "Then the gnome is *already* in Alaghôn, you fool," he said. "And our number is down to twenty-five. What makes you believe we can spare two warriors long enough to hunt down one gnome in a city that must have hundreds?"

Ajloon's complexion paled to the color of dusk, but he did not let his gaze drop. "The gnome might have seen how they are keeping the Eye hidden from your magic," he said. "And if nothing else, he can tell us more about our new foes from Marsember."

The argument was not unreasonable, and Yder liked how Ajloon had refused to look away in the face of a Prince's anger. The refusal to be intimidated reflected well on his ability to be an honest advisor—and it served to remind Yder that their losses were not Ajloon's doing, but the results of his own mistakes.

After a moment, Yder laid a hand on Ajloon's shoulder. "You are not a fool. But if you are to be second commander of my Night Guard, you must learn to think and then think again. If the gnome knew anything of value to us, why would the thieves have let him live?"

Ajloon's eyes darkened in comprehension. "They wouldn't."

"That's right," Yder said. "Now, think and think again. The thieves not only let him live, but let him *leave*. Why?"

"Because they *want* us to find him," Ajloon replied, growing more confident. "They hope to make us believe what they have made *him* believe."

"Exactly," Yder said. "These thieves may seem like fools and bunglers, but never forget that one of them is the Seraph of Lies and the other is the Thief of Hearts. We must question everything we see, doubt all that we hear—or suffer the wrath of the Mistress of the Night for failing her."

"And what of failing *Netheril*?" The new voice was deep and raspy and ghostly, and it seemed to come from the broken canes beneath their feet and the starlit sky above his head and the darkness all around. Ajloon and the scout glanced over Yder's shoulder and prostrated themselves at once. Then the rest of the company spun toward the voice and dropped to their stomachs.

"What of *my* wrath?" the voice demanded.

Yder turned to find the gloom-cloaked figure of his father looming behind him. With bright platinum eyes peering out from a blocky face cowled in shadow, Telamont Tanthul looked as much like an apparition as an actual living being, and even Yder found it impossible to tell whether he was standing before a phantasm or his father's true form.

"Most High." Yder clasped his hands before his stomach and bowed. "What have I done to earn your wrath?"

"It is what you *haven't* done," his father replied. "Suzail has yet to fall, and here you are—still chasing after orc trinkets."

Ignoring the fact that he had not yet been given permission to rise, Yder drew himself to his full height. "Perhaps the war is going poorly because you have angered the goddess."

His father flicked a hand. "The Lady of Loss and I have had an uneasy relationship for a thousand years—no doubt because I prefer that Netheril continue to exist . . . along with the world it inhabits."

"If you are referring to the Cycle of Night, you know Rivalen was driven mad by his divinity," Yder said. "You *know* he misinterpreted Shar's will."

"I know no such thing—and neither do *you*." The Most High's eyes blazed white, burning into Yder's shadowy essence. "Do not follow your brother's path, I warn you. I won't tolerate it again."

Yder forced himself to meet his father's glare—and felt his entire body growing warm. The longer he tried to lock gazes, the brighter the Most High's eyes seemed to glow—and the more Yder burned inside.

Finally, he could stand no more. "Even if you are right, the Cycle of Night has been stopped," he said. "Now you must serve Shar, if you wish her help in the war."

The Most High's eyes dimmed to their normal silver-white glow. "It's not Shar's blessing I need," he said. "It is blades—blades that are Netheril's by right."

A cold hollow formed inside Yder. "You're asking for the Night Guard?"

"Did it sound like I was asking?" The Most High's eyes began to blaze again. "The Hall of Shadows will be safe until their return."

Knowing better than to openly doubt his father's promise, Yder said simply, "Sadly, your retainers aren't the only ones who blame Shar for what became of Rivalen and Brennus. There are many noble houses that would like to see the Hall of Shadows brought low."

"And they will answer to me if they dare." The Most High's voice grew gentle, in the way it always did when he delivered a threat. "You mustn't defy me in this, my son. At least I am leaving you with the men you have here."

Knowing that his father would take them, too, if he did not yield, Yder sighed and nodded.

"I will send word at once," he said. "But the Mistress will not be happy. I cannot promise her favor in your attacks."

The Most High smiled, revealing his long fangs in a way that Yder had not seen in centuries. "But I *will* have it, Yder," he said. "Is not Netheril her only champion in this tournament of gods?"

With that, his shadowy figure dissolved into the night, and Yder finally knew he had been talking to but an apparition of his father, a phantasm of thought that the Most High had projected across the vast distance that separated the City of Shade from the lonely shore upon which he now found himself.

Yder turned to find his entire company still flat on the ground, looking up at him in obvious distress. He motioned them up.

"It's a ploy," Ajloon said, even before he had finished rising. "The moment the Night Guard departs, Hadrhune's allies will raze the Hall."

Yder thought for a moment, then caught Ajloon's eye and shook his head. "No," he said. "They won't."

Ajloon looked puzzled for a moment, then finally seemed to realize that Yder had something else in mind. "You mean to defy the Most High?"

"Not at all," Yder said. "I will send word to the Night Guard that it is to join the Most High in the fight against Cormyr. You will take ten warriors and return to Shade at once."

"To defend the Hall of Shadows?" Ajloon asked.

"To *protect* the Hall of Shadows—in the best way you can," Yder said. "Remember, Ajloon. Think, and think again."

Ajloon was silent for a moment, then finally seemed to grasp the full extent of what Yder was asking him to do—murder, coerce, blackmail, take hostages . . . whatever was necessary.

"We'll find a way," he said. "But *ten* warriors? That will leave *you* with only fifteen."

Yder could only nod. "Shar will provide," he said. "Perhaps it was she who sent the orcs, after all."

CHAPTER TEN

THE PLAIN AHEAD WAS ROLLING LIKE A SEA BEFORE A STORM, actually rising and falling and rising again in a slow undulating rhythm that made Joelle's mount skittish and her stomach queasy. The ground smelled of damp earth and rotting vegetation, and a pale green stubble of new growth rose through a mat of dead feather grass drowned by the Great Rain of a few months before. The sky hung low and golden between two mountain chains, with wisps of darkness and fire creeping across it in a never-ending battle for control of the heavens.

The world was on the cusp of a painful rebirth, and all across Toril, Chosen just like Joelle were fighting to decide the nature of that rebirth—whether it would bring forth the life-giving radiance of the gods of hope and love or let loose the living Hells of the lords of fire and darkness. She knew it was the outcomes of all of those thousands of battles that would determine whether the world to come was a place ruled by Lathander's hope-bringing light or Umberlee's storming rage or Cyric's truth-eating madness, but Joelle could not help feeling that her own fight was the most important, that if she and her companions failed to deliver the Eye to Grumbar's temple, then the Mistress of the Night would rule supreme forever.

And that responsibility terrified her. The unacknowledged daughter of a Berduskan lord, Joelle had been little more than an unrepentant jewel thief until a year earlier, when a threat against her beauty had prompted her to join the Church of Sune. Soon after, she had awoken one morning with flame-red hair and an innate ability to charm and heal. Then she'd had visions of a misshapen eye of badly sculpted quartz, and now here she was, in the middle of a quest to stop Shar from loosing the Shadowfell across Toril.

Fortunately, Sune had sent Kleef Kenric to help her.

After the escape from Yder's sea monster, Kleef had rowed the skiff ten leagues to shore and led his companions to a road. A few hours later, they had come across a caravan preparing to camp for the night, and a short demonstration of his fighting prowess had won the entire party a place in their company.

That had been eight days ago, and now Kleef was riding flank guard. Mounted on a huge courser and wearing an expensive suit of filigreed armor, he looked more like an elite mercenary knight than a common traveler earning his passage with his sword—which was no doubt why the caravan master had been so eager to lend him the horse and equipment. Even without the other guards arrayed around the column, Kleef cut such an imposing sight that Joelle felt certain he would give pause to any common band of thieves.

She glanced up at the mottled crimson disk that was the midday sun, then reached up to mop the dampness from her brow.

"Amaunator must be winning the godfights today," she said, glancing over at Malik. Like Joelle herself, the little man held the leads of a five-horse pack-string in one hand and the reins of his own mount in the other. "I'm ready to melt."

"Indeed. Faroz is a foolish oaf for making us ride in the heat of the day." Malik pointed east toward the Aphrunn Mountains, where a crooked line of trees marked the river that snaked along the base of the range. "In my own kingdom, we would be resting in the shade of those trees, watering our camels and feasting on dates until the coolness of evening."

"And in your country, would a band of orcs be lurking among those trees, waiting to ambush your caravan the instant it entered the wood?"

"Never in a hundred years," Malik replied. His round face had turned red and blotchy, and he smelled of death more strongly than usual. "The orcs would be resting, too. In my kingdom, *everyone* rests at highsun."

Joelle laughed. "Then you must come from a very civilized country." She looked back toward Kleef and—ignoring the fact that he was still sitting tall and straight in the saddle—said, "I think Kleef is beginning to slump. He must be growing thirsty."

"If the oaf is thirsty, he will drink," Malik replied. "Even Kleef is not such a fool that he has trouble finding his own lips."

"I think his waterskin must be empty," Joelle said. "He hasn't lifted it in the last hour. I've been watching him."

Malik's voice grew bitter. "I have no doubt."

Joelle turned to find her fellow Chosen glaring in Kleef's direction, his eyes filled with a smoky hatred that made her wonder what intentions the little man might be harboring for his "rival."

"Malik!" she scolded. "What did I tell you about jealousy?"

"That jealousy is the first refuge of a selfish heart," Malik recited. "But I am not jealous of the fool. I am only weary of watching you pursue the one man in Faerûn unwilling to be yours."

Joelle frowned. "Who says he's unwilling?"

"He does, every time you throw yourself at him," Malik said. "You have gone to him eighty times in eight days, and the fool has not come to you once. If *that* is willing, then I am a cloud giant."

Joelle sighed. Malik was not exaggerating much. She had been trying to recapture Kleef's heart since before they joined the caravan, always making sure that she was the one to bring him food and drink, asking for his help with little tasks she could have performed herself, sometimes even joining him on watch. His reaction was always friendly but restrained, an obvious attempt to hold her at arm's length.

Joelle knew he wanted her. She could see that much in the way the veins in his neck pulsed as she drew near, in how the air grew musky and warm after she smiled at him. But whenever she tried to move close, he was careful to hold himself apart, and whenever she tried to lock eyes with him, he always looked away the instant their gazes began to smolder.

Finally, she nodded to Malik. "I know how it looks," she said. "But Kleef is ready to fall in love with me. I can feel it. There's just something that holds him back."

"Perhaps that *something* is another woman."

"Lady Arietta?" Joelle shook her head. "Don't be ridiculous. It would never occur to Kleef to pursue a Cormyrean noblewoman—and Arietta would never invite him to."

Malik shrugged. "What does that have to do with their feelings?" he asked. "If what you say is true, Kleef has feelings for you and refuses to pursue them. Perhaps his feelings for Arietta are the reason."

Joelle thought for a moment, then let out her breath. "It's possible, I suppose," she said. "Arietta *is* quite beautiful."

"And do not overlook the temptation of forbidden fruit," Malik added. "A heart wants most what it can never have. On that account alone, Kleef and Arietta are a perfect match. They can lust after each other from afar—and feed their noble pride by resisting their desires."

"And that doesn't strike you as terribly sad, Malik?"

"The world is a sad place," Malik replied. "And Myrkul's embrace is the only true escape—"

"Sune's love is a pretty good escape, too." Joelle hated to be rude, but the Myrkul refrain was a familiar one, and she had a problem to solve. She glanced back toward Kleef, then added, "And it's my duty to make certain Kleef understands that."

"Foolish me," Malik replied. "I thought our duty was to deliver the Eye of Gruumsh to Grumbar's Temple in the Underchasm."

"Exactly," Joelle said, still watching Kleef. His helmet was turned slightly toward the treeline, though his loose shoulders and relaxed posture suggested that he was not alarmed by what he was watching. "And when we do, it must be in the company of someone who is utterly in love and totally devoted to me. That's the only way Sune's magic will work to bind Grumbar here on Toril."

"And you're just telling me this *now*?" Malik complained. "I could have saved you the embarrassment of trying to win a fool's heart. I have been in love with you since the moment you nearly put my eye out in Lundeth."

"Malik, spying on someone through a keyhole *isn't* love," Joelle said. "It's . . . appalling."

"It would be a tragedy to hold that against me," Malik countered. "I was only trying to see whether you were the woman I had been sent to help, and now I am utterly devoted to you—just as you require."

"What a sweet thing to say." Joelle reached over to pat Malik's cheek. Despite the heat, his flesh felt cold and spongy. "But you're *not*."

Malik's expression fell. "Not as you require?"

"Not *devoted*," Joelle replied. "You couldn't be."

"How can you know what is in a man's heart?" Malik demanded. "I'm as devoted to you as I am to my own god."

"Malik, you're bearing the *Eye of Gruumsh*," Joelle reminded him. "If you were capable of any devotion at all, you couldn't do that. The Eye would destroy you before you had carried it a hundred leagues."

"You would not be the first to underestimate me." Malik's voice grew menacing. "Every woman who has ever forsaken me has come to regret it."

Joelle felt her jaw drop. "Are you *threatening* me, Malik?"

"Never in a thousand lifetimes!" While Malik's tone was apologetic, his gaze remained ominous. "But I will not let you make a mistake you will surely regret for the rest of your life. I am too devoted to allow that."

Joelle hesitated, biting back a pointed reply. She disliked nothing more than being patronized, but the last thing she needed was for Malik to turn angry and resentful. She took a deep breath, then cocked her head and pretended to study him.

"Are you truly that devoted, Malik?" Joelle finally asked. "You would die for me?"

"*Die?*"

"You said you were devoted," Joelle reminded him. "Aren't you?"

Malik hesitated. "Would dying truly be necessary?"

"I'm afraid so." Joelle was careful to sound disappointed. "When we deliver the Eye, someone must die for his beloved. It's the only way Sune's magic will be strong enough to bind Grumbar."

Malik looked doubtful. "My devotion knows no bounds," he said. "But I fear my own god requires me among the living."

Joelle put on an apologetic smile. "Then I'm sorry, Malik," she said. "You *can't* be the one."

To Joelle's surprise, Malik did not continue arguing or even express any skepticism. Instead, he merely studied her for a moment—then looked almost panic-stricken.

"You are telling the truth!"

Joelle nodded. "Of course." She stretched out her arm, holding out her pack horse leads. "I wouldn't lie about something like that."

"You have no idea what you're asking," Malik said, ignoring the leads. "I have been dead before, and my god left me to wander the Fugue Plane for a hundred years. I cannot name all the horrors I endured—devils attempting to cheat me out of my soul, serpents trying to eat it, fiends seeking to enslave it. Would you ask that of someone you love?"

"Never." Joelle paused, then added, "And I shouldn't have to ask it of someone who loves *me*."

When Malik seemed too confused to reply, Joelle leaned across the space between their mounts and pressed the leads into his hand.

"It has to be Kleef," she said, speaking more gently. "Count yourself lucky."

Giving him no chance to continue the argument, Joelle wheeled her mount out of line and started toward Kleef at a trot. The caravan was spread along the road for a good quarter league, a double column of skittish beasts and nervous riders traveling along at a brisk pace. Most of the beasts were horses and most of the riders were swarthy humans, but there were a few mules and oxen—and even a handful of camels—mixed into the line as well. Near the middle of the column rode a small company of bronze-skinned eladrin, mounted on a white chargers with ivory manes and eyes as dark as obsidian. Although the eladrin tended to be aloof both while traveling and in camp, they never failed to acknowledge Joelle whenever she passed near.

She returned their nods with a smile, then caught Arietta watching her from the front of the column. Mounted on a golden palomino that Faroz had traded her for a gem pried from her sword scabbard, she was traveling with a small cluster of nobles who always rode at the head of the column. In the evenings, however, she returned to make camp with her traveling companions, recounting all she had learned by chatting with Faroz and her fellow nobles. It was an odd arrangement, but one that had provided a great deal of information on the various routes to the Underchasm—along with a fair idea of the hazards the companions could expect to face along the way and the hope that they might find help from the fey creatures of the Chondalwood.

With more than a hundred paces of undulating ground still separating Joelle from the front of the caravan, it was difficult to tell exactly where Arietta's eyes were focused. But it was possible to see the noblewoman's head turning as she looked toward Kleef, then back again, and Joelle began to think that Malik just might be right about the temptation of forbidden fruit.

Arietta dipped her head in an exaggerated motion that reminded Joelle of a sportsman wishing luck to an opponent, a gesture that was less than permission and yet an acknowledgment that they both wanted the same thing—Kleef's devotion.

And that was the whole problem with the noble class, as far as Joelle was concerned. They didn't know how to share. They were always hoarding—the land around their castles, the game in their forests, even the hearts of their men. They longed to own all they saw—and from the balconies atop their keeps, they saw very far indeed. It was a soul-crushing way of life, and one Joelle was sad to see someone as courageous Arietta had embraced.

She returned Arietta's nod with one of her own, then looked away and trotted her mount the rest of the way to Kleef's side. He waited until she was almost within arm's reach, then reluctantly turned to greet her.

"Back already?" His mouth smiled, but his eyes did not. "Malik talking too much again?"

"Malik *always* talks too much." Joelle reached down and took the waterskin off her saddle, then offered it to him. "I just wanted to be sure you had water."

"Thanks."

Kleef took the skin, then opened the top and tipped his head back to drink. It wasn't until he'd held the position for a few moments that Joelle realized nothing was coming out. He was pinching the neck shut, and his eyes were watching the tree line instead.

"What's wrong?" Joelle asked.

"Orcs," Kleef said, finally lowering the waterskin. "A lot of them. I think they're gathering a horde to hit us."

Joelle's heart climbed into her throat, but—knowing that the orc scouts would be watching them—resisted the temptation to study the trees. "How soon?"

"Hard to say," Kleef said. "They'll come at night, so it depends on a lot of things—where we camp, what the sky is like, whether we look ready to fight."

"In other words, at the worst possible time." Joelle hesitated, not really wanting to ask the next question, but knowing she must. "What about the Shadovar?"

"I haven't seen any," Kleef said. "But they're out there. They must be."

"You don't think they could have gone after the *Wave Wyvern* and lost the battle?"

"No," Kleef said. "Seasilver's men were in no shape to fight. If Yder had caught up to the *Wyvern*, he would have lost a few blades—but it wouldn't have been the Shadovar who ended up massacred."

Knowing that any words of reassurance about Jang's fate would ring hollow at best, Joelle said, "Then I hope Yder didn't go after the *Wyvern*. Jang is a good man."

Kleef nodded. "And a clever one. If there's anyone who can get the *Wyvern* back to Westgate without a fight, it's Jang." He paused, then offered a sly grin. "Besides, I can't see Yder *wanting* to chase down the *Wyvern*—not when he knew he would have to take Grand Duchess Elira hostage again."

Joelle smiled. "She's really that bad?"

"Even for a noble," Kleef said. "I pity Jang, if he's still alive."

Joelle chuckled, then grew more serious. "So, if Yder *is* out there, why hasn't he come for us again? Is he waiting for the orcs to attack?"

Kleef's expression grew clouded. "That's part of it," he said. "This is a big caravan, and that means a hard fight with plenty of magic. It would make sense to use the orc attack as a diversion."

"And the *other* part?" Joelle asked.

Kleef glanced back toward the tree line. "Me, I think," he said. "He's still coming to me in my dreams—usually three or four times a night. I think he's trying to wear me down."

Joelle cocked an eyebrow. She knew that Yder had been visiting Kleef in his dreams since the night he had offered to trade for Joelle and Malik. But she hadn't realized the visits were that frequent—or that Kleef found them quite so troubling.

"Wear you down, how?" Joelle asked. "By keeping you from sleeping?"

Kleef continued to study the tree line as it rose and fell, then finally said, "Something else. He wants me to steal the Eye for him."

Joelle fell silent, trying to fathom the idea of even *asking* one of Helm's Chosen to betray his companions. The thought would have been laughable, had anything the Shadovar ever did been quite what it seemed. Either Yder was working at something else or he didn't realize who Kleef *was*.

Or maybe the Shadovar were just that desperate.

"Good," Joelle said, forcing a smile. "That's very good news, indeed."

Kleef shot her a suspicious scowl. "I don't see how."

"Because it means Yder still can't find the Eye on his own," Joelle said. "He hasn't figured out how we're hiding it."

Kleef seemed to relax a little. "You think so?"

"Oh, *absolutely*." Joelle flashed a playful smile. "If Yder *knew* how to find the Eye, we'd all be dead by now."

Kleef laughed heartily. "I hadn't thought of that," he said. "Maybe Yder will protect us from the orcs."

Kleef sealed the waterskin again, but instead of passing it back to Joelle, he exchanged it for the one hanging from his saddle and passed *that* one over. It was even heavier than the skin she had given him, and it took a moment for her to realize he was trying to make her visit look like a routine water delivery.

"Who are you trying to fool?" she asked. "The shades or the orcs?"

"It would be nice to fool both," Kleef said. "But I'll settle for the orcs."

"And trading waterskins will keep them from wondering what I'm doing out here?"

"That's the idea," he said. "Orcs are hunters, and hunters notice the little things."

"I suppose so." Realizing the same scouts had probably been watching when she came out to flirt earlier, Joelle hung the waterskin on her saddle and continued to ride at Kleef's side—just as she had done two hours before. "Should I pass a warning along?"

"I wouldn't," Kleef said. "If people start getting nervous, the orcs will see that."

"So?"

"So then the *orcs* get nervous," Kleef said. "Maybe they attack too soon, before we have a chance to find good ground."

"That makes sense," Joelle said. She glanced over at the wall of leaves that was the distant tree line, then wondered how Kleef could see *anything* sneaking through the woods beyond. "There's just one problem. It we don't tell anyone there are orcs shadowing us, how does Faroz know to look for good ground?"

A smug look came to Kleef's face. "That's where you come in," he said. "You're spending more time with me than with your pack-string. Soon enough, Faroz will send a man over to chase you back to your horses."

"And you'll tell *him* about the orcs," Joelle surmised.

"Right," Kleef said. "And all the orcs will see is a caravan master trying to keep trail discipline."

"Interesting plan." Joelle hesitated, then added, "But maybe we should try something simpler."

"You don't think they'll buy it?" Kleef asked. "Orcs aren't that smart, you know."

"The orcs aren't the problem," Joelle said. "It's Faroz. He won't be sending anyone to chase me back."

"He won't?" Kleef lowered his brow. "Why not?"

Joelle smiled and batted her lashes—and saw the suspicion in Kleef's face change to understanding.

"Oh," he said. "Did you really need to charm him?"

"Yes, if I want to spend any time with you," Joelle said. "You're always on guard duty."

"Because I'm a guard," Kleef said. "But I'm never out of earshot."

"And I'm sure you'll arrive in time to staunch the bleeding." Joelle lowered her voice. "But that's not what I was talking about, and you know it."

An uncomfortable note came to Kleef's voice. "I do?"

"Yes," Joelle said. "In fact, Faroz loaned me a tent. I was hoping you might help me set it up tonight."

The color began to rise in Kleef's cheeks. "I can help you set it up," he said. "But then I have guard duty."

"Not *all* night, I trust."

Joelle was practically purring now, but Kleef was looking away, allowing his gaze to roam over the plain in a manner that suggested a certain faintness of heart. She couldn't decide whether to be offended or flattered—but she was definitely confused.

When her invitation continued to go unanswered, Joelle finally broke the silence. "Kleef, I need to ask you a question. Have you never shared yourself with a woman?"

Kleef's eyes grew as round as coins. "What kind of question is that? Of course I've been with women. Many times!"

"You don't have to snap," Joelle said. "I just thought that as one of Helm's Chosen, you might have taken a vow of celibacy. Or something."

"Why would I do that?" Kleef's voice remained sharp. "I'm not even sure that I *am* one of Helm's Chosen. You're the one who keeps saying that."

"But I'm not the only one who believes it," Joelle said. "Why do you think Yder keeps coming after you? He knows who's protecting us."

Kleef sighed. "All right, I'm Helm's Chosen," he said. "What does that have to do with being celibate?"

"I don't know," Joelle admitted. "But you've been avoiding me." Kleef's expression finally softened. "A little bit."

"Why would you do that?" Joelle was genuinely hurt, because—as much as she needed Kleef to love her—she already loved Kleef. "I thought we had feelings for each other."

"We do," Kleef said. "And they make it hard to keep my mind on my duty."

Joelle frowned. "You're avoiding me because I distract you?"

"You're more than a distraction, Joelle, and you know it." Kleef's voice grew almost ashamed. "Back at the reef, when Yder's sea monster took out the *Lonely Roamer*, I went after you first."

"Kleef, you can't be upset with yourself for that," Joelle said. "The fog was thick and the situation confused. Arietta was doing fine, and just because she happens to be nobility—"

"No, it wasn't because I went after you before *Arietta*," Kleef said. "Malik was in trouble, and Arietta wanted to go after him because he had the Eye. But I went after you first, and she had to jump in to save Malik. I chose *you* over duty."

"You chose . . . me." Joelle felt her stomach drop, for she knew what Kleef was about to tell her—that he could not be hers and remain true to his god—and he was right. It would have been a terrible failure for *any* follower of Helm to put his own desires before his duty. But for a Chosen of Helm . . . well, that had only happened because of who *Joelle* was, because of the power imbued in her as a Chosen of Sune. "And now, you're choosing duty."

Kleef nodded. "I'm sorry," he said. "But if I *am* a Chosen of Helm, I have no choice."

"Don't be silly, Kleef. You always have a choice." Joelle

kissed her fingers and touched them to his cheek. "But you're making the right one."

Kleef's face brightened with relief. "Thank you," he said. "I'm glad you understand."

"Better than you know." Joelle forced a smile. "Duty first. Even heartwarders understand that."

Joelle turned her horse away and started toward the front of the column, where Arietta was riding with Faroz and her fellow nobles.

After all, *someone* needed to tell Faroz about the orcs.

CHAPTER ELEVEN

THE RIVER ARRABAR WAS IN SLOW FLOOD AS THE SEA OF Fallen Stars seeped back to the Vilhon Reach, turning grassy plains into marshes and stands of timber into islands of yellow leaves. A hundred leagues distant, a jagged ridge marked the line of earthmotes the goddess Chauntea had dropped across the valley to hold the sea back and give her worshipers time to bring in the harvest. Closer by, a cluster of thatched roofs marked the location of a drowned village, and it seemed clear to Arietta that had the caravan tarried to rest along the way, it would never have reached the river in time to cross. As it was, the stone bridge ahead was nearly submerged, with its abutments hidden below the surface and muddy water lapping at the haunches of its arches.

"What a happy sight!" said Malik. He was riding next to Arietta, between her and Joelle. "Now that we've made it, perhaps Faroz will let us take the time to cook our meals before we eat them."

"We haven't made it yet." Joelle pointed to the far end of the bridge, where Kleef and twenty more guards were galloping ahead to scout the ground on the far side of the river. "This would be a good place for an attack."

"Who is there to attack us?" Malik asked. "Even Kleef has not seen an orc for three days. Perhaps we have finally outrun the brutes."

Arietta and Joelle turned to Malik simultaneously, both of them with a single eyebrow cocked in doubt. The orcs had been trailing the caravan for a couple of tendays now, mounting raids so frequently that Faroz had hired more guards at Xorhun. Arietta had even forsaken her place at the front of the column, choosing to ride with Joelle and Malik so she would be available to help defend the Eye.

After a moment, Arietta said, "I fear that's wishful thinking, Malik. Those orcs wouldn't quit that easily."

"Why should they not?" Malik asked. "They are on foot and the caravan is mounted. It is a wonder they keep catching us at all."

Malik had barely spoken when an alarm cry rose from the far bank of the river. Arietta turned to look and, fifty paces up the slope, saw a mob of stooped figures charging from a copse of duskwood trees. With stocky bodies armored in leather and thick gangling arms bearing two-handed axes, there could be little doubt they were orcs—and almost certainly orcs from the same horde that had been shadowing the caravan.

Arietta saw Kleef draw his sword and spur his courser into a charge. The other guards hesitated, clearly surprised by the maneuver, then grabbed their own weapons and raced after Kleef. Only a single rider remained behind, a gaunt figure in robes who dropped his reins and gestured, then drew something from a sleeve and flung it toward the orcs.

A thunderous *crack* rang out across the river, followed by a brilliant flash that flattened dozens of orcs. Kleef reached the mob a few breaths later, his huge horse pounding through a tangle of fallen orcs as he whirled to face those who were still standing. His great blade began to rise and fall, flinging heads and limbs and broken axes in every direction, and Arietta felt her heart rise into her throat.

Which was only natural, she told herself. Kleef was not only a courageous warrior and an honorable man, he was a fellow-in-arms. Surely, even her mother would have understood *that*.

Still, Arietta did not let her breath out until the rest of the guards had reached the mob and taken positions on Kleef's flanks. The horsemen quickly formed a line and became a galloping, wheeling wall of death that stopped the orc charge cold—even if it *did* fail to send the survivors running for the trees.

"It looks like they're serious this time," Joelle said. "Have you ever seen orcs fight like that before?"

"Never," Arietta said. "But then, I haven't seen many orcs fight before—only the ones who have been attacking the caravan."

Joelle smiled and started to reply, but stopped when the sound of galloping hooves rumbled up the road ahead. Arietta dropped her gaze to the near side of the river and found Faroz's golden-eyed second-in-command—a genasi earthsoul named Majeed—leading two dozen guards up from the bridge.

"Keep moving!" Majeed waved a hand toward the river, the energy lines on his skin blurring into a fan of golden radiance. "We cross *now*!"

For a moment, the caravan seemed too confused to obey. But, as Majeed and his men continued past, cries of alarm rose from the back of the column. Arietta strung her bow, then twisted around in her saddle and saw a second mob of orcs pouring from a tree line above and behind them. Like their fellows on the far side of the river, they were broad-bodied and muscular, with stooped postures and arms that reached almost to their knees. Most were armed with two-handed weapons—either battle-axes or spiked clubs—but some carried slings or crude bows instead.

Instead of mounting an uphill charge as Kleef had, Majeed and his men joined the rearguard and quickly formed a battle line across the hill. A wizard raised a wall of fire between them and their enemies, and the orcs vanished behind a blockade of crimson flame.

By then, the caravan was pouring onto the bridge. Taking care to keep abreast of Malik and Joelle, Arietta nocked an arrow and began to watch the terrain along the caravan track. Twice before, the Shadovar had taken advantage of an orc raid to come after the Eye, and though they had lost warriors each time, she was not fool enough to think they would hesitate to try it again.

Arietta was almost at the bridge when the cane grass downwind of the trail began to quiver. At first, she thought the motion might be caused by water seeping into a low-lying pocket of ground, but then the stalks began to divide, as though someone were running through them.

"Ambush!" she cried. "They're invisible!"

Arietta loosed her first arrow past Malik and Joelle— drawing cries of surprise from both—then heard the guttural groan of a wounded warrior. In the next instant, a flight of stones and arrows came arcing toward the caravan, and the grass grew thick with charging orcs.

"Down!" Joelle yelled.

Arietta was already flattening herself behind her horse's neck. She heard arrows whizzing over her head and felt her mount shudder as a stone bounced off his skull. He stumbled for an instant and nearly fell, then regained his footing and sprang forward. She glanced up to see a ribbon of blood running down the side of his head.

In the next moment, the air erupted with clacks and sizzles as the caravan returned the attack. A din of orc grunts and squeals joined the cacophony of shrieking humans and horses, and panicked voices behind Arietta yelled, "Go! Ride!"

She urged her mount forward, then looked over to find Joelle leading both strings of pack horses. Beyond the heart-warder were yet more orcs, charging up the slope, armed with hand axes and short swords and trampling their fallen fellows. Malik was nowhere in sight, and Arietta could only assume that the instant the battle began, he had used his god's blessing to go into hiding.

As her horse raced onto the bridge, Arietta nocked another arrow and twisted around to fire back over her shoulder. The fastest orcs were less than five paces from the road and were turning to charge onto the bridge behind her.

Arietta loosed and saw her shaft take the lead orc high in the chest, above his leather breastplate. It wasn't the throat shot she had been hoping for, but it made the brute stumble and pause to snap off the shaft.

Then a plummy voice rose from the party of eladrin traveling behind her, and a tremendous crackling erupted from the ground beneath the orcs. They continued to come, not even bothering to glance down until a tangle of thorny stems shot up to entangle first their feet, then their entire bodies.

A trio of the brutes managed to leap free and cut the horses from beneath a handful of riders. They were soon felled as the caravan raced past, attacking with everything from rusty sabers to coin-filled saddlebags to golden wands.

Someone well back in the column sent a fireball streaking into the thorn wall, and the entire hedge burst into flames. Arietta turned away quickly, but still found herself sickened by the sweet black smoke that billowed from the hedge.

And then Arietta and her companions were twenty paces onto the bridge, with no orcs in pursuit and dozens of riders between them and shore. Arietta hung her bow from her saddle horn, then loosened her sword in its scabbard and began to watch the bridge's walls for emerging Shadovar.

"That was too close." Joelle's voice was difficult to hear over the din of screams and squeals coming from the burning thorn wall. "I hope that blood is your horse's."

Arietta glanced down and realized her left side was coated in blood. Since she felt no unusual aches or numbnesses, she assumed it had all come from her horse's head wound.

"I'm fine, but I think my mount may need a few stitches," Arietta said. "What about you?"

"A few lumps." Joelle glanced down at her far thigh. "And an arrow wound."

"An *arrow* wound?"

Arietta reached across and took the reins of both pack-strings. They were nearly halfway across the bridge, and the sounds of the battle behind them were starting to fade. She glanced back and saw nothing to suggest that the fighting would spill onto the bridge—nor any sign that she and her companions were being pursued by orcs *or* Shadovar. Breathing a sigh of relief, she turned back to Joelle.

"How bad?"

"I don't think it's in very deep." Joelle switched her reins to her right hand, then lowered her left toward her thigh and instantly looked a little less anguished. "Nothing that can't wait until we're safe."

A muffled tumult rose ahead. Arietta feared for a moment that the orcs on the far side of the river had recovered from the cavalry charge and were mounting an attack. But when she looked, she saw Kleef riding back across the bridge, hugging the balustrade as his big courser pushed past the long line of nervous riders and jittery pack animals.

On the slope above, the few orcs who had survived the cavalry charge were racing for the trees. A company of guards rode back and forth behind the fleeing orcs, picking off stragglers and making sure the rest did not return to renew their attack. The caravan had a clear route onward—at least for now.

Kleef soon arrived, then drew up and studied the far end of the bridge for a moment. Once he seemed convinced the rearguard had the battle there in hand, he wheeled around to ride alongside Joelle. His gaze slid from Joelle's injured thigh, to Arietta's blood-soaked flank, to the empty space between the two women where Malik usually rode.

"Malik?" he asked.

"He's fine." Joelle glanced over her shoulder, looking back between the two strings of pack horses. "Behind us."

Arietta followed her gaze and saw nothing for a moment. Then a colorless blur appeared between the second horse in each string, and she realized there was another horse trotting between them. Lying stretched along the horse's back, clinging to its neck, was a scrawny figure in a shabby gray robe.

"He looks healthy enough to me," Kleef agreed. His gaze dropped back to Joelle's thigh. "You want me to snap off that arrow?"

"Not on your life," Joelle said, growing pale. "You can help me cut it out later."

Kleef shrugged. "Your choice, but it's going to be a while before the caravan can stop to regroup. You'll ride easier without the shaft swinging around like that."

"I'm *holding* it," Joelle snapped. "Don't you see that?"

Kleef looked more amused than offended. "Now that you mention it, I do." He peered past Joelle to Arietta, searching her flank for wounds. "How about you, my lady? Are you hurt?"

"The blood is my horse's," Arietta said. "I'm fine."

Kleef gave a nod of relief, then asked, "What happened?"

"What happened is that Faroz has entrusted our safety to a buffoon and a fool!" Malik answered. He sat upright in his saddle and urged his mount forward—until he found himself caught between the two sets of pack-leads that Arietta was holding. "You failed to scout the bridge approach. There were orcs hiding in the grass!"

Kleef glared at Malik as though considering whether to toss him off the bridge or cut him in half, then finally turned to Arietta. "What's he talking about? We *did* scout that ground."

"You wouldn't have seen them," Arietta said. "The orcs were invisible."

"*Invisible*?" Kleef frowned, thinking. "I didn't know orcs used that kind of magic."

"It gets worse," Joelle said. "They waited until *we* were the ones in front of them."

Now Kleef really began to look worried. The companions had already begun to suspect that the orcs were after the Eye of Gruumsh. But they had been hoping the reason the horde hadn't launched an all-out attack yet was because they didn't know exactly *who* they were after, that the same magic that kept the Eye hidden from the Shadovar was preventing the orcs from determining which humans had it.

After a moment, Kleef said, "There's no doubt now that the orcs and Shadovar are working together. That explains the invisibility magic *and* how they knew to look for Joelle and Malik."

Arietta shook her head. "Then where *are* the Shadovar? Why help the orcs at all, if they don't intend to take advantage of the attack?"

Kleef fell silent for a moment, and then his eyes slowly began to widen. "Because it wasn't the real attack."

"They were shooting at us with real arrows and pelting us with real rocks," Malik said. "If that is not a real attack, then I am not a real man."

"They were just trying to see how we would react, probing our defenses." Kleef looked forward again, to where Faroz and the nobles were starting to lead the caravan up the hill. "The attack will come later, after they've had time to consider what they saw."

"How much time do we have?" Joelle asked. "Enough to heal the wounded and prepare more magic?"

"No," Arietta said, taking Kleef's point. "They'll hit us sooner than that."

Kleef nodded. "Before morning." He scanned the slope above the bridge, his eyes lingering on the tree line. "I need to talk to Faroz. If the scouts can find defensible ground, we can stop early and spoil their plans—for today, at least."

"Then go," Joelle said. "If we protect the caravan, we

protect the Eye."

"Most likely," Kleef agreed. Before leaving, he reached down between his horse and Joelle's, then he looked up and said, "We're going to be riding hard. You need to let me do this."

Joelle hesitated, then took a deep breath . . . and a sharp *crack* sounded as Kleef snapped the arrow lodged in her leg. Her mouth fell open, and it looked as though she were fighting to stifle a scream.

Kleef did not look the least bit apologetic. "Give it a minute. You'll be fine."

He tossed the broken shaft aside, then rode off while Joelle's eyes were still wide with pain.

While they remained wide, Malik said, "This is what comes of trusting the clumsy oaf. He loves nothing more than the pain of others."

Arietta shot him an angry frown and snapped, "If you believe that, you are not only a coward, you are a fool."

Malik's eyes flashed with fury.

Looking away before he could reply, Arietta turned back to Joelle. "Are you all right?"

"I will . . . be." Joelle was clutching her reins so hard her knuckles had turned white. "Just give me a minute."

Arietta nodded, then glanced back to make certain there was no trouble coming up behind them.

With nearly a hundred riders between them and the curtain of black smoke at the end of the bridge, it was impossible to tell what had become of the orcs. But she saw no signs of panic, and no spells could be heard cracking or booming above the general din of alarm. The attack was starting to look very much like the probe Kleef had suggested, and by now, Arietta suspected the orcs were halfway up the slope, nursing their wounds and plotting their next attack.

When Arietta turned forward again, Joelle was riding easier, and much of the pain had drained from her face.

"Well, you *look* better."

Joelle nodded. "It still hurts, but Kleef was right." She smiled and added, "I just *hate* that in a man."

Arietta laughed. "So that's why you stopped pursuing him."

They reached the end of the bridge and started up the slope with the rest of the caravan. When the outriders took their places on the flanks of the column, Arietta decided it would be smart to keep her hands free so she could reach her bow. She passed the leads of both strings of pack horses to Malik—and had to endure five minutes of complaining because that forced him to ride behind her and Joelle instead of between them.

Soon after, a herald came back with word that stragglers would be abandoned to the orcs, and the caravan settled into a ground-eating pace that left Joelle clenching her teeth against the obvious pain of having her leg constantly jostled. Hoping that a little conversation would help keep Joelle's mind off her pain, Arietta eased her horse near enough that they could talk in quieter voices.

This drew a fresh round of muttering from Malik, but he was far enough behind them that Arietta simply chose to ignore it. She turned to Joelle and spoke in a chummy tone.

"So why *did* you stop pursuing Kleef?"

At first, Joelle seemed surprised by the question, but she recovered quickly and gave Arietta a sly smile.

"I didn't think you were paying attention when I *was* pursuing him."

"It was hard to miss," Arietta said. "Though I certainly don't blame you. Kleef is a good man."

Joelle's expression grew wistful. "He is, but it wasn't meant to be." She caught Arietta's gaze and held it. "His heart belongs to another."

"Is that so?" Arietta was disconcerted to feel her pulse pounding faster. "I hope you aren't referring to *me*."

"Would that be so terrible?"

"Perhaps not *terrible*," Arietta said. "But certainly inappropriate. He's just a watchman."

"He's a *Chosen of Helm*," Joelle countered.

"Yes . . . I suppose there's that," Arietta said. "But he still has no title, no lands. What could he bring to a marriage?"

"*Marriage?*" Joelle seemed genuinely amused. "Arietta, I'm talking love . . . not marriage."

Arietta felt the heat rising to her cheeks. "Oh," she said. "I see."

Joelle chuckled, then reached over and took Arietta's hand. "Trust me," she said. "Forbidden fruit is always the sweetest."

She squeezed, and Arietta's head began to spin.

CHAPTER TWELVE

As the caravan continued onward, Arietta and Joelle rode side by side, talking steadily in an attempt to keep Joelle's mind off her pain. They discussed men, Kleef and his code, the difference between romance and love, their lives before the world went mad. The longer they conversed, the more Arietta enjoyed Joelle's company, and it was not long before she realized she had never met anyone quite so open and willing to share her true feelings as the heartwarder.

Eventually, the conversation turned to how they had become Chosen, and Joelle revealed that she had become a Sune worshiper only after a threat against her beauty prompted her to offer a rather large tithe to the Firehair Church. Arietta confessed that she found most noblemen unworthy of her affections and had deliberately sabotaged her father's efforts to arrange a suitable marriage for her. It was not something she had ever admitted before, even to her maid Odelia, and Arietta began to understand what it was to have a true confidante, someone with whom she could share her most intimate feelings.

The only damper on their growing friendship was Malik, who often came forward to intrude on the conversation. His remarks were cutting toward Joelle and resentful of Arietta, and he soon became an angry presence smoldering just out of earshot behind them. His behavior was at least partially a reaction to Arietta's harsh words earlier, but she knew his hostility went deeper than that. Aboard the *Lonely Roamer*, Malik had made it clear he didn't want anyone else competing with him for Joelle's attention—and apparently that included women.

After a few hours, the caravan finally left the road to make camp atop a nearby butte. Littered with loose boulders and ringed on three sides by hundred-foot cliffs, it was a good place to regroup. While Kleef and the rest of the guards prepared their defenses, Arietta helped Joelle dig the arrow out of her leg and cleansed the wound.

The two women passed the night sleeping side by side in the open, and the next morning the caravan woke to find the butte surrounded by thousands of orcs. Faroz ordered the column to form up anyway, then had his wizards unleash a barrage of spells that rained sheets of fire and stone down on the orcs' heads. The horde fled in disarray, leaving half their number lying dead in the field behind them.

The caravan returned to the road and continued on its way toward Ormpetarr. That night, it made camp behind a circular thorn hedge raised by the eladrin traveling with the caravan—and the companions spent half the night listening to orcs being strangled to death by blood-sucking vines. The night after that, the caravan slept inside a ring of mud created by Faroz's wizards, and they had to endure an endless chorus of panicked squeals and snorts as the orcs tried different methods of sneaking across the moat.

On the fourth night after crossing the River Arrabar, the caravan made camp at the edge of the Chondalwood, inside the ruins of an ancient hilltop fortress. The citadel stood on a tor so high that anyone peering over its eastern walls found themselves looking at the forest canopy from above. A well in the courtyard still supplied clean sweet water, though its shaft was so deep that bringing a bucket of water up required several minutes of cranking the winch.

It was an hour after dark, and Arietta was changing the bandage on Joelle's arrow wound while Malik sat in front of the horse line, drinking tea by moonlight and glowering at them across a small campfire. Kleef was inside the doorless tent, trying to get some sleep before he took command of the late watch. He did not seem to be resting very well, as he was thrashing around in the throes of yet another nightmare, grunting and growling as though locked in a wrestling match. Finally, he gave an incoherent bellow and rolled up against the tent wall, where he lay mumbling and flailing against the canvas.

Joelle glanced at him and said, "It's worse than usual tonight."

"Much worse," Arietta agreed. "But Yder must know by now that Kleef will never break a vow. Why does he keep trying?"

"Because Yder sees what you do not," Malik said. "Kleef's greatest weakness is his bitterness, and Shar is the goddess of the embittered. Yder does not wonder if he will turn the oaf to Shar's service, but only how soon he will succeed."

Joelle shot him a frown. "That's a terrible thing to say."

"There are no truths more dangerous than terrible truths," Malik said. "Those are the kind no one wishes to see."

"And just what is it that we don't see?" Arietta demanded. "Kleef may resent those who turn their backs on their duty, but that doesn't mean he would ever betray his own vows. Quite the opposite, I assure you."

"You assure me?" Malik held her eyes just long enough to convey his disdain for her assurances, then said, "Oh, what a relief. I will certainly sleep easier tonight."

He took a sip of tea and looked into the fire. Arietta finished changing the bandage on Joelle's leg, and the trio spent the next quarter hour in uneasy silence, watching the flames and listening to Kleef toss and growl in his sleep.

Though Joelle insisted Malik was as dedicated to delivering the Eye of Gruumsh as she was, Arietta could not help thinking that was not entirely true. Malik seemed more interested in keeping the heartwarder to himself than he did in marshaling Kleef's help to stop Shar. That did not seem like someone who put his mission above all else, and Arietta wondered if the Eye itself could be affecting Malik, making him behave in a way that undermined his own cause.

Arietta was still pondering the question when an alarm horn sounded from the front of the citadel, where the steep road from the plain below ended in a pile of rubble that had once been the citadel's gatehouse. The caravan did not immediately spring into action, for the events of the last few nights had taught the travelers to trust in Faroz's defenses. Instead, a vague sense of expectation fell over the courtyard, and the drone of camp conversation quickly faded as all ears waited for a report.

Finally, it came. "Orcs, coming up the hill."

A gentle murmur spread across the caravan as travelers gathered their shields and weapons. Still, there was no rush to reinforce the gateway, nor even much movement in that direction. If help was needed, the guards would call for it—and if it wasn't, a bunch of travelers running about would only interfere with the wizards. Arietta strung her bow, then both she and Joelle buckled on their weapon belts. Malik did not even bother to do that much, continuing to sip his tea and leaving his sword on the ground next to him.

No one bothered to wake Kleef. If the watchman was needed, the din of battle would rouse him in plenty of time for the fight.

A long clatter echoed across the courtyard as the wizards sent mounds of rubble tumbling down on the orcs. The sound was followed a few seconds later by a distant chorus of shrieks and groans, and the guards gave a rousing cheer that suggested the assault had already been broken.

If Kleef heard any of it, the only sign he gave was that he began to thrash in his sleep even more wildly.

Then cries rang out over near the well. Arietta rose and looked toward the sound—and found her view blocked by the silhouettes of pack animals and other people. The chime of steel on steel echoed across the courtyard. Human voices shrieked in pain, and she glimpsed stooped figures charging through the moonlight.

"Orcs!" Arietta gasped. "Inside the perimeter."

"Malik, douse that fire," Joelle ordered. "And stay close until we figure out what's happening."

"We know what is happening," Malik said. A wet sizzle sounded from the fire, and the smell of steam and ash filled the air. "The brutes have tricked us!"

The well, of course.

Arietta had no way to guess how large a hiding place the orcs had dug inside the well, but she felt certain they could not be climbing out of the narrow shaft more than two at a time. To turn the trap against the brutes, all they had to do was reach the top of the well and hold it.

Kleef yelled something unintelligible, clearly still asleep. Arietta turned to wake him—and saw Joelle already ducking into the tent to do the same.

As soon as Joelle touched his shoulder, he sat up and caught her on his forearm, then hurled her out of the tent. Arietta barely had time to step out of the way before the heartwarder landed beside her and went tumbling.

"Kleef!" Arietta yelled. "Wake up!"

Kleef grabbed his sword and stumbled out of the tent, his eyes vacant and unfocused, his expression blank.

"Over there, you fool!" Malik cried. He was still holding the canvas bucket he'd used to douse the fire, and he swung it toward the well. "Orcs!"

Kleef pulled Watcher from its scabbard—but instead of heading for the well, he stepped toward Malik.

Arietta moved to intercept him. "Kleef—"

"Orcs!" Kleef said, cutting her off. He pointed across the fire pit, then sprang after Malik. "Filthy orcs."

Malik hurled the bucket at him and turned to flee, but Kleef was already on him. He caught the little man by his collar and raised Watcher. Coming in from the side, Arietta slapped her bow down across his wrist.

The blow did not land hard enough to make Kleef drop his sword—but it did make him glance back at her.

"Orcs!" he snarled. "Filthy orcs."

Arietta did not even see his foot move. She simply felt a huge boot plant itself in her abdomen, then her entire midsection blossomed in pain, and she went flying.

She landed in a breathless heap two paces away. Arietta saw dozens of figures out in the courtyard, their blades rising and falling as they did battle among the neighing pack animals. In the darkness and confusion, it was impossible to tell the orcs from the humans, but she had the sense that the fight was expanding rather than contracting—a sure sign that there were still orcs pouring from the well in the center of the courtyard.

As Arietta struggled to get her breath back, she saw that Joelle had recovered her feet and was on Kleef's far side, shouting for him to awaken. Malik had squirmed out of his drab robe and was standing in front of the horse line, brandishing his sword and demanding that Kleef return his robe.

"Orcs!" Kleef swung his blade at Malik's neck. "Filthy orcs!"

Malik threw himself to the ground shrieking, then rolled beneath the horse line and vanished. Before Kleef could pursue, Joelle leaped in front of him, palms raised.

"Kleef, look at me." She slipped inside his guard, then placed a hand on the wrist of his sword arm. "Do I look like an orc to you?"

Kleef jerked his sword arm free, and Arietta feared for a moment that an orc was exactly what Joelle looked like to him. Arietta rolled to her knees and rose.

Then Joelle flashed one of those radiant smiles of hers, and Kleef squinted like a man looking into a bright sun. His brow furrowed and his gaze came into focus.

"Joelle?" Kleef seemed confused for a moment, then he finally exhaled in relief and displayed the robe he had taken from Malik. "I have it back."

And that was when the agate on Watcher's crossguard began to glow. Realizing at once what had happened—that Yder had used Kleef's dreams to trick him into revealing the location of the Eye—Arietta nocked an arrow and scanned the perimeter of their little campsite.

Dark figures emerged from the gloom inside the tent, from the shadows between the horses, from the murk all around. Arietta chose a target coming up behind Joelle and loosed, then dived to the ground, rolled to a knee, and came up to find a shade splaying his fingers in her direction.

Behind her, Kleef boomed, "Down!"

Arietta hurled herself back to the ground and Kleef stepped over her, bringing Watcher down to intercept a disk of spinning shadow. The disk dissolved into a harmless spray, and a trio of white darts went streaking back in the opposite direction. They buried themselves in the shade's chest, and before he hit the ground, Joelle leaped in to behead him with her sword.

Kleef caught Arietta beneath the arm and pulled her to her feet, then pressed Malik's robe into her free hand and pointed after Joelle.

"Go!"

Giving Arietta no time to argue, he spun around and began whipping Watcher back and forth, cleaving shades with every stroke. Though he was too hard-pressed to stop for beheadings, he slowed their charge and gave Arietta time to reach Joelle.

The heartwarder was dancing back and forth between two shades, pivoting and ducking as she struggled to parry their attacks. Arietta used her bow to hook the nearest one's foot. He whirled on her, bringing his glassy blade around in a sweep that would have removed her head—had she not already been backing out of reach, her bow pulling his front foot from beneath him.

The shade hit the ground with a deep *thud*, but he remained alert enough to bring his sword back across his body in a clearing sweep. Arietta stepped back, then threw the robe over her shoulder and nocked an arrow. The Shadovar rolled and spun, coming to his knees ready to spring.

Arietta loosed and planted the shaft between his eyes.

By then, she could hear Kleef only a few steps behind her, huffing and grunting as he slowly gave ground. Knowing they were doomed if they did not break free of the ring of shades, Arietta slipped her bow over her shoulder and drew her sword, then stepped in to help Joelle.

They had barely lopped the heads off the fallen shades before they turned to find a pair of steel-blue eyes approaching, moving through the whirling mass of orcs and men without once stepping aside or even pausing to avoid becoming entangled in the battle. The silhouette of a gaunt face soon appeared around the glowing eyes, followed by a tall figure in a murk-swaddled cloak.

Yder.

Arietta started to move into a flanking position, but Joelle put a hand out to stop her. The heartwarder uttered a quick prayer to her goddess, and her long red hair began to emit a faint aura of fiery light. She pointed her sword in Yder's direction, then started to race toward him.

"Help me!" Joelle called. "Kill that one!"

Sune's magic carried Joelle's voice into the ears of their fellow travelers. All at once, dozens of fighters broke from their battle with the orcs and whirled on Yder, assailing him with everything from golden missiles of magic to spiked clubs. The prince vanished behind a wall of attackers, leaving

Arietta and Joelle with a clear path to . . . what? A courtyard filled with angry orcs?

Joelle breathed a sigh of relief, then said, "Let's take the high ground."

She pointed to their left, where the moonlit face of the citadel wall loomed above a handful of bustling campsites. Ascending the interior of the wall was the jagged line of a stairway—and the battle with the orcs had not yet spilled into that part of the courtyard.

Arietta nodded and started toward the stairway, which lay about thirty paces ahead. It made her stomach ache to let Kleef bring up the rear alone, but the first priority was protecting the Eye—and that meant she had to get away from the shades.

Before they had taken five steps, a tremendous hiss sounded from Yder's direction, and his attackers began to shriek and wail. Arietta glanced over to discover that the prince had surrounded himself with a whirling sphere of shadow. A dozen stunned men stood at its perimeter, staring at wisps of shadow where their sword arms used to be, watching in horror as their shoulders melted into shadow and drained into the hissing orb.

Arietta felt Joelle's hand on the small of her back, urging her to move faster. She raced around a campsite with three tents and a horse line that must have had thirty animals. And then the hiss ended as suddenly as it had begun. When she glanced over, Yder was standing alone in a ten-foot circle of emptiness, his gaze fixed on the last place he had seen his quarry. It did not take long for his eyes to turn in their direction again.

Kleef was still behind Arietta and Joelle, about even with the large campsite, pivoting and spinning as he held four shades at bay. But even he could not be in all places at once, and there were four more shadow warriors circling around the other side of the campsite, racing to catch Arietta and Joelle before they reached the stairwell. Judging by their speed, the shades were likely to succeed.

"We're not going to make it," Arietta said. "What now?"

"You return what was stolen from me." The reply came not from Joelle but from a nasal voice on Arietta's opposite shoulder. "That is what."

"Malik?" Arietta turned to find the little man running alongside her, his far hand holding his sword. "Where have you been?"

"Hiding from the thieving oaf who tried to kill me," Malik snarled. "Where else would I be?"

The three companions were less than ten paces from the stairs—about the same distance as the four Shadovar rushing to cut them off. Malik reached up with his free hand and tried to pull his drab robe off Arietta's shoulder, but it remained trapped beneath Arietta's bowstring and would not move. Before she could raise a hand to help, he brought his sword around and slipped the tip beneath the bowstring, clearly intending to cut it.

"No!" Arietta pushed an elbow into the side of his head and sent him stumbling, then pulled the robe from beneath her bowstring. "And don't you ever turn a sword my way again."

Arietta tossed the robe to him, then instantly lost sight of him as he dived to the ground and rolled into the shadows at the base of the wall. Seeing that Joelle had already taken a position about three paces from the stairwell, Arietta stopped next to her and turned to face their pursuers—only to discover the shades had changed directions and were already sinking into the shadows behind the nearest horse line.

Kleef, down to just two foes, was standing his ground no more than five paces from Arietta and Joelle. Beyond him, the battle against the orcs seemed to have stabilized, with wizards and mounted caravan guards working the perimeter of the fight, slowly forcing the enemy back toward the well.

Malik was nowhere in sight.

Realizing that the shades did not necessarily need to go through her and Joelle to reach the top of the citadel wall, Arietta spun around and looked up the stairs. Near the top, she saw a line of dark silhouettes emerging from the shadows, then continuing upward toward the top of the wall.

"Joelle, above us!"

Without waiting for a reply, Arietta charged up the stairs. Set into the wall itself, they were steep and narrow, with no handrail to offer support. Still, she managed to climb quickly and was more than halfway up when the fifth shade emerged from the shadows near the top and turned to face her.

A trio of Joelle's white darts came flashing up from the courtyard below. The shade managed to dodge one and catch two on a shield of shadow. By then, Arietta was on him, hacking at his knees, then driving her sword up into his torso. She angled the tip of her blade toward the citadel interior and sent him plunging into the courtyard below.

"Go!" Joelle called. A wet crunch sounded as she brought her blade down across his neck. "They're after Malik!"

Arietta nodded, then traded her sword for her bow. She nocked an arrow and, expecting to see a shadow disk flying toward her at any moment, crept the rest of the way up the stairs.

The attack never came, and when she reached the top, it was to find herself alone. The last four shades were moving along the wall in both directions, their glassy swords probing shadows and crannies as they searched for Malik in every conceivable hiding place.

Arietta stepped onto the top of the wall, then crouched in the shadows of the parapet. She heard Joelle's voice down at the base of the stairs, calling out to Kleef.

When Malik did not reveal himself, Arietta whispered, "Malik?"

Her only reply was the sound of Joelle's boots pounding up the stairs behind her, and the faint rustle of leaves, coming up from the trees on the other side of the parapet.

Or *were* they leaves?

Arietta rose high enough to peer over the parapet and found herself looking down on the vast Chondalwood forest. The canopy was perhaps twenty feet below, a billowing blanket of moonlit leaves that came up tight against the base of citadel walls. She saw no sign of niches or crannies in which the little man might hide, but the walls were rough enough that he could have climbed down to conceal himself among the trees.

Arietta leaned over the parapet, then called again, "Malik?"

This time, a soft scoff sounded behind her. Arietta turned to see a gray blur charging toward her, two outstretched hands leading the way.

"Malik!" Arietta let go of her bow and raised an arm to defend herself. "What are you—"

Then he hit her, and Arietta felt herself going over the parapet. She grabbed a handful of coarse wool, then realized it was too late to save herself, that she would only pull her attacker down with her. She tried to open her hand, but her feet were already in the air, Malik already coming down atop her.

"Thief!" he cried. "Harlot!"

They tumbled apart and crashed into the forest canopy, and the last thing Arietta saw before sinking into the leaves was Joelle's stunned face, peering over the parapet after her.

CHAPTER THIRTEEN

Kleef plunged into the forest canopy with his feet together and his arms held wide, snatching at branches and boughs as he dropped through the tangled darkness. He managed to grab hold of only twigs and leaves and began to realize just how reckless he had been to jump. But what choice had there been? He could not be sure that Arietta and Malik had survived their fall, and in the confusion of his dream, Kleef had revealed the Eye's hiding place. If Malik was dead and Yder located the body before Kleef did, Malik's robe would be lost.

Kleef's boots came down squarely atop a limb. Then the limb bounced and his knees buckled. He toppled off backward and went tumbling down through the branches, falling from bough to bough almost gently, his descent gradually slowing until he felt almost under control. Finally, he landed face-down on the tip of a particularly long limb, which slowly dipped until it had deposited him feet first on the forest floor.

Once the branch had risen out of the way, Kleef found himself looking at the base of an enormous duskwood tree. Though he stood less than five paces away, the forest gloom was so thick that he could barely make out what he was seeing and thought his eyes must be deceiving him. With a heavy beard of moss and a pair of horizontal ridges that looked like lips, the trunk resembled the profile of an old man's face—complete with a heavy brow ridge and crooked branch-stub that looked like a hooked nose.

Then something stirred above the branch-stub nose, and a pair of pale ovals appeared beneath the brow and swung in Kleef's direction.

Eyes.

The eyes seemed to study him for a moment, then blinked and swung away, looking in the opposite direction.

Kleef was too stunned to react. He had heard of treants, of course. But in the tales sailors told, treants were not kindly beings who caught hapless men as they fell from the sky. They were huge walking trees who guarded their forests against loggers and farmers and all manner of fire users—and who always seemed to be attacking some poor ship's crew as it tried to replace a broken mast.

An impatient rustle sounded from the far side of the treant. The pale ovals swung back in Kleef's direction and lingered on him expectantly, then a low creaking noise came from within the moss beard. Kleef may not have been able to understand the word, but its meaning was clear.

Go.

Kleef drew Watcher from its scabbard and started in the direction the treant had indicated. After a moment, a wall of dappled light appeared through the trees, and he soon realized it was moonlight reflecting off the cliff beneath the citadel. Standing in a small clearing at the base of the cliff were two figures, both holding swords and facing each other. They were not fighting, but the shorter figure was waving his blade around angrily and complaining in a whiny, nasal voice.

Malik and Arietta—both alive.

Kleef was about to call out to them when he glimpsed silhouettes moving through the undergrowth around them. He feared for an instant the shapes were orcs or shades, but they had curled horns on the sides of their heads and a strange bouncing gait that seemed more beast than humanoid. Uncertain of quite what he was watching, Kleef dropped into a crouch and paused to study them—only to have the figures glance in his direction, then vanish as quickly as they had appeared.

When the agate on Watcher's crossguard remained dark, Kleef decided that whatever the creatures were, they weren't Shadovar. He started forward again and began to make out Malik's complaints.

". . . almost killed me," the little man was whispering. "As it is, I can barely draw a breath."

"It's your own fault," Arietta hissed back. "You're the one who pushed me."

Pushed?

Kleef felt his stomach clench. He could not imagine why Malik would want to push Arietta off a cliff, but there was no doubting what he had just overheard—not with the pair holding weapons and facing off. Kleef stepped into the clearing and pointed Watcher at Malik.

"Throw down your sword," he ordered. "And stand away."

Malik looked in Kleef's direction, then his eyes bulged and he turned to flee. Giving the little man no time to use his ability to vanish, Kleef leaped after him.

"Kleef, wait," Arietta whispered. "Don't hurt—"

Kleef ignored the order and caught Malik by the wrist of his weapon hand. "Drop it, you worm."

When Malik shifted the sword to his other hand, Kleef lifted him into the air and heard a joint pop.

"Last chance," Kleef warned. He gave Malik a little shake. "Drop the sword."

"Stop!" Malik's voice was pained, but he continued to hold onto his sword. "You've broken my arm!"

Kleef doubted it was true, but the complaint was enough to make Arietta lay a hand on his arm.

"Stop," she ordered. "We still need him in one piece."

"A man can walk with a broken arm," Kleef said. "Right, Malik?"

Malik squirmed in Kleef's grasp, trying to swing his body around so he could bring his short sword to bear. Kleef brought Watcher's blade around to guard himself—and heard a female voice call out from near the base of the cliff.

"Kleef, no!"

Kleef glanced over to find Joelle stepping out of the undergrowth, Arietta's bow slung across her shoulders. She was still breathing hard from the long climb down the cliff, but that did not prevent her from rushing to protect Malik.

"You can't kill him," Joelle said. She took the sword from Malik's hand. "You can't even hurt him."

Kleef frowned. Joelle was the one who had told him that Malik and Arietta had fallen into the forest, just before she slipped over the parapet to climb down the cliff face. But she had not said anything about Arietta being pushed—and she did not seem all that surprised to find Kleef ready to lop off an arm.

After a moment, Kleef said, "You knew."

"That Malik pushed her?" Joelle hesitated, then reluctantly nodded. "I thought it was possible."

"And you didn't tell me?"

"I was afraid of how you would react." Joelle waved at Malik's still-dangling form. "Apparently, I was right about that. Besides, I couldn't be sure of what I had seen."

"Because this is all a tragic mistake," Malik said, quick to seize on her doubt. "The shades were coming, and there was nowhere else to go. I was only trying to save her."

Kleef looked to Arietta for a denial, but she was studying the gloom-shrouded forest around them, clearly more interested in keeping watch than anything Malik had said. He turned back to find Joelle rolling her eyes at the little man's latest lie.

"I was right behind you, Malik," she said. "The shades were nowhere near when you went over."

Malik's gaze flickered away. "Perhaps not," he allowed. "But the oaf and his noble lady are a threat to the Eye. You saw how they worked together to steal it from me."

"First you're saving Arietta's life, then you're protecting the Eye?" Kleef demanded. He was beginning to understand why Joelle had wanted to protect Malik from his wrath—because he could feel himself growing angrier by the moment. He shook his head in disgust, then turned to Arietta and Joelle. "Under Helm's Law, a man who attempts murder can be cast out or have a hand taken. Let's pick one and be done with it before the shades show up again."

"What?" Malik cried. "I need my hand to protect the Eye!"

"I can carry the Eye," Kleef said. He was still holding Malik up by the wrist.

Joelle shook her head. "Not for long," she said. "And even if you could, you're not a Chosen of Myrkul. When the time comes, how will you retrieve the Eye from the Fugue Plane?"

Kleef had no answer for that, of course. He hadn't even realized that was where the Eye went when Malik slipped it into his robe.

"And that would suggest we can't cast him out, either," Arietta said. She took Malik's sword from Joelle, then stepped close to the little man. "I can only imagine you attacked me because of some of the things that have passed between us on the trail. For that, you have my regrets."

A look of triumph came to Malik's face. "Did I not warn you to watch your tongue?"

Arietta's eyes grew cold. "And I shall," she said. "But if you attack me again, I'll have Kleef cut out your tongue and feed it to you. Do you understand?"

Malik's face clouded with anger, but he reluctantly nodded.

"Good." Arietta returned Malik's sword and motioned for Kleef to put him down. Then she turned toward the heart of the forest. "Because someone is trying to get our attention."

At first, Kleef saw nothing but gloom. Then, as he grew

accustomed to looking into the darkness, he realized there were dozens of silhouettes ahead, standing in the undergrowth without trying to hide. They had the same curled horns as the figures he had glimpsed earlier, but now he could also see that they had large, heavy legs that seemed to bend backward at the knees.

"Satyrs!" Joelle gasped. "What a welcome surprise."

She started forward, until Kleef caught her by the arm.

"You know them?" he asked.

"Not by name," Joelle said. "But we'll be fine. Satyrs are special to Sune."

As she spoke, a tall satyr in the center of the clan stepped forward, then abruptly turned away and vanished into the gloom. The rest remained where they were, the dark silhouettes of their heads turned as though they were watching the four humans.

A moment later, the tall satyr returned and approached to within ten paces of the companions. Kleef could see now that he had a thin, rugged face with a tuft of beard on his chin. He carried a long, curved bow, and on his belt he wore a short, thick-bladed sword.

Joelle smiled and stepped forward to greet him.

The satyr quickly turned away, then ran a few steps in the opposite direction and paused to look back.

"He seems to want us to follow him," Arietta whispered.

"Then let's do it," Joelle said.

Before Kleef could object, both women started after the satyr.

"That cannot be good," Malik said.

"It'll be worse if we lose sight of them." Kleef grabbed Malik's arm and shoved him forward. "You first."

They had taken no more than three steps before a distant crashing reverberated through the trees—no doubt an orc mob entering the Chondalwood in pursuit of Kleef and his companions. The satyrs turned toward the sound and started to string bows, then moved off one at a time, vanishing into the gloom as silently as they had appeared.

Kleef could only assume the tribe was rushing off to defend the Chondalwood from the Eye's pursuers. But were they also trying to protect Joelle and her companions? It seemed as hard to believe as a treant breaking his fall from the cliff top, yet there seemed no other explanation for the satyrs' behavior—especially the behavior of the tall one, who was clearly leading them deeper into the forest.

Kleef and Malik continued to follow, stumbling and staggering through the darkness as they tried to keep Arietta's blonde hair in sight. Malik maintained a constant litany of complaints, whining about the pain in his injured arm—even though he never shied away from using that same arm to break a fall. Kleef did his best to ignore the mewling and watch for shades, though the latter seemed impossible in so much gloom.

After a few minutes, a distant thudding rumbled through the forest, growing steadily louder and closer. Then the ground began to shudder. Their pace slowed, and Kleef and Malik came up behind Arietta and Joelle just as their satyr guide stopped entirely, his arms spread wide to hold everyone behind him.

Moonlight danced down through the leaf canopy, and Kleef saw the looming pillars of tree trunks crossing in front of them.

Treants, on the march.

As the last one passed, he turned his pale eyes toward the satyr. He groaned something in a voice barely audible above his booming footfalls, then shook a leafy bough behind him. The satyr dipped his head in acknowledgment and, motioning for the companions to follow, angled off in the direction from which the treants had come.

A hundred steps later, the ground grew soft and spongy beneath their feet. The satyr spoke in a wispy language Kleef did not recognize, and a narrow band of soft green light arose from the mossy ground beneath their feet. The light extended for perhaps ten paces—just enough distance to reveal that they had entered a narrow forest corridor that ran through a thick stand of hawthorn trees.

And, just where the light ran out, the corridor ended in a tangled wall of thorny branches.

"Trap!"

Kleef reached past Arietta, grabbing for the satyr's shoulder—and met Joelle spinning around to push him back.

"I wouldn't do that," she warned. "Satyrs hold a grudge."

"Grudge?" Kleef glanced at the satyr, who was watching their exchange, looking more confused than dangerous. "He's led us into a chokepoint. We're about to be ambushed!"

Joelle chuckled. "Not likely," she said. "They're forest children, and forest children are not fans of the Shadowfell. I'm sure the Forest Queen sent them to help us. The treants, too."

"You're just assuming," Kleef said. "There's no way Mielikki sent them, because she couldn't have known we'd jump off that cliff into the Chondalwood. *We* didn't even know."

"But she did know we'd be going through the Chondalwood," Joelle replied. "It's the only way to reach the Underchasm from where we were."

Kleef frowned. "How does Mielikki know where we're going?"

"The Lady of Love is hardly the only god who wants to stop Shar," Joelle said. "Sune's allies have been sending help all along. Myrkul sent Malik, Helm sent you, Siamorphe sent Arietta—and Mielikki sent the children of the forest."

As Joelle spoke, the satyr said something in a melodic language Kleef recognized as Elvish. Arietta held up a finger, then pulled a pinch of something from a cloak pocket and tossed it into the air, at the same time speaking the twisted syllables of a spellcasting.

When she was finished, she turned and touched the satyr's shoulder. "What is it?"

The satyr spoke for a few seconds, then looked up the

path—to where Malik was already ten paces ahead of the rest of the group and still moving. To Kleef's surprise, the moss was still glowing ahead of him, and the wall of thorny branches had pulled back to create an open corridor.

Arietta turned back to the others. "Theamont says we need to trust him," she said. "The forest children are no friends to orcs or Shadovar, but that doesn't mean they will let us hide in the Chondalwood forever."

Joelle smiled and motioned him forward. "By all means, Theamont," she said. "Lead the way."

She fell in behind the satyr, leaving Kleef and Arietta to bring up the rear. As they started forward, he looked over at her and raised his brow.

"You know magic?"

Arietta shrugged. "I've picked up a few spells along the way," she said. "Unfortunately, they tend to be more useful in handling court intrigue than in surviving a fight."

They caught up to the others and continued down the enchanted pathway. Still concerned about pursuers, Kleef made a habit of checking the trail behind them. All he ever saw was the glow fading from the moss and the corridor closing behind them, but it did not make him feel any safer. An impassible tangle of hawthorn branches might prevent the orc horde from pursuing them, but it would also cut off any possibility of retreat.

How long they continued to flee down the corridor was impossible to say. With nothing but darkness around them and a soft green glow ahead of them, he soon lost all sense of time. Malik's elbow swelled to twice its normal size, and they paused long enough for Joelle to make a sling and assure him it was only sprained. Arietta grew so weary she started to stumble, and Kleef convinced her to let him take her arm and help her along. Soon after, Joelle had to call on Sune for strength, and she began to give off a faint aura as the goddess's divine power flooded into her.

Still, Theamont led them onward. When the gray glow of false dawn began to filter through the hawthorn branches ahead, he urged them to move faster. Eventually, Kleef found himself almost carrying Arietta, and Joelle and Theamont had to resort to dragging Malik along by his armpits.

When even that did not seem fast enough for the satyr, Arietta cast her spell again. Theamont did not even slow his pace as he explained.

"He says the Forest Way's magic ends at dawn," Arietta said. "If we haven't reached the end before then, we'll be trapped inside."

"Would that be so bad?" Malik asked. "I could sleep the entire day."

Arietta hesitated, as though debating whether she wanted to answer Malik at all, then finally said, "He didn't mean until nightfall. His actual words were 'when the thorns close.'"

The threat of death-by-perforation was enough to reinvigorate the companions, at least temporarily. Malik no longer had to be dragged, and Arietta grabbed onto Kleef's belt and insisted that he pull her along at whatever pace Theamont set.

The gray glow filtering through the branches became a pearly gleam. Leaves rustled in the morning breeze, and the sound of purling water arose somewhere beyond the thorny wall ahead. Theamont gestured more vigorously, at once urging them to hurry and beaming as though the end were in sight. The pearly gleam became a silver radiance, and the glow began to fade from the mossy ground.

Theamont waved them onward one last time, then broke into a sprint and raced down the path. The hawthorn branches continued to open ahead of him—but more slowly, and at times it seemed he would crash into the thorn wall before it divided.

Then there were no more branches ahead, just Theamont running up the Forest Way, silhouetted against a circle of silver sky. After a few steps, he stopped and stood panting for breath, his gaze fixed on the far horizon. Finally, he turned and pointed at the ground, beaming and nodding to indicate that they had reached the end.

Joelle arrived next, so exhausted that when she finally stopping running, she stumbled and nearly pitched over. Theamont grabbed her arm and pulled her back to her feet.

By then, the first golden rays of sunlight were shooting across the horizon beyond them. A soft hissing arose from the walls of the path, and the hawthorn branches crept inward.

"Hold on!" Kleef called.

He reached back and grabbed Malik by the arm, then sprinted the last dozen paces to the end of the path—and nearly ran over Joelle as she stepped in front of him, her palms raised.

"Kleef, wait!" she yelled. "It's a chasm!"

Kleef jammed his front heel into the ground and threw his weight back, then felt his feet go out from beneath him. He released Malik's arm and hurled himself away from Arietta— then felt Theamont's big hoof land between his shoulder blades and stop his slide by pinning him face-down against the mossy ground.

Beneath his feet, Kleef felt nothing but air.

"All that running for this?" Malik cried out. He was a few steps to Kleef's left, somewhere near Joelle. "It is nothing but a dead end."

Once Theamont had removed his hoof, Kleef rolled over, sat up, and found himself looking across twenty paces of gorge. He couldn't see the bottom from where he was, but from somewhere below came the purling sound he had started to hear earlier.

Theamont said something in his own language, and Kleef looked up to see the satyr pointing down the canyon.

"He says we can rest on that island," Arietta translated. "The Shadovar won't be able to find us, and the orcs are a hundred leagues behind."

"A hundred leagues?" Kleef asked, rising. "How far did the Forest Way take us?"

Theamont studied Kleef with a blank expression for a moment, then turned back to Arietta. As the satyr spoke, Kleef peered down into the gorge and saw that they were forty feet above a dark, slow-moving river. The water filled the canyon from wall to wall.

After a moment, Theamont fell silent, and Arietta turned to her companions. "He says we're free to make a raft, as long as we use only dead wood," she said. "But the river empties into the Underchasm, so we should leave the water as soon as we hear the canyon roaring."

"A raft is well and good," Malik said, peering over the edge. "But how are we to reach the island—or the river, for that matter?"

Theamont smiled and used his fingers to make a running motion toward the river, then spoke a single word that needed no translation.

Jump.

CHAPTER FOURTEEN

They hit the water hard, and Malik felt the river rip him free of Kleef's tight embrace and carry him away, and he saw what a fool he had been to place his fate in the hands of an oaf. Yet what choice had there been? Joelle and Arietta were in the water already, and the satyr had threatened to throw Malik in after them if he did not jump himself. In the end, it had seemed safer to trust Kleef than to test their guide's resolve.

It was a mistake Malik feared would drown him. The water was as cold as it was dark, and it had seeped into his boots and soaked his robe, until he was caught in his own clothes like a fish in a net. The current dragged him down to the bottom of the river and sent him tumbling along the riverbed, bouncing off boulders and raking through gravel, sliding along sunken logs and scraping past shelves of bedrock. It dropped him into the narrow channel between two outcroppings and squeezed him out the other end, and his breath left him in a stream of bubbles.

And then Malik called out to Cyric in his thoughts. *Do not abandon me now, Mighty One,* he warned, *or you will spend eternity serving as Shar's toe-licker in the Tower of—*

His boot soles struck the top of a boulder, and Malik knew his god had answered his prayers. He pushed off at once. His head broke the water's surface in the same heartbeat, and he found himself in the center of a river that filled the gorge so completely that its waters ran tight against the canyon walls. The island they sought was but a blurry green dot on the downstream horizon, an impossible distance for Malik to swim in his sodden robes and water-filled boots.

Fortunately, Kleef was treading water off to the right, no more than three arm lengths away. But the oaf was looking downstream, his blocky head swiveling back and forth as he searched for his lost companion. Malik gulped down a few breaths and opened his mouth to call out to the oaf—and felt something wet grab his ankle.

Malik looked down and, through the dark water, he saw a crooked arm reaching out to hold his foot between a pair of scaly pincers.

"Kkk—"

He managed only a single sound before he was pulled under, and his cry for help became a gurgle. Fearing the worst, he reached for his sword with his good hand and felt himself being pulled deeper. He scraped along the rocky bottom for longer than he thought any man could bear, his weapon hand taking such a beating that at last he left his sword in its scabbard and drew his arm back.

His captor continued to pull, bringing him upstream, and up to the surface. At last, Malik was able to spin around to face his attacker.

It was a dead tree.

Or rather, it was a twenty-foot section of tree, with a handful of dead limbs reaching out from its trunk like so many crooked arms. Malik's foot was caught beneath a narrow crotch where two leafless branches came together, and one of those branches had splintered halfway through and then bent across Malik's ankle to trap his foot.

This was no act of random chance, Malik knew, for it was through such haphazard events that the gods worked their schemes, disguising their true intentions from mortals and fellow gods alike. Knowing that any effort to free himself would be in vain, Malik made circles with his free leg and waved his uninjured arm through the water, all in an effort to keep his head above the surface.

"Mighty One?"

No sooner had Malik asked this than the water grew so cold and still that he felt as if he were floating in slush. In the tree trunk in front of him, a pair of knotholes deepened into bottomless black eyes, a nesting hole became the cavity beneath a long-rotted nose, and the last few shreds of peeling bark became the jagged teeth in a lipless grin of a grinning skull's face.

Serving, Malik? The skull's mouth spoke not with one voice, but with a thousand, all as cold and sharp as cracking ice. *Toe-licker? You dare threaten me?*

The tree rolled, pulling Malik back beneath the water and holding him there until he thought his lungs would burst.

It was not a threat, Mighty One, Malik said in his thoughts. *I was only thinking of you, and what your fate would be if I died in this river and failed in my quest to deliver the Eye.*

Cyric's wrath seemed to fade a little, and he allowed the tree to roll again and bring Malik's head back above the surface.

You think I would count on you alone to stop Shar? Cyric asked. *That I have no other plans afoot?*

In truth, that was exactly what Malik thought, for though the One and All was brilliant in his scheming, he was confident to a fault and always assumed his plans would work exactly as he foresaw.

"I would never presume to know all your plans, Mighty One," Malik said carefully. "I only know that if this one is to succeed, I needed to make you hear my call."

A pair of cold blue flames appeared in the depths of Cyric's eyes. *I always hear your call, Malik,* he said. *There is no escaping me. You should know that by now.*

"I would never try to escape you," Malik said. "I am your most devoted servant."

Then why do you betray me? Cyric demanded. The tree rolled, and Malik sank beneath the surface again. *Why do you work so hard to undo all my plans?*

As Malik had no idea what plans the One meant, it was impossible to answer. As far as he knew, Cyric's plan required only that he help Joelle deliver the Eye of Gruumsh to Grumbar's Temple in the Underchasm and then murder her at the exact moment of their triumph. This would prove the spark that ignited the flaming glory of Cyric's mystical schemes, unleashing such a tide of strife and betrayal across Toril that, when the Sundering was finished, he would be guaranteed a place high in the divine hierarchy.

At last, Malik could hold his breath no longer. He sucked in a mouthful of river and began to cough and sputter, which caused him to take in more water and cough even harder. Finally, the One relented and rolled him to the surface again.

Well? Cyric asked.

"How have I . . . betrayed you, Mighty One?" Malik asked, coughing. "I'm still carrying the Eye, and if the accursed satyr is to be believed, we will soon be in the Underchasm."

Cyric waved off the explanation with the flick a dead branch. *That is not what angers me. What angers me is that you tried to kill Arietta.*

"That little thing?" Malik asked, truly surprised that the god of murder would be angered by the attempt. "I was only planning ahead, Mighty One."

You were jealous, Cyric said. *And you sought revenge for her slights.*

"Perhaps a little," Malik admitted. "Yet, there is more. To make Sune's magic bind Grumbar to Toril, Joelle must entice some fool to fall so much in love with her that he is willing to die for her. But Arietta has convinced Kleef that falling in love with Joelle would be a violation of his duty."

So you tried to remove Arietta, hoping that doing so would free Kleef to become Joelle's sacrifice. Cyric pulled Malik beneath the water again. *Do you think me such a fool that I failed to see that?*

Malik was quick to shake his head, and Cyric allowed him above water again.

"Forgive me, Mighty One," Malik said. "I am only a moth flickering around the brilliance of your wisdom, but I fail to see how removing Arietta can be anything but good for your plan. If she reaches the temple with us, she will only steal a small part of your glory for Siamorphe."

No, Malik. She will be Joelle's sacrifice.

"Arietta?" Malik was not such a fool that he had never heard of one woman falling in love with another, but he shook his head nonetheless. "It would never happen, Mighty One. Arietta may fall in love with another woman, but she is a slave to her noble title. She would never allow her heart to set a course so certain to bring scandal to her name."

Scandal? The very word seemed to perplex the One. *Her father his dead, her home is gone, her realm is falling, and her world is ending. Why would she worry about what people think?*

"Because Arietta is a noblewoman," Malik said, shrugging. "And she is convinced that she is a Chosen of Siamorphe. She will not even admit that she finds Kleef handsome because the oaf is too far below her station."

Chosen? Arietta? Cyric fell silent, the blue flames in his eyes flickering in thought. Finally, he shook his head and said, *You're wrong, Malik—as usual. Arietta will fall in love with Joelle. And you'll see to it that she does.*

"I will?" Malik took a long gulp of air, then asked, "How can I do that? I have no power over the hearts of others."

You don't need power over her heart, Malik. Cyric's eyes grew steady and cold. *All you need is the truth. Show that to her, and you will set her free.*

The truth was hardly Malik's favorite weapon, but there had

185

been a time when it was all he had, and he had learned to use it well enough to understand what Cyric was asking of him.

"You are a genius among gods, Mighty One," Malik said. "But if Arietta is to be the sacrifice, what of Kleef?"

Yes, what of Kleef? Cyric's skull-faced smile stretched even wider, until it seemed to Malik that it encircled the whole tree trunk. *Kleef will enhance my plan.*

Malik began to have a sinking feeling. "Enhance, Mighty One?"

Exactly, Cyric said. *The more Chosen you murder, the more powerful the effect. Kill Joelle and Kleef, and my magic will drown Toril in strife and betrayal.*

"Kill Kleef, too?" Malik gasped. "Impossible! He is a Chosen of Helm."

And you are one of mine. Cyric's voice turned icy, and the river grew so cold that Malik began to shiver. *Are you telling me I chose poorly?*

Malik's felt the bile of his fear rise into his throat. "Never, Mighty One," he said. "I will find a way."

Good, Cyric said. *And remember, it must be in the moment of their triumph. Do that, and it won't be Shar who rules supreme. It will be me.*

Knowing what a mistake it would be to point out that Cyric was asking the impossible, Malik merely swallowed and said, "As you command, Mighty One."

Cyric remained silent for a moment, the tiny flames in his eyes so intense that Malik felt as though they were burning inside his head. Finally, he said, *You'll need help.*

"It might be wise," Malik said. "Kleef is not only larger and stronger, he is also a better swordsman."

Then it's a good thing you're a murderer. Cyric bent a branch down toward the water in front of Malik. *Give me your dagger.*

Malik withdrew his dagger from inside his robe and passed it over, then watched in horror as Cyric plunged the blade into the knothole of his own empty eye socket—and continued to talk.

You see, Malik? I can be as reasonable as the next god. He remained silent for a moment, then pulled the dagger free and passed it back. *Now you have the advantage.*

Malik accepted the weapon back and saw that the blade had turned as black as Cyric's heart. "Indeed," he said. "I shall cherish it."

Don't cherish it, Malik, Cyric said. *Use it.*

CHAPTER FIFTEEN

Aᴀ̀ᴛᴇʀ ᴛʜʀᴇᴇ ʜᴏᴜʀꜱ ᴏꜰ ᴡᴏʀᴋ, ᴛʜᴇ ʀᴀꜰᴛ ᴡᴀꜱ ᴄᴏᴍɪɴɢ along even better than Arietta had expected. Malik had floated ashore on a huge dead tree, which Kleef had hacked into a pair of pontoons that would provide enough buoyancy to keep them above water. Joelle was kneeling next to the raft, lashing the driftwood deck in place. Kleef was down at the river's edge, using his dagger to put the final touches on a pair of oars. Arietta was atop the deck, peering down through a gap between logs as she tried to slide an oarlock post into place between two crossbars below.

For the fifth time in as many minutes, the bottom of the post missed the crossbars and dropped into the sand. Arietta sighed, then rose and turned toward a nearby tree, where Malik sat with his eyes closed and his back against the trunk. His sore arm was tucked back into its sling, but the elbow was no longer swollen, and twice Arietta had seen him use that hand to scratch his nose.

"Malik," she said. "Didn't you hear me ask for help?"

Malik opened a single eye. "And did you hear me agree?" He raised his sling. "I need to rest my elbow."

"Perhaps you can rest it on the river." Arietta had to fight to keep a civil tongue. "After the raft is built."

Malik shook his head. "There's no need for that. The satyr said we'd be safe on this island until the raft is built. Only a fool would rush to finish it."

Arietta sighed in exasperation and started to pull the oarlock post back up—then saw Joelle rise and peer across the raft at Malik.

"Don't be such a dolt, Malik," the heartwarder said. "Theamont doesn't know the Shadovar like we do."

"And he doesn't know about Kleef's dreams," Arietta added. Knowing how badly Kleef felt about revealing the Eye's location to the enemy, she kept her voice low so it wouldn't carry to the river's edge. "If Yder can use them to discover the Eye's hiding place, he can use them to find us."

"Then we must use his dreams to draw the Shadovar off," Malik said. "Take the oaf on the raft with you, and leave Joelle and me here to rest."

"And you don't think Yder would see where they left us in Kleef's dreams?" Joelle asked. "You would only divide our strength, and the Shadovar would find us anyway."

Malik thought for a moment, then conceded the point with a nod. "If the oaf has been tricked once, he will be tricked again." He shot a spiteful glance in Arietta's direction. "Do you see what you have done? Had you taken the oaf back to Marsember as I begged, the Shadovar would still be looking for us on the Lake of Dragons."

Joelle's brow shot up. "As you *begged*, Malik?" she asked. "You tried to make them leave—behind my back?"

"What else was I to do?" Malik answered. "You were convinced Sune had sent them to us—and if that is true, she did us no favors. Kleef is an oaf who cannot keep his own dreams to himself, and Arietta is a silly maiden who is no more a Chosen of Siamorphe than the orcs who have been chasing us."

Too shocked to be angry, Arietta let her jaw fall. "Why would you say such a thing?"

"Because it is true," Malik said, finally rising. "Joelle can charm with a smile and heal with a touch. I can always sense a lie and hide from those who wish me harm. Kleef can fight like a giant and tell when there are Shadovar near. What blessing has your god granted you?"

"Blessing?" Arietta could sense a trap in the question, but she couldn't see its nature—or figure out what Malik hoped to accomplish. "Honestly, I give more thought to what I owe Siamorphe than what she owes me. I should think it's the same with all Chosen."

"Which only proves you understand nothing of being one," Malik replied. "The gods chose us because we are useful to them, not because they wish to reward our devotion."

"Malik, that's enough." Joelle's tone was protective. "You know as well as I do that each god chooses differently."

"But always for the same purpose—to serve them." Malik continued to glare at Arietta. "And to serve them well, Chosen must have power. What power do you have, Arietta?"

More troubled by Joelle's attempt to shield her than by Malik's words themselves, Arietta glanced over at her friend and saw sympathy in her eyes. Not anger or doubt, but sympathy—as though she believed there was reason for Malik's words to trouble her.

Arietta lifted her chin and turned to Malik. "You know very well what my blessing is," she said. "Leadership. Perhaps you haven't noticed because you're busy hiding when a fight breaks out, but soldiers stand firm when I'm there. That was true back in Marsember, when I led my father's men-at-arms onto Deepwater Bridge. It was true when Kleef's watchmen volunteered to sail after the Shadovar with us. And it was true every time I helped Faroz's caravan guards turn back an orc raid."

Malik only smirked. "Are you such a ninny that you failed to notice who else was there?" He shot a defiant glance at Joelle, almost daring her to interrupt, then said, "Kleef. He is the one who has been inspiring the soldiers. You've only been one of the fools standing at his side, looking at his shadow and thinking it belongs to you."

The smugness in Malik's voice made Arietta's blood boil, but her discourse tutor had taught her to always question her anger—that it was often a mask that disguised something she didn't wish to face. She paused and thought back to all of the battles she had fought, and—with an growing sense of embarrassment—she realized that Malik was right. Kleef *had* always been there, too.

And most of the time, he had been the one leading the fight.

Finally, Arietta nodded. "You make a good point about Kleef," she said, trying not to sound resentful. "It may be that the soldiers draw their inspiration from him."

"Or from both of you," Joelle said, sounding more supportive than convinced. "Why not? A woman charging into battle has a way of making men ignore their own fears."

Arietta flashed a grateful smile. "Perhaps," she said. "But Malik is right. It was foolish of me to assume the soldiers were responding to me, when Kleef has always been the one leading the fight."

"It was?" Malik looked distressed rather than surprised. "And you are not troubled that you've been such a fool?"

"I'm a bit embarrassed, naturally," Arietta admitted. "Perhaps inspiring soldiers isn't one of my Chosen powers, after all. But better to have my error corrected than have my friends laughing at it behind my back."

"No one was laughing," Joelle said. "Because it doesn't matter. You're honest, devoted, and courageous. Those are the things that make you a worthy companion."

As kind as they were, Joelle's words hit Arietta like a kick to the stomach. She was trying to reassure Arietta about more than a mistaken assumption about her powers. Joelle was trying to tell her that she didn't need powers—that she still mattered without any.

"You think Malik's right, don't you?" Arietta asked.

"You think that I don't have any other powers—that I'm not Chosen at all."

"What I think is that we wouldn't have made it this far without you," Joelle said. She smiled, and that almost reversed the growing hollow in Arietta's stomach—almost. "Besides, it's not for me—or Malik—to say who Siamorphe's Chosen are."

"But we all know Siamorphe is the goddess of noble rule," Malik said quickly. "So, would not her true Chosen be able to command obedience?"

Joelle scowled at Malik. "Since when do you know how gods think?"

"It is only common wisdom," Malik said. Keeping his gaze fixed on Arietta, he raised the arm in the sling. "And you could not even stop the oaf from breaking my elbow."

"I keep telling you it's not broken," Joelle said. "And, considering what you did to Arietta, you should consider yourself lucky."

"What I did is of no concern," Malik replied. "The oaf still attacked me, and Arietta could not command him to stop. If she is a Chosen of Siamorphe, then I am a Chosen of Tempus."

Arietta barely heard the rest of their argument, for her head was spinning and her pulse was pounding in her ears like a drum. She had no doubt that, having failed to avenge himself by pushing her off the citadel walls, Malik was now trying to destroy her by other means.

But that didn't make him wrong. Arietta should have been able to command Kleef to stand down after the attack, but it had been Joelle who had finally calmed him down. And Kleef was a loyal Cormyrean, dutiful to a fault. If she could not command him, even in the heat of the moment, then Malik was right—she did not carry the divine power of a Chosen.

Which shouldn't have surprised her, really. Arietta had never received the kind of vision Joelle had described, or been charged by her god with some impossible mission the way

Malik had, or even found herself in possession of unexpected blessings as Kleef had. She had simply been a dutiful young girl who embraced the worship of Siamorphe as the obligation of every Cormyrean noble, then done her best to live by the goddess's teachings. After she revealed that she occasionally saw Siamorphe in her dreams, the temple priests began to flatter her and indulge her with special favors, which only increased in extravagance when her father rewarded their attention with frequent donations.

By the time she reached the age of eligibility, she believed only a Chosen of Siamorphe could be the subject of so much adoration and special treatment. When the temple priests did nothing to disabuse her of the notion, the rest of the congregation accepted the status as fact, and Arietta had begun to dispense wisdom and advice to her peers as though she were a true Chosen of Siamorphe.

What a fool.

Arietta could see now that the priests had only been afraid of losing her father's lavish support, and they had been willing to let her deceive herself and the rest of the congregation rather than tell her the truth. She could not help imagining them in their opulent refectory, toasting her folly with free wine from her father's vineyards. And that was not the worst of it. Surely, many of the other noble families had seen through the charade. How many of them had been snickering up their sleeves each time the priests mentioned her father's latest gift, how many of her peers had been biting their cheeks as she held forth on their duty to Siamorphe?

More than she cared to know, Arietta was certain.

Realizing the argument had fallen silent, Arietta looked up to find the eyes of both Joelle and Malik fixed on her. Joelle's brows were arched and her mouth drawn into a sympathetic smile. Malik looked smug and triumphant, as though he had just emerged victorious in the bitter rivalry that only he seemed to truly understand.

Arietta swallowed hard, then looked him in the eye and said, "It seems I find myself once again indebted to your candor, if not your tact. Thank you for dispelling my illusions."

"Think nothing of it," Malik said. "I'm only doing what is best for our mission."

Arietta responded with a tight smile. "Rest assured I'll do the same." Hoping for some privacy to compose herself, she made a show of glancing at the leathra vines coiled in the sand next to Joelle, then said, "It looks as though we're running low on lashing cord. I'll go cut some more."

No sooner had she stepped off the raft than Malik appeared in front of her.

"There is no need to trouble yourself."

He reached inside his robe and withdrew a large coil of greasy gray cord. The stuff stank of death and decay, and it looked more like fish intestines than rope.

"A gift from Myrkul." Malik tossed the coil on the pile of leathra vines, then sneered, "That is what a real Chosen can do."

Joelle picked up the rope and made a sour face, but continued to hold it as she turned to Malik.

"You've made your point," she said. "Now, either help finish the raft, or I'll use this rope to drag you along behind it."

Malik's expression remained victorious. "There is no need for threats." He withdrew his arm from the sling and said, "All you had to do was ask."

He dropped onto his back and slinked under the deck to help Arietta place the oarlocks, and an hour later the raft was complete. They foraged an early highsunfeast of chufa roots and currants, made a set of long tridents for spearing fish, and then finally launched the raft.

Despite the crudeness of their materials, the raft was both stable and sturdy—due in no small part to the skills Arietta had developed as a ten-year-old, when her beleaguered father had finally assigned his best shipwright to help her build her own canal raft. That craft had been fitted with a great many luxuries that this one lacked, including a canopy, a rudder, and a foot-operated paddlewheel. But she had never forgotten the care the shipwright had taken in fitting each piece and making certain that the lashings were secure without being inflexible. By the time Arietta and her companions had been on the river twenty minutes, they felt secure enough in their work to take turns sleeping on the deck.

The river was gentle and swift. Aside from the occasional island or stretch of riverbank, the water filled the gorge from wall to wall. Occasionally, Kleef had to row them around an eddy or steer them away from a waterfall plunging down from above. But generally, the travel was easy, and Kleef had little to do but watch for river hazards and enemies skulking on the canyon rim.

Arietta passed much of the time sitting on the front edge of the raft, watching for fish and holding a trident poised to strike. But her mind was elsewhere, and she missed a chance at a big carp because her thoughts were consumed by Malik's revelation that she was not Chosen. She was angry at the temple priests for encouraging her self-deception, angry at her father for using his wealth to encourage their behavior, angry at herself for being such a fool. But most of all, she was angry at Siamorphe for rewarding her unwavering faith with cruel mockery. Arietta had lived her entire life by the tenets of the church, donating vast sums to the local temple and refusing to consider any suitor who did not share her faith. She had preached the canon of noble obligation to her peers with a condescension that could only be described as overbearing, and she had imposed on her parents a code of behavior they clearly could not accept.

And how had Siamorphe responded? By allowing her priests to make Arietta the butt of jokes across all of Marsember—and probably the entire realm of Cormyr. She could not understand why Siamorphe would allow such a thing—why the goddess had deemed her unworthy of being one of her true Chosen. In Siamorphe's name, Arietta had dragged her family into a fight they wanted no part of— a fight that had cost her mother a finger and her family its fortune. Her father had died for a cause he did not believe in, and Arietta was to blame. She felt cheated and angry and guilty.

Guilty—she felt that more than anything.

After several hours of brooding, Arietta finally began to calm down and turn her thoughts to her companions. Malik and Joelle were both sleeping on the deck, but Kleef had been at the oars since they'd launched at midday. He was a man of incredible strength and endurance, and Arietta suspected that Helm would sustain him far beyond what a normal person could abide. But he was still only human, and she knew that standing all that time could only be wearing him out faster.

Stepping past Malik's sleeping form, Arietta rose and went aft to Kleef's side. "How are you feeling?" she asked. "I can pilot the raft for a while, if you'd like to sit down."

Kleef shook his head. "No sitting for me," he said. "I'll fall asleep."

"And Yder will come?"

"Without a doubt." Kleef began to row gently, moving them away from a ripple in the river that suggested a submerged rock. "And the last time he entered my dreams, we almost lost the Eye."

"I know," Arietta said. "But we have to think of something. You can't stay awake forever."

"I can stay awake for a while," Kleef said.

"And if the Shadovar find us anyway, when you're not rested?" she asked. "That would be just as bad. It could be worse."

Kleef was silent for a moment, then said, "They won't find us—not if I don't fall asleep."

"Because Theamont said so?" Arietta shook her head. "I'm sure he believed that, but the Shadovar are very resourceful— and very determined."

Kleef stopped rowing and looked over. "Where's this going?" he asked. "Are you telling me you have a better idea?"

Arietta paused, surprised by the note of desperation in Kleef's voice. It hadn't occurred to her that he might be worried, too, that his stoic demeanor might be no more than a mask hiding his own fears.

After a moment, she said, "I'm sorry, but I don't have one. I was just hoping there might be a more workable solution."

Kleef continued to study her for a moment, then said, "Maybe there is." He turned back to the river. "It might be best for me to leave the group and climb out of the canyon."

Arietta's stomach clenched. "Kleef, forgive me for saying so, but that would be very stupid. How long do you think it would take Yder to locate the rest of us after he found you?"

"That depends on how long I can stay awake," Kleef said. "If I can last three or four days—"

"Kleef, we built a raft," Arietta interrupted. "We're floating down a canyon. You don't think Yder would see some hint of that in your dreams?"

Kleef clenched his jaw, then nodded. "I guess he would."

"So there's nothing to be gained by leaving." Arietta laid a hand on his forearm and gave it a soft squeeze. "Everyone is better off with you here, believe me."

Kleef looked at the hand on his arm, then smiled and dipped his head. "You leave me no choice, my lady," he said. "I'll stay."

"Good. And thank you." Arietta returned his smile, then realized that—no matter how angry she was with Siamorphe— it would be wrong to reward his loyalty by continuing to deceive him about who she was. "Kleef, there's something you should know. I'm not exactly who I've been claiming."

Kleef frowned. "I thought we'd been through that," he said. "Are you not Arietta Seasilver after all?"

"No, I am Arietta," she said. "But I'm afraid I've been fooling myself about being one of the Chosen. I'm sorry to have misled you."

Kleef's jaw dropped, and he stared at her without speaking a word.

After a moment, Arietta grew uncomfortable. She could not bear the thought of Kleef thinking of her as a self-deceiving fool, but it was better that he hear the truth from her than Malik.

"Is it really such a terrible mistake?" she asked. "I would have told you earlier, but I just discovered it myself."

"Not so terrible," Kleef said. "It's just that you . . . well, you apologized."

Arietta raised her brow. "Yes, I suppose I did." She was as surprised as Kleef, for it was an unspoken rule of life in Marsember that a noble never apologized to a commoner. Fortunately, Arietta was no longer in Marsember. "And I meant it. I wouldn't deceive you on purpose. Not again."

A look of mock suspicion came to Kleef's face. "Are you really Arietta Seasilver?"

Arietta smiled. "It's hard to believe, I know," she said. "I'm still a little stunned myself."

"Well enough," Kleef said, laughing. "Apology accepted—not that I needed one."

Arietta did not find the remark reassuring. "Why not?" she asked. "Because you don't care that I'm not Chosen? Or because you already knew? Please be honest."

"Because what you call yourself isn't as important as what you do," Kleef said. "You're here, trying to do right by your god and your realm. That's all that matters to me."

"That's not an answer."

"But it's honest," Kleef said. "That's what you asked for—and it's all you're going to get from me."

Arietta smiled wistfully. "Then I guess I have my answer." She rose onto her toes and kissed his cheek. "Thank you for being so gentle."

Kleef's jaw dropped in disbelief. He studied her openly for

a moment, his expression slowly changing from surprise to delight, then he nodded to himself and, smiling, looked back to the river. Arietta returned to her perch at the front of the raft, took up the trident again, and they continued to float down the canyon.

Kleef's pragmatic dodge had made her realize that she was behaving like the worst sort of noble, worrying about appearances rather than substance. Kleef and Joelle had never cared whether she was Chosen or not, only that she was there with an arrow when the need arose. And Malik had cared only because her delusion gave him a way to avenge his wounded pride.

But Kleef was right. The best thing she could do for her companions—and the mission—was to let go of her wounded pride. She had to accept herself for who she truly was, then do everything in her power to deliver the Eye to Grumbar's Temple.

With her mind at ease, Arietta soon caught two large river gar that they roasted over the cooking fire that evening. Determined not to sleep, Kleef insisted on standing vigil all night, then rowing all day.

As incredible as Kleef's stamina was, Arietta and Joelle knew it couldn't last forever. By the third day, they'd thought of several ways to keep Yder away, such as asking Sune to guard Kleef in his sleep or allowing him to rest only during the day, when Yder might not be searching for a way into his dreams. But Kleef rejected them all, and in the end the two women resorted to simply keeping him company, maintaining a constant stream of chatter to make certain he did not fall asleep.

The gorge continued to deepen and darken, with waterfalls and tributaries feeding the river from both sides. The sky became a jagged band of light trapped between the rocky walls of the canyon. As often as not, the sky was filled with rippling fans of color—green and gold, sometimes even crimson and purple— but it was never blue. When the sun appeared at all, it was dim and mottled, or shaped like a sickle or a spider or a skull.

On the fifth day, Kleef said, "Someone's watching us."

Arietta grabbed her bow, then stood and followed his gaze down river. He seemed to be looking about fifty feet up the canyon wall, where a lone dragon tree clung to a small ledge.

"Where?" Arietta asked. "All I see is a tree."

"Under the tree," Kleef said. He had bags beneath his eyes the size of Arietta's thumbs, and his posture was so slouched and awkward it looked as though he might collapse any moment. "There's a man in a robe. Bald and thin, sunken gray eyes."

Arietta stepped to Kleef's side, then double-checked his line of sight and saw that he was still looking toward the ledge. She glanced back at Joelle, who had been seated next to her in the back of the raft, and gave her head a worried shake. Joelle nodded and stepped to Kleef's other side.

"I don't see him, either," Joelle said. "Can you point him out?"

"No," Kleef said. "Then he'll know we've seen him."

"He probably knows already." Arietta waggled the tip of her bow. "I'm afraid I wasn't very subtle when you said we were being watched."

Kleef frowned, taking far longer to consider her words than he should have. Finally, he removed a hand from an oar and pointed at the tree.

"There," Kleef said. "It's the second time I've seen him."

"When was the first time?" Arietta asked, trying not to show her growing concern. "And why didn't you tell us?"

"Because I wasn't sure," Kleef snapped. "But I am now."

"That's good," Joelle said, in a tone of exaggerated patience. "Where did you see him the first time?"

"In the mouth of that little cave we passed," Kleef said. "I thought it was just a trick of the shadows—"

"Until you saw his eyes follow us down the river," Malik finished. He was in the front of the raft, and had just sat up.

"You saw him, too." Kleef looked toward the little man. "Why didn't you say something?"

"Because then he raised his cowl and disappeared," Malik said. "I thought my eyes were deceiving me."

"They weren't," Kleef said. "I saw him pull his cowl up, too."

"Perhaps the shadows were playing tricks on both of you," Joelle suggested. "And even if you did see someone, wasn't the cave on the other side of the river? How would he get across and up to that ledge?"

Kleef furrowed his brow and looked down river again, and his eyes grew doubtful.

Seeing that they were thirty paces from the ledge, Arietta said, "There's an easy way to find out. Just move the raft closer to the cliff. If he's there, maybe Joelle and I will see him, too."

Kleef looked back down river, then shook his head. "It's too late," he said. "He's gone."

Arietta exchanged worried looks with Joelle and realized they had both come to the same conclusion. She tucked her bow back beneath the security line they had rigged to keep their equipment from falling off the raft, then returned to Kleef's side.

"I'll take the oars for a while," she said. "You can rest, and Joelle will ask Sune to guard your dreams."

Kleef refused to yield the oars. "I'm not imagining things."

"All the more reason to get some sleep," Joelle said. "If someone has been watching us, it may be that the Shadovar have found us on their own."

"He didn't look like a Shadovar," Kleef said. "Too pale."

"And yet, he emerges from the shadows on both sides of the canyon," Joelle said. "Who else could cross the river and appear in front of us so easily?"

Kleef looked uncertain.

"Kleef, even Helm can sustain you only so long," Arietta said. "Your thinking is clouded and slow, and you can barely stand. You are going to fall asleep."

"And it's better to do it now, when we can try to protect you," Joelle said. "And when Yder may not be looking for your dreams."

"Indeed," Malik agreed. "It has been so long since you have dreamed that Yder may even believe you've finally figured out how to keep him away."

"Finally?" Arietta asked. Fighting to keep the anger out of her voice, she turned toward the little man. "Are you saying you already know how to keep Yder away?"

Malik looked genuinely confused. "You do not?"

"No." Joelle's voice was seething. "If we knew, why wouldn't we have tried it four days ago?"

Malik shrugged. "Because it is not for you to try." He looked toward Kleef, then said, "And I can only believe the oaf has never tried it because it is easier to fight shades than to forsake his bitterness."

"Bitterness?" Kleef asked. He leaned so far forward between the oars that Arietta reached out and caught him by the arm. "What does that have to do with my dreams?"

"You are angry at your god," Malik said. "And that is what gives Shar power over you. Give up your anger, and we will all be the safer. Yder won't be able to use his goddess's power to enter your dreams."

Kleef scowled and shook his head. "I'm not angry at Helm," he said. "Why should I be? Helm's been dead for the last hundred years."

"And yet, you've spent your whole life serving him," Arietta said. She was not happy to find herself agreeing with Malik, but her recent disappointment with Siamorphe gave her some insight into what Kleef must have been feeling all those years. "You've kept faith with Helm's Law and honored your duty, all while watching your superiors profit outrageously by turning their backs on everything you stand for. Of course you're angry. Who wouldn't be?"

Kleef turned to her with a confused look. "You think Malik is right?"

"So do I," Joelle said. She laid a hand on his arm and smiled. "And so do you, if you look inside yourself. Will you try to give up your anger? For us?"

"And for our quest," Malik added. "After your mistake at the citadel, it is the least you can do to protect the Eye from our enemies."

Kleef glowered at the little man for a moment, then finally nodded. "I'll try." He relinquished the oars to Arietta, then stepped to the back of raft and said, "If I start to talk or thrash around—"

"I'll wake you," Joelle promised. "But you won't. Sune and I will be watching over your sleep, too."

Kleef's only response was an unintelligible grunt, then the raft rocked as he dropped onto the deck and stretched out. Arietta heard Joelle whisper a soft prayer to Sune, and two breaths later, Kleef was snoring. Instead of dropping back into his usual repose, Malik remained alert and anxious, scanning the canyon rims and studying every shadow they passed. Once, he raised his arm as though to point, but quickly lowered it again and announced that he was no better than Kleef. He thought he had seen the bald-headed man again, but it had only turned out to be a turtle resting on a boulder.

Arietta spent the rest of the day keeping them in the middle of the river, where it would be difficult for the Shadovar or anyone else to launch an attack. Then, toward the end of the afternoon, the current started to move much faster, and the gorge grew so deep that the bottom was cloaked in permanent twilight. They began to hear a faint whispering in the canyon ahead, and soon the whispering became a constant drone.

Finally, the drone became a steady thrum, and Arietta said, "We must be getting near the end. That's beginning to sound like the waterfall Theamont warned us about."

"I am sure it is." Malik pointed toward a hanging ravine on the south wall of the gorge. "And there is our way out."

Arietta barely glanced at it before shaking her head. Although there was a small gravel bank beneath the ravine where they could beach the raft, the mouth was nearly fifty feet up a sheer cliff.

"We're not that close to the waterfall yet," Arietta said. "There's bound to be a bigger gulch or side canyon before we reach it."

"Perhaps, but it is not the waterfall I am worried about," Malik said. "It is that."

He pointed again, this time straight down the canyon. At first, it was difficult for Arietta to identify the source of his concern. All she could see was the river disappearing into the gloom that filled the bottom of the gorge.

And then she realized that the gloom *was* his concern. It lay on the water like the approaching dusk, a gray dimness seeping into the air above, spreading upriver toward the raft, creeping along the canyon walls around them.

It was the Shadowfell, and it was coming for them.

CHAPTER SIXTEEN

THE MOUTH OF THE RAVINE HUNG FIFTY FEET ABOVE THE ground, a gray wedge of nothingness opening into the cliff's craggy dark face. While there were no crevices into which a fist or foot could be jammed while a climber paused to rest, there were plenty of rough-textured knobs and flat-bottomed divots to use as handholds and toe rests. The ascent was going to be tiring but fairly safe—and not really much of a challenge compared to some of the palace towers Joelle had climbed in her time as a jewel thief.

Satisfied that she was not likely to encounter any unexpected obstacles during the climb, Joelle returned to the river's edge, where her companions sat among a tangle of logs. As she approached, Malik rose and offered her a coil of braided rope, which he had spent the last two hours creating from the vines they had used to lash the logs into a raft.

"It will hold anything," he promised. "Even the oaf."

"You're sure?" Joelle asked. "Because you'll be coming up third. If it breaks before then, you'll be trapped down here with Kleef."

"Anything," Malik assured her. "I took extra care because I knew my own life would depend on its strength."

Joelle rewarded him with an approving smile. "I'm glad you understand."

She accepted the coil and slung it over her shoulder, then stepped over to where Arietta was sitting with Kleef's head in her lap, monitoring his slumber for any sign of bad dreams. After more than eight hours of sleep, the big watchmen was starting to look more like himself. The bags beneath his eyes had retracted into mere circles, and even his cheeks seemed a little less hollow.

Joelle dropped to her haunches next to Arietta and asked, "Any sign of trouble?"

Arietta shook her head. "Nothing yet."

"Then let him sleep until I finish the climb," Joelle said. "Once I'm in the ravine, it will take a little time to tie off the rope."

Arietta nodded. "I'll keep an eye out."

"Good." Joelle glanced downriver toward the hazy dimness that was the Shadowfell creeping toward them. "The sooner we're out of here, the better."

Joelle started to rise, but stopped when she felt Arietta's hand close on hers.

Arietta didn't say anything. She just looked at Joelle with soft eyes and an arched brow, and Joelle saw the confusion inside her—the conflict between what Arietta was feeling and what she thought she should be feeling, the conviction that she should be the master of her emotions rather than a servant to them.

That was wrong, of course. Sune's worshipers knew that emotions were the true guide to happiness, that only by paying attention to their desires and their anger and their joy could they come to know their own souls and live in harmony with their true natures. Unfortunately, that was not something Joelle could simply explain. It was something that everyone needed to discover in her own way—and that included Arietta.

After a moment, Joelle smiled, then raised the hand Arietta was holding. "Yes?" she asked. "Was there something else?"

Finally seeming to realize what she had done, Arietta blushed and shook her head. "No, not really." She released Joelle's hand, then said, "Just . . . be careful."

Joelle laughed. "Be careful? Where's the fun in that?"

She leaned down and kissed Arietta full on the mouth. At first, the noblewoman seemed too stunned to react, but her lips finally began to soften—and that was when Joelle broke off and looked into Arietta's eyes.

"For luck," she said. "I hope you don't mind."

Arietta seemed barely able to shake her head. "N-not at all."

"Good." Joelle smiled and turned to climb the cliff. "Maybe we'll do it again."

In the dream, Kleef and Arietta sit side by side at a campfire. They are nestled against a log somewhere in Faerûn, looking out over a moonlit river. Malik and Joelle are long gone, though Kleef doesn't know whether they are dead or have simply parted ways.

Arietta reaches over and takes his hand. She says nothing, does not even look at him. She just watches the flames and twines her fingers into his, and Kleef knows that she is the one.

Arietta understands him in a way no one else can. She sees the despair that weighs on those who keep faith in a dead god, and the rancor that eats at those who honor their vows while others grow rich by flaunting theirs. But most of all, she recognizes the strength it takes to stand firm in a sea of corruption, to remain true to a sworn duty while the tide of depravity pulls the sand from beneath one's feet.

Kleef knows that Arietta sees all this because she is a kindred spirit. Like him, she values honor and duty for their own sake, and she believes that the gifts a person receives in life carry a sacred duty to use them in the service of others.

And Kleef knows he and Arietta were meant for each other. He can feel it in the aura of warmth and comfort that shields them from despair, in the love and joy that armors them against the immorality all around them. As long as they have each other, they are invincible.

Then Kleef feels a strip of cold metal between his fingers, and he looks down to discover that the hand holding his wears a golden ring. It is huge and gaudy, with a setting that holds a moonstone carved into the image of a striking wyvern. The ring is the signet of House Seasilver, and that can only mean he is holding the hand of Grand Duchess Arietta Seasilver.

Now, the love that has been armoring them is gone. No matter how much she might want to, a grand duchess can never marry a mere watchman. Take him for a paramour, perhaps even keep him in the house disguised as a loyal retainer. But wed? The scandal would weaken her entire house. The Seasilvers would find themselves shunned by noble and royal alike, quietly demoted to the status of mere merchants—to be tolerated when necessary, but not to be courted or befriended.

Kleef feels the old bitterness seeping back. The only way he can have Arietta is through subterfuge and deception, and he cannot dishonor either of them in such a manner. He would be destroying the very thing he loved.

No sooner has Kleef come to this conclusion than Arietta's hand turns cold. It starts to shrivel and wither, and the nails grow long and yellow. It becomes the hand of a crone. When he gasps and looks up, her face is gaunt and gray and hard. She is wearing a queen's crown, and the light in her eyes has gone dim and malevolent.

"Have courage, Kleef," The voice is soft and wispy and familiar—and it is not Arietta's. "Ask Shar, and I can be yours."

But Kleef has been in these dreams before, and he knows that the words are a diversion—that Yder has found him again. He shakes his head and tries to will himself awake.

Arietta's face grows harsh and wrinkled. Her mouth drops into an angry frown, and she glares at him in hatred.

"Kleef, you could have saved me," she says. "All you had to do was ask."

Arietta jerks her hand from Kleef's grasp, and then he feels it on his shoulder, squeezing hard and shaking.

"Kleef!" This time, the voice was Arietta's, and it was filled not with hatred and disappointment but with impatience. "Kleef, wake up!"

Kleef opened his eyes and found a tent of blonde hair hanging down above him. In the middle was a slender female face with a long nose and full lips. Arietta, as beautiful as ever—with Kleef's head resting in her lap.

Could it be that some part of his dream had been real? Could it be that the Arietta in his dreams had grown cold and cruel not because of their love but because he turned away from it?

Kleef smiled, then reached up to take the hand that was shaking his shoulder. "We can't let them tell us who to love."

Arietta's eyes grew round with surprise. "What?"

"This is important," Kleef said. "Follow your heart. It's the only way to save yourself."

Arietta's jaw dropped. She seemed to study Kleef for a moment without really seeing him, then finally said, "Good advice." She looked up the gravelly slope. "Perhaps I'll take it."

Kleef followed her gaze toward the canyon wall and was surprised to see Joelle clambering into the mouth of a hanging ravine. She had a coil of rope slung across her shoulder and did not look all that tired for a woman who had just completed a fifty-foot climb.

"Where's she going?" he asked.

"Time to leave the river."

Arietta pointed down the canyon, to where a blanket of dark shadow lay thick on the water. It seemed to be spreading, pushing slowly upriver and creeping along the canyon walls.

Kleef sat upright. "Tell me that's just fog."

"I wish I could," Arietta said. "But we both know it's not."

Stomach knotting and eyes fixed on the remnants of the Shadowfell, Kleef rose. "Where's Malik?"

"Have no fear." Malik's voice came from behind him. "I am here."

Kleef breathed a sigh of relief, then turned to the little man. "We need to get you out of here."

"That's the idea," Arietta said. "As soon as Joelle secures the rope, we're climbing out."

Kleef looked back up the slope and saw that Joelle had vanished into the interior of the ravine.

"We might not have that long." Kleef drew Watcher, then slung the sword's scabbard across his back. "I couldn't do it. I let them in."

"Who?" Malik asked.

"Who do you think?" Kleef replied. "Shar. Yder."

Malik's expression grew angry. "Do not snarl at *me*," he said. "You are the one who cannot forgive his own god."

"That's enough," Arietta said, crossing to the canyon wall. "The Shadovar were bound to find us sooner or later, and we were still on the river when Kleef went to sleep. If we're lucky, we can be out of here and halfway to Grumbar's Temple before they realize we've left the canyon."

Kleef doubted they would be so lucky, but—at least if he remembered his dream correctly—the Shadovar had not been with him long before Arietta awakened him. Keeping a careful eye on the shadows around them, he followed Arietta and Malik up to the canyon wall.

They did not have to wait long before Joelle tossed the rope down. Arietta made the climb first, pausing twice to twine the line around her legs so she could rest her arms. Malik was not strong enough to make the climb on his own, so he tied the rope around his waist and spent several minutes complaining while the two women hauled him up. Kleef brought up the rear, hauling himself up hand over hand.

He was nearly at the top when the twang of a bowstring

rang out inside the ravine. It was followed by a strangled gasp and the scuff of running boots, then another *twang*.

Malik's head appeared above, peering down over the cliff. "What is taking you so long?" he demanded. "There are orcs!"

Kleef practically flew up the last ten feet, pulling so hard that the rope stretched and bounced each time he grabbed hold of it. By the time he reached the ravine mouth, his breath was coming hard and his arms were trembling with fatigue. Still, he clambered over the edge and rolled, then came up on a knee with Watcher in hand.

The hanging ravine narrowed almost immediately into a slot canyon, and Kleef found himself looking up a rocky, sheer-sided passage not much wider than he was tall. Malik was to his right, crouching behind a small boulder. Arietta stood ten paces ahead, peering around a sharp bend. She had an arrow nocked and her bow raised, but had not yet drawn the string back. Joelle was nowhere to be seen.

Kleef went to Arietta's side. A short distance ahead, a pair of orc legs lay on a small boulder, the body above them concealed by another bend in the stony passage. Next to the legs, a second orc slumped against the canyon wall. He had an arrow in his throat and a look of surprise on his brutish face. Like the orcs that had been harassing Faroz's caravan, he was broad-bodied and muscular, with stooped shoulders and long gangling arms. He also wore the same kind of armor—a boiled leather breastplate reinforced with bands of waxed wood.

"Where's Joelle?" Kleef asked.

"Scouting ahead." Arietta gestured at the orc with the arrow in his throat. "What do you think? The same tribe as before?"

"That would be my guess," Kleef said. "It makes more sense than orcs living in the Chondalwood."

"Then the Shadovar must have walked them through the Shadowfell," Arietta said. "There's no way they came through the Chondalwood—not this fast, and certainly not with the treants and satyrs against them."

"I know," Kleef said. "Yder's found us again—and it's my fault."

"Because you had to sleep?" Arietta shook her head. "You stayed awake for five days. No one else could have done such a thing."

"Not because I had to sleep—because Malik's right." Kleef glanced back. The only sign of the little man was the rope snaking across the rocky ground toward the boulder where he was hiding. "I'm bitter and resentful, and Yder is using that against us."

Arietta reluctantly nodded. "You've certainly had reason to be resentful in the past." She pointed at his sword. "But Helm is back now. Perhaps that will make it easier to let go of your anger."

Kleef was still considering her words when Joelle raced around the bend, coming so fast she nearly ran into Kleef.

"Hurry!" she whispered. "We don't have much time."

"Before what?" Kleef asked.

"Orcs." Joelle turned to start back up the narrow gorge. "Dozens, at least—maybe the whole horde."

Arietta started after her, but Kleef remained where he was.

"Why are we going toward them?" he asked.

Joelle paused and craned her neck, looking up the rocky face of the wall beside them. It was as sheer as the cliff they had just ascended—and easily ten times higher.

"Because we can't climb that," she said. "And if we turn back, the only place to go is into the river."

With that, she and Arietta disappeared up the narrow canyon. Kleef was still confused, but there was no remaining behind. He turned to summon Malik and found the little man already on the move, his short sword in hand and a worried look in his eyes.

"I am sure she has a plan," he said. "Even if it is only to limit our suffering by seeing that we die sooner rather than later."

Reluctant to leave Malik alone at the rear of the line, Kleef fell in behind the little man, then checked the agate on Watcher's crossguard. It did not make him feel much safer to see the stone still dark. There could be no doubt now that Yder had found them, so if the Shadovar were not showing themselves yet, it could only mean they were preparing some more perilous trap.

Following the two women up the narrow passage was difficult and tiring. At first, the canyon floor was blanketed in so much soft sand that it was almost impossible to run. After a hundred steps, it became packed with boulders, and they had to clamber and crawl as though climbing through a cavern. Then it sprouted a dense thicket of willow that prevented them from seeing more than a few feet ahead.

The sound of clacking stones and jangling steel began to ring down the canyon. Joelle and Arietta started to hang back with Malik, at times taking him by the arms and dragging him along. Muffled grunts and angry snarls began to punctuate the approaching noise, and Kleef moved into the lead, certain they were about to run headlong into the front of the orc column.

He was just starting to make out individual voices when Joelle caught him by the arm and quietly pulled him toward the canyon wall. For a moment, he didn't understand what she was doing. All he saw was another rocky face, slightly lighter than the stone around it.

Then she drew him toward the downhill side of the light area, where a curving black line marked the seam between the dark rock of the canyon wall and the lighter stone of a boulder. About twelve feet up, the seam widened into the shape of a wedge, and disappearing into this space was Malik's boot.

Joelle quickly wedged her hands into the seam, then scrambled to the top of the boulder and reached down for Watcher. Kleef passed the sword to her and followed her example, and seconds later he found himself looking up a steep rocky chute choked with boulders, loose stones, and long-dead trees. Malik and Arietta were crouched behind a gray log just a few feet above, side by side with their weapons at the ready. A thousand paces beyond them, the chute ended in a small, circular cliff that looked no higher than the one they had climbed just a short time before.

With the willows rustling down in the canyon and the sound of orc voices practically beneath them, they did not dare risk moving. Kleef took his sword back from Joelle, then lay atop the boulder to watch the orcs pass.

At first, the thicket was too dense for him to see much more than an occasional double-bladed axe or bear-skull helmet. But soon enough, the willows fell victim to the constant tramping of the orc column, and he could see that the horde was descending the narrow passage two abreast. The canyon was too serpentine for him to see the length of the column, but the orcs were moving at a steady pace, and Kleef and his companions were still watching more than a quarter hour later.

When the rear of the column finally came into sight, the warriors appeared to be much larger and stronger than those who had passed before. Instead of leather, they were armored in steel scale, and most carried both swords and pikes. And in the center of this bunch marched a huge orc with broad shoulders and tusks long enough to gut a bear. Wearing ornate plate armor and armed with a two-handed sword, he appeared to be their chieftain. Next to him limped a tall, lanky orc in a snakeskin cape over thigh-length chain mail. With a finger bone through his nose and one eye burned out, he was almost certainly a shaman of Gruumsh.

If any Shadovar were accompanying the pair, Kleef saw no sign of them.

As the two orcs passed beneath the chute, the shaman suddenly slowed his pace. He started to look up toward the canyon walls—until the chieftain snarled and cuffed him in the back of the head. The shaman grunted and started forward again, but his gaze drifted back to the chute.

Kleef cursed under his breath and gathered himself to

spring, but Joelle laid a hand on his arm and squeezed. The shaman limped another couple of steps, then stumbled and finally looked away.

The column passed out of view a few minutes later, but the companions remained tense and still until the sound of clattering stones and jangling weapons had faded into nothingness. And even then, when they rose and began to ascend the chute, they said nothing and did their best to climb in silence.

It was a futile effort. No matter how carefully they moved, gravel rattled, stones clattered, and dead branches snapped. Knowing it would not be long before the first orcs reached the end of the slot canyon and passed word back about the dead scouts, Kleef kept one eye on the chute entrance. The shaman had clearly sensed something as he passed, and when it grew apparent that their quarry had escaped, the chute would be the first place the orcs searched.

The companions were about a third of the way up, ascending a field of rocks, when a head-sized stone rolled from beneath Arietta's foot and came tumbling down the slope. Kleef pulled Malik aside, then watched in dismay as the rock bounced off a boulder and went crashing down the chute.

Arietta looked horrified by the misstep, until Joelle turned and reached down the steep slope to give her shoulder a reassuring squeeze.

"I'm surprised it didn't happen sooner," the heartwarder said. "And now, we worry only about getting out of here."

Joelle smiled, and Arietta began to look a little less mortified. The companions began to ascend as fast as possible, doing their best to avoid climbing behind one another so nobody would get hit by a bouncing rock. At times, the slope was so steep they had to scramble on all fours, and often Kleef had to boost Malik over a boulder or up an outcropping. Soon, they were all sweating and huffing, but every step carried them visibly closer to safety, and even Malik did not allow his fatigue to slow him.

They were only a few hundred steps from the top when a signal horn rang out below. It was impossible to see their pursuers over the jumble of boulders and logs between them and the chute entrance, but there could be little doubt that the orcs had picked up their trail. Kleef pointed at the crescent of low cliffs that ringed the top of the slope.

"Almost . . . there," he panted. "Still have plenty of time."

They scrambled over one more boulder field and found only a short, steep slope of loose gravel between them and the cliffs. Kleef stopped there and climbed onto the largest boulder he could find. Then he turned to study the chute below.

The orcs were starting to come into a view, a swarm of hunched figures clambering over boulders and logs, their weapons slung across their backs, their long arms pulling them up the steep slope almost as fast as a human could run. But as they climbed, they were unleashing a small avalanche of stones, filling the chute with a torrent of bouncing stones that felled a steady stream of warriors.

Kleef remained on the boulder for a long while, watching the orcs and trying to catch a glimpse of their leader. He knew better than to think killing the chieftain would make the orcs forsake the Eye of Gruumsh, but it might cause a power struggle and distract them for a while—perhaps long enough for him and his companions to deliver the Eye to Grumbar's Temple.

Unfortunately, the chieftain was nowhere to be seen—no doubt because he was too smart to lead the way into such an obvious deathtrap. Kleef waited until the first orcs were halfway up the chute, then jumped off the boulder.

By then, Joelle had climbed the small cliff and was just disappearing over the top. Malik was at the base, waiting for her to toss the rope down to him. Arietta had stayed behind with Kleef and was standing between two large boulders, her bow in hand and her quiver hanging from her left hip.

Clearly, she thought Kleef intended to do this the hard way. He spent a moment studying the boulder field to be sure that wouldn't be necessary, then waved Arietta toward the cliff.

"Malik will be exposed while he's going up," he said. "That will go faster if you're on top, helping Joelle pull him. I can handle things here."

Arietta cocked an eyebrow. "Kleef, that isn't necessary," she said. "You have nothing to feel guilty about."

Kleef frowned. "Guilty?"

"About your anger with Helm," Arietta said. "After five days without sleep, you were in no condition to contemplate such things."

"You think I'm going to make some kind of last stand? Against hundreds of orcs?"

"Aren't you?"

Kleef shook his head. "No," he said. "That's crazy."

"Then what are you going to do?"

A soft clatter sounded from the base of the cliff. Kleef glanced toward the sound to find the end of the rope lying in the gravel and Malik stepping over to retrieve it.

"I'm just going to slow them down," Kleef said, waving toward one of the boulders he had selected. "Maybe reduce their numbers a bit. You'll see."

Arietta studied the boulder for a moment, then finally nodded. "You'd better not be deceiving me, Kleef." She started up the slope. "I want you climbing that cliff as soon as we have Malik on top."

Kleef smiled. "As you command, my lady."

Now that a rope was hanging over the cliff, the orcs redoubled their efforts and came up the slope even faster than before. They were still too far away for their slings and crude bows to be effective, but that would not remain true for long. Kleef went to a waist-high boulder resting atop another larger stone, then pressed his shoulder to it and pushed.

The boulder slid off so easily that Kleef nearly fell over

headlong. It rolled once, twice—then dropped between two huge monoliths and stopped dead.

The orcs saw what he was attempting and began to break out slings and bows. Kleef picked up a rock the size of his own chest and hurled it down the slope. It bounced off a larger boulder and went arcing through the air, picking up speed as it dropped through the chute. When it hit a second time, it knocked half a dozen smaller stones free, most of which began to roll and pick up momentum. Within moments there were a couple of dozen head-sized stones following the boulder down toward the orcs.

The orcs answered by launching a flight of arrows and stones that was doomed to fall short. Kleef ignored the volley and hurled another boulder down the slope. The result was much the same as the last time, and soon there was a second small avalanche of rocks tumbling down toward the orcs. By the time he had picked up a third boulder, the second was bouncing through the enemy swarm, leaving behind a trail of billowing dust and broken, groaning bodies.

With a river of tumbling rock following close in that second boulder's wake, the survivors scrambled for shelter beneath outcroppings and behind huge monoliths. It was impossible to see how well the strategy protected them, but it allowed Kleef plenty of time to feed the avalanche. He continued to push and hurl boulders as fast as he could move them. Soon, his muscles were trembling and he was out of breath, but the avalanche had become a crashing, rumbling thing that shook the ground and filled the chute with billowing clouds of dust.

Kleef turned away and saw that Malik was already halfway up the cliff, clutching the rope with both hands and walking his feet along the sheer face as Arietta and Joelle pulled him up. Knowing this would be when the little man would be most vulnerable to a Shadovar attack, Kleef pulled Watcher off his back and scrambled up the slope.

But the agate on Watcher's crossguard remained dark, even when he reached the base of the cliff. And that only made him worry more. The orcs could not have found Kleef and his companions without Shadovar help. Yet the Shadovar were nowhere to be seen—even now, when it would be difficult for Malik's companions to defend him.

Kleef could not quite figure out what that meant. Perhaps the orcs were not in constant communication with their allies, or perhaps they did not entirely trust the Shadovar. But what Kleef feared—the thought that was tying his gut into knots—was that the Shadovar were using the orcs to herd them into a trap.

Kleef was still pondering these fears when Malik reached the top of the cliff and disappeared. When none of his companions reappeared in the next couple of minutes, Kleef began to worry that the cliff *had* been the trap, that perhaps it had been the Shadovar pulling Malik up.

Then, finally, Arietta peered over the edge and smiled. "I suppose another apology is in order."

"An apology, my lady?"

"For underestimating you." Arietta glanced down into the dust-choked chute, where the rumble of the avalanche was just starting to fade. "That was a lot more than a hundred orcs you just killed."

She threw the rope down.

Kleef climbed to the cliff-top and saw that the companions had floated so far down the river they had left the Chondalwood behind. Now, they stood on the edge of a wide flat plain with yellow flowers rising from a blanket of new grass. A few leagues distant, the expanse dropped away into a jagged-edged abyss so deep and immense that its shadows seemed to swallow even the far horizon. Above the chasm, a vortex of purple clouds hung swirling with sheet-lightning and balls of green flame.

He was looking at the Underchasm, Kleef realized, and now he knew why the Shadovar had given up the chase.

Now, they could wait for the Eye to come to them.

CHAPTER SEVENTEEN

Aᶠᵗᵉʳ TWO DAYS OF EIGHTEEN-HOUR MARCHES ON NOT
much sleep, Arietta was so foggy-headed that she didn't
realize Joelle had stopped moving until she felt the heartwarder's back against her chest. She quickly reached up and
caught Joelle by the shoulder, steadying them both.

"My apologies," Arietta said. "I wasn't paying—"

"No need to apologize." Joelle placed her hand over Arietta's
and left it there. "We're beyond that now, don't you think?"

Arietta allowed herself a hint of a smile. "I suppose we are."
In truth, she wasn't quite sure how she felt about the night
before—except that it gave her a secret thrill to hear Joelle
mention their intimacies. "But that doesn't give me leave to
run you over."

Joelle shot her a sly grin. "Maybe that was the idea."

Arietta's cheeks grew warm. While it was true that she had
developed a deep and passionate affection for Joelle, it was
equally true that she was just growing accustomed to the idea
of being in love with another woman. She cast a nervous glance
back at Kleef and Malik, who were coming up the gentle rise
behind them, then slipped her hand from beneath Joelle's.

"Bad timing, I'm afraid."

Joelle laughed. "Concerned about what our friends may think?" she asked. "I thought you were done worrying about your noble decorum."

"I am." Arietta stepped around to Joelle's side, where their bodies would not be in such obvious contact. "But there's a difference between following one's heart and making a spectacle of oneself."

"As you wish." Joelle feigned a tone of disappointment. "I suppose I'll just have to control myself until we make camp."

By then, Kleef and Malik had joined them atop the rise. Malik looked from Arietta to Joelle with a smug little grin that suggested he'd seen what had passed between the two and knew exactly what it meant. Kleef simply avoided their eyes and stopped alongside Malik, his gaze fixed on their destination.

From this close, the Underchasm looked like the end of the world, an immense dark void falling away from the jagged edge of a grassy, windswept plain. Here and there, thumb-sized crags of gray stone rose out of the murk like islands out of a foggy sea. A couple of the crags were connected by pale lines that seemed to be ropes or bridges, and the largest was topped by a crownlike shape that suggested a castle and its turrets.

After a moment, Kleef worked his gaze across the grassy plain ahead, no doubt searching for an orc scouting party or Shadovar ambush. When he spotted neither, he frowned and said, "I don't see anything."

"Out in the Underchasm," Joelle said. She pointed at the large stone crag with the crown of castle turrets. "That's our destination: Sadrach's Spire."

"That's where Grumbar's Temple is?" Arietta asked, confused. "A castle aerie?"

"Grumbar's Temple is beneath the castle," Malik said. "Sadrach was a student of elemental magic. He kept temples to all of the Elemental Lords in his home."

"That castle must be leagues from the nearest solid ground," Kleef said. "How do we reach it?"

Arietta pointed at the pale lines she had observed earlier. "Across those bridges, I would wager."

"Bridges?" Kleef's face fell, and he turned to Joelle. "Is there another way across?"

"Not that I'm aware of," Joelle said. "Unless you can fly."

"Or we wish to climb down and go through the Underdark," Malik added. He cast a wary glance toward the angry sky, where a boiling red rift was opening between two banks of purple clouds. "But I do not think we have time for that."

Kleef let out his breath, then said, "Well, at least we know where the Shadovar mean to ambush us."

Arietta saw what he was thinking and nodded. "On the bridges."

"How can you know that?" Malik asked. "The Shadovar are many things, but seldom predictable."

"They are this time." Kleef glanced back over his shoulder, toward a distant, brownish-gray blur—the orc horde coming over the horizon behind them. "Yder has been using the orcs to wear us down. When we reach the bridges, he'll use them to push us into his trap."

"So we destroy the bridges behind us," Arietta said. No sooner had she said this than an even more alarming thought occurred to her. "Unless the Shadovar have *already* destroyed the bridges."

Kleef was quick to shake his head. "They haven't."

"Why not?" Arietta asked. "It would prevent us from delivering the Eye to Grumbar's Temple."

"It would force us to try something desperate," Kleef said. "They'd rather have us on the bridges, where they can anticipate our moves."

"Nor would it be easy for them to undo Sadrach's magic," Malik said. "Those bridges have been there since the Spellplague. If they could be destroyed, I am sure someone would have done it by now."

Arietta frowned. "Why would anyone want to destroy those bridges?" she asked, instantly suspicious. "There's something you haven't told us."

"Nothing of concern," Malik said. "Only that Sadrach and his servants were much changed by the Spellplague, and I doubt the nomads of the Shaar are fond of having them visit in the night."

"Changed how?" Kleef asked.

Malik shrugged. "I know only what my god has shared with me, which is little enough," he said. "But have no fear. He has promised to protect us."

Kleef looked skeptical. "He'd better keep that promise," he said. "Because if one of these servants so much as looks at us wrong, I'm throwing you to the orcs myself."

Malik grew pale. "There is no need for threats," he said. "We are all here to stop Shar."

"Just remember that." Arietta caught Kleef's eye, then added, "But if Malik is right about those bridges being indestructible, we have a more urgent problem. We can't allow ourselves to become trapped between the orcs and the Shadovar."

"Good point." Kleef glanced back toward the orc horde, then started toward the Underchasm. "We need to keep moving."

It wasn't quite what Arietta had meant, but she saw no harm in talking while they walked. She fell in beside the watchman and started through the tall grass.

"Actually, I was thinking of something a bit more unexpected," Arietta said. "We need to find a way to pit the orcs and Shadovar against each other."

"Perhaps you could ask Siamorphe to fly us across the chasm," Malik suggested, squeezing in between Kleef and Arietta. "Surely, even she is more likely to grant such a miracle than are the Shadovar and the orcs."

Kleef scowled at the little man's rudeness, then turned to Arietta. "I hate to say it, but he has a point."

Arietta shook her head. "It doesn't take a miracle—not if we can make them see that their interests are no longer aligned. For instance, if Gruumsh were to recover his eye, what's the first thing he would do?"

"Take horrible vengeance on Luthic, without a doubt," Malik said. "But what good is that to us? Then Luthic would be dead, and Grumbar would have no reason to stay on Toril."

"Wrong." Kleef was starting to sound interested. "Grumbar wouldn't let it go that far. He'd be honor-bound to protect his lover."

"Which means he would have to stay on Toril," Arietta said. "And that's exactly what the Shadovar *don't* want."

"Wait—you want to give the Eye to the orcs?" Joelle's voice was aghast. "Please tell me that's not what you're saying."

"Not quite," Arietta said. "I'm just saying that if we want to reach Grumbar's Temple alive, we need to make the orcs see that the Shadovar are no more on their side than ours."

The companions continued toward the Underchasm, refining Arietta's plan as they walked. Malik favored trying to strike a deal with the orcs, then double-crossing them when the Shadovar arrived to interfere. Kleef thought it made more sense to challenge the orc chieftain to single combat and put the Eye up as the prize. In the end, they realized they needed to be subtler—that it wasn't the orcs they needed to trick, it was the Shadovar.

They stopped long enough to make a few preparations, then resumed their march. Although they were now so close to their goal they could actually see it, the scale of the Underchasm made it difficult to estimate the remaining distance. For the next two hours, the swath of grassy plain in front of them never seemed to narrow, nor the stone crags out in the abyss to grow much larger or more distinct. Only the red rift in the sky appeared to draw nearer, becoming wider and brighter and driving the two banks of purple clouds down toward the horizon.

Every now and then, a blazing white vortex would form somewhere inside the rift and drop a swirling column of flame down into the Underchasm. The plain would shudder and the wind would boom and shriek, and sometimes there would come a blast of heat so ferocious that grass withered and dirt smoked. Other times, ranks of lightning would dance across the horizon, seeming to wall off some distant part of the world and cleave it away forever. Once, a sheet of blue ice dropped from the sky and sliced into the ground alongside them, opening up a mile-long fissure that immediately began to vent a curtain of frigid white fog.

Finally, the grassy plain began to narrow, and the rim of the Underchasm drew visibly closer. The nearest of the stone crags slowly swelled into a mountaintop, and the pale line that connected it to the lip of the abyss became an impossibly long bridge. A pair of stone pylons appeared on the brink of the chasm, serving as the entrance to the bridge and anchoring the thick, translucent cables that held it suspended in the air.

Kleef removed his sword and scabbard from his back and, keeping one eye on the agate on Watcher's crossguard, cautiously led the way forward. As the companions drew nearer to the bridge, the plain grew barren and lifeless, exposing a powdery brown loam that had been compacted into a network of foot trails. The trails converged at the bridge entrance, where a dozen wood poles stood, planted in a rough semicircle. Some were no more that waist-height, and a couple were as tall as Kleef. But all had a chain dangling from the top and a carpet of bones scattered around the base.

Lying chained to one of the shorter posts was a black-and-brown billy goat. When he noticed the companions, he staggered to his feet and turned to watch them approach. His eyes were wary and pale, with elongated horizontal pupils that reminded Arietta of the agate on Kleef's sword.

Kleef stopped a few paces away and asked no one in particular, "What's this? An offering?"

"Or perhaps a gift," Malik suggested. "If the nomads leave food here, Sadrach's servants will have less reason to visit their camps at night."

Kleef studied the goat for a moment, then went to his side and kneeled next to his head. The goat shied away, but Kleef reached out and gently drew him back, then began to fiddle with the iron collar around his neck.

"Are you mad?" Malik demanded. "You will turn Sadrach's servants against us if you steal what is meant for them!"

Kleef continued to work on the collar. "Sadrach's monsters have nothing to be angry about," he said. "The only ones I'm stealing from are the orcs."

He looked back the way they'd come, to where the orc horde had become a churning mass of flesh and iron, spreading across the plain behind them. Arietta could already see the advance guard out in front, distant knots of stooped shapes that left ribbons of trampled grass in their wake, and she knew it would not be long before the first scouts arrived at the bridge.

"Kleef's right," Arietta said. "The first orcs are going to be here within the hour—and there's no need to appease *them*."

She retrieved the top of a human skull from among the bones surrounding one of the tall poles, then filled it with water and kneeled down in front of the goat. The beast fixed his eerie eyes on hers, and for an instant she felt as though she were staring into the heavens themselves, a realm of iridescent clouds and mountains the color of molten gold, of endless silver waterfalls and alabaster palaces reflected in shimmering lakes.

Then the goat lowered his nose, and the image vanished from Arietta's mind so quickly she was not even sure she had seen it. The goat drank until the skull was empty, then nosed the makeshift bowl from Arietta's hands and turned his gaze on Kleef. A moment later, the iron collar finally snapped open, and the goat bleated in what may well have been gratitude.

Kleef pointed in the direction opposite the approaching horde. "You'd better hurry," he said. "You don't want those orcs catching sight of you."

The goat looked from him to Arietta, and a tree of

lightning snaked across the red sky. A heartbeat later, a peal of thunder crashed over the Underchasm, so sudden and loud that Arietta found herself curled into a ball on the still-shuddering ground, with dust billowing up around her and no clear memory of how she had gotten there. Kleef was next to her, and Malik and Joelle were close by, also on the ground and looking frightened and confused.

Only the goat remained standing, his eerie eyes watching them with an expression that seemed both expectant and mocking. He shook the dust from his coat and trotted over to stand between the stone pylons that served as the gateway onto the bridge.

Kleef looked over at Arietta, his brow raised in bewilderment. "What do you make of that?"

"I have no idea." Arietta returned to her feet. "But did you notice that his eyes—"

"Look like Helm's Eye?" Kleef stood and retrieved Watcher, then turned the agate on the crossguard upward and spent a moment examining it. "How could I miss it?"

"Then perhaps we should take that as a sign and keep moving," Joelle said, joining them. "We aren't all that far ahead of the orcs."

Malik also joined them, and they stepped between the pylons with the goat. For a moment, they all stood waiting, looking down at the beast and half-expecting it to lead the way.

Finally, Malik let out an exasperated snort. "It is just a stupid animal that does not have the sense to run from its own destiny."

The goat looked up at him and bleated.

"Sadrach's servants are going to eat you alive," Malik said. "That is your destiny."

The goat lowered his horns as though he were going to butt Malik, then simply backed away and looked at Kleef.

Kleef laughed. "I'd like to kill Malik, too," he said. "But Joelle keeps saying we need him."

He led the way onto the bridge itself, with the goat close behind. Malik followed, and Arietta and Joelle brought up the rear, walking side by side on a thin metal deck barely wide enough to hold a donkey cart. As they moved away from the anchoring pylons on the rim of the Underchasm, the deck began to shudder and bounce beneath their footfalls. But the translucent suspension cables, which looked more like twisted glass than any sort of metal, remained taut and unmoving. Arietta thought about the weight of the orc horde pursuing them and wondered if the structure was as indestructible as Malik had implied. She tried to take comfort from the goat, which seemed completely at home on the bridge, trotting along close on Kleef's heels and nonchalantly peering between the support lines into the abyss below.

When Arietta finally gathered the courage to look for herself, her heart sank. Hundreds of feet below lay a gray blanket of shadowstuff, its surface an indistinct zone of slowly expanding murk. She looked back at the rim of the Underchasm and saw a dark stain creeping up the wall, just a little above the shadowstuff itself.

"It's started," Joelle said, also peering over the side of the bridge. "Time is against us."

Arietta looked toward the center of the Underchasm and found herself inclined to agree. Though she could see a second bridge curving out from behind the mountaintop ahead, it quickly narrowed into imperceptibility, and she could not tell which of the distant crags it led to—or how many more such bridges there might be between them and Sadrach's Spire. But they clearly had a long walk ahead—and plenty of trouble to face along the way.

They continued along the bridge at a steady but unhurried pace, deliberately giving the orcs time to close the gap behind them. Given the rising sea of shadowstuff and the uncertain distance to their destination, it was a nerve-racking way to travel—but far better than running headlong into a Shadovar trap.

Soon enough, a line of distant figures appeared on the bridge and rapidly began to swell into the stooped shapes of running orcs. As the column grew longer and more distinct, the decking began to tremble and thrum beneath the pounding of hundreds of hobnailed boots. Arietta looked back to check on the ever-growing column and was surprised to find the orcs running down a slight incline. It didn't make sense, but that was definitely the way it appeared.

Whether the bridge had always run at a slight downward angle or had simply begun to sag beneath the weight of the horde, she could not say. But after a while, the suspension cables began to hum and shimmer, and when she looked over her shoulder again, she found that the orc column extended a full league behind her, all the way back to the chasm rim.

And the front of the column was only three arrow flights away—close enough to make out the gray-yellow ovals of individual faces. Arietta turned forward again, where a jagged wall of stone—the first of the stony crags they had seen from the plain—now loomed over the far end of the bridge. They weren't close enough yet to tell how the suspension cables were attached to the mountainside, but it looked as though the bridge simply entered a tunnel that had been cut into the sheer face of a cliff.

Kleef and the goat were now traveling side by side, with Malik three paces behind them and Arietta and Joelle bringing up the rear. Joelle's brow was furrowed in concentration, and she was glancing back and forth between the orcs behind them and the crag ahead. No doubt, she was wondering the same thing as Arietta—whether the tunnel was where the Shadovar were waiting to ambush them.

Joelle caught Arietta's eye. "Is it time?"

Arietta nodded. "I think it is." She looked forward again, then yelled, "Kleef, let's move along!"

Kleef glanced back at the long line of orcs, then drew Watcher from its scabbard and set off at a brisk trot. The goat continued to keep pace, loping alongside him with an oddly wolflike gait. Malik lasted perhaps a quarter of a league before he began to fall behind, and Arietta and Joelle soon found themselves half-dragging him along by the arms.

The decking growled and shuddered as the orc vanguard broke into a full sprint. Arietta glanced back and felt her heart rise into her throat. The leading orcs were less than two arrow-flights away and coming fast.

"Why the big eyes?" Joelle asked, looking over at Arietta. "This is the plan . . . right?"

Arietta nodded. "Right," she said. "As long as we don't let them catch us before we reach the Shadovar ambush."

"And there is the weakness in . . . your mad plan," Malik said, huffing for breath. "They are going to catch us whether we let them or not."

Arietta looked forward, toward the end of the bridge. They were so close to the crag that all she could see was the square maw of a tunnel entrance surrounded by a jagged wall of dun-colored cliff. To her surprise, the bridge's suspension cables were not anchored to the stone by any sort of device. Instead, they emerged from the crag as a cluster of huge, limpid crystals that came together in a twisting mass of glasslike cable, then kinked sharply upward.

Arietta stopped and leaned over the side of the bridge, peering down toward the foot of the cliff. With the Shadowfell emerging out of the depths of the Underchasm, it was impossible to see the bottom of the crag. But she could see enough to tell that its base was narrowing instead of expanding, and she did not like what the shape seemed to suggest.

The crag wasn't a mountaintop at all; it was an earth-mote. And it wasn't supporting the bridge—the bridge was supporting *it*.

The growl in the decking swelled to a rumble, and the hum in the suspension cables began to rise and fall in pitch. Malik grabbed her by the elbow and tugged her toward the tunnel.

"This is no time to sulk," he said. "Your plan may be a reckless one, but it is certainly better than giving up!"

Arietta started forward again, half-expecting to find herself plunging into the Underchasm at any moment. With its suspension cables of living crystal and earthmote anchoring piers, the bridge was a marvel of elemental magic. But the earthmotes of Faerûn had fallen many tendays ago, and now the ones on the way to Sadrach's Spire were dragging the bridge down instead of supporting it. Could that be because the air primordial, Akadi, had already left Toril?

And if Akadi was already gone, how long could it be before Grumbar followed? Arietta had only to look at the fiery rift in the sky to know that Abeir and Toril were parting fast, and it seemed obvious that the earth primordial would need to make his choice soon—perhaps even before Arietta and her companions had a chance to deliver Luthic's token of love.

The companions had closed to within fifty paces of the cliff face when Kleef finally drew up short and raised his sword, the hilt turned to display the glowing agate. The goat stepped in front of him, his body positioned crosswise between him and the mouth of the tunnel. His head was lowered and his tail twitching, and Arietta half-expected the beast to break into a charge.

Arietta and the others stopped behind Kleef and peered into the murky depths ahead. The tunnel was the same width as the bridge and a little higher than Kleef was tall, with a tiny square of light at the far end that suggested it was both straight and long. There were no figures silhouetted against the light, but Arietta knew better than to think the tunnel empty. Even if there were no niches or alcoves along the walls, the Shadovar could be lurking within the shadows themselves, waiting to emerge until the companions had entered their trap.

She turned to Malik. "Are you ready?"

Malik shrugged and reached inside his robe. "Does it

matter?" he asked. "Your foolish plan will either save us or kill us, and the time has come to find out which."

He withdrew the Eye of Gruumsh from its hiding place, and Arietta sensed its profane gaze on her, a cold nettling touch that made her feel sick and weak and vile. When she looked away, the touch became an icy chill that raced down her spine in a shiver of fear and revulsion. Had Arietta not experienced the sensation twice before, she might have cowered in terror or fled in a blind panic. As it was, she merely looked behind them and saw that the orcs were more frenzied than ever, battering and shoving each other in their lust to reach the Eye first.

Good.

Now that they had it in sight, they wouldn't want anyone else leaving with it—not even their Shadovar allies. The orcs in front raised their bows and began to loose on the run. Their arrows rarely landed on the bridge and fell short when they did, but Arietta knew that would change all too soon. She stepped to Malik's side, then motioned for Joelle to take the opposite flank.

"Hold the Eye over your head," she said. "Make certain it's looking in their direction."

Malik did as she asked. The orcs broke into a roaring battle cry, and the decking began to shudder with the fury of their charge.

"This will never work," Malik complained. "We are only inflaming their lust for our blood."

"Give it time," Arietta said.

She took her bow off her shoulder, then watched as an orc loosed an arrow in their direction. The shaft dropped a dozen paces short and came sliding along the bridge in their direction. She nocked her own arrow and returned the attack.

Her shaft took its target high in the chest and sent him sprawling into the warriors behind him. Half a dozen fell, and Arietta saw three figures tumble out beneath the suspension cables and plummet into the Shadowfell far below. She loosed another arrow and downed a second target, with much the same effect as the first, and the orc charge became more of a churning snarl.

"Now, Malik," Arietta said. "Let them see what happens if they keep coming."

Keeping the Eye high in the air, Malik stepped to the side of the bridge and held it out over the Underchasm. At the same time, Joelle raised both hands toward the orcs.

"Stop!" she yelled. "Stop, or he'll drop it!"

Whether or not the orcs comprehended Joelle's exact words, they understood the message, and the column came to a slow, lurching halt. The warriors in front nocked arrows or loaded their slings and stood just seventy paces away, their angry glares shifting back and forth between the Eye of Gruumsh and Arietta and her companions.

A murmur rolled forth from deep in the column, and Arietta soon saw warriors scrambling to make way for a huge orc in ornate plate mail. Following close behind him was a lanky, one-eyed orc with a finger bone through his nose.

"Kleef, it looks like the chieftain and his shaman are coming," Arietta said over her shoulder. "Any sign of the Shadovar?"

"Not yet," Kleef replied. "Just stick to the plan. They'll be out."

Arietta watched as the chieftain and his shaman shouldered their way to the front of column, then continued forward at a walk, leading the rest of the column behind them. Arietta allowed them to approach to within fifty paces before finally nocking an arrow.

"Close enough," she said, raising her bow. "We can talk from there."

The chieftain continued to approach, his long tusks glistening with saliva and his crimson eyes burning with malice. Arietta dropped her aim and let fly, putting the arrow through the thin metal of the bridge decking where his foot was about to come down.

The orc snapped the arrow beneath his boot and continued to approach, the shaman still at his side—and the rest of the horde at his back. Arietta nocked another arrow and aimed at the chieftain's head.

"One warning is all you get," she said. "Any closer and you die first."

The chieftain paused, then locked gazes with her and signaled the column to wait. He leaned toward his shaman and appeared to ask for a translation, then started forward again. The shaman walked at his side, making a show of gesturing at Arietta and the Eye as he spoke, but Arietta suspected it was all a ruse. The chieftain's quick reaction to her threat suggested he had understood exactly what she had said. He was just pretending to need a translation in order to work his way closer.

After a few steps, the chieftain growled something to the shaman, and the shaman called out, "If you return Gruumsh's Eye now, Hadarog will give you quick deaths." His voice was deep and raspy, but with a brittle edge that made it seem as though he were in pain. "But for every minute you make him wait, you will suffer an hour."

"Or we could just drop the Eye into the Shadowfell and let Shar have it," Arietta replied. "I'm sure she'll be happy to return it to Gruumsh—when the time suits her."

A flash of alarm shot through Hadarog's red eyes, but he recovered quickly and managed to mask his concern as he pretended to listen to his shaman. The two orcs were less than forty paces away now and still coming, and Arietta had no doubt that the chieftain intended to attack once he drew near enough.

After a moment, the shaman said, "Hadarog says the choice is yours. The Shadovar are our allies, and he is certain the Mistress of the Night will return Gruumsh's Eye as soon as she receives it."

Arietta cocked a brow. "Is that so?" She drew her bowstring back and shifted her aim to Hadarog's left eye. "Then go ahead. Call the attack and see how Gruumsh rewards you in the next life."

Hadarog finally stopped, his heavy jaw clenching in anger.

Arietta smiled. "You didn't become a leader by being stupid, I see." She let the tension off her bow, but kept the arrow pointed at the orc's face. "If you let Shar have the Eye, she'll use it to make a slave of Gruumsh."

The shaman started to translate, but Hadarog silenced him with a snarl. He took another step forward, then asked, "What you want?"

"Not much," Arietta said. "We give you the Eye, and you give us a five-minute head start."

The shaman spoke to Hadarog in their own language. Arietta would have liked to know what they were saying, but her language magic only worked when she touched the subject—and the last thing she wanted to do right now was get close enough to an orc to touch him.

After a short conversation, the shaman said, "Hadarog says you would do better to let him kill you now. The Shadovar are waiting to ambush you, and you have no place to go."

"Not yet." Arietta kept her gaze fixed on Hadarog. "But once you have the Eye, that will change."

Hadarog narrowed his red eyes. "Change how?"

"The Shadovar can't allow you to return the Eye to Gruumsh." Arietta needed to be both quick and direct in her explanation, as she would not have much time to make Hadarog doubt his allies. "Once Gruumsh has his eye back, he'll retaliate against Luthic for stealing it—and then Grumbar will be forced to stay and defend her."

Hadarog scowled and looked to his shaman. The pair held a brief, testy conversation that Arietta knew could come to only one conclusion. Whether they believed her or not, they would want to recover the Eye themselves and claim the credit for returning it to Gruumsh. The only thing they could be debating now was whether Arietta and her friends were trying to trick them.

Arietta glanced back at Malik, who groaned on cue and let his hands drop a few inches.

"If you do not hurry, my weary arms will make their own choice," he warned. "The Eye is as heavy as a boulder. I cannot hold it another minute."

Arietta nodded, then turned back to Hadarog. "Do we have a bargain?" she asked. "Or shall we fight and let Shar sort it out?"

She pulled her bowstring back, making it clear who would be the first to die if Hadarog chose to fight.

Hadarog glared at the tip of the arrow for so long Arietta began to fear he might fight. Then, finally, he met her gaze again.

"No fighting. Yet," he said. "Leave the Eye, and we give you a head start. But you're wrong. The Shadovar don't care about the Eye. They only want you stopped."

"We'll see." Arietta shot him a smirk, then called over her shoulder, "All right, Malik. Bring the Eye over."

"At last!" Malik drew the Eye back toward his chest, then stepped to Arietta's side and whispered, "What now?"

"Buy time," Kleef said, also whispering. "Here come the shades."

Resisting the impulse to look back at the tunnel, Arietta kept her attention fixed on Hadarog. "Back away fifty paces, then we'll put the Eye on the bridge and leave."

Hadarog shook his head. "Give the Eye and leave now. We will give you your five-minute lead."

"I don't think so," Arietta said. She continued to hold the arrow on her bowstring. "As soon as we're far enough away, you'll just snatch the Eye and attack us anyway."

"Glomred keeps good track of time." Hadarog clapped his shaman—Glomred—on the shoulder, then attempted a smile that came out as more of a snarl. "Honest."

Arietta scowled, pretending to think. "Let me ask my friends."

She leaned toward Joelle, pretending to consult—then saw Glomred's single eye go wide with alarm. The shaman turned to Hadarog, pointed past the companions toward the earthmote, and spoke rapidly in their own language. Arietta glanced back and saw the Shadovar rushing out of the tunnel, their tall prince leading the way. Yder's steel-colored eyes went straight to Kleef.

"Fool!" the prince said. "You are going to lose the Eye either way. Bring it to us, and Shar will reward you all."

Kleef's shoulders sagged, and he spoke over his shoulder to his companions. "I don't know if this is going to work," he said. "I think he knows what—"

"It's going to work," Arietta said, realizing that Yder still had a hold on Kleef. "You mustn't let him into your thoughts. You *won't*."

Arietta spoke the last two words in a tone of command, and Kleef's shoulders immediately squared. He raised his sword and braced his feet.

"You want the Eye?" he asked. "Then come and get it."

Yder's eyes flashed silver. Then he raised a hand and sent five tentacles of shadowstuff writhing down the bridge.

A furious bellow erupted from Hadarog's direction, and the bridge began to shudder and bounce as the orc horde resumed its charge. Arietta saw Kleef raise Watcher and step past the goat to meet Yder's shadow tentacles, then she looked back at Hadarog.

The orc chieftain had drawn a huge two-handed sword and was no more than twenty paces away. But Glomred worried Arietta most. The shaman had drawn a dagger of sharpened bone and was jabbing it into his own thigh, at the same time gesturing in their direction and calling out to Gruumsh in his own language.

Arietta shifted her aim and loosed.

The arrow took Glomred square in the chest, piercing his chain mail hauberk and sending him staggering back. As he struggled to stay upright, the shaman managed to curl his fingers into the shape of a claw, and Arietta felt something icy and sharp rake down her ribcage.

Her left side erupted into deep throbbing pain, and her bow arm went weak. She staggered back, watching in horror as a trio of Joelle's white darts burned through Hadarog's ornate armor and failed to slow his charge.

Behind her, Malik asked, "Now?"

Arietta and Joelle answered together, "Yes!"

The Eye of Gruumsh's dark hunger vanished as Malik slipped the orb back into its hiding place, and then Hadarog was in front of them, his huge sword sweeping across the bridge at neck height. Arietta felt Joelle's hand on the back of her collar, pulling her down, and they landed on their backs side by side.

Arietta shifted her bow to her right hand and pushed it beneath the orc chieftain's feet as he charged past. She managed to hook his far ankle. Then, as he tried to take his next step, she jerked the bow, pulling his front foot from beneath him.

Hadarog slammed down face-first, so hard the decking jumped.

A few paces beyond the orc chieftain, Kleef and the goat were making a stand against the Shadovar, Kleef's sword flashing and whirling as he hacked limbs and blocked shadow magic. The goat danced through the shadow warriors' legs, butting and bleating and somehow not getting himself killed. Malik was nowhere to be seen, of course, though Arietta could not imagine where he had found to hide.

Behind her, the roaring of the orc horde was approaching fast, and the bridge was shaking beneath their feet. She felt Joelle push her toward the orc chieftain.

"Take him!" Joelle said, jumping up. "I'll slow the others."

Arietta dropped her bow, then rose to a knee. She felt as though her entire side were peeling away from her ribs.

She glanced down and saw nothing but blood and flaps of hanging skin, and her vision began to narrow.

She reached for her sword anyway, but by then Hadarog had rolled into a sitting position and was bringing his own blade around at chest height. Arietta went cold and weak inside and knew she was going to die—until she saw Malik pulling himself up over the edge of the bridge, a black dagger in his hand and his gaze fixed on the back of the orc's head.

Hadarog seemed to sense the attack coming and leaned away at the last instant, and instead of sinking into the back of the orc's skull, the dagger opened a long gash along the side of his neck.

It didn't matter. The color drained from Hadarog's face in an instant, then the sword slipped from his hands and went spinning between the support lines to tumble down into the Underchasm.

A deafening roar sounded from the direction of the orc horde. Malik glanced toward the cacophony, and his face went pale with fear. For an instant, Arietta thought he would use his Chosen ability to vanish again—which would have been the smart thing to do, given that he was still carrying the Eye.

Instead, Malik clambered over Hadarog's body and pulled her to her feet. "I should never have doubted you," he said, tucking the black dagger back into his robe. "Your plan is working beautifully."

Arietta glanced back and found Joelle racing toward them at a sprint, with a long line of orcs just a half-dozen steps behind her. She took Arietta's arm from Malik, then stepped past Hadarog's corpse to take a position close behind Kleef. Malik positioned himself in the center of the group, his ability to vanish so effective that were he not pressed against her, even Arietta would not have known where he was hiding.

"Now, Kleef!" she said. "And make it fast!"

Kleef quickly pivoted to one side, then used the flat of Watcher's blade to send first one, then two shades stumbling past them toward the charging orc horde.

The result was instantaneous, a cacophony of sizzling shadow magic and clanging blades, punctuated by the screams and squeals of dying orcs. Kleef pivoted toward the opposite side of the bridge and, aided by some timely butts from the goat, sent three more shades staggering into the fray.

After that, the battle quickly became the chaotic three-sided melee that Arietta had hoped for. Kleef killed another shade, and the goat knocked one off the bridge into the Underchasm. Malik slipped away from the group and vanished into the general confusion, and the orcs continued to push the fight back toward the earthmote. Finally, there was just Yder ahead, standing in the mouth of the tunnel, less than a dozen steps ahead.

Yder studied the companions for a moment, glaring, then raised his hand and sent a disk of shadow spinning down the bridge toward them.

Kleef leaped to defend them, bringing his sword around to deflect the attack. The disk divided on Watcher's blade, then hit the support lines beneath the suspension cables.

Arietta felt her stomach rise into her chest, half-expecting to feel the bridge fall away and find herself plummeting into the Underchasm below, but that didn't happen. Sadrach's magic was still too strong, and it was the shadow disk that dissolved into a spray of darkness.

Yder smiled, displaying a mouthful of long, white fangs.

"Not yet," he said. "But soon."

The Shadovar stepped back into the tunnel and vanished into the murk.

CHAPTER EIGHTEEN

THE GOAT REARED UP ON HIS HIND LEGS, THEN DROPPED HIS head and slammed his horns into the castle gates. A hollow *boom* echoed through the entryway, and the goat staggered back, bleating and shaking his head. It was the fifth time the beast had rammed the gates, and Kleef saw no sign that he intended to stop until he had battered them down.

"There is something wrong with that goat," Malik said. "Surely, even a stupid beast can see that the only thing he is cracking is his own skull."

"Determination is a virtue," Kleef said, glancing around. "Besides, he has the right idea. That looks like our only way in."

After a long, arduous flight across dozens of bridges and sagging earthmotes, the companions had finally reached Sadrach's Spire and were now stalled inside a small entrance grotto. The walls and ceiling had been carved from native stone, without any of the arrow loops or murder holes that would have lined the entry vault of a typical gatehouse. Beyond the grotto, a fierce fire-hail raged over the entire Underchasm, hammering the bridge they had just crossed with pellets of yellow flame—and forestalling any attempt to scale the castle walls.

Out on the bridge, only a few hundred paces distant, the orc horde was just coming into view through the fire-hail. They were advancing at a snail's pace, crouched down low and creeping across the bridge with their breastplates held over their heads. Kleef was too far away to tell how well the makeshift shields were protecting them, but it would not be long, he suspected, before they saw the dark shape of the grotto's mouth and grew eager to reach shelter.

Another *boom* echoed through the grotto, and Kleef turned to find the goat staggering back from the gate again. Deciding to take his cue from the beast and try something, Kleef drew Watcher and stepped forward to start hacking—then heard stone crackling beside him.

He turned to find a horizontal viewing slot opening in the grotto wall. A pair of large brown eyes appeared behind the slot and stared out at him. Rimmed in kohl and set into a face the color of alabaster, they were young and female—and so distant and expressionless that Kleef was not quite sure they belonged to a human.

"Well met," Kleef said. "My friends and I beg leave to come inside. It's important."

The eyes flickered from Kleef to the goat to the front of the grotto, where Joelle was cleaning the four long slashes that ran down Arietta's ribcage. Despite Joelle's best efforts to heal them, the wounds had started to fester, and Arietta's brow was beaded with fever. Malik claimed the purulence was because Gruumsh's fury was stronger than Sune's love, and Kleef was beginning to fear the little man was right.

A small voice arose from the other side of the viewing slot. "But she's not dead yet."

"No," Kleef said, puzzled by the odd response. "She's been wounded, but she's a long way from dead."

The eyes clouded with confusion. "Then why bring her here?"

"Because we weren't about to leave her behind," Kleef said. "We've traveled a long way to—"

"But you're not dead, either."

"Not yet," Kleef said, glancing toward Malik. He was starting to think that there was something the little man had neglected to tell them about Sadrach's Spire. "But that may change soon, if you don't let us in."

Again, the eyes clouded with confusion. "You want to come inside while you're still alive?"

Kleef nodded. "That's right," he said. "We need to deliver—"

"No, that can't happen." The eyes vanished from view, and the voice grew muffled. "Come back when you're dead."

The goat hit the gate again, this time so hard Kleef could hear the *boom* echoing inside the gate tower itself. The kohl-rimmed eyes appeared again immediately.

"And make Peox stop that," the woman said. "He'll wake Grandfather."

"Peox?" Kleef repeated. "You know this goat?"

"Of course," the woman replied. "He was one of the wall-bound, but now he makes too much noise. That's why I left him for the tribes."

Before Kleef could ask what the wallbound were—or who the woman was—the eyes vanished from the viewport again.

"Wait!"

Kleef rapped on the grotto wall—then cried out in astonishment as a stone hand emerged beneath the viewport and grabbed his arm. He tried to jerk free, only to have the hand clamp down and stop him. A heavy-jawed face formed out of the rock above the viewport and glared out at him.

"Quiet!" The voice was deep and grating. "Gingrid is right. You'll wake Sadrach—and nobody wants that."

Kleef resisted the urge to attempt freeing himself again. "Then let us inside," he said. "We need to reach Grumbar's Temple."

The stony hand clamped down so hard Kleef feared his arm would break. "Your need means nothing to me," he said. "And you are in no position to threaten."

Kleef started to raise Watcher to free himself, but Malik was already at his side, pushing the sword down.

"We are here to threaten no one," the little man said. "Please forgive the oaf his poor choice of words. He is a fool who will be dead soon enough as it is."

The face continued to glare at Kleef for a moment, then finally said, "Until that happens, see that he stays quiet."

The hand released Kleef's arm, then it and the face melted back into the grotto wall.

Kleef whirled on Malik, forcing him back against the gate. "What is this place?"

Malik spread his hands. "How should I know?"

"Because they keep saying we can't come inside until we're dead." Kleef caught Malik by his collar. "And you're a Chosen of Myrkul."

"I know only what my god has shared with me," Malik said, repeating something he had told Kleef before. "That we would find Grumbar's Temple in the catacombs beneath Sadrach's Castle."

"Catacombs?" Kleef had a sinking feeling he understood why Gingrid refused to let them inside alive—and why Malik had been so reluctant to share what he knew about the castle. "Is this some kind of charnel house?"

The goat hit the gate again. Another loud *boom* echoed through the entryway, then half a dozen stony faces and twice as many arms emerged from the grotto walls, demanding quiet and grabbing for any living thing they could reach.

Peox danced into the center of the grotto and stood bleating at his attackers. A pair of hands grabbed at Joelle, while a third caught Arietta's shoulder and pulled her against the wall.

Kleef saved Joelle by using Malik like a club to knock aside the hands grabbing for her, then he slapped the flat of Watcher's blade into the hand holding Arietta. To his relief, the sword's magic was powerful enough to make the stony fingers flex open. He quickly spun around and, still using the flat of the blade, slapped aside a second attempt to grab both women. By then, Joelle and Arietta were retreating into the center of the grotto.

Kleef wasted no time stepping into the mouth, where he held Malik just inches from the bridge, turned so the little man could look out at the fire-hail bouncing and smoking off the thin metal decking. The orcs had crept to within two-hundred paces and were now more visible, a long line of stooped figures cowering beneath their breast-plates and inching steadily closer to Sadrach's Castle.

Malik's eyes grew as round as coins. "Have you lost your mind?" he cried. "Think of the Eye!"

Kleef hesitated. The Eye was the problem, of course. They couldn't retrieve it without Malik, and that meant Kleef couldn't drop him into the Underchasm or toss him to the orcs—no matter how badly the little man had betrayed his companions.

But Kleef still needed to know what they were walking into.

"The Eye won't matter if we don't survive to deliver it." He brought his arm back, as though preparing to toss Malik out into the fire-hail. "And you were warned. I told you what would happen if you lied about this place."

"But I spoke no lies," Malik said. "Once we are inside, my god will protect us. I swear!"

"Sure he will," Kleef said. "Once we're all undead."

Hoping to scare Malik into blurting out the rest of the truth, he started to bring his arm forward—only to have a hand catch him beneath the elbow.

"Kleef, wait." Arietta's voice was weak, but still strong enough to make it clear she was giving him an order. "We need to hear him out."

Joelle caught Kleef's other arm. "Please." She spoke in a soothing tone, and the anger began to drain out of him. "Sune wouldn't have sent us here to die. Give him a chance to explain."

"What's to explain?" Kleef demanded, fighting to resist

her charm magic. He nodded back toward the grotto wall. "You heard them. They won't let us into the castle until we're dead—and Malik is a Chosen of Myrkul. He's been planning to turn us into undead from the start."

"Not so!" Malik said. "I am here to *protect* you from the undead."

"Then why won't they open the gate?" Kleef demanded.

"How am I to know?" Malik turned to Joelle. "Perhaps this is why Sune sent the oaf to us in the first place. He has certainly brought nothing but trouble otherwise."

It took an act of will for Kleef not to bring his arm forward and send Malik tumbling down the bridge. He settled for knotting the little man's collar tighter, then he turned to Arietta and cocked an eyebrow.

Arietta sighed. "He's trying to shift the blame. I see that." She paused, then added, "But I believe him—at least the part about not planning this."

"You do?" Kleef asked. "Why? He tried to kill you once himself."

"And then he risked his life to save me from Hadarog," Arietta reminded him. "If Malik was just planning to let me die here, why would he take a chance like that?"

Kleef frowned. "I don't know." He had already heard a description of the orc chieftain's death, so the only thing that came as a surprise was the part about the little man endangering himself. He looked to Malik, then asked, "You risked your life?"

"Indeed," Malik said. "There were a thousand orcs coming from one direction and a dozen shades from the other, but when I saw the danger that had befallen Arietta, I did not give a second thought to putting my own life at risk."

"Sure you didn't," Kleef said, more suspicious than ever. "And what about the Eye?"

Malik's expression turned wary. "What of it?"

"You didn't worry about putting the Eye at risk?" Kleef

asked. "Because that, I just can't imagine. The one thing you do well is protect the Eye."

"With no thanks to you," Malik said, too quickly. "After you revealed its hiding place to the Shadovar, it is a wonder I still have shoulders for my robe to hang on."

"And now, you're just trying to change the subject." Arietta removed her hand from Kleef's elbow, then asked, "You're hiding something again. Why did you save my life?"

When Malik did not respond quickly enough, Kleef started to pivot his hips around, as though preparing to send Malik tumbling out onto the bridge.

"Because Joelle needs your love!" Malik cried. "It is the only way to tie Grumbar to this world."

Kleef stopped midpivot and drew Malik back into the shelter of the grotto. He didn't understand what the little man was implying, but he did know the ring of truth when he heard it. He glanced over and saw a gleam of recognition creeping into Joelle's eyes. He turned back to Malik.

"Joelle needs Arietta's love *why*, exactly?" Kleef asked. "And don't even think about dodging the question. We have no time for guessing games."

To drive home the point, he pointed his chin down the bridge. The orcs had crept to within a hundred and fifty paces, close enough that he was starting to see red eyes and gnashing tusks.

Malik turned to Arietta. "It will be a great honor," he said. "You will be the one who stops Shar."

"By doing what?" Kleef whipped Malik toward the fire-hail, then pulled him back at the last second. "Final chance."

"I think Malik is referring to the binding ritual." Joelle's voice was warm and kind—a sure sign that she was trying to use her charm magic. "When the Eye of Gruumsh is placed on Grumbar's altar, it must be done by someone utterly devoted to her beloved."

Knowing how his resolve would weaken if he turned to

address Joelle, Kleef was careful to keep his attention on Malik. "And then what happens to her?" He brought Watcher's tip up and pressed it beneath Malik's chin. "Be truthful."

"I know only that she must die for her lover," Malik said. "It is the only way to make Sune's magic work—and since you were too selfish to accept the job yourself, the duty has fallen on poor Arietta."

Kleef felt a dark ball of rage forming inside his chest. He had already guessed from Malik's evasions that there was a sacrifice involved, but something inside him had not wanted to believe Joelle capable of such treachery.

Something naive and foolish, he saw now.

It was the same mistake Kleef had been making his whole life—placing his trust where it wasn't warranted, honoring duties no one else valued. He had wanted to trust Joelle because of her beauty and charm, been eager to believe in her because he was desperate to find someone else devoted to a greater cause. But she had turned out to be no different than Malik, just someone trying to manipulate others for her own purposes.

A cold bitterness seeped into Kleef's heart. He tossed Malik into the back of the grotto, then whirled on Joelle.

"Is it true?" he demanded.

Joelle did not flinch from Kleef's anger. "As far as it goes," she said. "Love is sacrifice, and love is the only way to bind Grumbar—"

"And you didn't tell us?" Kleef interrupted. He shook his head, the bitterness inside him building into cold fury. "You're worse than Yder. At least he was honest about what he wanted. At least *he* offered something in return."

Joelle reached for his arm. "Kleef, I don't know exactly what's going to happen." She was using her warm voice, the one that made others want to please her. "There needs to be a sacrifice, but whether that's—"

"Don't." Kleef jerked his arm from her grasp. "Don't try to charm me. Don't even talk to me."

He stepped to the edge of the grotto and looked out onto the bridge, where the orcs had drawn to within a hundred paces. They still cowered beneath their breastplates, trying to stay out of the fire-hail, but he knew it would not be long before the orcs were close enough to risk a charge—and once that happened, there would be no question of delivering the Eye to Grumbar's Temple. The companions would be dead, and the Eye would be returned to Gruumsh.

Kleef peered down into the Underchasm. The Shadowfell was less than fifty feet below, so close he could almost feel Yder inside it, looking up and watching them, waiting for his opportunity to snatch the Eye.

Kleef turned back toward Malik, who cowered against the gate with a small black dagger in his hand, and he felt his bitterness become a physical thing, a cold throbbing tumor where once there had been a heart.

Perhaps the time had come to stop believing in dead gods, to live in the world as it was instead of as he *wished* it was—to do what was practical instead of what was right.

Kleef started across the grotto.

Malik glanced toward the walls, looking for an escape that did not exist.

"There's nowhere to run," Kleef said. "Just give me the Eye, and we'll get out of this alive."

"Kleef!" Arietta said. "What are you doing?"

"Saving us," Kleef said. "We're never going to reach Grumbar's Temple anyway."

"So you want to do what, exactly?" Arietta stepped to his side and grabbed him by the arm. "Strike a deal with Yder?"

"No choice," Kleef said. "The orcs have us cornered. They'll never agree—"

"No." Arietta slipped in front of him, blocking his way. "This is wrong."

"There is no wrong." Kleef glanced over his shoulder toward Joelle. "I've finally learned that."

"Because Joelle didn't tell us someone might have to die?"

"Because she used us," Kleef said. "Because she used *you*."

"Tell me how that matters," Arietta said. "This isn't about me, and it's not about your hurt feelings. It's about stopping Shar."

Kleef raised his brow. "You don't care?"

"Not at all. In fact, if I must die at the end of this, I'm glad she *didn't* tell me." Arietta turned to Joelle and said, "That was very kind."

Tears welled in Joelle's eyes, and Kleef began to feel a little petty in his anger.

"Then you're willing to be the sacrifice?" he asked.

Arietta nodded. "As I know you would be, were the situation reversed." She paused for a moment, then glanced back toward the Underchasm. A mischievous smile crept across her face, and she said, "Besides, look at what's happening out there. You'd have to be a damned fool to think any of us are going to survive."

The goat slammed into the gates again, and Kleef broke out chuckling. He could not help himself. Arietta's selfless courage was both a call to duty and an admonishment to rise above his own petty anger, and her easy humor was an inspiration to him, a reminder that their lives were less important than the cause they served. He felt the cold drain from his heart, and just like that, his bitterness was gone. Arietta was the one he had been waiting for his entire life, a noble who honored her vows and served a cause greater than herself. She not only deserved his trust, she was entitled to it—and to his loyalty, as well.

Kleef dropped to a knee in front of her, then laid Watcher's hilt across his forearm—and was nearly blinded as a blue radiance blossomed in Helm's Eye. For an instant, the agate seemed to become a window into a realm of pure, shining light—and then the light was outside the stone, flooding the grotto with a fierce blue heat that made their hair stand on end and set their blades to humming.

The goat bleated in alarm, and his fur crackled with tiny forks of dancing static. His eyes began to shine with the same blue light that had arisen from Helm's Eye. Blue haloes formed around his horns. He reared up on his hind legs, and for just an instant he seemed to take the form of a gauntlet with a blue eye on the back.

Then he hit the gates again.

This time, there was no boom, only the *crack* of splintering planks and the *bang* of a snapping crossbar. The gates swung open, revealing the cramped confines of the small bailey beyond. The goat dropped back to all fours and stood between the gates, shaking his head from side to side and watching the yellow pellets of flame pelt the cobblestone courtyard ahead.

The light in the grotto swirled along the walls, drawing itself into an ever-tightening spiral that finally coalesced into the shape of a knight in blue plate. The knight stepped out onto the bridge and swelled to the size of giant. Paying no attention to the fire-hail pinging off his armor and helmet, he stood looking out on the world, his eyes moving from the orcs cowering on the bridge ahead, to the Shadowfell seeping up from below, to the raging fire-filled sky. Finally, the blue knight squared his shoulders and spread his arms, expanding his chest and drawing in a long, hot breath of brimstone-laced air.

If the knight ever exhaled, there was no sign of it in his shoulders. He simply took a step forward, then turned to look back into the grotto.

It was impossible to see the face behind the helmet's lowered visor, but Kleef could feel Helm's gaze upon him, boring down into his very soul, taking stock and passing judgment. He found himself trembling at the memory of the bitterness that had ruled his life for so long, of the doubt and resentment that had nearly led him into Shar's darkness, and he wondered how such a weak man could ever be worthy of being one of Helm's Chosen.

The hidden face continued to study Kleef for what seemed both an eternity and the mere blink of an eye, and a single word rang off the grotto walls.

Vigilance.

And with that word, Helm's power came flooding into Kleef, filling him with strength and magic and a perception beyond anything he had ever imagined possible. He could smell the orcs out on the bridge, a cloud of sour leather and rotten breath less than a hundred paces away. He could feel the Shadovar watching from the shadows in the corners of the grotto, a cold patient malice awaiting their next chance to strike. He could hear the wallbound moving through the stone around them, a long lingering whisper filled with loneliness and despair.

Kleef dipped his head in the blue knight's direction, acknowledging both the gift and the obligation, then repeated, "Vigilance."

The knight nodded once. He stepped over the bridge cables into the Underchasm and started to walk across the Shadowfell, heading toward a distant curtain of lightning.

Kleef was still on a knee in front of Arietta, who was staring after the knight, her mouth gaping as the giant warrior faded into the raging storm. Her wounds had stopped festering and were closing before his eyes, no doubt healed by the divine magic that had filled the grotto.

Once the blue knight had vanished completely from sight, Arietta turned back to Kleef. "Was that . . ." She paused, perhaps too awestricken to speak the god's name aloud. "Was that who I think it was?"

Kleef nodded, then added, "You can say his name. After all, Helm has you to thank for his return."

"Me?" Arietta asked. "How?"

"By restoring my faith." Kleef presented Watcher's hilt to her. "I will always be yours to command."

Arietta arched an eyebrow, then looked back out into the fire-hail. "Don't you have a higher master now?"

"I do," Kleef said. "And his first law is to serve those who are worthy."

Arietta smiled. "In that case, I accept." She touched Watcher's hilt to formalize their bond, then motioned for him to stand. "Now rise, Sir Kenric, and let's go find Grumbar's Temple."

CHAPTER NINETEEN

THEY CAME UPON THE GIRL DEEP WITHIN THE CASTLE, inside a long-abandoned barracks tucked against the base of the inner curtain walls. She was dressed in a simple gray shift and hard at work building one of the eerily beautiful bone walls that lined so many halls throughout the structure, carefully placing freshly scrubbed skulls atop a row of femurs stacked two-feet high. She was surrounded by a dozen ghouls and twice as many zombies, and Arietta felt sure she could see the shimmer of several ghosts floating high in the corners of the room.

With alabaster skin and brown, kohl-rimmed eyes devoid of any apparent emotion, the girl appeared to be the same one who had addressed the companions through the viewing slot in the castle entryway. She had a strong, sinewy build and a hollow-cheeked face lacking any childhood softness, so it was impossible to be certain of her age. She might have been more a young woman than a girl.

In either case, she was only the second living being the companions had encountered since entering the gruesome castle. The first had been the goat, Peox, which they had come across again in a storeroom near the entrance. The chamber had been lined by rotting corpses that were being torn apart and slowly devoured by the wallbound. Peox had been bleating in protest, springing back and forth as he grabbed mouthfuls for himself. After seeing that, the companions had been all too happy to leave the goat to his own devices and continue exploring on their own.

What they had encountered were hundreds of undead, mostly withered ghouls and rotting zombies. Fortunately, Malik had made good on his promise to protect his companions by having them hold the hem of his robe, and the group had simply eased past the undead without the creatures taking notice. It was hardly the complete command Arietta had imagined Myrkul's Chosen to have over the undead, but as long as it worked, she wasn't inclined to start asking questions.

Besides, judging by the muffled clamor behind them, it seemed likely Malik had chosen his method with the orcs in mind. Certainly, the brutes had been too busy fighting undead to catch up with the companions.

After observing the young woman through the barracks entrance for a time, Malik turned to his companions and lifted a querying eyebrow. Arietta was quick to raise a finger to her lips and point down the bone-lined passage ahead. The castle crypt stood next to the keep tower, just across the inner bailey from where they were now.

As determined as Arietta was to go through with the sacrifice and activate Sune's binding magic, it would have been a lie to say her resolve was not wavering. Every step deeper into Sadrach's Castle seemed to bring with it a fresh reminder of what she would be leaving behind—a hand squeeze from Joelle, a reassuring smile from Kleef, even a solicitous nod from Malik. These people were her friends and fighting companions, and the longer it took the group to reach Grumbar's Temple, the less she wanted to leave them behind.

Joelle and Kleef quickly added their own nods to Arietta's, then Malik raised a hand, motioning them to await his signal. When the young woman turned to take a fresh skull from one of her ghouls, he finally pointed his arm and started across the doorway.

Without turning around, the young woman called, "You're acting like thieves." She turned and placed the skull on the wall she was building. "And you don't want to see what Grandfather does to thieves." She shook her head. "Truly, you don't."

Malik stopped midway across the doorway—which meant the rest of the group did, too.

"We have not come to steal a thing," he said. "We were only trying to pass quietly because we had no wish to interrupt your work."

"And because you hope to break into the family crypt." She stepped back from her work and turned to face the companions. "Though you won't find what you're looking for there. Grumbar's Temple isn't beneath the crypt."

"How do you know what we're looking for?" Kleef demanded.

The young woman—Arietta recalled one of the wallbound calling her Gingrid—pointed toward the side of the barracks.

"The walls have ears." As Gingrid spoke, a female face emerged from the stone and turned its head to the side, displaying an ear. A thin smiled flashed across Gingrid's mouth and vanished as quickly as it had appeared. Then she added, "And what the walls hear, I hear."

"Then you must know we didn't come to steal anything," Joelle said, using her warmest voice. "You would be doing me a great favor by telling us how to find Grumbar's Temple."

"I am sure I would." Gingrid let her gaze fall on Joelle's face, and for a moment, it seemed the heartwarder's magic would work. Then Gingrid looked away. "But no."

"Why be unreasonable?" Malik asked. "We mean no harm to you or anyone in this place."

"And yet, the castle gates hang open and Grandfather's

servants are forced to eat orc." Gingrid's eyes narrowed. "And they don't like orc."

She turned to her undead companions and looked expectant.

The ghouls looked back at her. The zombies dropped the skulls in their hands and shuffled around randomly, while the ghosts remained in their corners and keened.

Gingrid's eyes widened, and she looked back to Malik with her head cocked in wary regard.

"It is no use commanding them to attack," Malik said, sounding a little too smug for the circumstances. "They will never harm a Chosen of Myrkul."

"You? A Chosen of Myrkul?" Gingrid studied Malik for a time, then shook her head. "I don't believe that."

"Believe what you will," Malik said. "I wandered the Plane of the Lost for a hundred years before I was Chosen. I still carry the smell of the place in my own flesh."

"It's true," Kleef said. "Not that you'd ever smell it in here."

"A death priestess would," Gingrid said. An odd gleam came to her eye, and her gaze remained fixed on Malik. "You have walked the Fugue Plane?"

"Indeed." Malik extended his arm toward her. "Smell for yourself."

Gingrid started to approach—then took another look at Kleef and stopped. "You come here."

"Who are you to give orders to a Chosen of Myrkul?" Arietta demanded. She was less interested in defending Malik's dignity than in keeping the hem of his robe securely within their grasp. "He has given you leave to approach him, and you will do it or suffer for your arrogance."

Gingrid actually cringed, then shifted her gaze back to Malik. "I meant no offense." She dropped her eyes and said, "With your permission."

"Very well." Malik glanced at Arietta with an expression that was half astonishment and half reassessment, then added, "You are forgiven."

Gingrid hesitated—perhaps offended by being offered a forgiveness she had not even requested—but she glanced back to Arietta and quickly came to the barracks doorway. Keeping a nervous eye on Kleef, she took Malik's hand and leaned over to smell it.

She was only halfway down when she abruptly stopped. "It's true!" She looked up at Malik, then dropped to her knee. "I—I thought I was the only one who still worshiped the Lord of Bones. But you—you have actually walked with him!"

"You could say that, yes," Malik replied. He motioned her to her feet. "Now, let us attend to the matter at—"

"Not yet," Kleef interrupted. His gaze was fixed on a shadowy alcove about ten paces down the corridor, where the passage took a sharp bend and started toward the crypt at the far end of the castle. "I think we've found what we're looking for."

Malik frowned. "We have?" he asked, clearly not grasping the true meaning of what Kleef was saying. "How can you know—"

"Because Kleef has Helm's Sight, Doomlord." Arietta addressed Malik by a title once used by Myrkul's most feared servants. "He can often see things that elude even you."

"Of course . . . Helm's Sight," Malik said, finally seeming to catch on. "And what is it Kleef sees?"

"The entrance, I'm sure." As Arietta spoke, she caught Kleef's eye, then tipped her head toward the barracks. When he nodded, she nudged Malik forward. "In there."

Malik balked at the door. "Are you certain?" he asked, eyeing the roomful of undead. "I would hate to disturb Gingrid's work for nothing."

"This is the place," Joelle said, no doubt recognizing the same advantage as had Kleef and Arietta. "Bring out the Eye. This will be quick."

Malik sighed. "Let us hope."

He motioned for Gingrid to lead the way, then stepped

across the threshold behind her. Arietta and the others followed close on his heels, still holding the hem of his robe to protect them from the undead. As they walked, Gingrid glanced back at Arietta and the others, her brow furrowed and her gaze on the three sets of hands clinging to the hem of Malik's robe.

"It mustn't touch the floor by accident," Joelle said, speaking in the hushed tone of a confidence being shared. "It's how the doomlord spreads his decay."

The suspicion vanished from Gingrid's eyes, then she nodded sagely and turned back to Malik.

"Whatever your servant sees in here, it isn't Grumbar's Temple," she said, leaning close. "That would be beneath Grandfather's—"

"Perhaps you can tell us later," Arietta interrupted, worried about the location being overheard. "At the moment, I'm sure the doomlord is more interested in showing you the Eye of Fate."

She poked Malik in the back, prodding him to bring out the Eye as Joelle had suggested. If Kleef's plan was to work, they needed to press the Shadovar into making their move now—before Malik managed to disaffect his new disciple.

"Yes, of course," Malik said. "All of the Reaper's priests must look upon the Eye of Fate."

Malik made a great show of traveling to the center of the room, where they would be away from dark corners and surrounded by Gingrid's hideous assistants. The stench here was even worse than in the rest of the castle, for the zombies' flesh reeked of fresh decay and the ghouls' breath stank from meals better left unimagined, but the creatures remained oblivious to the companions' presence—even when Kleef had to shoulder a zombie aside to make room for them all.

Malik reached into his robe and withdrew the Eye of Gruumsh. Arietta felt a shiver of revulsion as its savage hunger filled the room, but Gingrid gasped in awe and seemed unable to look away from its pulsing veins.

"It's beautiful . . . and terrifying." She stepped so close her torso was almost pressed to the thing, then raised her hands as though to grasp it by its sides. "What happens if I touch it?"

Her response came in the form of Kleef yelling, "Move!"

Arietta felt his arm slam into her back, pushing the entire group down onto the floor.

"Shades!"

They landed as a group, then Arietta heard the cold sizzle of shadow balls descending from all sides of the room. She rolled onto her back and saw a volley of the dark spheres converging on the spot where the group had just been standing, ripping holes through ghouls and zombies alike. Several of the orbs missed and simply drilled down through the stone floor deep into the dirt beneath.

Behind the orbs came the shades, a half-dozen warriors dropping down from the gloomy corners of the room. Joelle felled one instantly, hitting him with a trio of magic darts that lodged themselves in a neat line from the pit of his throat to the center of his brow. The wallbound killed a second warrior, catching him in a tangle of stone arms and pulling him back to die a screaming death beneath their gnashing teeth.

The other four landed intact, scattering bones and skulls in every direction as they drew their glossy swords and charged toward the center of the room.

Kleef was already on his feet, dodging ghouls and shouldering zombies aside as he rushed to meet Yder. Arietta rolled to a knee, drawing her own sword—and using the flat of the blade to slap aside the lashing claw of a nearby ghoul.

"Malik, not us!" she cried. "Turn them on the shades!"

Joelle came up beside her, simultaneously kicking a zombie back and sending a fresh trio of darts flying toward a charging shade. This time, the warrior was prepared to counter, raising a shield of shadowstuff to absorb the first two darts, then simply twisting away from the third . . . straight into the claws of a hungry ghoul.

The shade went rigid as the first claw raked across his neck, then stood wide-eyed and helpless as the ghoul's poison did its work. The thing opened its mouth and twisted its head around to bite at the warrior's throat, and Arietta turned her attention to more immediate threats.

Buoyed by his resurrected faith—and the spark of divine magic he now carried as one of Helm's Chosen—Kleef had Yder well in hand. He whirled Watcher through a dizzying blur of attacks, driving the prince toward a tangle of wallbound at the far end of the barracks. The shade was counterattacking with everything he had, dodging in close to slash at Kleef's legs, flinging shadow tentacles high and low, spinning into head-high power chops, hurling disks of shadowstuff left and right.

Each time, Kleef was ready. When Yder slashed low, Kleef pivoted and opened a slash across the Shadovar's shoulder. When Yder hurled his shadow magic, Kleef leaped in to attack, dodging and deflecting as he drove the prince back. When Yder tried to spin away, Kleef lashed out with a snap kick and cut off his escape.

Finding no immediate threats on that side of the group, Arietta turned to find a trio of ghouls watching her from a bone pile two paces away, their yellow eyes locked on her throat. Unsure of their intentions, she put the point of her sword between her and the middle one's eyes.

"Malik," she said, glancing over. "About those undead . . ."

It was Gingrid who called them off. "Not her," she said. "The dark ones."

The ghouls lingered long enough for the middle one to bare its fangs at her, then all three bounded off to join the mass of undead swarming the last of the shades. Arietta breathed a sigh of relief, then joined Joelle next to Malik and Gingrid.

"Where are the rest of Yder's warriors?" she asked.

"I don't know," Joelle said. "Maybe we killed—"

She was interrupted by the wet crunch of bodies coming

apart, and Arietta saw the tip of a shadow scythe slicing through the mass of undead. One after the other, zombie and ghoul torsos fell away from the legs beneath. In the blink of an eye, she had a clear view into the heart of the swarm, where both shades remained on their feet.

One was swinging the scythe. The other brought his arm forward, about to fling a shadow spell in their direction.

"Down!"

Joelle was already pulling Malik down, so Arietta grabbed Gingrid and sprang in the other direction. Or tried to. The young woman had gone limp, perhaps from the shock of seeing—or feeling—the destruction of so many of her undead at once. Arietta had no choice but to release her and dive into a neatly stacked row of femurs.

The shade's spell sizzled by a few feet behind her. Arietta spun to a knee and saw the dark band of a shadow disk streak past—straight toward the fight at the far end of the barracks.

Arietta turned to shout a warning, but Kleef was already spinning around, bringing Watcher down to defend himself. He caught the disk on the blade's edge and sent it spinning off in three hissing pieces.

By then, Yder was on him, bringing his glassy blade around in a vicious overhand strike that looked as if it would split Kleef from collar to navel—until the watchman landed an equally vicious back kick in the middle of the shade's chest.

Yder doubled over—and still managed to drag his blade down the length of Kleef's back, opening a wound so deep that Arietta saw the blood spray from twenty feet away.

Kleef roared in pain and whipped Watcher around one-handed—catching Yder on the elbow and dropping a murky forearm onto the floor. Then the battle continued as before, with Kleef pressing the fight and Yder giving ground, retreating inexorably toward the waiting arms of the wallbound.

Closer by, Gingrid lay on the floor, unconscious but not obviously injured. Malik and Joelle were just gathering themselves up, Malik tucking the Eye back inside his robe while Joelle drew her sword. The two Shadow warriors quickly advanced, hacking and blasting their way through a steady stream of undead.

Arietta rose and started across the bone-strewn floor to help defend the Eye—and quickly found her path blocked by the withered forms of two snarling ghouls.

"Out of my way." She waved them aside, then pointed her sword at Malik. "I'm with him."

The ghouls hissed, but reluctantly took a single step apart—then seemed to catch themselves and leaped forward to attack.

Arietta was so surprised that she barely managed to duck away as the nearest one's claws raked through the air above her. She pushed her sword up through its chin, deep into its brain. Then, dragging the blade free as she moved, she spun around behind it and drove the tip through the back of the second ghoul's skull.

When she turned back toward her friends, it was to find a trio of zombies shuffling away from the Shadovar toward her. The two shades quickly took advantage of the shift to break free of the other undead and rush Malik and Joelle.

Arietta charged straight at the zombies, then changed course at the last second and launched herself into a flying dropkick that caught the nearest zombie square in the chest. The zombie went over backward, clawing and clutching at her legs. She landed atop him with bent knees, then quickly freed herself with a couple of quick slashes to the wrists.

By then, the Shadovar were on Malik and Joelle, the larger one hammering at Joelle's guard, driving her away from Malik and forcing her sword farther down with every strike. The smaller shade had Malik pinned to the floor, his foot in the middle of the little man's chest and his sword tip pressed to Malik's throat.

"No need to die," the shade was saying. "Give me the Eye and—"

Arietta slashed her sword across the back of his neck as she raced past, then reversed her stroke and buried her blade deep into the side of the larger shade's throat. Joelle finished the job by lopping off the head completely.

Arietta turned to find Malik withdrawing his little black dagger from the other attacker's chest. It was hardly a beheading, but with the shade's body withering into a shriveled black husk, the shadow warrior was clearly just as dead as the one Joelle had killed.

Before Arietta could ask after the Eye, the three zombies she had eluded a moment before came shuffling toward her. She backed away, then looked to Malik.

"Aren't you supposed to be protecting us?"

Malik rose. "As I have been." He took Arietta's arm, and the zombies instantly turned to shamble after Joelle. "But I warned you, Myrkul's magic will only protect you when we are touching."

"What?" Arietta glanced toward the far end of the barracks, where Kleef and Yder were battling a handful of undead as well as each other. "You can't even command the undead?"

Malik straightened his shoulders. "I have commanded them not to see us so, have I not?"

"That's not very strong magic for one of Myrkul's Chosen," Joelle said. She slipped behind Arietta and grabbed the hem of Malik's robe, and the zombies turned toward Kleef and Yder. "Especially when Gingrid can control them with a thought."

"Gingrid has lived with them all her life," Malik said. "I have only just—"

"No more excuses." Arietta grabbed Malik's arm and started toward Kleef. "We do what we can."

They quickly caught up to the three zombies and cut them down from behind, then Arietta and Joelle grabbed Malik beneath the arms and practically carried him into the battle.

Yder saw them coming and twice attempted to retreat into the shadows. Kleef made him pay in shadow and blood, slashing him behind the knee the first time and slamming him in the head with the end of Watcher's crossguard the second. The Shadovar finally countered by smashing an elbow into Kleef's nose and driving him back into the arms of a lunging ghoul.

The ghoul raked open one side of Kleef's face, and the watchman staggered a single step forward, blinded by his own blood. For a heartbeat, his legs seemed to go rigid, and it appeared he had been immobilized by the creature's poison.

Yder turned to flee.

Then Watcher's tip came shooting out through the ghoul's back, and Kleef whipped his sword around, slamming the thing into Yder and sending him sprawling.

Arietta and Joelle arrived in the next breath, leaving Malik's side and tearing into the nearest undead. Kleef shook the blood from his eyes and sprang after Yder, bringing his sword down in an overhand strike that the prince escaped by a mere inch.

Yder rolled onto his back and swung at a knee—only to have Watcher's tip come up beneath his blade and send it spinning away. Kleef's boot caught the shade beneath the ribs, lifting him completely off the floor.

Yder planted a foot on the ground and twisted into a standing position, his remaining hand already dipping into a pouch on his belt. Kleef feinted a sword strike, then skipped forward and planted a stomp kick in the Shadovar's chest and that sent him flying backward.

Into the stony arms of the wallbound.

The arms pulled him tight against the wall, and then a pair of heads emerged from the stone and bit into his murky flesh. Yder screamed and pulled his hand from the pouch on his belt. Kleef quickly stepped forward and brought his sword down across the prince's neck.

Yder's head fell free and bounced off Kleef's boot—but the hand opened anyway. A tiny ball of shadowstuff slipped

TROY DENNING

from between the dead fingers and sank into the wall. A dark stain slowly blossomed around the spot, and the *pop-crack* of crumbling stone shook the room.

Gingrid stumbled to her feet, looking dazed and alarmed, but otherwise none the worse for her recent collapse. She stopped in front of the wall and watched the dark circle expand for a few moments. Then, when a steady cascade of dust and pebbles began to spill out onto the floor, she turned to Malik.

"Grandfather won't be happy about this," she said. "He won't be happy at all."

CHAPTER TWENTY

THE DARKNESS HAD ALREADY DEVOURED THE BARRACKS
where Yder had died. Now it was blossoming inside the
curtain walls, slowly eating its way around the bailey to
the little gatehouse where Kleef and his companions stood
debating their next move. Across a small drawbridge in front of
them, Sadrach Keep shuddered with wallbound fury, its stones
grinding and clacking as though it might collapse any moment.

A stony face glared out from each side of the keep, its
appearance exactly the same on all four walls: an immense,
gaunt visage with a hooked nose and a long beard hanging
from the narrow chin of an old man. Beneath each face, a pair
of thin, stony hands gestured furiously, hurling spell after spell
across the bailey, blasting orcs and undead and even other
wallbound with wave after wave of fire, force, and lightning.

Kleef pointed at the nearest face. "I take it *that* is your
grandfather," he said, glancing at Gingrid. "Sadrach?"

Gingrid nodded. "I've never seen him this bad," she said.
"I don't think we can make it inside."

"And that's where Grumbar's Temple is?" Arietta asked.
"Beneath the keep?"

Again, Gingrid nodded. "Beneath the dungeon catacombs,"

she said. "The temple is easy enough to find—but not when he's like this."

The companions were atop the curtain wall, studying the keep from the upper level of the little gatehouse. The drawbridge that led to the keep was lowered, and the portcullis that protected the doors was raised. The fire-hail had finally stopped falling, and the wounds that Kleef had suffered against Yder were already closed, healed by the spark of Helm's divine essence that Kleef now carried. But it was growing clearer by the moment that entering the keep would be far more challenging than simply crossing the bridge and booting open the doors.

Sooner or later, they would have to risk Sadrach's ire.

After a moment, Joelle asked, "How did Sadrach come to *be* like this?" She waved her hand around the bailey. "How did they *all* come to be like this?"

"It was during the Spellplague," Gingrid answered. "When the Underchasm opened, Grandfather believed his magic was powerful enough to protect Castle Sadrach. And it was—but you can see what became of us. Those who were not wallbound became spellscarred or plaguechanged."

"*Us?*" Arietta asked. "Then you were here? A hundred years ago?"

Gingrid nodded. "That is my curse," she said. "To live among the dead and never age."

"I know a woman in Westgate who would pay her entire fortune for the second part of your curse," Malik said. "But we lack the time to wait out your grandfather's temper. Surely, there is another way into the dungeon?"

Gingrid shook her head. "No."

Malik studied the drawbridge for a time, then turned to Arietta. "We have only one choice," he said. "You must command Sadrach to let us inside."

Arietta frowned. "Me?" she asked. "How?"

"Just as you commanded Gingrid." Malik looked up at the wizard's wallbound face. "I cannot be certain your blessing will work on him, but even if you fail, your death will be no worse than ours."

Arietta looked confused. "Blessing?" she asked. "I have no idea what you're talking about."

"I am talking about Siamorphe," Malik replied. "Surely, you have felt her presence since we entered the castle?"

Arietta thought for a moment, then shook her head. "Most of the time, I've just been scared."

"That means nothing," Malik said, too quickly. "I have always found being Chosen a most frightening thing."

Kleef saw Arietta's eyes light with pride—and he immediately grew suspicious of Malik's motives.

"Whatever you're trying to do, stop it," he ordered the little man. "We'll find another way inside."

"No, you won't," Gingrid said, watching Arietta. "And the doomlord is right. I felt Arietta's power when she summoned me to obedience. She's certainly *someone's* Chosen."

"It must have happened when you agreed to offer your life for Toril," Malik said, continuing to speak to Arietta. "Surely, that is the kind of self-sacrifice any god values."

"*Enough,*" Kleef said, stepping toward Malik. "One more word from you and I'll tear out your tongue."

"No, Kleef." Arietta raised a palm to stop him. "I think Malik may be right."

"*What?*" Kleef saw the hurt flash across her face and instantly regretted his reaction. "What I mean is, Malik could be playing on your emotions. You know how tricky he is."

"I'm aware of that." Arietta's voice was reserved without being hostile, but even Kleef knew she resented his doubts. "I'm also aware of what happened in the barracks—and no one is in a better position to reflect on those events than I am."

"Maybe," Kleef said. "But even if Malik is right—"

"If Arietta thinks Malik is right, then I'm sure he is," Joelle said. She took Kleef by the elbow. "Unless you know of some easier way into the keep, there's nothing to be gained by questioning her judgment."

As Joelle spoke those last few words, she squeezed Kleef's elbow hard, and he realized he was only undermining Arietta's confidence in a decision she had already made.

And that was one of the things Kleef loved most about Arietta, her determination to be worthy. He nodded reluctantly and stepped back.

"Forgive my rudeness." He shot a warning glance in Malik's direction, then added, "When it comes to our doomlord, I find it hard not to be suspicious."

"As do I," Arietta said, giving him a warm smile. "But I saw the same reaction Malik did."

Keeping a watchful eye on the orcs' progress across the bailey, the companions spent the next few minutes developing a plan, asking Gingrid about her grandfather's personality and discussing how Arietta should phrase her commands. Kleef was careful to avoid casting any doubt on her chances of success, though inside he was aching to take her place and simply charge the keep. He tried to remind himself that Malik would not risk Arietta's life lightly, since the little man still believed that only she could trigger Sune's binding magic. But the thought wasn't much comfort. Malik was just too unpredictable.

All too soon, Arietta gave Joelle a long, lingering kiss and stepped out onto the drawbridge. As they had discussed, she made no effort to hurry or attract attention, but simply walked purposefully toward the keep until she saw Sadrach's eyes drop in her direction.

The wizard's stony fingers immediately began to weave a spell.

Arietta raised an arm and wagged her finger at him. "I'll have none of that, Sadrach," she called, continuing across the bridge. "You are not to harm me or my friends in any way."

The face on Arietta's side of the keep lowered its arched brows, and the hands gestured more frantically. Kleef had to resist the urge to draw Watcher and rush out beside her—which would only have gotten them both killed, he suspected.

Arietta continued to stride forward. "You will *not* cast magic at me or my friends."

Her voice was commanding but nervous, and Sadrach's hands paused for only a moment before renewing their gestures. Arietta continued across the bridge at the same steady pace, her stride just awkward enough to betray the doubt Kleef wished he had not planted in her mind.

A sudden *bang* sounded from the mouth of the gatehouse, and Arietta's knees seemed to buckle just a little. Kleef was halfway to the door before Gingrid caught him by the arm and dragged him back.

"Look," she said, pointing through the window. "Your friend's blessing is working, or Grandfather would have killed her by now."

Arietta was three-quarters of the way across the bridge and still striding confidently forward, her gaze fixed on the stony face above.

"And you will *stop* behaving like an ogre." This time, there was nothing but anger in her voice. "Your granddaughter is terrified of you, as are the rest of the people you trapped in the walls of your castle. If you cannot free them, then you will at least stop tormenting them."

Arietta reached the archway at the far end of the bridge, which sheltered the closed doors. Once she was in the alcove, there was no way the face on the wall could continue watching her—nor could the stony hands cast a spell in her direction.

But the keep began trembling even more fiercely—so fiercely that Kleef feared Sadrach might soon loosen the keystone above Arietta's head. He shot an angry glare in Malik's direction, but it was clear that Arietta would never have made it across the bridge, had the little man not been right about her becoming one of the Chosen. If Arietta's powers failed her now, it would only be because of the doubt *Kleef* had placed in her mind.

Malik returned Kleef's glare with a smug little smile, then shifted his gaze back to the keep, where the stones had finally stopped trembling. The mad anger soon drained from all four of Sadrach's faces, and his hands stopped weaving their spells. The door to the keep swung open.

Kleef breathed a sigh of relief, then nodded to Malik. "It seems I owe you an apology."

"Yes, and I will accept one later," Malik said, heading for the drawbridge. "*After* we have delivered the Eye."

The group was less than a quarter of the way across when the orcs spotted them and began to stream across the bailey toward the keep. Gingrid volunteered to stay behind and handle the problem—no doubt using the undead and the wallbound. She told them how to find the entrance to Grumbar's Temple, and ten minutes later, Kleef was leading the way down a narrow, spiraling passage deep beneath the keep. An eerie gray glow lit the way, always seeming to come from just around the bend. Like the passage itself, the steps had been hewn from the surrounding stone, and they were so narrow that two men could not stand on them side by side. The air was dank and musty, but still fresh enough that the only obvious whiff of decay came from Malik.

Kleef kept expecting to see a warning glow rise from the agate on Watcher's crossguard, or to feel a band of Shadovar lurking around the bend ahead, but the only enemies they encountered were the phantoms of his own imagination.

Finally, the passage opened into a small, seven-sided chamber with uncut gems glowing from the walls in seven different colors. In the center of the room stood a mountain-shaped dais with seven slopes, each veined with a different native metal. The summit of the dais rose into the shape of a huge seven-fingered hand, held open and flat. The palm was large enough for a man to sit upon, and Kleef could imagine Sadrach seated atop the strange throne, meditating on the changeless nature of the earthlord.

"At last!" Malik slipped past Kleef and started for the dais. "No one will be happier than me to see this done."

He was no more than halfway there when a cold pool of darkness began to seep from the base of the stone walls around them. It was impossible to guess whether Shar was coming for them or the boundary between the physical realm and the Shadowfell had simply grown that tenuous, but the result was the same—Malik stopped and looked down in horror.

Kleef rushed to Malik's side. "Don't stop now!" He slipped a hand beneath the little man's arm, then glanced back to find Arietta and Joelle close behind. "What next?"

Joelle pointed at the dais. "Deliver the Eye," she said. "The rest is for fate to decide."

By the time she finished speaking, the darkness had congealed into a blanket of gloom and spread across the entire floor. Kleef could feel the murky stuff drawing the warmth and sensation from his feet, turning them into numb bricks of ice. He lifted Malik off the floor and carried him the last few steps to the center of the room, then placed him on the edge of the dais.

Kleef felt the darkness swirl around his ankles.

"Hurry!"

Malik reached up, grabbing hold of the seven-fingered hand and using it to pull himself up a gold-veined slope to the top. He reached into his robe, and Kleef felt the Eye of Gruumsh hunting for him, a profane hunger searching for a bitterness that no longer existed.

The darkness climbed toward Kleef's knees, and he could no longer think of it as anything but the Shadowfell, Shar's cold oblivion rising up to take the world.

Malik placed the Eye in Grumbar's stony hand.

"A token from your beloved," he said. "Your rival's only eye."

A soft rumble arose inside the dais, so deep and sonorous that Kleef heard it more in his stomach than in his ears. The entire temple began to shudder in a slow, pulsing rhythm, and the muffled crump of grinding stones reverberated from the temple walls.

Then the veins on the Eye began to throb, and the savage

fury of Gruumsh became a burning fear in the pit of Kleef's stomach. He wanted nothing more than to flee and leave Toril's fate to the gods, but he could not. He had sworn a vow.

The Shadowfell was seeping in from all sides now. Malik slid back down to the edge of the dais, his gaze fixed on Arietta.

"I hope you have said your farewells," he said. "I fear we are at the end of our time."

Arietta nodded. "I'm ready." She stood a few paces from Kleef, holding Joelle's hand, her eyes moist, her chin held high. She turned to Joelle and asked, "How do we do this?"

"We *don't*—not you, my lady." Kleef turned to Joelle. "I can't allow it."

Joelle's eyes glimmered with approval, as though she had actually been expecting his declaration, but behind Kleef, Malik was aghast.

"What do you mean you can't allow it?" he demanded. "Sune must have her love sacrifice."

"And she will," Kleef said, directing his answer to Joelle. "When Arietta offered her life, it was because she knew it was the only way to save Toril."

Joelle nodded, her eyes patient and knowing. "I had the same thought."

Arietta's eyes widened in alarm.

Kleef gave her no time to object. "But you are not the only one who loves Arietta." He flipped Watcher around, setting the hilt on the floor and bracing it in place by leaning his chest against the tip. "And when I offer my life, it will be to save hers."

Arietta's jaw fell, and she shook her head. "You can't!"

"Of course he can," Malik said. He looked to Joelle. "The question is, will sacrificing Kleef work instead?"

Joelle glanced past Kleef toward Malik, her eyes cold with dislike. "Probably better."

"Good," Kleef said.

The Shadowfell was swirling around his thighs now, and would soon reach the top of the dais and begin its advance toward the Eye. Kleef's legs had gone cold and numb from the knees down, and he felt as though he were standing on pillars of ice. He looked up and met Arietta's eyes, then steeled himself to begin the long fall forward.

"Kleef," she said. "Please—"

Her sentence came to an abrupt end when Malik leaped into view, a little black dagger in his upraised hand, his eyes locked firmly on Arietta's heart.

"For the One and All!" He swung the dagger toward Arietta. "For the Prince—"

His cry ended as Joelle hurled herself into Malik's side, driving him back onto the dais. As the dagger came down, it opened a shallow gash across Joelle's back, then they both dropped into the Shadowfell and vanished from sight.

Arietta screamed and lunged after them.

Kleef rolled himself off Watcher's tip. Blood was seeping into his tunic, and his chest ached where the sword had already started to drive through his breastbone. He kicked the hilt into the air and grabbed it on the move, then stepped to Arietta's side as she plunged her arms down into the swirling darkness.

She cried out in dismay, but when she rose into a kneeling position, her arms wrapped around her beloved's torso. Too late. The color had already vanished from Joelle's face, and her lips had gone blue with death.

A tremendous crunching sounded atop the dais. The dull rumbling that had filled the temple faded and the shuddering stopped, and the muffled grinding of stone became the hushed hissing of shifting soil. The temple smelled dank and earthy and pure again, and the profane hunger of Gruumsh's searching Eye became just a passing moment of revulsion.

Too concerned about what Malik would do next to look away from Arietta, Kleef plunged Watcher into the swirling darkness—and felt the tip sink into something too soft to be flesh. He brought the sword around in a clearing arc and felt it drag through something thick and loose, then raised the blade—and found fresh dirt clinging to it.

When Kleef raised his feet, he felt the ground tugging at his boots—and Malik quickly became a secondary concern. He slipped a hand beneath Arietta's arm and pulled her to her feet.

"It's done," he said. "Time to go—before we get buried."

Arietta rose with tears streaming down her face. She tried to pull Joelle's body up after her, but managed to lift the heartwarder only about halfway out of the congealing darkness.

"Kleef, something has her!"

"Malik?"

Arietta shook her head and thrust an arm toward the temple entrance. Malik was stepping from the chamber into the mouth of the passage beyond, still holding the dagger that had killed Joelle. He looked back in their direction and raised the dagger as if to throw it—then saw Kleef glaring at him. He shrugged and lowered his arm, then turned to flee up the stairs.

"We'll deal with him later." Arietta wrapped her arms around Joelle's waist, then said, "First, help me get her out of here."

Kleef swept Watcher through the darkness again, and was dismayed to feel the dirt already twice as deep as before. He stooped down and slipped his free arm around the lifeless heartwarder and tried to pull her free—only to have a seven-fingered hand rise from the floor and wrap her in its earthen grasp.

Arietta cried out and fell backward, but she refused to let go of Joelle. She gathered her feet beneath her and began to pull.

A clatter sounded beside them, and Kleef turned. The hand atop the dais had closed, and a cascade of crushed quartz—all that remained of the Eye of Gruumsh—was streaming from between its stony fingers.

Kleef took Arietta by the arm and gently drew her to her feet.

"Arietta, we have to go . . . we have to leave her behind," he said. "That's *our* sacrifice."

EPILOGUE

The silhouette could not have been a shade.

Arietta was almost certain of it. She had only glimpsed the figure briefly, as he crossed in front of the arrow loops that overlooked the drawbridge. But she had seen enough Shadovar in the last few months to feel confident in her conclusions. The figure had been too short, more swaddled in darkness than a part of it. And his head was too round, his shoulders too slouched.

Definitely not a shade.

Arietta started to reach for Kleef's sleeve, then thought better of it and drew her hand back. Malik would not be easy prey to hunt down, not with his god's blessings and his inherent cunning. If she wanted justice for Joelle's death, it would be better to let the little man come to them.

Besides, Kleef was a Chosen of Helm, ever vigilant and always aware. If he had not paused when the silhouette crossed in front of the arrow loops, it was because he'd already known someone was there.

As they started across the anteroom toward the drawbridge doors, Kleef lengthened his stride and began to pull away. Arietta let him, knowing he was only making space to fight. They had been expecting this attack since fleeing Grumbar's Temple, so they both had their swords in hand. Neither one of them knew why Malik wanted Arietta dead, but since he had tried to kill her twice already, it seemed wise to expect a third attempt.

Kleef was just reaching for the drawbridge doors when

a dark figure dropped from the ceiling shadows, his dagger leading the way. Arietta yelled a warning, but Kleef was trapped against the still-closed doors with nowhere to leap free.

Instead, he pivoted around, slamming his forearm into his attacker's elbow. The dagger came flying back at Arietta, passing so close to her ear that she felt the air stir before it clattered off a wall behind her.

Malik landed on his feet behind Kleef, clutching his broken elbow and howling in pain. Kleef kicked the little man's feet from beneath him, then planted a boot in the center of his chest and started to bring Watcher down.

Arietta raised her hand to stop him. "Hold."

"Hold?" Kleef looked up. "*Seriously?*"

"For now." Arietta came forward, then looked down into Malik's bulging eyes and asked, "Why?"

"Why what?" Malik replied. "Why should you release me before my god sends his unliving—"

"*Your* god," Arietta interrupted. "Would that be the One and All?"

Malik's eyes bulged wide. "That is but one of his many names."

"And another would be the Prince of Lies?" Arietta asked. "It *was* him you were calling out to when you attacked me, was it not?" She pressed the tip of her sword to his throat. "Cyric?"

The fear in Malik's eyes gave way to resignation. "So it would seem," he said. "The Most Mighty was as eager as Sune to see Shar stopped."

"That much, I believe," Arietta said. "But why claim to be a Chosen of Myrkul?"

"So Sune would accept the One's help," Malik said, looking her straight in the eye. "She is a jealous goddess who demands all the glory—"

"The *truth*, Malik." Arietta pressed down until the tip of her sword drew a bubble of blood so dark it was black. "Or I'll tell Gingrid who you are and let her feed you to her friends."

Malik swallowed, then said, "Perhaps the One also wished to claim Myrkul's old throne."

"What's that have to do with Arietta?" Kleef demanded. "Why do you keep trying to kill *her*?"

Malik hesitated, no doubt wondering whether he would suffer more by remaining silent or telling the truth. Kleef answered that question by putting more weight on the foot pinning Malik to the floor.

"It was never to be just . . . Arietta," Malik gasped. "I was to slay you all."

Kleef paused expectantly, then finally seemed to realize Malik was serious and broke out laughing. "You, kill *all* of us?" he asked. "What were you thinking?"

"It wasn't . . . my idea," Malik said. "The Mighty One desired his own ritual."

Arietta frowned. "A ritual to do what?"

"How am I to know?" Malik demanded. "And why should I tell you anyway? I failed the One, and for that I will suffer a fate worse than any of *you* can offer."

"Don't be too sure about that," Kleef said. "The punishments for things you have done—"

"Then deliver them . . . all."

As Malik spoke, he threw his head back, arching his neck up so quickly that Arietta barely had time to pull her sword away. Even so, he managed to open a bloody gash along the side of his throat. Had it been a finger's width to one side, it would have severed an artery.

Kleef quieted him by slamming the flat of Watcher's blade into the side of his head. Then he looked up at Arietta.

"Your call, my lady," he said. "But I think we've learned as much as we're going to—at least without hauling him all the way back to Cormyr for a proper interrogation."

Arietta was quick to shake her head. "Please, no," she said. "I couldn't stand his company that long."

Kleef nodded, then looked down into Malik's eyes. "That

just leaves the question of justice," he said. "For what he's done, we'd be within the Law to kill him."

"Which he obviously doesn't fear." Arietta studied the gash he had opened in the side of his neck, then said, "At least not as much as he fears having failed Cyric."

Beads of sweat rolled down Malik's brow. "Leave me alive, and you will never be safe," he said. "I will hunt you down and—"

Kleef's boot crashed into the side of Malik's head, bringing the threat to an abrupt end as the little man's eyes rolled back in their sockets.

Kleef kneeled down and moved Malik's head back and forth to make sure he was truly unconscious, then looked up and asked, "You still want to leave him alive?"

Arietta nodded. "Serving Cyric brings its own justice, I suspect," she said. "And killing him would do no honor to Joelle. Better to leave him to meet his fate with Gingrid and her unliving friends."

Kleef nodded his agreement. "Well said." He unbuckled Malik's sword belt. "But there's no reason to make it easy for him to come after us, either."

Arietta retrieved the black dagger that had almost killed her earlier. Despite a lopsided hilt and a notch at the base of the blade, the dagger was a fine weapon, light and slender and surprisingly well-balanced. She tucked it into her belt, then turned toward Kleef.

"I think the time has come to look to our future," Arietta said. She started across the anteroom. "Will you see me home, Sir Kenric?"

Kleef smiled and bowed. "As you command, my lady."

He opened the door, and they stepped cautiously out onto the drawbridge.

Sadrach Castle lay in ruins. Much of its stonework had been eaten to the ground by the spell Yder had released into the barracks wall. The inner bailey was filled with orc corpses and the undead who were feasting upon them. Meanwhile, dozens of dazed-looking humans—wallbound released by the destruction of their stony prison—wandered about, searching for their lost friends and relatives.

Beyond the castle stretched an endless plain of raw brown earth, still churning and billowing upward as it filled the vast void that had once been the Underchasm. As Arietta followed Kleef across the drawbridge, she heard a sound coming from a window high behind her. Somewhere in the keep, an old man was weeping with joy, at once cackling and sobbing, thanking the gods that his long nightmare had come to an end.